Si...

"[A] twisty, realisti...   ...ry-
teller."   —*Houston Chronicle*

"[A] tantalizing thriller. . . . Bell keeps readers on edge
throughout."   —*Publishers Weekly*

"David Bell is a definite natural storyteller and a first-class
writer. . . . A great thriller . . . that you most definitely will
devour."   —*Suspense Magazine*

"A gripping and suspense-filled novel with plenty of eye-
popping surprises."   —HuffPost

Praise for David Bell and his novels

"When six students are trapped inside Hyde House, so,
too, is the reader—helpless to escape until the final page is
turned. Smart and compelling."
—Charlie Donlea, *USA Today* bestselling
author of *Twenty Years Later*

"*The Finalists* is proof positive that David Bell is one of the
best thriller writers working today."
—Alma Katsu, author of *Red Widow*

"Will keep you guessing until the very end. Not to be
missed!"
—Hannah Mary McKinnon, international bestselling
author of *Never Coming Home*

"Utterly riveting. . . . I couldn't put it down!"
—May Cobb, author of *My Summer Darlings*

"A terrifically tense thriller . . . will keep you guessing until the very end."

—Riley Sager, *New York Times* bestselling author of *Survive the Night*

"David Bell is a top-notch storyteller. . . . I flew through this twisty, riveting psychological thriller at breakneck speed, hooked from the first page right up through the book's breathless conclusion."

—Cristina Alger, *New York Times* bestselling author of *Girls Like Us*

"Grabs you by the throat and never lets go . . . will keep you reading late into the night, with a twist you'll never see coming."

—Liv Constantine, bestselling author of *The Last Mrs. Parrish*

"A whirlwind story about secrets, regrets, and sacrifice . . . a deliciously infectious thriller."

—Alafair Burke, *New York Times* bestselling author of *The Better Sister*

"[A] page-turning whodunit where every character's a suspect and no one can be trusted."

—Mary Kubica, *New York Times* bestselling author of *Local Woman Missing*

"[A] compulsive, twisty, race-against-the-clock thriller . . . [a] smart and unrelenting page-turner!"

—Lisa Unger, *New York Times* bestselling author of *Confessions on the 7:45*

"[A] suspenseful, page-turning thriller."   —HelloGiggles

ALSO BY DAVID BELL

Cemetery Girl
The Hiding Place
Never Come Back
The Forgotten Girl
Somebody I Used to Know
Bring Her Home
Somebody's Daughter
Layover
The Request
Kill All Your Darlings
The Finalists

SINCE SHE WENT AWAY

DAVID BELL

BERKLEY

NEW YORK

BERKLEY
An imprint of Penguin Random House LLC
penguinrandomhouse.com

Copyright © 2016 by David J. Bell
Readers Guide copyright © 2016 by Penguin Random House LLC
Excerpt from *The Finalists* copyright © 2022 by David J. Bell
Penguin Random House supports copyright. Copyright fuels creativity, encourages
diverse voices, promotes free speech, and creates a vibrant culture. Thank you for buying
an authorized edition of this book and for complying with copyright laws by not
reproducing, scanning, or distributing any part of it in any form without permission.
You are supporting writers and allowing Penguin Random House to continue to
publish books for every reader.

BERKLEY and the BERKLEY & B colophon are registered
trademarks of Penguin Random House LLC.

ISBN: 9780593546376

New American Library trade paperback edition / June 2016
First Berkley mass-market edition / August 2022
Second Berkley mass-market edition / November 2022

Printed in the United States of America
1   3   5   7   9   10   8   6   4   2

This is a work of fiction. Names, characters, places, and incidents either are the product
of the author's imagination or are used fictitiously, and any resemblance to actual persons,
living or dead, business establishments, events, or locales is entirely coincidental.

If you purchased this book without a cover, you should be aware that this book is stolen
property. It was reported as "unsold and destroyed" to the publisher, and neither the author
nor the publisher has received any payment for this "stripped book."

For Molly

CHAPTER ONE

Five police cars. Three news vans. And one coroner's wagon.

Jenna Barton saw them as she made the turn onto the last county lane. The vehicles were fanned out around the old weathered barn with one wall collapsing and the others hanging on for dear life.

The fields around her on either side, stretching away for miles to the edges of the county, were empty and barren, still marked by patches of snow from an uncharacteristically heavy storm for that part of Kentucky. The soil was dark and lumpy, the remnants of cornstalks sticking out like spikes.

As she came closer, the dirt and gravel on the narrow road pinging against the underside of her car, she saw the people as well. County sheriffs in their pale green uniforms and Smokey Bear hats. News reporters in their nice clothes, their hair perfect, were being followed by cameramen in flannel shirts and heavy boots. And a scattering of onlookers, the curious good old boys who heard the call on their scanners or read about it on Twitter, were standing around in their feed caps, hands thrust deep into pockets against the cold, hoping for a glimpse of something horrific. Something gory or gross, some story they could tell later that night in the Downtowner while they sipped beers or threw darts.

Yeah, they'd say, their bravado mostly covering their unease, *I saw them bring the body out. Wasn't hardly anything left . . .*

Jenna parked next to a sheriff's cruiser, but she didn't get out. She sat in the car, hands clenching the wheel, and took a few deep breaths. She told herself this was probably nothing, another false alarm, one of many she had experienced over the past three months. Every time an unidentified woman's body was found in central Kentucky, along an interstate or in a culvert, an abandoned house or the woods, someone called her. Usually the media but sometimes the police, and Jenna would have to wait it out, wondering whether this would be the time they'd tell her they'd found Celia. As she sat in the car, her eyes closed, the heater making the cabin of her Civic feel even closer and more cramped than it already was, she wondered whether she wanted to know the truth or if she could keep her eyes shut and hide forever. Would she finally feel relief when they found her best friend's body?

The thoughts swirled through her brain like some twisted Zen koan:

I want to know.

I don't want to know.

A light tapping against the window brought her eyes open. Jenna blinked a few times, turned her head. She saw a smiling face, one wearing a pound of makeup. Becky McGee from Local 40 News. Becky gave a short wave, her shoulders rising in anticipation of Jenna's response.

Jenna turned the car off and stepped out. She'd been at work when Becky called and still wore her light blue scrubs. She'd rushed out of the office so fast she barely had time to grab her keys and purse. A damp winter chill hit Jenna as she straightened up, so she pulled her coat tighter, felt the light sting of the wind against her cheeks.

Becky placed her hand gently on Jenna's upper arm. "How are you?" she asked, her voice cooing as if she were talking to an invalid or a frightened child. "Tough day, huh?"

"Is it her?" Jenna asked.

"They don't know anything," Becky said. "Or they won't tell us anything. They've been poking around in there for the last thirty minutes. It's a potential crime scene, so they have to take their time. . . ."

Becky's voice trailed off as Jenna's eyes wandered to the old barn. Some cops stood at the opening where a door once hung, staring inside. One of them said something and then smiled, looking to the man next to him for a laugh as well. They were close to fifty feet away from Jenna, so she couldn't hear them, and she envied their ease at the scene, their lack of emotional involvement in the outcome of the search. She looked around. She was the only one truly invested, the only one who would buckle with pain if Celia's body was discovered in the shitty, run-down barn.

Jenna turned back to Becky. The camera guy, Stan, loomed behind her, the equipment in his hand but not shooting. Jenna had learned over the past few months what the red light meant. "What did they find?" she asked. "You said on the phone it was a body."

"Well, it's—" The cheer and lilt quickly went out of Becky's voice. She was a little older than Jenna, probably in her early forties, but her voice still sounded like the high school cheerleader she had once been. "Bones. I guess *a* bone to be more specific." Becky nodded, confirming the fact. "Yes, they found *a* bone. A surveying crew was out here, and they went inside the barn to get out of the cold or to take a smoke break, and they found a leg bone. Now they're digging around in there, looking for more." Becky made an exaggerated frown to show how awful she found the whole situation.

"Did someone call Ian?" Jenna asked.

"I did. He said he wasn't going to come. You know he never makes it out to anything like this." Becky lowered her voice. "I think he mistrusts any potential display of emotion. Plus, you know, a lot of people still think he's guilty."

"The police cleared him," Jenna said.

"Mostly," Becky said, her voice low.

Jenna wished she could be as strong as Ian, could so easily and readily draw lines and never cross them. It was easier for men. People accepted it if a man was cold and distant. "He's smarter than me, I guess. It's so cold out here."

Jenna saw the other reporters and their cameramen moving her way. They recognized her, of course, after all the stories and interviews, after all the features and updates on Celia's case. They knew she was good for a quote or two, knew the viewers loved to hear from her, even the ones who took to online forums and social media to criticize her. It was Jenna whom Celia was leaving the house to see that night back in November. It was Jenna who first called Ian when Celia didn't arrive at their designated meeting place. It was Jenna, Celia's best friend since high school, who could tell the viewers anything they wanted to know about Celia.

Jenna knew the reporters were using her, but she couldn't help herself. She felt obligated to speak to them out of loyalty to Celia, even though she always received crank calls—at work and at home—and hateful comments on Twitter and Facebook. People offered support too, plenty of people, she reminded herself. But the nasty ones stuck with her.

Becky nodded to Stan, easing toward Jenna, reaching out with one hand to brush something off her coat. "You know what would be great? We'd love to be able to get your reaction now, you know, and have it as part of the story tonight. And I've already heard from New York. Reena wants to do a live remote tonight, put it all over CNN. Of course she'd love to have you again. She thinks you're great." Becky tilted her head to one side, studying Jenna. "This is so cool that you wore your work uniform. It's so real. If you could slip your coat off and—"

"Please, Becky." She didn't want to be rude, didn't want

to snap at the reporter, who Jenna knew was only doing her job and who had always been decent to her. Jenna tried to soften her words with a smile, but it felt forced, like squeezing toothpaste back into a tube. "It's cold out here."

"You want the coat on?" Becky asked. "That's fine. It's a little brisk, even for February."

"No, I don't want to talk right now," Jenna said, her voice friendly but firm. "Not *before*."

Becky was a professional, but that didn't mean she could hide all her emotions. One side of her mouth crinkled when Jenna told her no, and a glossy coldness passed over her eyes. "You don't want to talk now?" Becky's eyes darted around. She scooted closer, lowering her voice and adding a steely edge. "You're not going to talk to someone else, are you?"

"I'm not going to talk to another reporter, no. Of course not." Jenna sighed. "Whatever happens, I'll talk to you first."

"Good. Because you and I—" Becky's glance darted to the other reporters, who stood just out of earshot. She eyed them like a school of circling sharks, which in a way they were. "We've always had a rapport, ever since this happened. And with Reena in New York helping me—"

"After," Jenna said. "Okay? Let's just talk after."

"After what?" Becky asked.

"After we find out what's—*who's*—really in that barn."

"Are you sure?" Becky asked. She lowered her voice again. "You know it could take a while for them to identify anything. I mean, they have to use the dental records at this point. And you always have something interesting to say. And this whole town has been on edge for the past few months. Things like this don't happen here."

Jenna felt the heat rise in her cheeks, and as it did, the molars at the back of her mouth ground together like shifting tectonic plates. She didn't want to say the wrong thing. She had a tendency to do that, to blurt things out. The wrong things at the wrong times. Jokes at a funeral, curses in front of someone's grandmother. They never came out the way she intended, and sometimes she hurt people or offended them. She never seemed to know how her words would land, and she wished she could learn to keep her mouth shut.

But Becky read the look and nodded, reaching up to pat her hair. "You're right," she said, smiling, doing her best to set Jenna's mind at ease. "After will be better."

Better, Jenna thought. Better? Would any of this ever be better?

CHAPTER TWO

It was a first for Jared Barton: a beautiful girl in his bedroom.

Yes, he'd fooled around with girls before. At parties or in the park, fumbling in the dark, the sweet taste of some kind of flavored vodka on the girl's breath while they kissed, their tongues swirling like clothes in a dryer. And he remembered the ever-present fear of interruptions that hung over those encounters: other kids barging into the bedroom or, worst of all, police chasing them from the park, the flashlight blast in the eyes, the smug cops hustling them away with smirks on their faces. *Okay, Romeo, the park's closed now. . . .*

But even though his mom worked full-time and his dad was long gone, Jared had never managed to bring a girl home. At fifteen, he felt a little behind. He had friends at school who boasted of blow jobs and even sex, and Jared listened to the stories in awe, not saying much for fear of betraying the fact that he'd never made it past second base, a private shame he kept to himself. But here she was, standing in his room after school on a Tuesday afternoon, the amazing Tabitha Burke.

Jared told himself to remain calm and to not—for the love of all that was holy—blow this chance.

Tabitha leaned over his desk, her long fingers picking up items and then placing them down, almost as though she was shopping in a store and didn't know what she wanted to buy. When they'd come in, Jared silently thanked whatever god dwelled above that his room was relatively clean, that there were no dirty boxer shorts on the floor, no stained socks or wet bath towels littering the carpet. For once he was glad his mom rode his ass about keeping things clean. He wanted to make the best impression possible, and he didn't think Tabitha would be the kind of girl who would leave dirty clothes on the floor or dirty dishes on her desk. Not that he'd ever been close to her house, let alone inside.

"Do you want a drink or something?" Jared asked. "I think we have some Cokes. Maybe my mom made iced tea."

"I'm fine," Tabitha said. She looked back at him, offering a smile that revealed a dimple on her left cheek.

Jared loved the smile—even though her teeth weren't perfectly straight—and he loved the dimple. He liked to caress her cheeks when they were close, making out and kissing her lips, her ears, her neck, running his fingers over her soft skin because he'd never felt anything like it. But that answer to his question about the drink. *I'm fine.* Tabitha said it all the time about almost everything. He thought of it as her motto, her catchall response to most questions, and Jared couldn't help thinking of it as a line in the sand, something that always reminded him he'd know her some, but not as much as he wanted. He hoped—and kept hoping—that would change, that he'd hear that phrase less and less as time went by.

He'd only met her three weeks earlier on the icy January day she showed up at Brereton Jones High School in Hawks Mill, Kentucky. The semester had already started and, in homeroom that first day, Tabitha was escorted in by a guidance counselor. She carried no backpack or pens, no papers or books, and she looked tired, like someone who'd just come off a twelve-hour shift in a factory. Jared didn't care. Tired or not, Tabitha was beautiful: almost as tall as he was, with fair freckled skin and green eyes. Her hair looked a little greasy that day, and she wore it back, but that only called more attention to her full lips, which Jared stared at while Tabitha explained to another girl that she'd just moved to Hawks Mill from Florida. They'd driven all night, she said, she and her dad. He'd just started a new job in town. . . .

But Jared didn't care about the details. He wanted to—*needed to*—meet her. He wasn't sure he'd ever wanted anything—*anyone*—so much in his life. It felt like hunger, a physical craving.

And he did meet her that very first day during sixth period. Jared went to the library instead of the cafeteria, where he normally spent his study halls, goofing around with his friends, drinking Cokes and watching stupid videos on their phones. But he knew he had a math quiz that day, and he knew if he went to the cafeteria he'd fail.

He hadn't stopped thinking about Tabitha since seeing her in homeroom. He'd spent the whole day hoping she'd end up in another one of his classes, and short of that, he hoped for a glimpse of her in the hallway. But those things didn't happen, so when he walked into the library and saw her sitting alone at a table, reading—of all things—a book by Dean Koontz, his heart raced like a motorboat.

She liked Dean Koontz. Jared loved Dean Koontz. And she just so happened to be reading one of Jared's favorites: *Whispers.*

Jared didn't stop. He didn't open his math book, and he didn't sit at another table. He went right up to Tabitha and complimented her on her taste in books. He knew he was taking a risk, approaching the new, very pretty girl and striking up a conversation. Jared felt the same that day in the library as the time he first went off the high dive at the community pool. He remembered the slow climb up the ladder, the terrifying view of the blue water on all sides. He knew kids were lined up behind him, and to turn away or back down meant instant humiliation.

So he jumped.

And how good it felt—the free fall through the air, the glorious splash into the water. The bubbles streaming from his mouth as he sank, and then the steady rise back to daylight. The terror and the glory.

He jumped with Tabitha too. He didn't think, didn't turn around and walk away.

He jumped.

She looked up from *Whispers* and smiled, the dimple catching his eye. "I read this before, a few years ago. And then I found it on the shelf here. It's one of my favorites, so I just started rereading it."

"It's one of my favorites too," Jared said, slipping into a chair across from her. She hadn't asked, and he didn't care. He acted, his body taken over by some force that allowed him to behave like a confident, mature human being. They talked about other books they liked. And movies. And food.

He never even opened the math book. He later failed the quiz.

He didn't care.

It all seemed to be leading to this moment in his room.

And so she stood before him, gently tucking a strand of hair behind her ear with one hand as she studied the books on the shelf next to his desk. "You really do like Dean Koontz," she said.

"He's the man who brought us together."

She turned and smiled again, then picked up the framed photograph on the top of the shelf. "Who's this?" she asked. "Is this your dad and your brothers?"

"Half brothers. Yes, that's them."

"Your dad looks like you. I can see it in the eyes."

"I guess so." Jared didn't want to talk about his dad. Not because his absence was particularly painful. It really wasn't anymore. His dad had left when he was five, and he remembered that pain very well. It felt as if he cried for weeks, stumbling around with his vision blurred by tears, asking if Dad was ever going to come back. His mom put on her best face for him, but even then he could see how much it hurt her. At night, after she put him to bed, he'd hear her crying through the thin walls of the apartment they lived in back then. Nothing ever scared him as much as the sound of an adult crying. "I can never see those things," he said to Tabitha.

"Didn't you say you don't really know your half brothers?" Tabitha tapped the glass with the end of her finger.

"I visited a couple of years ago. Dad paid for the plane ticket, so I went." Jared's first plane ride. He loved the window seat, looking out and watching the huge patches of nothingness beneath the wings. So much room in the country, so many places to go. "It was weird. It felt like I was staying with strangers. I mean, his new wife is okay. Shelly. And the kids are good kids. I guess. But how much can you get to know people in a week? Dad . . . I barely remember him, and he doesn't know me at all."

Tabitha nodded. She placed the frame back in the exact spot she found it, as though she were handling a precious work of art.

Jared waited, hoping she'd signal a willingness to talk more about her own family. He didn't want to press or push if she didn't offer any signs, even though he wanted to ask almost as much as he wanted to do anything else. *Almost.* There were other things he wanted to do with Tabitha more.

But he didn't know where Tabitha's mother was. On the few occasions the subject came up, Tabitha was evasive, suggesting only that her parents were separated, and her mother lived in another part of the country. Tabitha didn't seem to have much contact with her mother, if any. He wondered if her mother had problems, emotional or something else.

Jared knew only that Tabitha lived with her dad in Hawks Mill. Beyond that . . . not much. And most of his inquiries in those first few days they walked home from school together or hung out in study hall were met with some variation of the standard *I'm fine*. Since then, he'd kind of let the subject go, hoping that over time she'd open up more. But weren't relationships supposed to work the other way? Wasn't the guy supposed to be closed off and the girl the one who always wanted to talk about her feelings?

"I heard something about your mom today," Tabitha said. She still stared at the photo of Jared's dad and brothers, a photo Jared put out only because his mom said it would be a nice gesture. He didn't know who the gesture was for, since his dad was never coming back, but he did it to appease his mom.

"Oh." Jared tensed. The muscles in his stomach tightened as though bracing for a blow. She could mean only one thing. "People say a lot of stuff."

"Yeah, some kids at school told me something about her friend disappearing. Is that true? I didn't know if it was just some weird gossip or exaggeration."

Jared hesitated before answering. Okay, he had to admit, Tabitha wasn't the only one holding things back. He hadn't mentioned much to her about his mom at all, except to say she worked as a nurse and she was pretty easy to get along with. He left out the part about Celia, knowing he'd have to tell Tabitha someday but hoping they'd know each other better when they went down that rabbit hole. A shared love for Dean Koontz was a much better icebreaker than *So, my mom's best friend disappeared without a trace and is probably dead. . . .*

"It's true, yeah."

When he started speaking, Tabitha turned to face him, leaning back against his desk and folding her arms under the gentle curve of her breasts. She didn't say anything but seemed to be listening with a particularly sharp focus, as though every word that came out of Jared's mouth mattered a great deal to her.

"It's kind of weird to talk about," he said. "Are you sure you want to hear about it?"

Tabitha nodded.

"Okay. My mom's been friends with Celia ever since they were in high school. I've known Celia my whole life. Back in early November, they were supposed to go out together. They were meeting near Caldwell Park. Do you know where that is?"

Tabitha looked confused. "I don't know where anything is yet."

"It's not far. They were meeting late at night, almost like they were sneaking out. I don't know why. I think they were trying to re-create some of the wild times they had in high school. But Celia didn't show up. At first Mom just assumed she'd changed her plans or something. Celia's married and has a kid." He snapped his fingers in the air. "Maybe you know her? Ursula Walters? She's in our grade."

"There's a girl named Ursula in a couple of my classes."

"She's kind of a pain in the ass," Jared said.

"She seems like a bully to me."

"Really? Why?"

Tabitha lifted one shoulder, a halfhearted shrug. "She just strikes me as the kind of person who thinks she should always get what she wants. I've known other people like that."

Jared waited for her to say more, but she didn't. "I've known Ursula since I was a kid. My mom thinks maybe Celia wasn't around for her enough. You know, Celia and Ursula's dad, Ian, were kind of wrapped up in their own thing too much instead of paying attention to Ursula. But that's another story. Anyway, Mom texted Celia and called her, never got an answer. She called Celia's husband. And then they called the cops, but they couldn't find her." Jared straightened up, scooting forward on the bed. "Wait a minute—have you really not heard about any of this? I mean, not until today?"

"No," she said. "I just moved to town. I don't know many people."

"But it's a national story. Or it was for a month or so, until they didn't find Celia and everybody decided to move on to some other kidnapping or plane crash or whatever. It was on CNN every night. That weird lady on the crime show? The one with the gray, poofy hair, Reena Huffman? She practically moved here." He almost smiled at the strangeness of the blank look on Tabitha's face. He didn't think it was possible not to have heard of Celia's case, given how much it played on the news. "Have you never heard of the Diamond Mom?"

"The what?"

"The Diamond Mom? That's what they call Celia." He looked around the room, trying to see if there was a clipping from the local paper he could show her, but he didn't see any. "Celia disappeared by the park, and the cops found this diamond earring at the scene. One of her earrings. Like it fell out when the maniac or serial killer grabbed her. Her husband and her mom identified it. They're worth a crap ton of money, I guess, the earrings. They're heirlooms, and Celia never went anywhere without them. She wouldn't just let them fall out and not notice. Celia's family is rich too. Anyway, that Reena Huffman lady started calling Celia the Diamond Mom. That popped up on the screen every night when she talked about Celia's disappearance. It's a play on some old song. 'Diamond Girl' or something. And I guess it makes Celia sound rich. The news shows love that stuff."

Tabitha's mouth hung open a little. Her eyes glistened, as though she might cry, as though the story about Celia had happened to someone she knew well. "So how's your mom?" she asked, her voice a little shaky.

"She's doing her best. The first couple of months after Celia disappeared were a disaster for her. She tried to act tough and cool and everything, but I knew it was killing her. You know how parents are. They feel like they have to be strong for us, but it really put her through hell. The media kept bugging her. People looked at her funny at work or the store, even though she didn't do anything. She blames herself, you know? She feels guilty about the whole thing." Jared felt a protective instinct swelling in his chest, some desire to shield his mom from the scorn and the pain and the attention. "It can't be her fault. After Celia disappeared, her husband told the cops she thought someone was following her."

"Really?"

"Some creep, I guess. But then, how do you prove that? I guess she just felt freaked out a few times when she went places, like a car was following her or something. But maybe she was imagining it. How can anyone know?" He shrugged. "The whole town's kind of gone crazy, you know? People have bought guns and security systems and dogs. They think a madman is on the loose. Maybe one is. It's been hard on Mom. I know she thinks about it all the time."

"That's terrible," Tabitha said, and her voice carried a weight that seemed heavier than her years. "Does everybody think she's dead?"

Jared noticed that Tabitha didn't pull any punches. So many people tiptoed around the topic of death. They said "passed away" or "deceased," but not Tabitha. She didn't play coy.

"I think everyone assumes that," Jared said. "Once someone has been gone that long, everyone thinks the worst. And maybe some creep was stalking her. . . . Sometimes I watch those cop shows on TV. After forty-eight hours, it's like impossible for them to find someone alive."

"I know," she said, again with the heavy weight in her voice.

Jared didn't want her to be sad, so he tried to say something hopeful. "People do think they've seen Celia. More than once someone in another town, sometimes way across the country, says they've seen Celia somewhere. The cops always try to check it out, but they haven't found her yet."

"And they haven't found her body?"

"No."

"I guess that's good. Kind of."

"You must live in some kind of cave, or a news media blackout, if you've never heard of the Diamond Mom," he said, trying to sound joking and casual.

Tabitha's cheeks flushed. Her lips, which had remained parted, clamped tight into a wire-thin line. The sympathetic emotion in her eyes grew hard and flat, almost like a light going out.

"That's not funny," she said.

"What's not?"

"That cave comment." Her words came out in rhythmic bursts, like steel banging against steel. "It's not funny."

"It's just an expression. Everybody says it."

"I should go." In one quick, fluid motion, she pushed herself away from the desk and grabbed her coat, moving to the door like someone rushing to catch a bus.

Jared barely had time to move. He walked a couple of

steps behind her as she glided through the bedroom door, turning to the right and the front of the house. "Tabitha? Wait."

He followed her, hurrying. The denim from her jeans made a sharp brushing noise as she walked away from him, and Jared had to jog to reach her before she made it to the living room.

"Wait. Please."

She stopped. He started to reach out and touch her arm, but some instinct told him to back off, that no one as angry as Tabitha was wanted to be touched at a moment like this.

But she had stopped.

She kept her back to him, her shoulders moving as she breathed heavily with anger.

"I'm sorry," he said again. "I was just . . . I didn't mean anything."

She didn't respond. But she didn't leave. He took that as a good sign, one that meant he still had a chance to keep her in the house for a little while longer.

"I didn't mean to insult you or your dad. I don't care where you live. I was just being a smart-ass. I do that sometimes."

"It's not . . . That's not what I'm mad about."

"What, then?"

"Forget it," she said. "I should go."

"No, I want you to stay. Please?" Jared decided to pull out all the stops, open up the way he wanted her to. If he was going to lay it all on the line, he figured this was the time to do it. "I want to tell you something else. About Celia. And my mom. About what I had to do with her disappearing."

She turned to face him, her eyes open wide.

And she stayed.

CHAPTER THREE

Jenna wandered away from the reporters, her feet crunching over the cold, uneven ground. She shivered, and not just because of the rising wind and the thickening clouds that blocked out the already meager and distant sun. Tension rose inside her as she waited for something to happen, a growing pressure that made her bones and muscles so taut she thought she'd explode.

She couldn't escape the feeling that the whole thing was a farce, a dog and pony show orchestrated by the media and the police. The police, who wanted to look as if they were still working on Celia's case, and the media, who needed the ratings. Jenna just wasn't sure whether she was the dog or the pony. Or both.

She pulled out her phone and texted Jared. He'd be out of school and heading home, and she didn't want him to hear on the news or from social media that something related to Celia's case was brewing. He'd never said much about Celia's disappearance or the media storm that blew up in its aftermath. Jenna got the feeling he didn't know what to say to her, and she understood the two of them already existed in a tricky, difficult-to-manage space. Single mother, teenage son. She tried not to lean on him too much, tried not to make him her confidant, her sounding board in the absence of a husband or a serious boyfriend, and that choice meant some distance had grown between them, a cautious boundary Jared respected but perhaps didn't fully understand. He'd certainly been supportive of her in the months since Celia disappeared. He'd treated her with great kindness and deference, but that served only to make Jenna feel even worse. Wasn't she supposed to be looking out for him?

Call me!!!

She studied the text for a moment. Were three exclamation marks too much? Or did they adequately convey her concern, her need to speak with him? She went ahead and hit SEND. Jared was a little secretive, a little private, but what teenager wasn't? He possessed a good sense of humor, one that was less cutting and drier than hers. He was sensitive, every bit as likely to read a book as to camp in front of a football game on TV. She didn't know what she'd have done if he'd been a meathead jock. What would they talk about then?

Then she texted Ursula, Celia's daughter. Her only child. She'd be out of school as well—she was the same age as Jared—and Jenna hated to think of her hearing about this on the news.

Can you give me a call?

She needed to talk to Ursula more, be more of a

presence for the girl, who hadn't had a mother for several months.

A text came right back from Ursula: Dad warned me. Thx.

Jenna wondered once again how her life had ended up like this—having to tell her son and her best friend's daughter she was at a crime scene where a part of a woman's body had been found. But Jenna knew exactly how it had happened. She was the one who invited Celia to go out. She was the one who proposed they meet near the park. She was the one running late—

"Jenna?"

Becky's voice—more cautious, less cheery—brought her back to the reality of the barn. And what—or who— might be resting inside. Jenna turned and saw Becky approaching, taking careful steps like someone walking through a minefield.

"Something's going on over there," she said.

Jenna looked beyond the reporter's shellacked hair and saw a flurry of activity near the barn. More cops gathered at the opening, and more rushed to join them, their movements full of hustle and energy. A broad-shouldered man in a dark jacket with the word "Coroner" stitched across the back in gold letters joined the cops, his hand clutching the kind of black bag an old-time doctor brought on a house call.

Jenna started forward, her feet propelling her whether she wanted to move or not. The cold seemed to have departed her legs and torso, replaced by a flushing heat, something that spread through her body so quickly she reached up and undid the buttons of her coat, letting it swing open to the cool air. The reporters ignored her. They instructed their cameramen to heft their equipment back onto their shoulders, the lights glowing in the gray winter afternoon. She sensed Becky next to her, the reporter no different from the rest of them, caught up in the excitement and anticipation over what might be revealed from inside that barn.

Jenna cursed herself for losing control of her emotions, for thinking something important and relevant was about to happen, but how could she stop the feelings from surging? She felt hot and sick, almost like a feverish child, as the events of that November night came back to her. She'd called Celia, yes, begging her to go out. The two women had drifted apart over the previous few years. They were both raising children, both working, and Jenna knew that happened to friends sometimes as time went by, even the best of friends. But they both had high hopes for that night, a chance to reconnect away from their kids, their jobs, their everyday lives. A chance to be free and even a little wild again just like when they were teenagers.

But Jenna blew it.

She'd shown up fifteen minutes late. Fifteen minutes Celia waited for her, standing near the entrance to Caldwell Park. Celia, who was always on time, and Jenna, who was always late. Didn't that say so much about them? Celia the perfectly punctual one, and Jenna the straggler bringing up the rear?

If only she'd shown up on time for once . . . if only

she'd gotten there when she was supposed to . . . would Celia still be alive?

The what-ifs played on a loop in her head like the trailer for a lousy movie.

And after Celia was gone and the cops were involved, Ian revealed that Celia once thought someone was following her. What if by being late, Jenna had led Celia right into the hands of some kind of stalker? Someone who had been planning to do her harm all along?

"Get that, Stan," Becky said, her voice low and tense. "Are you getting that?"

"I'm on it."

"What are they doing?" Becky asked. "Can you see?"

Jenna could see, but she didn't understand.

One of the cops laughed and shook his head. And the guy in the coroner's jacket started doing the same thing. He turned around, shrugging, the black bag still in his hand, and walked away, back toward his van. More of the cops were laughing, some of them leaving the barn with the coroner.

But most of them stayed, still lingering in their places as though something else was going to happen, something they didn't want to miss.

Jenna turned. "What is it, Becky? What did they find?"

"I don't know," she said. "Give it a . . . Wait."

The cops at the barn door parted, creating a lane as though someone was about to emerge. A uniformed sheriff's deputy appeared, and he held something in his hands, lifting it up above his head like a trophy.

The flush across Jenna's face grew hotter, a trickle of sweat running down behind her ear. She felt sick as she tried to make out what the cop was holding.

Something jagged and gray, the color of old marble, and it made the other cops laugh.

"What is it, Becky?"

But even as she asked she understood. Bones. The cop was holding up bones. A rib cage or something.

How could he? How could they stand around, laughing and making light of somebody's body? Somebody's bones.

Maybe Celia's bones.

"Becky, stop them," Jenna said.

"Stop them?"

Then the cop lifted the bones and placed them on the top of his head.

Antlers. They were antlers.

"Oh, Jesus," Jenna said, trying to breathe.

Her mouth was dry, and an ache grew in the pit of her stomach.

"Oh, shit," Becky said. "It's a deer. A deer's bones."

"Crap." Stan lowered the camera. "Some hunter probably dragged the thing in there to dress it. Or maybe the deer just went in and croaked."

"Oh, gosh." Becky turned to Jenna, the cheer returning to her voice in full force. "Well, isn't that fantastic, Jenna? It's not a person at all. It's just a deer. It's not Celia. Aren't you relieved?"

Jenna still felt hot. She fanned her face with her hand while the reporter smiled at her. The smile was so white and blinding that it hurt Jenna's eyes, made them ache. It matched the ache in her stomach and the one forming in her head, just behind her left temple.

She took a couple of steps toward her car and leaned down by the side door. A hot stream of vomit shot out of her mouth, splattering the hard ground.

She spit a few times, wishing she had water, the remnants of the vomit stinging her cheeks. She wiped her mouth with the back of her hand, then just remained there, hands on knees, making sure there was nothing more to come out.

Her sides ached and cramped, and the headache remained, as if someone had jammed a knitting needle into her brain.

"Oh," Becky said behind her. "Oh, dear."

"Damn," Stan said. "Gross."

"Stan," Becky said as if she were correcting a naughty child. "Are you working or hanging out in a frat house?"

Jenna straightened up. She rested her right hand against the side of the car, bracing herself. She felt light-headed, and for a moment the world tilted, but then quickly settled. She heard a shuffling beside her, feet moving over the broken ground. A hand rubbed against her back.

Becky.

"Are you okay, hon?" she asked.

"Fine."

"It's been a crazy day, hasn't it?"

"Not the craziest of the last few months," Jenna said. "Unfortunately." She turned around, intending to thank Becky for her concern. But Becky was right there, right in her face, microphone in hand. She nodded to Stan, who had the camera up on his shoulder again, the bright light rigging on top burning, the red dot glowing.

"What are you doing, Becky?" Jenna asked, her eyes darting between the camera's eye and the made-up face of the reporter.

"You said we'd talk after we knew. Well, now it's after. And we know. So just real quick give me your reaction to what happened here today. Just your own words about how relieved you are or how scared you are. Something like that. Maybe remind everyone how much you miss Celia."

Jenna stood frozen, the sour taste of the vomit churning in her mouth.

She wanted to storm off. She wanted to shove Becky to the ground.

"How the fuck do you think I feel, Becky? Jesus."

Jenna turned away, her hands shaking as she pulled the car door open and climbed in. When she sped off, she hoped she hit them both—Becky and her juvenile sidekick—with the gravel the tires churned up.

CHAPTER FOUR

They moved toward the bedroom, Tabitha and Jared.

His gut burned as they held hands, walking down the hallway again, and the contact between his skin and hers, the intertwining of their fingers, sent surges of something close to electricity up his arm and into his chest. Jared guided her to the bed, where she sat down and slipped her hand out of his. He sat down next to her, studied her face in profile as he had so many times over the past few weeks.

Tabitha still seemed closed off but not exactly angry. They'd never had a fight or disagreement of any kind. But it was hard to fight when they were almost never really able to do anything. Tabitha's father enforced a strict curfew, so their time together was limited to the moments after school before he came home from work. They'd never had a weekend night together. They'd never even gone on a real date to a movie or a basketball game or even a trip to McDonald's. Jared kept hoping it would happen soon, that her old man would loosen up the longer they lived in Hawks Mill.

"Okay," he said. "I told you how my mom's friend disappeared."

Tabitha looked him in the eye, her gaze piercing and intense. "I don't know how that could be your fault."

When Jared was seven, his appendix became inflamed. It felt as if someone had taken a blowtorch and lit it inside his body. He writhed in his bed, sweat pouring down his face.

He felt the same way inside when Celia's story came up. Except he knew the feeling wasn't his appendix. It was guilt. Burning, searing guilt. He tried not to think about it, tried to push it aside like the remnants of a bad dream. But it always came back. A burning in his gut. A sick taste in his mouth as if he was about to puke.

"My mom was supposed to meet Celia, like I said, but my mom ended up running late. My mom always runs late. She doesn't do it for work, although she always cuts it close, but for everything else—going to meet a friend, going to a movie, whatever—she runs late. And it used to drive Celia nuts. Really nuts. It was the only thing they fought about. So Mom was determined to be on time that night. She told me she absolutely didn't want Celia to have to wait. And she made it. She was ready to walk out the door right on time."

"So, what's the problem?"

"Jesus, it's so stupid." He remembered the night well, felt his cheeks burn with embarrassment just thinking of it. "You know my friend Mike. He's a little wild. He's a jerk sometimes, to be honest. He got ahold of this bottle of whiskey. I think he stole it from his dad. He wanted us to drink it that coming weekend, me and him and our other friend Syd. But Mike couldn't keep it in his house, so he gave it to me to hide."

"And your mom found it?"

"She came in to say good night and the damn bottle was sitting out. I'd taken it out of my bag for just a minute, and I forgot to hide it. She saw it sitting there and started asking me a bunch of questions. You see, she can be cool about stuff like that. She trusts me. I told her the truth. I said it was Mike's. She believed me, but we still had to have this talk about alcohol and responsibility. She wanted to cancel her plans with Celia, you know? She said she didn't feel right running off with this hanging over us. But I told her to go, even though she was late."

Tabitha nodded, her gaze still locked on his. "You were holding something for your friend. It's not a big deal."

"I know, but I think . . . I think about it. She beats herself up over Celia, and it was me who caused it."

Some of the burning in his gut eased. A little of the pressure lifted. Tabitha's understanding washed over him like a cool rain.

"Have you talked to her about it?" Tabitha asked.

"I should, but I'm always afraid to bring up the whole thing. I don't know if she wants to talk about it, or if she wants to pretend the whole thing isn't happening. Even though it is."

"It's sweet that you worry about her like that," she said. "It really is. But I'm sure she understands."

"Do you know she never told the police about it? Nobody knows but her and me. I lied to Mike about it. I told him I got caught, but not that night."

"And now I know." She looked pleased.

"And now you. She figured it didn't matter *why* she was late that night. Just that she was late. She protected me from having everyone know. She was afraid that the whole town would hear about Mike and me having the alcohol, and they'd judge us and they'd judge her. People talk a lot in a town like this. They lay into people for every little mistake. Mom figured none of us needed that hassle. She made me dump the booze out, and she told Mike's parents. He was pretty pissed for a while." Jared ran his hands through his hair, running against his scalp. "I wonder if I'll ever be able to forget that. Or forgive myself."

Tabitha looked lost in thought. Her eyes grew duller, and she raised her hand to her mouth and started nibbling on the nail on her index finger. He thought she was checked out, but she said, "Parents can be pretty sensitive sometimes. They go through a lot of stuff. We have to remember that."

Jared saw the opening. He decided to jump.

"Is that what your parents are like?" he asked, feeling very much like a man sliding along potentially thin ice. "Your dad, I guess . . . or your mom when she was living with you?"

Tabitha's eyes focused again. Jared worried that he'd pushed too hard, that she'd be angry again. He knew if she stormed off this time he wouldn't be able to convince her to stay. And if she walked out the door of their house angry, he might never get this close to her again.

But he took the chance. He wanted to know. Wanted to know *her*.

As his mom always said, *"You have to live with whatever consequences you create."* He understood that all too well.

But Tabitha didn't storm off. Her features softened, and she slid her hand along the inside of his thigh, creeping ever closer to the bulge growing against the fabric of his jeans.

"My parents," she said. She shook her head and leaned in close, kissing him once and then twice. "Shit. It's so complicated. . . ."

"Your mom? Is something—?"

"Shhhh," she said.

And then they were kissing more, her hand on top of the bulge. And Jared had no trouble forgetting everything except her.

CHAPTER FIVE

The sun was slipping away as Jenna drove home. They lived at the eastern edge of the central time zone, which meant it started to get dark by four thirty. Jared usually remembered to flip the porch light on for her, but it was out when Jenna pulled into the driveway. Was the bulb dead or was he not home? He was supposed to be home.

Jenna's hand shook as she reached out. The front doorknob turned and opened without her key, and she stepped into the darkened living room. The door shouldn't be unlocked, even if he was home.

No answer. Unlocked door.

"Jared?"

Jenna tried not to smother him, tried not to let Celia's disappearance color the way she treated her son, but she couldn't help it. She worried about him more. The day after Celia disappeared, Jenna called a locksmith—every door received a dead bolt and a chain. Everybody in town probably did the same thing. A wave of suspicion swept through Hawks Mill once Celia was kidnapped. There was a palpable edge, a tension that seemed to grow between everyone, pushing them back, making them scared. No one felt the same about the town or the people in it.

On the day after Celia disappeared, Jenna found an old baseball bat in the garage, one that Jared used in grade school, and she'd slept with it next to her bed ever since. She carried pepper spray on her key chain and kept one in the drawer of her bedside table. She checked in with him more, texted him more.

But she hadn't heard from him after school. He never responded to the text she sent from the barn. She took deep breaths, told herself to be cool.

All was quiet inside the house. No music, no TV. She turned on a lamp, which cast a faint halo of yellow light on the space. The house looked neat and orderly, just the way she liked it. The place wasn't much, about fifteen hundred square feet, and it still needed work. But it was hers, slowly being paid for by her job as a nurse. Didn't this make her an adult: a job, a house, a kid? It wasn't bad for a single working mom, right?

How did having a missing and possibly murdered friend fit into the picture?

She went down the hallway to his bedroom, stepping lightly, the floorboards creaking under her feet. He could have fallen asleep. She remembered her own teenage years, the endless naps, the sleeping in on weekends. Was that one of the worst things time took away? The ability to sleep long, lazy hours?

Faint light seeped through the bottom of his bedroom door. She knocked lightly.

Did something rustle? Did she hear a voice?

"Jared?"

She pushed the door open. A quick scrambling, two bodies moving away from each other like repelled magnets. It took Jenna a moment. Jared was on the bed, his hands fumbling with his belt. And was that . . . ? A girl? Was there really a girl in Jared's room?

"Jesus, Mom. Don't you knock anymore?"

Jenna was paralyzed by both shock and embarrassment. Embarrassment for herself more than for the kids. After all, they were just being kids. She'd done the same things when she was fifteen. But as the bumbling adult walking in on them, she felt more the fool. Could she not have imagined Jared might have a girl in their house after school?

"Oh, shit, honey," she said, her words rushed. "I didn't know."

The girl—*the beautiful girl*—was straightening her shirt, smoothing it back down over her jeans. Jenna did the only thing she could do—she stepped back, pulling the door shut behind her.

Jenna wandered out to the kitchen in something of a daze. A girlfriend? How did she not know? She turned on the light above the sink. The darkened window gave back her own reflection. She'd never given him rules about having girls in the house. She'd never given him many rules about anything, so she had no reason to be angry. Not about that. She was a little pissed he hadn't returned her text or locked the front door, but she knew her worries were her own problem, letting the dog and pony show at the barn get inside her head. Jared was fifteen. He didn't have to stay in constant contact with his frazzled mother.

Jenna opened the refrigerator and pulled out a bottle of beer, which seemed essential after the day she'd had. She popped the cap and took a long drink, feeling the pleasant burn as it ran down her throat.

She stared at the bottle. A couple of beers or glasses of wine became the norm after Celia disappeared. Sometimes more than a couple. She needed them. Every night she needed them.

That's when she heard Jared's door open followed by footsteps coming down the hallway.

"Mom? I'm walking Tabitha home."

Jenna turned and saw Jared's head peeking into the kitchen. She recognized the look on his face. He wanted to rush out of the house, make a break before she could say or do anything else. No way, she thought. She wasn't going to let everybody go their separate ways on that crazy note of embarrassment.

"Come on in here," Jenna said, making a waving gesture with her hand.

"Mom," Jared said, teeth gritted.

"I want to meet . . . Did you say Tabitha? Come on."

"Are you kidding?" Jared asked.

"Tabitha?" Jenna called. "Can you come here for a minute?"

Jared looked as if someone had just dropped a ton of

bricks on his shoulders. He possessed the teenager's ability to overexaggerate even the slightest indignity.

Jenna walked to the hallway and saw the girl making
her way toward her. Jenna's quick first impression in the
bedroom had been correct—the girl *was* beautiful. Bright
green eyes and a long neck. She'd pulled on a winter coat,
a little too big and two seasons out of style even to Jenna's
eyes, but it wasn't zipped yet, and Jenna saw the slender,
shapely figure that almost every teenage girl seemed to be
blessed with. Once upon a time, Jenna had had that body
too, and she cursed herself daily for not appreciating hers
when it was in full bloom.

Jenna held out her hand. "I'm Jenna Barton. Jared's
mom."

"Hi." The girl took her hand in a limp shake. Her skin
was warm, a little sweaty.

"I'm sorry I walked in that way," Jenna said. "I had a
long day, and I wasn't thinking. You're welcome here
anytime."

The girl smiled, but the look seemed forced, as though
she didn't want to show her teeth. Jenna couldn't tell if she
was shy or embarrassed or both. Up close, Jenna saw that
the girl's haircut looked unprofessional, as if someone just
trimmed the edges straight across every once in a while.
Maybe she even cut it herself. And her clothes weren't
anything special either. Knockoff jeans and a fading top,
the sneakers, once white, scuffed and dirty. A kid without
a lot of money, which made her beauty all the more impressive. It wasn't enhanced by the clothes or the haircut
or orthodontics. She was the real deal, a stunner.

"What did you say your last name was?" Jenna asked.

"Tabitha Burke."

The girl didn't look up and meet Jenna's eye. But there was something about her face, and not just its youthful beauty. Something about the shape, the set of the eyes looked familiar.

"Burke," Jenna said, leaning against the hallway wall. "Are you related to Tommy Burke? He manages that electrical supply company out on the bypass."

Tabitha shook her head. "No."

"Mom, Tabitha doesn't have relatives here. She's new to town. Don't start asking her about everyone you went to high school with."

"I was just asking about the Burkes I know."

"We have to get going, okay? I'm walking Tabitha home."

"Do you want me to drive you? It's dark and cold."

"I've got this, Mom. Okay?"

"Are you sure? I mean—" Jenna stopped herself. Life had to go on. They couldn't hide inside all the time.

"Mom."

And Jenna knew he was right. She needed to back off and let him walk the girl home if that was what he wanted to do. It was early, and there'd be a lot of cars and people out despite the darkness. She sighed, letting go. She tried very hard to let go.

"Okay," Jenna said. The girl, Tabitha, still looked sullen and stiff, her eyes fixed on the floor as though Jenna's shoes were fascinating. But Jenna couldn't shake the sense she'd seen the girl before. And recently. Maybe she'd been a patient at Family Medicine. Jenna couldn't ask about that, couldn't run the risk of violating the girl's privacy. Walking in on her dry-humping her son was enough humiliation for one night. And if the girl had the guts to come back, to stick around after that inauspicious beginning, then Jenna would admire her. "Well, I'm sure your mom appreciates the fact that you have someone to walk you home in the dark."

Jared's eyes rolled to the ceiling and back, as if Jenna had just offered the queen or the pope a hit from a joint.

Tabitha raised her head a little, her cold green eyes meeting Jenna's. "My mother . . . ," she said, her voice flat.

"You mother? Is something . . . ?" Jenna lifted her hand to her mouth. "Oh, honey, I'm sorry. Did she pass away?"

If there'd been a hole to crawl in, Jenna would have jumped in with both feet. And pulled the top shut behind her. First catching them in the bedroom and then that comment. It made cursing at Becky seem like a minor miscue. She'd made the ridiculous mistake of assuming that everyone else's life was better than hers, that she could be a single mom but Tabitha's family was perfectly intact.

"Not that," the girl said. She held Jenna's gaze. "It's kind of an unusual situation, I guess. I live with my dad. Here. My mom . . . moved away. She's—she's had some problems."

Jenna waited. The girl seemed on the brink of adding something else, but she stopped herself. Jenna decided not to prod. She'd already trodden uncomfortable ground. She didn't need to pry into her parents' marital troubles.

"I see," Jenna said, trying to sound neutral.

"We're going, Mom." Jared reached out and gently guided Tabitha toward the door. "Tabitha's late."

The two of them walked side by side, but Tabitha turned back and looked at Jenna again. "I'm sorry about your friend," she said, her voice still flat and cool. "It's messed up when these things happen. When people just disappear."

And then they were gone.

CHAPTER SIX

T hey walked side by side through the dark, close but not holding hands. Jared wanted to reach out, to fold Tabitha's hand into his, but she walked with her head down, her eyes fixed on the ground as though she was afraid she might trip. And they never held hands in public. She didn't want someone to see and tell her dad. So Jared didn't push it.

And Tabitha did this at times, slipped away into someplace in her mind and acted as if the rest of the world, including him, didn't exist. Jared wanted to chalk it up to the embarrassment of his mom walking in, and then her slip of the tongue about Tabitha's mom, but he suspected something more. He'd seen her withdraw that way on an almost daily basis, and whenever he'd ask what was wrong, she'd simply say, "I'm fine."

"I'm sorry about my mom," he said. "She really is pretty mellow, but sometimes she says stuff. It's kind of like if there's an embarrassing situation, she feels the need to acknowledge it or talk about it more instead of just letting it go away."

Tabitha kept walking, eyes down. In the street beside them, cars zipped by, the headlights catching their figures in the glow and making Jared squint. He couldn't wait to get his license, to no longer have to be dependent on walking across town in the cold or rain. Or taking rides from his mom or his friends' parents.

"She was probably a little shocked to see a girl in my room," he said. "It's never really happened. I mean, I've been with girls and stuff, just not in my room."

Tabitha looked up, turning to face him. But she still didn't say anything.

"Is that okay? Should I have not said that?"

"No, you're lucky," she said.

"Lucky?" He didn't understand what she meant. Lucky? Because he hadn't had a lot of girls in his room? "You mean because I have a mom looking out for me?" he asked.

She didn't answer right away, but then she said, "Yes, that."

"Will your dad be pissed that you're late? I know you're supposed to be home before it gets dark."

Tabitha spoke but barely moved her lips. "I don't know."

The nature of their relationship—if he was even allowed to call it that—had always seemed strange to Jared. They spent a lot of time together but only in the most narrow, limited way. Tabitha's father insisted she come home right after school every day, which meant they rushed out of the building carrying their books. Only a couple of times—including today—had Tabitha defied her father and done something else. Mostly the two of them ate lunch together and talked all through study hall in the cafeteria, to the point that Jared's best friends— Mike and Syd—had taken to shaking their heads at him for being so quickly and completely in love.

Tabitha texted him from time to time outside of school, but she never called, and the messages stopped in the early evening, long before either one of them would have been going to bed.

They crossed Washington Street, lights glowing in all the houses. Through some of the windows, Jared saw families sitting down to dinner together or watching TV, like some kind of sickeningly perfect Norman Rockwell scene. He'd never had that in his life, at least not in the ten years since his dad left. But how many kids did? Half of his friends' parents were divorced, and he'd been in enough homes and around enough families to see the strain and tensions that simmered in even the most normal places.

A few blocks later, the houses started to change. He and his mom lived in what she called a "working-class neighborhood," which as far as he could tell meant they were surrounded by store clerks and mechanics and men and women who worked in factories. They all took good care of their yards and kept a careful eye on their kids. Occasionally somebody threw a party, and there'd be loud music and whooping and hollering and beer cans in the yard the next morning. But the beer cans always got picked up, usually by the homeowners themselves, tired and looking hungover, sweating out their booze as they tossed the empties into an orange recycling bin.

The few blocks around Washington Street were nicer. The homes were older and bigger, made out of brick with wide front porches and bay windows. Those houses had beautifully cared-for yards as well, but the people who lived there didn't do the work. They paid someone else to cut and trim and weed and plant. Jared knew a few kids from school who lived there, the sons and daughters of doctors and lawyers and executives.

But across Washington, as they headed into Tabitha's neighborhood, the houses looked different from the way they did anywhere else. They were small and dirty, the yards filled with toys and trash. The cars in the street were dented and damaged, leaking oil and hoisted on blocks. People sat on their porches a lot over there when the weather was nice, but Jared didn't get the sense it was because they were looking out for anybody else. Those people gave off a boredom that bordered on desperation, a thick, palpable sense of being lost and adrift. He couldn't imagine what else they did with their time, if anything.

And with a woman kidnapped in the town, they probably grew more scared, more withdrawn and suspicious.

Tabitha's house was two blocks ahead on a little side street called Nutwood. He'd walked her home nearly every day for the past three weeks, but not once had he so much as set foot in her yard. At her insistence, they always said their good-byes at the corner, and while she'd once pointed her house out to him—four doors down on the left, a boxy little structure with a cramped porch and a loose shutter—he'd never come any closer than that. He should have known the cave comment would hurt her feelings. Even compared to the modest house he shared with his mom, Tabitha's looked small and dingy. Was it simple embarrassment that kept her from letting him get any closer?

Once again, they stopped at the corner. Fewer cars went by, and the ones that did pass made their presence known through their apparent lack of mufflers. The houses on Nutwood looked darker too. Most of the shades and curtains were drawn, smothering any light that might have escaped.

"Oh, shit," Tabitha said.

"What?"

She turned toward Jared, placing both of her hands on his chest and giving him a hard shove that sent him stumbling back on his heels. "Go," she said, her voice cutting through the dark like a laser. "Just go."

But Jared stepped forward again, closer to her. "What is it?"

She turned and started hustling down the street toward her house, moving away from him quickly for the second time that afternoon. Jared looked in the direction she hurried, and on the porch of the fourth house on the left, a man stood, pacing back and forth, the red glow from a cigarette burning in the darkness.

Jared couldn't make out the man's features. He looked broad, even a little heavy through his chest and stomach. And he paced like a panther Jared had once seen in the

Louisville Zoo, a desperate-looking animal that simply moved from one end of its cage to the other. The animal depressed Jared, even as a child, because the big cat seemed so eager to run, to charge, to hunt, but it couldn't.

Jared jogged after Tabitha. "Wait. If that's your dad, I can tell him it's my fault. I'll say my mom was talking to you—"

She wheeled around. Even in the dark, he saw the tears glistening in her eyes, about to spill over. She jabbed the air with her index finger, the stubby nail pointing directly at his heart.

"Go," she said. "Please. Go. Now."

She didn't wait for a response but turned back around and kept walking away. Jared turned and left, not sure if the smoking man—Tabitha's father—had seen them together or not. And if he had seen them, what would it mean for Tabitha when she entered her house?

CHAPTER SEVEN

Jenna saw Celia again.

Her best friend walked along the edge of Caldwell Park, wearing a white nightgown. Celia's hair was down, lifting in the light breeze. The trees were colored by autumn—vivid reds, oranges, and yellows—even though it was dark. The trees practically burned. And on the porch of every house a jack-o'-lantern glowed.

Jenna knew when the scene was taking place. A week after Halloween. The week Celia disappeared.

Jenna watched her friend through thick hedges, the leaves and branches jabbing at her and tickling her face. She tried to extract herself but couldn't move. She couldn't slip out of their grip. She couldn't step forward onto the sidewalk where her friend walked.

And then the car. Always a different car. Sometimes a white van, sometimes a hearse. It pulled alongside Celia, and a hand reached out to grab her. Never a full body.

Never a face. Only that bone-white hand reaching through the dark to take her friend.

Celia looked back. She knew Jenna was there, trapped in the bushes. Celia didn't speak, didn't scream or call for help. But she looked back, terror etched on her face like a frozen mask.

Jenna couldn't make a sound. She tried to shout, tried to scream, but she couldn't make a sound. Her voice was choked off, silenced—

The chiming of her phone woke her on the couch.

Her heart thumped, even though she'd had some version of the dream . . . how many times? Fifteen at least. She vowed to stop counting, vowed to not let the image of Celia's terrified face haunt her anymore.

But how could it not? How could she not contemplate, in her darkest, most desperate moments, what must have happened to her friend?

Jenna sat up on the couch. Her neck ached from the crooked angle. She felt lonelier than ever, the dull ache of Celia's loss worming through her body. She missed Celia so badly. Missed her laugh, missed the sound of her voice. It felt as if someone had cut a piece out of her on that November night.

An empty beer bottle sat on the coffee table, and her head swam a little. *Good work, Jenna,* she told herself. *Puke. Don't eat anything else. And then drink a beer. And you're a nurse. Shouldn't you know better?* For the twentieth time since November, she promised herself to drink less. To maybe—just maybe—stop drinking altogether.

The phone chimed three straight times. She checked her watch. Six ten. How long had she slept? Thirty minutes or so?

The house around her was quiet. She replayed the events that had occurred right before she dozed off. Jared left to walk his girlfriend—*girlfriend*?—home. Jenna's face flushed with embarrassment, and she had to laugh. What an introduction for that kid. Nowhere to go but up.

"Jared?"

She scrolled through her texts, but they didn't make sense. They came mostly from her group of friends and a cousin who lived in Ohio.

Nice one, Jenna!

Whoa, you were pissed!

Way to stick it to the media.

Um, call me?

And one from Jared: I'm staying at Tabitha's for a while.

Jenna wrote back. Okay, but not too late. Call if you want a ride.

She hoped things went better on that end than they had gone on hers. Maybe the girl's dad was cool and smooth, the kind who played old music for the kids and told stories about the summer in college when he followed U2 across the country, hitchhiking and chasing girls. Or maybe he and Jared would talk about sports or cars or Stephen King novels, and the guy would send him away with some poetry by Rimbaud.

I think you're ready for this now, he'd say, clapping her son on the back and shaking his hand, and Jared would go along, accepting his lesson on masculinity.

Someone knocked on the door, and on her way to answer it the landline rang.

"Good God," Jenna said. "Now what?"

She grabbed the phone first, and before she could even say hello, her mother's voice came through.

"Are you okay?"

"Mom? Hold on."

"You really didn't look that great—"

She laid the phone aside and went to the door. She peeked through the window, and in the glow of the porch light—not burned out, just not turned on while Jared swapped spit with Tabitha—she saw her coworker Sally. Jenna hustled to undo the locks, and when she pulled the door open, her friend stood there with a bottle of wine in one hand and a large grin across her face.

"What's the occasion?" Jenna asked, and Sally stepped past her and into the living room. "Did you say you were coming over and I forgot?"

"I figured you needed a pick-me-up."

"Because of today? Sure, I guess. Hold on, my mom's on the phone."

Jenna picked up the receiver again. "Mom? Can I call you back? Sally's here."

"That's fine. You don't have to call me back. I just want you to know, I have no problem with women speaking their minds." Her mother's voice was rough and gravelly, a by-product of years of cigarette smoking. "I taught you to do anything a man can do, you know that. I didn't raise a shrinking violet. I just wish you wouldn't be quite so *assertive* in public that way. It's . . . coarse. People judge you for those things."

Jenna said, "Am I supposed to know what you're talking about?"

Just then her phone received a few more texts, the chiming sounding more urgent.

"You weren't watching?" her mom asked. "Oh, boy."

Jenna watched herself on the television several times. Reena Huffman seemed to be enjoying playing the clip. Jenna saw herself on camera, her face paler than she could ever have thought possible. The lights from Stan's camera hit her at such an angle that she looked like something that had just crawled from beneath a rock.

"How the fuck do you think I feel, Becky? Jesus."

The offending words were replaced with long, angry bleeps, leaving it up to the viewer's imagination to wonder what she had really said.

"I didn't know they would show that, Sally. I'd literally just puked. I thought they were carrying Celia's bones out of that barn."

"I don't think people around here will mind the 'fuck' as much as they'll mind the 'Jesus.' If they can read lips . . ." Sally poured herself another glass of wine. "Everybody's on edge around here. Everybody's scared. It won't take much to make them angry." She wore loose-fitting jeans and a bulky sweater, and her hair was piled on top of her head and held in place with a pencil. A pair of glasses dangled from a chain around her neck. Sally was fifteen years older than Jenna, and since Celia's disappearance, she had been increasingly playing the roles of both mentor and friend. Jenna had a mother, but the phone call about her appearance on TV epitomized their relationship—it never lost its air of judgment, the sense that Jenna needed constant correction and guidance.

Sally held the wine bottle up. "More?"

Jenna shook her head, which still hurt. She always drank with Sally. It was one of the pillars of their friendship—alcohol consumption. The glass of wine on top of the beer made Jenna's head feel as if it had been stuffed with cotton.

"I've told you before that Becky McGee is a pill," Sally said. "I knew her older sister in high school. She was a brat when she was a little kid, and I bet she still is."

"She's always seemed decent."

"As long as the story is flowing her way, she's decent," Sally said. "But there haven't been any new leads. The story has to go somewhere."

Jenna saw a freeze frame of her face on the screen. "Oh, God. That's the worst image ever. I'm going to turn it up."

"Jenna—"

"I want to hear it."

Reena Huffman was ranting in her high, grating voice.

". . . been holding off on saying some of these things. I always try to be respectful of the friends and family members of a crime victim. And make no mistake, what happened to Celia Walters is a crime. It's a tragedy. But someone knows something about it. A young, beautiful woman like this, this Diamond Mom, doesn't just disappear without a trace without someone knowing something about it."

The images on the screen shifted. Jenna's pale, ugly photo remained, but it was joined by a portrait of Celia, the one most widely distributed in the wake of her disappearance. In the photo, Celia looked radiant. Perfect smile, shining brown hair. Wide brown eyes. She looked like everybody's sister, friend, daughter, girlfriend. The all-American dream.

"This friend, this Jenna Barton, I'm starting to wonder if she has been entirely forthcoming about the events of that night, November the fourth. She says the two women, who had been best friends since junior high, were just going out for some girl time. But why were they going out at midnight? Who does that? Why did Jenna call Celia up that night and invite her out for a drink at midnight? Jenna says they were just reliving their old glory days when they were wild and free young people. But who does that? Who does that when they're parents? Both of these women are parents to teenagers. And Jenna is a single mom, so who was home with her son when she went out that night? Who does those things at that age? I think there's much more to know here, and I hope . . . no, I pray that the police start asking these questions of Jenna Barton. This language she used today . . . it tells me this is not a normal person."

Jenna groaned.

Sally fumbled around, looking for the remote.

But Reena shifted gears.

"As if this case wasn't getting strange enough," she said.

"Wait," Jenna said. And Sally stopped looking.

"There's another piece of news breaking about this case, and maybe, just maybe, we'll finally get some light shed on these events."

Jenna's mind raced. What else could be going on besides the bones in the barn?

"This is breaking news," Reena said, "something we are just learning as we went on the air. Apparently the earring, the match to the earring that was found near the park where Celia Walters is believed to have disappeared, has been found."

Jenna stood up, her hands hanging limp and useless at her sides.

"We're still learning about this, and we'll have more to report as the show goes on here. But what we know is that someone was taken into custody just this evening for trying to sell that earring, the match to the one that belongs to Celia Walters, at a pawnshop. Police have taken a man into custody, and that's all we know right now. But we'll keep you up-to-date. And we'll be right back."

"No," Jenna said, stepping toward the screen. "No. You can't do that. You can't just start and stop like that."

"It's a commercial," Sally said. "She'll be back. She's teasing us because she doesn't know anything."

Sally muted the TV. Jenna stared at the images. The

president talking at a lectern, a teaser for a foreign affairs show. And then a commercial for orange juice.

"Honey." Sally came up beside her and placed her hands on Jenna's shoulders. "It will be okay. They'll come back."

"What if they found the guy?" Jenna asked, not really addressing her words to anybody. "What if this is it?"

Sally guided her to a chair. Jenna dropped into it, her body moving without any conscious thought on her part. She felt like a robot, an automaton.

"We'll know more in a minute," Sally said. "Well, maybe not even then. They're piecing the story together. Becky is probably running around bugging the shit out of the cops."

"I should call Detective Poole."

"Why don't you wait and see what Reena says? Here." She handed Jenna a glass of wine. "Let's see if it comes back on."

Jenna finished the little bit of wine in the glass.

The show returned, but Reena went to another story, something about a woman who discovered she had a sister she didn't know about until her mother was murdered.

Sally muted it. "Let's talk while they go through these other things."

They sat in silence for a moment, and then Jenna grabbed the wine bottle and filled her glass. She needed it. She could slow down tomorrow. She took a long drink and then said, "I haven't eaten anything."

"Do you want to order something?" Sally asked. "Or

do you want me to make you some eggs? Or a sandwich?"

"I'm good."

"Do you want to be alone?" Sally asked.

"No. No way." Jenna gave Sally a smile that she hoped
conveyed the depth of her gratitude. "I like your company. I like having someone to talk to. It's been hard to
talk to some of my other friends about all this. It's so
freaking awkward." She pointed to the TV screen. "I
think this is what everybody thinks about me. People I've
known for years. They have these questions. They blame
me. You just said that everybody's scared and on edge in
town. You've felt it. When people get scared, they look for
someone to blame. No one will say it, but they do blame
me. I wish they'd actually just say it instead of dancing
around it."

"I doubt they feel that way about you. I think a lot of
this is in your head. It's guilt talking."

"I don't know. . . ."

Sally took a swallow from her own glass. She looked
thoughtful. "I've never asked you anything about the
case because I figured you'd had your fill of talking about
it. And we've only started to get to know each other
well."

"You asked me to your book club the month Celia
disappeared."

"Was that rude?" Sally asked.

"It was a lifesaver," Jenna said. "You were the first
person to treat me like I was normal. That's all I wanted,
for people to act normal."

Sally laughed. "No one ever accused me of that," she said. "Well, there is something I've always wanted to ask you."

"What's that?" Jenna asked.

"What the hell were you doing, going out that night?"

Jenna took another big swallow of wine. She nodded, ready to go on.

CHAPTER EIGHT

Jared froze on the sidewalk in front of Tabitha's house. The curtains were drawn, the porch light out.

He'd started home, cursing himself for letting Tabitha run late and cursing himself for not having the guts to walk her all the way to the door. All he had to do was stick out his hand and introduce himself to her father. Wasn't that what boyfriends were supposed to do? Go to the door, shake hands with the dad? Times like that, he did wish he had a father, someone who could guide him through the complicated waters of manhood. But Jared knew he made a good impression on adults. He was clean-cut, well dressed, polite, and friendly. He needed to take the heat so Tabitha wouldn't have to.

But he couldn't will himself up the front walk to the door. He couldn't stop thinking about the look on Tabitha's face, the combination of fear and sadness. She'd shoved him with a force he couldn't have guessed she'd have in her body, almost knocking him down. What if he rang the bell like an idiot and made it all worse? He didn't want to be like his mom, barging into any situation and then thinking about the consequences later.

Jared needed to go home. His mom would be waiting, and he had homework to do, things he would have been working on except he spent that time with Tabitha. But he wouldn't hear from her all evening. There'd be no texts or calls, no messages. He'd have to go home and work, all the while wondering if she ended up in trouble with her dad—and if she did, what kind of trouble might inspire so much fear? If the guy was so strict about everything else, might he hurt her if she came home late? And what if he had happened to look up the street and see her saying good-bye to a boy?

Jared looked to the houses on either side of Tabitha's. They were dark, as still and quiet in the night as empty tombs. Jared took a few steps up the city sidewalk, moving parallel to the houses, then turned to his left, cutting across the grass between Tabitha's house and their neighbors'. It was getting colder, and he'd forgotten to bring gloves. His fingertips tingled, so he stuffed his hands in his pockets.

The door of Tabitha's house came open, a shaft of light spilling across the lawn.

Jared acted without thinking. He dropped to the grass, face-first. He pressed his body against the ground, hugging it as tightly as he could. The blades of grass tickled his face, and the cold seeped into his clothes, clinging to his skin like a tight suit.

He risked a look, moving his eyeballs slowly to the

left. The man stood on the porch, his large body obscuring most of the light. He tossed a cigarette out into the yard, its glowing tip landing ten feet from Jared's head.

Jared waited. Every atom in his body clenched. A pressure rose in his bladder, a painful surging of liquid. He gritted his teeth until he thought they'd chip.

Then the door closed. The man was gone, back inside.

Jared waited as long as he could. When he thought it was okay to stand up, he counted to twenty and then rose.

He was colder, his pulse racing. But he didn't stop.

At the back of Tabitha's house, a light burned in a window and then spilled into the darkness. Given the window's placement, he guessed it was the kitchen. Jared felt a churning in his gut as he moved closer, a swirling of adrenaline and nerves that seemed to be on the brink of bursting through his skin. He still needed to pee. He knew if he was seen, if someone from the neighborhood or Tabitha's father called the police on him, then Tabitha would know he'd been sneaking around. The relationship would be over. Game, set, match. But he needed to know she was safe. He'd seen guilt over Celia's kidnapping rip his mother apart, felt his own guilt over that night like broken glass in his stomach. Did he want to feel the same way about Tabitha if something happened to her?

He came to within ten feet of the window. A dog started barking nearby, a harsh ripping sound that cut through the night, freezing Jared in his tracks. His breath came in quick huffs, but he realized the dog wasn't barking at him. Somebody a few houses away shouted at the dog to be quiet, and the barking stopped. He willed his body to move forward again, avoiding the spill of light from the Burkes' kitchen window.

He saw a row of brown cabinets, and a light fixture hanging from the ceiling by a decorative chain. The wallpaper was yellow and faded, a couple of corners peeling loose and curling away from the plaster.

Tabitha sat at the kitchen table. Her head rested in her hands, so Jared couldn't see her face. Her shoulders rose and fell once as though she'd heaved a big sigh. Was she crying? A coil of anger wound its way through Jared's chest. If someone hurt her, if someone made her cry . . .

Then the man came into the room, the same man he'd seen on the porch. He was close to fifty and overweight, his midsection straining against the confines of a stained sweatshirt. His face was flat and broad, and in the harsh overhead light of the kitchen, Jared saw pockmarks on either side of his bulbous nose. The lids of his eyes looked heavy, and his graying hair was greasy and thick. He lifted a newly lit cigarette to his lips and took a long drag, his eyes squinting as the smoke curled up toward the ceiling. Then he made a jabbing motion against the table, stubbing the cigarette out.

Tabitha hadn't moved. Jared couldn't even bring himself to look for a physical resemblance between such an ugly man and beautiful Tabitha. The thought was too distasteful. Jared's anger switched to something else, something similar and even more pointed and painful. He understood it, even though he hadn't experienced it in quite this way before. But the man's proximity to

Tabitha, the fact that he could be in the same house with her and know her so well, made Jared seethe. Jared was jealous, and the distance between him and Tabitha never felt greater. What else didn't he know about her if he didn't know what went on in her house?

The man said something, and Tabitha looked up. She didn't appear to be crying, although she didn't look happy either. Her face was a mask of caution as she considered her father from the corners of her eyes.

The man continued to speak, wagging his index finger in the air for emphasis. He didn't seem angry, didn't appear to be losing control of his emotions, but the lecture continued for several minutes while Tabitha listened without responding or moving.

And then the man stopped his talking. He stared down at Tabitha as though he was waiting for something. Finally Tabitha nodded, moving her head up and down three times.

The man moved closer to Tabitha. He hovered over her, looming like a massive shadow. Tabitha looked small. Young. Defenseless.

CHAPTER NINE

Jenna had met Celia Springer on the first day of junior high. They ended up sitting next to each other in homeroom, and at first, Celia acted as if Jenna weren't there. Maybe that made the possibility of her friendship more appealing. Maybe it made Jenna want to work harder to earn that friendship from her. While the teacher, an older man with a comb-over named Mr. Phelps, read announcements, Celia studied her perfectly manicured nails, occasionally looking up with a casual flip of her flawless brown hair.

Then Mr. Phelps provided the opening for Jenna. At the end of his speech, he looked at them sincerely, not quite aware of what an object of derision he was in their eyes. Jenna felt sorry for him because he was trying so hard. But that didn't mean she wouldn't make fun of him.

"I think," Mr. Phelps said, "this might be hard, but if we work together we can handle it."

Without missing a beat, Jenna whispered out of the side of her mouth, "I bet he says that to his wife."

Celia tried to contain her laughter, but it burst out. She lifted her hand, cupping it over her mouth. But it was too late. And then Jenna laughed too, but louder, a sound that to her own ears sounded like a bray.

Mr. Phelps pounced, threatening them with detention. Celia controlled herself. Jenna couldn't. It wasn't even that funny, but Jenna ended up in detention alone. And then the next day, Celia didn't ignore her in homeroom. They talked before the bell rang. They both loved George Michael, even though they wondered if he was gay. They both watched *The Wonder Years* religiously and admitted to daydreaming about Fred Savage, who they *knew* wasn't gay. Celia had seen the movie *Hairspray* and looked disappointed when Jenna said she hadn't. Jenna tried to recover by saying she intended to see it as soon as she could, maybe that coming weekend.

"I might want to see it again," Celia said, her voice noncommittal.

Jenna prayed that Celia would go with her. And Celia did. After the movie, Celia invited Jenna to spend the night. Jenna had read *Charlie and the Chocolate Factory* several times by that point in her life. As she fell asleep in Celia's large and comfortable home that night, she felt she'd discovered her own personal golden ticket.

"We've been best friends ever since," she said to Sally.

The wine bottle on the coffee table was nearly empty,

and Jenna felt a drunken tingling forming at the back of her neck. But she didn't feel sick anymore. She was hungry, her stomach sending gnawing messages to her brain. It felt good to talk to someone, someone who seemed content to listen without judgment. Talking of Celia made Jenna feel lonely and guilty again, but the pain wasn't as sharp.

She looked at the TV. Reena came back from yet another commercial, so Sally turned up the volume. Jenna checked the clock. It was nearing the end of the show's time slot.

"No," she muttered to herself.

"If you're just joining us, we're covering the breaking news that an earring, an apparent match to the one apparently lost by Celia Walters on the night she disappeared, has been found. What we know now is that a man tried to sell this earring at a pawnshop in Hawks Mill, Kentucky, and an alert clerk notified the police. The man is in custody, but the authorities aren't saying anything else at this time. Tune in to our coverage at eleven o'clock tonight, after *The Foreign Affairs Hour*, which is coming up next."

"No." Jenna jumped up. She scrambled around the living room until she found her phone and dialed Detective Poole. "Come on, come on." It went straight to voice mail. She tried three more times, feeling Sally hovering behind her. The detective still didn't answer.

"She's busy," Sally said. "A new can of worms just opened."

"Drive me to the police station."

Sally reached over and gently took the phone out of

her hand. "No. Let them do their jobs. The cops are having a hard enough time around here. Everybody's buying
guns and jumping at their own shadows, even three
months later. No one's relaxed. Are you hungry?"

"You're trying to change the subject."

"Yes. Are you hungry?"

Jenna gave in. "I could eat something," she said. "And
that wine's almost gone. But I have more in the kitchen."

Jenna pulled some grapes and decent cheese out of the
refrigerator and found a box of crackers in the cupboard.
She pointed across the room. "There's another bottle in
there. Cabernet if you want to open it."

Please, she thought. *Let me learn something about this
case. Something real.*

Even if I have to wait until tomorrow.

I promise I'll drink less.

"I have to pace myself," Sally said.

Jenna looked up at the clock. Seven o'clock. "Shit."

"What is it?" Sally asked. She dug in a few different
drawers until she found the wine opener, and then she
went to work on the bottle.

"Jared. Get a load of this." She tried to shift away
from Celia. From the earring. *A man in custody.* "Did
your sons ever have girls in the house? I mean, without
you knowing it?"

"Probably all the time. I don't want to know what
they did." She poured them each a glass. "Ignorance is
bliss."

"I came home today after all that crap at the barn. I
walk into his room, and he has this girl on top of him.

I'd never seen her before, didn't even know he was hanging out with a girl. What am I supposed to do with that?"

"Buy him some condoms," she said.

Jenna had just started chewing a cracker with cheese on top, but she paused to give Sally a look. "That's all the motherly wisdom you could come up with? He's over at this girl's house now. But how do I know that? Should I call over there? Or go over?"

"Relax. Kids are going to do what they're going to do. I thought you trusted him."

"I do. But how do I know I trust her?"

"You think she's a bad influence?"

"I just met her. And ever since Celia disappeared . . . I try not to be too paranoid or crazy about what Jared does."

"But it seeps in."

"Exactly. It colors everything I do. I check the back of my car before I get in, even in broad daylight. I rush from the car to the front door like the bogeyman is about to get me. Like I'm a dumb girl in a horror movie. And I worry about Jared when he leaves the house. He's a boy, so I figure he's a little safer. But still . . . he's young. He could be a target for something." Jenna sipped her wine, then threw a grape into her mouth and bit down. She pictured the girl, Tabitha, in her mind again, tried to re-examine her first and only impression of the girl objectively. "And there was something about this girl, Sally. Something about the look in her eye. There was an edge to her, a toughness, something you wouldn't acquire just growing up the way Jared did. Even with his dad leaving us high and dry."

"A lot of kids come from shitty homes," Sally said.

"It wasn't just that, although I suspect her home life isn't great. She basically said her parents are separated. It kind of sounded like she doesn't have any contact with her mother. And her clothes looked . . . Well, I suspect she's poor. But her eyes . . . they didn't have the spark of youth the way you'd expect to see it. There was something off there, something cold."

"Maybe she thought climbing on top of Jared would keep her warm."

Jenna picked up a grape and threw it at Sally. "Aren't you supposed to be helping me?" She laughed despite the long, shitty day. The wine had helped her get there.

"It's good to hear you laugh," Sally said. "Hell, I almost feel bad."

"About what?"

"The serious stuff we've been talking about. We can forget it if you want. Or talk about it another day."

But Jenna was shaking her head, even before Sally finished speaking.

"Are you kidding?" Jenna asked. "I'm glad you finally asked."

CHAPTER TEN

Jared's hands were no longer cold. He flexed them in the darkness, felt an aching heat in his knuckles. Light rain started to fall, frigid drops pinging against the top of his head and dotting his face. He wished the man would walk away, leave the room, leave Tabitha alone.

The man moved even closer to Tabitha, who stared up at him with a look that seemed to waver somewhere between fear and disgust. He made a quick lunging gesture with his left hand. Tabitha flinched, as though she thought he was going to hit her. Jared tensed, took a step forward.

But her father's hand—fat and broad like a large cut of steak—stopped inches from her face. It brushed along her cheek and tucked a loose strand of hair behind her ear. Her father spoke to her, the words lost to Jared, as he continued to stroke her hair. Tabitha's eyes remained wide, but some of the tension drained from the rest of her face. The skin around her mouth relaxed, and the rising and falling of her shoulders as she breathed settled into a more natural rhythm.

She nodded to something he said, her eyes staring up at him with nearly complete attention and devotion.

Jared felt the jealousy twisting in his guts again, an irrational but powerful surge he couldn't stop. He needed to turn away, to let Tabitha be with her father without his spying on her.

But he didn't go. He watched as her father bent down at the table and placed a quick, gentle kiss on Tabitha's lips. It wasn't a long, lingering kiss. Their lips made just the barest of contact with each other's. And when her father straightened up, keeping his hand resting on Tabitha's shoulder, she wore a slight, uncertain smile, as though the kiss had reassured her of something she'd been doubting.

But it seemed wrong to Jared. A violation.

Those lips. He'd just been kissing them.

Without thinking, he bent down, lowering his hands to the cold earth. He fumbled, his hands passing over brittle blades of grass and dirt. Then his hand closed around a rock, small and jagged like a throwing star.

In one motion, he straightened up and threw it toward the window, hoping to stop the scene playing out before him.

It made a short, sharp crunching sound as it passed through the windowpane. Both Tabitha and her father flinched as the rock bounced off the wall behind them. The look on her father's face transformed. From doting love to defensive. He started toward the window.

"Shit." Jared turned and ran back out to the street, his legs pumping so fast they seemed about to lift him off the ground. He ran and ran, the cold air in his face, his heart pounding. The dog barked again, and then a voice called after him.

"Hey!"

But he didn't break stride. He kept running and running, the increasing rain like a frozen river on his face.

CHAPTER ELEVEN

—————————

I wish the media could capture and really convey what good friends Celia and I were," Jenna said. *"Are."* They'd moved back into the living room, the snacks and the new bottle of wine on the coffee table before them. Jenna settled into an overstuffed chair while Sally sat on the couch. "We went through everything together. Everything over the last . . . Shit, we've known each other for twenty-seven years."

"Everyone needs a friend like that. Women especially."

"Do you have someone like that?" Jenna asked.

"My friend Dee. She lives in Atlanta now, but we talk almost every day. And we go see each other."

"Exactly. Celia and I, we went through losing our virginity, prom, falling in love, and getting married. She was there during my divorce. She really encouraged me to go back to school after Marty left. She helped with watching Jared while I did it. If it wasn't my mom, it was Celia. Always."

"And you kept it up all these years?"

Jenna didn't say anything for a moment. She ran one hand along the puffy contours of the armrest while the other held a full glass of wine. She felt Sally watching her, waiting for more. "It hasn't been quite the same the last few years. Not that we weren't close, Celia and I, but we hadn't spent as much time together. Her husband, Ian, his family runs the Walters Foundry."

"I know who they are."

"Ian's been taking a bigger and bigger role at the company as his dad gets older. They've become part of a different social circle. I'll be honest—I worried about her as a mother. Was she spending enough time at home? They spend more time at the country club, more time traveling to places I could never afford to go. Barcelona. Costa Rica. I'd love to visit those places, don't get me wrong."

"But a nurse who's a single mom can't just jet off to Spain."

"Exactly." Jenna tried to find the right words to describe what had changed between her and Celia. It wasn't anything big. It wasn't the kind of shift that ends a friendship or even fundamentally alters it. There were just times when they'd see each other or talk that they seemed to be speaking different dialects of the same language. How could Jenna compete with stories of seaside dining in Saint-Tropez? "There was a little barrier between us the last few years. Not a wall. Not even a curtain. Maybe I'd describe it as mesh. Something sheer and see-through, but I was still aware it was there. And I think Celia felt it too."

"Friendships, even the best ones, can go up and down."

"Yeah." Jenna looked around the room. Her house. Her space. Pictures of Jared from all stages of his life. A framed college diploma. She'd made a life, and she hated that sometimes, like an insecure teenager, she still held it up next to others to see how it compared. She thought she'd made her peace, way back in high school, with the fact that she'd never measure up to Celia in certain departments: looks, money, decorum, boyfriend. But she had other things. She knew she did. She had a life she'd built mostly by herself. "We used to sneak out all the time in high school. Weekdays, weekends, it didn't matter. We'd sneak out after our parents went to bed, usually around midnight, and we'd meet at Caldwell Park. Sometimes there'd be boys or other friends to meet up with. Sometimes we'd just talk and wander around on our own."

"And that's what you were doing that night? Reliving your wild single-girl years?"

"It sounds idiotic."

"Not really. It sounds like fun."

"I was thinking about Celia that night. I heard a stupid song on the radio, one we used to dance to when we were kids. 'Girls Just Want to Have Fun'? It's a Cyndi Lauper song."

"I'm not that old, girlfriend."

"Sorry. I sat here in the house thinking of Celia and that stupid sheer curtain, and I decided it didn't have to be there. We could just rip it down by acting like we used to act. So I texted her and said, 'Want to meet in the park at twelve?' I expected her to say no, but she said yes. One word. 'Yes!' So we were on. We would be kids again."

Jenna took another drink of wine. She remembered the night so well. It was warm, Indian summer. And as she'd dressed she felt a flutter of excitement in her belly she hadn't felt in years. Once she was ready, she told Jared where she was going and that she wouldn't be gone long. He was reading a novel, something with a creepy clown's face on the cover, and she made him promise to keep the doors locked and to text her if he needed anything. She expected to get a grunting response, something that indicated an utter lack of interest in his mother's activities, even if the timing of her departure was a little strange.

But then she saw the bottle on his desk. Jim Beam. She never knew him to take a drink, never knew him to show any interest in the stuff, although she also knew that day would come soon enough. She went into full mom mode, asking a ton of questions about where it came from and who it belonged to.

She decided not to go, to call Celia and cancel the plans.

But Jared told her to go, that they could work it all out. He dumped the booze down the sink right in front of her.

And she didn't want to cancel. Didn't want to let her friend down again.

"So I was late," Jenna said. "I was always late. But that night I never heard from her. She didn't show up. I texted and texted but didn't hear back. I figured something came up. Hell, something came up with my son. I figured maybe it was Celia's daughter, Ursula, or maybe Ian. I called Ian finally, and he reported her missing. He thought she was with me. I thought she was with him. And then later I found out she thought someone might have been following her. She never told me that, so it hit home that we weren't as close. I could have picked her up. We could have done it all differently."

"Wow. I'm sorry, honey. But you can't beat yourself up over that. It's just . . . a coincidence. A horrible coincidence, but that's all it is."

"I try to tell myself that."

"Are you sure she didn't run away?" Sally asked. "You know people say things. They speculate. Would she leave her life that way?"

"Leave her child?" Jenna asked. "Like I said, she wasn't a perfect mom. And Ursula, her daughter . . . she's shown it a little bit."

"Wild?"

"Not that so much," Jenna said. "Just . . . unhappy, I guess. Kind of an angry kid once she hit her teenage years. A couple of weeks after Celia disappeared, she got into a fight with a girl at school. No big deal, really. No one was hurt. They pulled Ursula off the other girl before it got too bad."

"And if her mother just disappeared, you could understand her anger."

"Sure. Look, Celia could be impulsive. She could be emotional. Every once in a while, she'd get mad at me and shut me out. She did it about four years ago."

"Why?"

"We were out with friends, and I mentioned this guy she hooked up with in college. She and Ian were on a break back then, and I thought all our friends knew she had this thing with this guy on the swim team. Apparently not everyone did. She froze me out for two weeks. I didn't even know what my crime was."

"So she had some places she wouldn't let people go."

"Doesn't everybody?"

But Sally looked as though she had something else on her mind, something else she wanted to say.

"What?" Jenna asked.

"It's nothing. It's—I'm sure you've thought of it. It's kind of a morbid thought."

Jenna didn't push her, but she knew exactly what Sally was thinking. She knew the same question lurked in the minds of everybody in town. Yes, if Jenna had been on time, Celia might not have been taken.

But what if she'd been on time and suffered the same fate?

That scenario ran through Jenna's mind at least one hundred times a day. She couldn't count the number of nights she lay in bed, the room and the house dark, the red glow from the bedside clock in her peripheral vision. She felt the guilt—and she felt a painful, almost sickeningly sweet sense of relief.

What if she'd been there? And what if she'd been the one taken away?

And every time Jenna considered her life—all the things she had and all the things she would have left behind. Like Jared. Her mother.

Everything.

And she always reached the same conclusion: When push came to shove, she wouldn't have traded her life for Celia's. *No way. No way.*

CHAPTER TWELVE

The rain let up, but Jared didn't notice. He walked through Caldwell Park, his feet splashing through small puddles, which would soon be turning to ice, the sweat from his exertion drying and cooling against his skin. His heart still thudded but was slowing down, and the frantic energy that had been running through his body since he first approached Tabitha's house wound down like a clock with a dying battery.

He couldn't believe he'd thrown a rock through Tabitha's window.

They couldn't have seen him, could they? He felt sick to his stomach, like a child in trouble with his parents. Which made him think of home. He pulled out his phone.

His mom would be freaked. He wandered around in the cold and the wet while she sat at home stewing. And they hadn't even talked about Tabitha, about her being in the house. In his room, on top of him after school.

Hell, that was unlikely to ever happen again. If she knew or suspected he'd been spying on her and then busted her kitchen window while her dad stood and watched—he could kiss all of it good-bye.

Her dad. He couldn't get the image out of his head. His hulking size. Those meaty hands.

That kiss.

But girls kissed their fathers all the time. His own mom occasionally pecked him on the cheek, even as a teenager, although he squirmed away when she did. But that was on the cheek. And she knew he couldn't stand it. He knew she did it just to irritate him.

He wished he could erase the image. He wished he had never looked.

Honey, where are you? Getting late.

He wrote back: On my way home. No worries.

He stopped his wandering and headed in the direction of their house.

He told himself to be calm. No, Tabitha and her dad hadn't seen him throw the rock. Tabitha told him to go home, and as far as she knew, he did. They couldn't see out the kitchen window into the darkness. And even if they'd caught a glimpse of him running away in the night, he'd have been a darkened shadow, a figure in a heavy coat moving away. It could have been anybody.

But where had the anger come from, the insanely spiking jealousy that drove him to do something so out of character? He knew some of his friends—acquaintances, really—liked to go out and damage property from time to time. They smashed pumpkins in the fall. They lit discarded Christmas trees on fire after the holidays. Jared never went along. They weren't his good friends, and he didn't want to get caught. He hated getting in trouble with his mom. It rarely happened, but when it did, she conveyed her disappointment loud and clear. He hated that part the most. The disappointment, the tone in her voice and the look in her eye that said *I expected more from you.*

So Jared bargained with the universe. He vowed never to do it or anything like it again. And he vowed never to be so irrationally angry and jealous again.

But that kiss. He couldn't shake it.

It wasn't just that her father had kissed her. It was all of it together. The lecturing, the looming. The control he seemed to be exerting over every other aspect of Tabitha's life. The curfew and the limited use of the phone.

Was the guy some kind of creep? Or was he a strict and controlling father, trying to keep a very careful eye on his beautiful daughter in a new town?

Tabitha never said much about him, never indicated that he hurt her in any way. She seemed in awe of him, as though her father was an impressive, powerful figure, like a wizard in a kid's storybook. And she seemed a little afraid of him, a little like she'd do just about anything the man asked. Jared figured a lot of girls were like that about their dads. And the guy *was* a single dad, trying to raise a teenage girl. Who knew where her mother was or what role she played in Tabitha's life?

He retraced the steps he'd taken while walking Tabitha home earlier. He wished he could go back in time to that moment, or the moments in his bedroom. How had it all gone wrong so quickly, just when everything was going well? Was it possible to feel nostalgia for something so recently in the past? The houses he walked past again really hadn't changed. Families still gathered in front of the TV. Kids did their homework, looking forward to the day to come.

These families were safe and secure, wrapped in their cocoon of comfort and privilege.

But was Tabitha safe? Was she really?

CHAPTER THIRTEEN

Jenna said good-bye to Sally at the door, hugging her friend and making her promise to drive safely even though the rain had stopped.

"It could be icy. And you've had a couple of glasses of wine," Jenna said.

"Are you kidding? I have that every night."

"I can't afford to lose anyone else," Jenna said.

The words just slipped out. She hadn't meant to sound like such a sad sack, but there it was. And Sally responded with another hug and an assurance that tomorrow would be a better day. Jenna felt a little lift.

She locked the door behind Sally and checked her phone. The texts kept coming in, proof that Reena Huffman's show reached a lot of people in Hawks Mill. She ignored them. She'd said what she'd said and done what she'd done. Tomorrow Reena would be dropping the hammer on someone else if Jenna was lucky.

But she did see the text from Jared telling her he was on his way home.

Relief coursed through her. She turned around and unlocked the door again, offering him easy access to the house. *Hurry up,* she thought. *Just get back here.*

She started straightening up the kitchen to distract herself from waiting for Jared. She knew she had to address the girl in his room, but to be honest, she didn't really care about that anymore. She told herself if he came home safe and sound, if he walked through the door again, she wouldn't say much of anything about it at all. Hell, shouldn't she be happy that he was opening himself up and spending time with a girl? At least someone in the house was getting some romantic action.

She smiled as the landline rang.

It rarely did. She certainly hadn't given that number out to any reporters. Jenna figured it was her mother calling back, offering more advice on how a proper lady conducted herself on CNN. But when she picked it up, no one was there.

She heard the sound of breathing and a rustling on the other end, a movement of some kind.

"Hello?" she said. "Mom?"

Then a voice came through, low and raspy. "Do you kiss your mother with that filthy mouth, bitch?"

The words hit Jenna like a slap. "Who is this?"

"Why don't you go away, bitch? You might as well as offed her yourself—"

She slammed the phone down, her hand shaking as she lifted it from the receiver. The calls had come before, mostly in the first month after Celia disappeared. Kids and cranks, weirdos offering their own theories of where Celia was and who took her. But sometimes a man like this called, one who seemed to be calling only to inflict some kind of emotional pain, to take a dig at Jenna and probe her wounds. No wonder she thought people in town blamed her.

"Mom?"

She spun and jumped at the same time. Jared stood in the kitchen doorway, his hair and coat wet. Under the harsh kitchen lights, his cheeks glowed from the cold. "You scared me."

"I told you I was on my way home."

"I know. I'm glad you're here."

He pointed to the phone, sniffling a little. "Another crank caller?"

"Some creep. Yes. It's no big deal."

"I told you to get rid of the landline. You don't need it, and you keep the number listed. Anyone can call and say whatever shit they want to you."

"We've been over this," Jenna said. She was glad—no, thrilled—he was finally home. She wanted to hug him but didn't, knowing he would grow rigid under her touch and back away in protest. "Did you lock the door?"

"Yes. Of course. I know the protocol."

"Because you didn't lock it earlier today when I came home."

"Mom."

"Okay, okay."

"If Celia comes back or wants to find you, she knows

your cell number. You don't have to keep a landline listed for her."

Jenna moved across the kitchen and continued with her cleaning. "I know it isn't logical, okay? None of it is. I just want to make sure there are multiple ways for her to find me. I think you can understand that."

"I get it. Really, I do." He gave her a little smile, an expression of sympathy. Most of the time, he tolerated his strange mother very well.

"You should get out of those wet things," she said. "It's cold."

"Yeah."

But he didn't move. He lingered in the doorway of the kitchen while Jenna rinsed glasses and plates and put them in the dishwasher.

"Aren't you going to say anything about Tabitha?" he asked.

Jenna stopped what she was doing, dried her hands on a relatively clean towel. "I am sorry I walked in on you two. You know I try to respect your privacy. Like I said, I was a little frazzled today." She watched his face. He seemed curious, his eyes intently watching her. "They thought they found a body out in an old barn." She shook her head at the mad emotional rush the whole thing had brought down on her. How had she given in to it so easily? "I went out there for nothing. It was a deer skeleton. They found the leg bone and thought it was a person. Then they dug around and found antlers and everything else. So I let myself get worked up. When I came home and the door was open and I thought you weren't here, I freaked a little. Sally came over tonight and calmed me down."

"That's messed up."

"It is. Better yet, I cursed on camera, and they ran it on CNN tonight."

Jared's face brightened. "Really? What did you say?"

Jenna warmed to the conversation with her son, realizing that they could bond over this. After all, who would appreciate someone cursing on national TV more than a teenager?

"I dropped an *f*-bomb. And I used the Lord's name in vain. A daily double."

Jared laughed, but his eyes remained serious. Something was bothering him, and she waited to see if he'd share it.

"Can I ask you something?" he said.

"Sure." Jenna tossed the towel aside. "Do you want to change first?"

"No." He seemed to be choosing his words, trying to think of the best way to say what he had to say. "Did Grandpa ever kiss you?"

"Kiss me? You mean like a peck on the cheek?"

"I was thinking on the lips," Jared said.

"You remember Grandpa, right? He wasn't the warmest guy. I don't think he ever kissed Grandma on the lips. Why are you asking me about that?"

He seemed to be working up to another question, his eyes trained on the floor. But then he shook his head. "Forget it. I haven't done any of my homework."

"Wait." Even as she spoke, Jenna knew she was violating her own rules. She was pushing the conversation, pushing at her son. She hated when she acted that way, maybe all mothers did, but she couldn't stop herself because she thought something might be wrong. "Is there something about Tabitha?"

Jared stood still for a moment, wavering between walking away and staying. "It's nothing, Mom. Don't worry about it."

"It's just that there was something about her. She looked familiar to me, and I couldn't figure out where I'd seen her before. But I've been thinking about it, and here you are, having some kind of issue."

"There's no *issue*," he said, his voice getting louder.

"Maybe I know her dad. Maybe that's why she looked familiar. What I'm saying is I might be able to help with whatever's going on."

"Mom, stop." He held his hands in the air, chest high, in exasperation. "Just . . . I never should have brought it up. I'm going to change and do my homework."

"Jared, wait."

She wanted to tell him about the earring, about the man in custody, but she'd blown it. She'd really blown it.

CHAPTER FOURTEEN

Tabitha didn't come to homeroom. Jared sat in his seat, a row behind hers, and waited, trying not to appear eager or concerned. His friend Syd, slightly overweight with thick glasses, a kid he'd known since first grade, sat on his left and wanted to talk about a college basketball game he'd watched the night before. He knew Jared didn't watch much basketball, but he kept bringing it up, even nudging Jared in the side to keep his attention.

"Isn't it time you got excited about following the Wildcats?" Syd said for the third time. "What if they go all the way, and you didn't pay attention?"

"Yeah, I'll watch," Jared said, but he didn't even know what he was agreeing to.

"What's the matter? Is your girl sick?"

"I guess so."

The night before, Jared had dreamed of being chased. He couldn't see who was behind him or what they wanted, but Jared knew, in the dream, he'd done something wrong. And if whoever was behind him caught up he'd be in big trouble. His eyeballs felt as if they'd been scoured with a Brillo pad, as if he'd slept about ten minutes.

"Didn't she text you and tell you what was going on?" Syd asked.

"She doesn't text much."

"So text her. You know if you weren't here she'd be texting you."

Jared tried to laugh it off, to play along with the banter. He wondered if Syd had ever been with a girl, if he'd ever so much as made out with someone. And in that moment, he found himself feeling envious of his friend's easy, uncomplicated life.

As the day went on, he looked for Tabitha in the hallways between classes, but he didn't have much hope. Something was going on, he knew, something relating to her father and the events of the previous night. Kids came down with stomach bugs and colds all the time, especially when the weather was as shitty as it had been. But Jared refused to allow himself to accept an illness as the cause of Tabitha's absence. He'd kept her out too late, and then made things worse with the rock.

At lunch he returned to the table with Syd and Mike. He'd been eating with Tabitha every day since she arrived at their school. He knew he'd get shit from them for coming back, but he also wanted the company and the distraction from his constantly racing thoughts.

"The prodigal returns," Mike said when Jared sat down. Mike was the best-looking friend Jared had. His hair was thick, his clothes always perfect. Mike liked to boast about the girls he'd been with, and if he had been anyone else, Jared would have doubted the stories. But Jared knew the way the girls in the school talked about Mike—as if he were a rock star, just stepped off the stage. Mike had moved to Hawks Mill in the second grade, and he and Syd and Jared had been a tight-knit group of friends ever since. "Your girl wasn't in history today."

"She's sick or something," Jared said.

"And you can't text her or anything? Is this all because her dad's so strict?"

"Yeah." Jared tried to concentrate on the slice of pizza before him, but he wasn't hungry.

"And you've never met the guy?" Mike's voice was full of awe. "That's unprecedented. You're walking this girl home every day, messing around with her, and the guy doesn't want to meet you and check you out."

"He's never been inside the house," Syd said. "Never even in the yard."

Jared wanted to curse at Syd. He told him things in homeroom he'd never tell Mike. But the floodgates were open. Jared was going to face the full force of Mike's interrogation and wisdom.

"Is that for real?" he asked. "Never set foot in the yard? Is she ashamed of you?"

"Easy, Mike," Syd said.

"What I mean is, her dad works, right? And where's her mom?"

Jared tried to think of the right words. "Her mom's . . . missing in action. They're separated. I don't think she knows where her mom lives. It's kind of like she left them, I think."

"Weird. Usually mothers don't leave," Syd said. "Fathers do."

"She acts evasive about her mom, like there's something else going on."

"So you could be in that house every day after school," Mike said. "When do you think all the good stuff happens? It's in that time between school letting out and the time the parents get home from work. I call it the Magic Hour. I guess your mom works too, but she's pretty smart. She'd know. Dads are clueless for the most part."

"I brought her to my house yesterday," Jared said, trying to lighten the mood. "My mom walked in on us."

Both Mike's and Syd's eyebrows shot up.

Mike said, "In the middle of the act?"

"Starting down that road," Jared said.

"Holy shit," Syd said. "I wonder what Jenna's face looked like when she saw that."

Mike laughed and laughed, the food he was chewing on full display. Jared hadn't planned on telling him anything, but the sharing of information made him feel more closely connected to his friends. It provided a sense of comfort and ease he hadn't felt since he walked Tabitha home the night before.

"Mom was cool," Jared said. "She really was. She has other stuff on her mind."

"Oh, yeah," Syd said. "She was on TV last night. My mom saw it. She dropped an *f*-bomb on Reena Huffman's show."

Mike laughed even more and asked Syd to find the clip on YouTube so he could watch it. Jared started eating, started feeling a little more normal. Maybe Tabitha *was* just sick. Maybe she needed a mental health day. His mom let him have those on occasion. He didn't have to be sick and she'd let him stay home and mellow out in his room, so long as he promised to keep up with the work, which he always did.

"I swear," Mike said, "your mom is so freaking cool. She makes my parents looks like the mom and dad on *All in the Family*."

Jared remembered the dustup with his mom the night before, all of which came about because he'd tried to open up to her and then changed course in midstream. He never liked losing his cool with her. He understood the pressures she felt, and she'd already opened up to him about the shitty day she'd had. But he wished she'd just learn to read the signals, to know when to back off and let him be. She didn't have to have the answer to everything all the time. Over breakfast that morning, they both behaved normally. Neither one mentioned the disagreement. They did that sometimes—let things go. He wished he could do that with Tabitha, just turn the page and go back to the way things were almost twenty-four hours earlier.

"Let me ask you guys something," Jared said once the laughing and the jokes about his mom's *f*-bomb settled down. "You know how Tabitha doesn't really text and she has the strict curfew and all that, right?"

"Practically Amish," Mike said.

"Exactly." For a moment, Jared wondered if that was

it. Were Tabitha and her father part of some Amish splinter sect? Was the strictness and lack of communication and even the kissing just a cultural or religious custom? "Have you ever Googled her?"

"Googled Tabitha?" Syd asked.

"Yes."

"Why would I Google someone?" Mike asked.

Syd looked at him. "You don't Google people? I Google a lot of people. Teachers, students. Not Tabitha, though. I looked for her on Twitter and Facebook once."

"I don't Google regular people," Mike said. "Not kids I know. Not that I really know Tabitha."

"Well, I have Googled her," Jared said. "I know the town she came from in Florida and her middle name. I figure maybe there'd be something. You know, honor roll. Soccer team. School project."

"Graduation lists," Syd said. "They always print lists of graduates in every town, so when she finished junior high they might have listed her."

"You think about this too much," Mike said, looking at Syd from the corner of his eye.

"He's right, Mike. There's nothing. There are other Tabitha Burkes in the country. The name isn't that unusual. But nothing about her. No social media, no school or sports stuff."

Syd pulled his phone out and started typing with his thumbs. While he did that, Mike looked at Jared and said, "Maybe she didn't do any activities. She seems pretty much like a recluse, don't you agree? I guess she gets out with you a little. She doesn't have any girlfriends." He leaned forward, his hands folded on the tabletop. "To be honest, the other girls think she's a little standoffish. You know? She's pretty and all that, but she's quiet. Maybe even aloof. She probably was like that at her old school."

"You're right," Syd said. "Nothing comes up. What's her dad's name? Maybe he shows up, and then you can at least know she didn't just materialize out of thin air."

Jared didn't even know where her dad worked.

He was starting to realize how little he did know.

CHAPTER FIFTEEN

Jenna vowed she'd have a better day.

Driving to work, she recited a list of all the things she intended to leave behind: the scene at the barn, the cursing on TV, the disagreement with Jared. And something else, some other lingering unpleasantness. Yes, the prank phone call. It all belonged to yesterday.

She scanned through the stations, checking for news. The man and the earring were mentioned on a local station, but they didn't seem to know anything else. She'd called Detective Poole once before leaving the house and hung up when it went to voice mail again.

A great song came on the radio. "These Are Days" by 10,000 Maniacs. Yes, she needed to hear that. The sun was bright, the temperature slightly warmer. Soon it would be spring and then summer. Things had to get better, didn't they?

Times like this, when she needed a pick-me-up, she didn't pray or meditate. She talked to Celia. Sometimes she heard the conversations in her head, but sometimes, usually when she was alone in the house or the car, she'd say things out loud and wish she could once again hear Celia's voice or her laugh.

"You would have liked the show I put on last night," Jenna said.

She made sure to stop talking before she reached a traffic light. She didn't want the people next to her—and in a town like Hawks Mill, it very well could be someone she knew—thinking she had totally lost her mind. But as she accelerated down the road, the music playing in the background, she told Celia all about the interview with Becky and the bleeped *f*-bomb on CNN.

"You'd have gotten a kick out of that one, C," she said. "You would have shaken your head and laughed. You would have found the clip on the Web and shared it on social media. You would have had a good time at my expense, as usual."

Celia always laughed at Jenna's missteps, the things she said wrong, the times she messed up. But she almost always followed up with something more: a pat on the back, a smile, or a hug. *"That's our Jenna,"* she used to say. *"We love you for it all, babe."*

Jenna came to a light and felt emotion welling in her throat. Once she was moving, she pounded the steering wheel with the flat of her hand. "Where the fuck did you go, C? Where the fuck did you go?"

She didn't let herself cry. She choked it all back, reminding herself once again that a new day had dawned. When she walked in to Hawks Mill Family Medicine, she

saw Detective Poole waiting for her, and the whole notion of a new day went out the window.

Naomi Poole was about fifty-five. She wore her hair cut
short and used the knuckle on her right index finger to
push her owlish eyeglasses up the bridge of her nose every
few minutes. She'd taken the lead on Celia's case and had
spent more hours than Jenna could remember asking
questions and then more questions about Celia's life and
their plans on the night she disappeared. Jenna liked
Naomi Poole and mostly trusted her, but couldn't escape
the feeling that the detective, as a consequence of her job,
was always sizing Jenna up, sifting through every piece of
information and reevaluating her. Jenna believed Naomi
turned that critical eye on everyone she met.

"Hey, Jenna," Naomi said, as casual as anything. She
pushed the glasses up her nose. If someone didn't know
any better, they'd think Naomi and Jenna worked together, and the older woman was just greeting her at the
start of another day. "I'm sorry to show up this way, but
I needed to talk to you."

Jenna knew the detective's arrival wasn't as casual as
she'd made it seem. Naomi could have returned her call
or could have texted. She'd done it before for smaller
things about the case. She could have caught Jenna on
her lunch break or even at home before she left. If there
was one thing Jenna had learned since the night Celia
disappeared, it was that detectives liked to talk to people
on their own terms. They liked to decide the time and

place of the conversation. They set the tone and the ground rules, even if it seemed that they weren't. Jenna knew Naomi had something on her mind.

"Maybe we can sit on those benches over there?"

"Can I at least—"

Naomi smiled, the wise woman who had thought of everything in advance. "I already told them you'd be a few minutes late. They're fine with it."

They walked across the spacious lobby, where everyone who entered the Medical Arts Building came in and studied the board to find out which floor their physician worked on. Functional, comfortable sofas and chairs ringed the perimeter of the room, and a security guard in a blue uniform sat at a desk, pretending not to be texting as patients started wandering in.

Naomi led Jenna to a sofa on the far side of the room, against a large window that allowed the morning light to stream in. Jenna placed her lunch and coat on the floor as the two women sat.

"What is the deal with this earring they found? And this guy? I've been going nuts and there's no news about it."

"We're still piecing it together."

It drove Jenna crazy that Naomi could be so calm and detached even in the midst of a crisis. Jenna knew it was part of her job to be cool, but would it have killed her just once to be as riled up as Jenna was?

"Just tell me anything," Jenna said.

"Yesterday a man went into Will's Pawnshop, the one out on Hammond Pike? He tried to sell an earring. The clerk was on his game. He recognized it from the hot sheet and called us. A cruiser got there while the guy was still in the store. He claims he found the earring in a field on Western Avenue. He was out looking for aluminum cans and came across it in the grass. The snow had just started to melt. He says he's heard about Celia's case but didn't put the two together when he found the earring."

"Who is he, Naomi?" Jenna asked.

"His name is Benjamin Ludlow. He's forty."

"Benjamin Ludlow . . ." Something scratched below the surface of Jenna's brain, something itching to get out.

"What is it?" Naomi asked.

"We went to high school with him."

"I thought you might have. He's a local guy, your age."

"Jesus, Naomi. He's a total creep. At least he was in high school. He was one of those guys who was always slinking around the corners of the building, leering at the girls but never actually talking to them. He scared us." Jenna felt flushed. "Is he a suspect? Did he hurt Celia?"

"Everything's on the table right now. This guy's kind of rootless. Grew up here, as you know, and then served in the army. Moved around in the South and came back here about a year ago." She stopped talking, but Jenna saw there was more.

"What is it?" she asked. "Don't keep me hanging."

"He has an arrest for sexual assault. It was ten years ago, and he served six months. This was down in Georgia."

If Jenna's hand hadn't been resting against her thigh, it would have been shaking. She stared at the floor, the intricate pattern in the tile.

"Did he do it?" Jenna asked. "Did he hurt her?"

"He's saying no. By the way, we're trying to keep as much of this as possible out of the press until we've had a chance to look into this guy more. That's why it's so quiet this morning."

"Do you believe him?" Jenna asked. "Naomi, he was a scary guy in high school, one of those guys you just assumed would end up in prison someday."

"I've been a cop so long I don't believe anybody. I'm sorry, Jenna—you're going to have to be patient on this one. We just got this guy into our hands yesterday. I've barely filled Ian in on it."

"I think I'm going to die being patient."

"Have you seen him since high school? Benjamin Ludlow?"

"Benny, everybody called him. And no, I haven't seen him. If I saw him, I'd run the other way." Jenna rubbed her temple. "What a week this is turning into."

"I'm sorry about what happened yesterday," Naomi said. She had a way of talking that made every word seem easy and natural. Nothing to be stressed about here. No crisis, no fears. *Sure, we might have a suspect in custody, but it's nothing to get worked up over.* "I hope you know I never would have called you to that scene. None of our officers would have."

"It was Becky McGee."

"I know," Naomi said. "She wanted a story, and she got one. Not the one she envisioned, but a story nonetheless."

"I walked right into it. I should have stayed at work, but

I couldn't say no. I wondered . . . I wondered about it really being Celia. If it was, shouldn't I be there and not leave her alone to be handled by a bunch of strangers?" Jenna studied Naomi's face, evaluating her. "Is that morbid?"

"Not at all." She reached over and patted Jenna on the knee. "It makes perfect sense."

"You don't have to apologize for a reporter's behavior."

"I havé to ask you about something else."

"Is this about Benny? Benjamin or whatever?"

Jenna wondered why she felt a different kind of guilt when a police officer wanted to ask her a question. It wasn't the guilt she felt over Celia's disappearance. That was a guilt she lived with every day, a duller ache, like a nagging cavity that sometimes—rarely—managed to slip below her consciousness.

But when a cop wanted to ask her something, she felt an acute sense of guilt, a feeling that the officer knew something about Jenna that she might not even understand herself.

"Not exactly," Naomi said.

"Do I want to know what this is?" Jenna asked, the question slipping out of her mouth with an edge she hadn't intended. It was the kind of quick, tart response that so often landed her in trouble.

Naomi studied her for a moment, a practiced pause that had the desired effect of putting Jenna back on her heels.

"I'm happy to help if I can," Jenna said. "Is this something else about Celia's case?"

"Maybe," Naomi said, taking her time. A woman was

pushing a crying baby in a stroller, the child's screams echoing off the high ceiling. Naomi looked over and gave the mother a sympathetic smile. It occurred to Jenna that she knew very little about Naomi's life. She wore a wedding ring but hadn't mentioned children. The whole relationship seemed asymmetrical. Naomi could turn Jenna's life inside out, while Jenna had no such recourse toward her. "Do you know someone named Holly Crenshaw?"

"Holly Crenshaw." Jenna thought it over, trying to be certain before she opened her mouth again. "I don't think so."

"She lives over in Clay County, about twenty miles from here."

"Should I know her?"

"She disappeared two days ago. She went out with some friends while her husband was away on business. It took a little while for anyone to know something was wrong. She's young, twenty-three. She doesn't have any kids and only works part-time." Naomi brought out her phone. She opened a picture and showed it to Jenna. "See? A pretty girl, isn't she?"

Jenna's hands shook as she took the phone. The girl looked young, even younger than her twenty-three years. She was a kid, not much older than Jared. And she was beautiful, almost as pretty as Celia was at the same age. Jenna saw right away the general resemblance between the two women. The hair color and length most notably, the fresh-scrubbed beauty.

"You think there's a connection," Jenna said, handing the phone back.

"We're wondering," Naomi said.

Jenna waited a moment and then said, "There has to be a reason for you to wonder. What is it?"

"Holly worked at the country club Celia and Ian belong to."

CHAPTER SIXTEEN

The only thing Jenna managed to say sounded defensive and petty. "I'm not a member of that country club. I've never even been there."

"The country club may not be a connection. There may be no connection." Naomi studied the screen for a moment, then slipped the phone away. "So far it doesn't look like Celia and Holly Crenshaw knew each other. Maybe they were passing acquaintances and nothing more. Holly worked in human resources, so she probably didn't have a lot of contact with the members."

Jenna looked around the lobby. More people came and went, and she studied the faces, wondering about each and every one of them. Did they all carry pain and regret like hers? "So there could be some kind of killer in the area, someone who is preying on women? Do you think it's Benjamin?"

Naomi was shaking her head. "We don't know any of these things. The town's nervous enough as it is. This is going to dial that up even higher. We can't jump to any conclusions."

But Jenna already knew people would. She could imagine the field day someone like Reena Huffman would have with that kind of news. A killer on the loose, beautiful women being targeted in small-town America. What tagline would she come up with next? *Maniac in the Heartland*? *Killer in Kentucky*?

"Don't jump to any conclusions?" Jenna said, repeating Naomi's words and adding her own sarcastic edge. "I'll stay nice and calm when the creeps call me on the phone. Or the next time I get summoned to a crime scene."

"You're still getting those phone calls? You know we can look into them again."

"I got one last night, but that's only because of my performance on CNN."

Jenna wondered if Naomi would say anything about that, but she didn't. She directed the conversation an entirely different way, still sounding casual. "Any other thoughts on Celia's marriage?"

Naomi made it sound as though the two women had just been discussing the topic a few minutes earlier.

"Other thoughts? I answered fifty questions about their marriage when Celia disappeared."

"I know." Naomi looked calm, unruffled. "But sometimes I like to check back with people close to the case in the event something new has occurred to them. The mind is a tricky thing. Thoughts can emerge from places we aren't even aware of."

"I'd tell you the same thing now I told you then. They

weren't perfect, but they seemed happy. I hate to say it, but I felt maybe neither one of them was paying enough attention to Ursula. Ian worked a lot. Celia had an active social life. And all of that was going on right when their daughter was hitting puberty and adolescence. But I'm a single mom. I'm not home when my son gets out of school." She'd seen the Jim Beam bottle in Jared's room the night Celia disappeared. Her interruption of Jared and Tabitha just the day before. No, she couldn't throw stones at any other parents. Everyone did their best. And then they hoped. "Some people have suggested that Celia ran away and wasn't taken. There's no way that's true. She wouldn't leave Ian or Ursula."

"Who's suggesting she ran away?" Naomi asked.

"People online mostly. I go to those message boards sometimes, especially the one at the Dealey Society." As Naomi well knew, the Dealey Society was an organization, founded by Paul and Pam Dealey, dedicated to discovering answers about missing persons cases involving adults. The site featured a clearinghouse of names, photos, and other information, as well as a message board where anyone could log on and discuss active and closed cases. They'd gained national attention over the past five years when members of their online community helped solve a couple of long-cold cases. The Dealeys started the site when their twenty-eight-year-old daughter, Sheila, was kidnapped and murdered. "I know I shouldn't. I know it just stirs up difficult emotions. But there's something comforting about talking to other people. It feels like there are individuals who really care."

"And you feel like you're being useful," Naomi said. "You're helping."

"Yeah," Jenna said, her voice trailing away. It hardly seemed like any form of real help. And it also required interacting with the occasional crazies who made the creeps on the phone seem normal and well adjusted. More than once, Jenna made vows to never go back, to stop dipping her toe in the online waters of the Dealey message board. But she inevitably went back, drawn there by the constant stream of new information, the ongoing sense that a group of people was trying to keep Celia's memory and case alive.

"So nothing about the marriage," Naomi said, drawing her back to the matter at hand.

"I'm hardly the person to evaluate that." Jenna tried to sound light and joking, but she could still feel a small measure of shame over the failure of her own marriage. Conversations with her mother or chats with other, happily married couples could still sting. "Mine flamed out pretty spectacularly."

"You're not alone in that category," Naomi said.

"I haven't spoken to Ian since Celia disappeared."

"Really? Still?"

"I told you we were never that close. I was friends with Celia, not really with Ian."

"Sometimes events bring people closer."

Jenna thought she detected something, an ever-so-slight emphasis on the word "closer" as Naomi completed her sentence. Or was she imagining things? If the emphasis had been there and not simply in Jenna's head, what did it mean? If the people who knew Celia and Jenna and Ian the best, the friends they'd had since high school, remembered everything accurately and told the truth about the past, then the police would know that it was Jenna whom Ian first showed interest in when they were all fifteen years old, that it was Jenna who first caught Ian's eye when they all ended up in the same chemistry class during their sophomore year at Hawks Mill High School.

Celia knew it, although the two friends never, ever talked about it. But Jenna remembered how high Celia turned up the volume on her thousand-watt smile as soon as she saw Ian's interest in Jenna. Once Celia set her sights on Ian, Jenna knew she didn't have a chance. Celia was prettier, more polished. Celia came from a better family, one almost equal in stature to Ian's in Hawks Mill. Like a fighter who knew when she'd met her match, Jenna bowed out gracefully and let things progress the way they were supposed to.

Despite Celia's easy victory, or maybe because of it, a barrier always existed between Jenna and Ian, an invisible force field that seemed to repel them away from each other in even the most mundane situations. They rarely shared a joke or made much more than small talk. As the years went by, Ian worked more, spent more and more time invested in his career. The truth was, Jenna and Celia's friendship existed independently of Ian and almost never involved him.

"That hasn't been the case with us," Jenna said, hoping the line of questioning would end. She was late for work, and if Naomi expected to hear something new from her about Celia's marriage, she would be waiting a long time. "You've talked to Ian more recently than I have."

"I guess so, then."

"How is he doing?" Jenna asked.

"He's holding up as well as he can."

"He was treated pretty poorly when Celia disappeared," Jenna said. "People assumed . . ."

"We didn't."

"But you questioned him. For a long time. Repeatedly."

"Wasn't I supposed to do my job?" Naomi asked, her voice acquiring a little edge. "Wasn't I supposed to do that for Celia?"

"Of course." Jenna felt bad for implying that the detective had been too hard on Ian. He was the missing woman's spouse. Everyone knew the odds. And Ian could take care of himself. "I can only tell you what I know from Celia about their marriage, and that's that they were doing as well as they always were."

Naomi didn't speak, but she held her gaze on Jenna's face for a longer period of time than seemed normal. Something flickered in the woman's eyes, a poker player's glint that said she might just know something Jenna didn't. But again, just like the emphasis on the word "closer," was it something Jenna was simply imagining in her own off-kilter state?

"Well, I'll let you get to work," Naomi said.

They stood and shook hands, and Naomi promised to be in touch if she needed anything else.

"Can you do me a favor, Detective?" Jenna asked.

"Sure."

"Can you tell Holly Crenshaw's family I'm thinking of them? I know what this is like. I hate to think of other people going through it as well."

"I'll pass it along."

"And you'll let me know—"

"If we learn anything from Ludlow, anything I can share, I'll call."

As Jenna walked across the lobby, heading toward the entrance to Family Medicine, the sense came over her that Naomi was watching her walk away. Jenna didn't want to turn around, didn't want to know the truth, but couldn't help herself. She craned her neck around and looked, but Naomi was gone.

CHAPTER SEVENTEEN

Jenna fell into the easy rhythms of the workday. She tried not to think about Ian. Or Celia. Or Benny Ludlow. She never thought she'd be thinking about Benny Ludlow again.

But how did he end up with Celia's earring?

Were Celia and Holly Crenshaw hurt by the same person?

Was it Benny Ludlow?

Sally distracted her. They traded notes over how tired they were when they woke up that morning. "Are you kidding? The wine helps me sleep," Sally said. "That's why I drink some every night. Doctor's orders."

Jenna admitted her sleep had been lousy, the lingering effects of the previous day's events, particularly the disagreement with Jared.

"The boys," Sally said, shaking her head. "They develop the sassiest mouths. If mine hadn't been so big, I would have kept right on spanking them."

Just before eleven, Jenna stepped out to the lobby and called a patient back. A middle-aged man, someone she had never seen in the office before. Possibly a new patient or someone she simply hadn't crossed paths with yet. When she called the man's name, he looked up, a hopeful smile on his face. People usually smiled when they were called back. Their wait was ending. They were that much closer to getting an answer from the doctor or receiving treatment. More than anything, they didn't have to wait anymore.

But as the man came closer to Jenna, the look on his face changed. His brow wrinkled, the smile disappeared. When she attempted to make the usual small talk—*How are you today? Is it any warmer out there?*—the man grunted.

She understood. Some people didn't want to talk. They wanted the business conducted without any of the frills. Except the smile the man first showed marked him as a talker . . .

When they entered the exam room, Jenna pulled out the blood pressure cuff.

"Just relax your arm," she said. "No need to roll up your sleeve."

The man cleared his throat. "Is there another nurse who can do this?"

"Excuse me?"

"Another nurse," he said. "Besides you."

Jenna didn't follow. The man refused to meet her eye. "Is something wrong, sir?"

Then he looked up. "I don't want to be helped by

someone with a foul mouth, a troublemaker. It's just not my values, that's all."

It took a moment to understand what he referred to, but then she knew. The TV interview. Reena Huffman. In the lobby, his face fell because he recognized her.

"Are you serious?" Jenna asked.

"What you've put that family through," he said. "They're pillars of the community."

Some other "foul" words popped into her mind, and she wished she could share them. But she didn't. She stepped out of the room without saying anything else and handed the chart off to one of her colleagues.

The receptionist in the lobby of Walters Foundry, a young woman with a bright smile and hair the color of straw, informed Jenna that there was simply no way she could see Mr. Ian Walters today. She offered to call upstairs to his private office and schedule the appointment herself with Ian's secretary.

But Jenna didn't feel like being turned away.

Something Naomi said stuck with her. Jenna did surf those Web sites and message boards because it made her feel as though she was doing something productive, even though, deep in her heart of hearts, she knew her little gestures didn't make a bit of difference. Jenna remembered those first days after Celia's disappearance. She walked the woods and hills of Hawks Mill with a group of volunteers. She manned a phone bank, dutifully writing down tips and leads.

None of it made any difference as far as she could tell. Celia remained lost, out of reach of all of them.

The other volunteers, as well as the observers and the citizens who casually followed the case around the country, they too slipped back to their daily lives, and the story barely left a mark on them. Another crime or crisis would pop up in the news, another distraction, and if something came up regarding Celia, they could flip the channel right back and pick up where they'd left off. The Reena Huffmans of the world would be sure nobody missed a detail.

Jenna, and those closest to Celia, floundered in the mire. No path forward presented itself. There was only looking back and regretting. Jenna wondered if she was stuck most of all. She wasn't a member of the inner circle, a tight group she imagined included Celia's mother, her sister, Ian, Ursula, and perhaps other friends Jenna didn't know well, and she couldn't walk away. Patience had become her watchword. Answers, if they came at all, wouldn't come quickly. She understood the harsh truths: Even if they did find Celia's body—in a rotten barn, a ditch, or a forest—they wouldn't necessarily be any closer to knowing what had happened to her, unless they could firmly tie it to somebody. Benny Ludlow or anybody else. They'd only know she was dead, an unpleasant truth Jenna tried to push from her mind whenever it crept in.

She needed to do something.

So Jenna told the secretary—*insisted*—that she call up to Mr. Ian Walters's private office and tell him Jenna Barton was here to see him.

Needed to see him.

The cheery young woman did as she was asked, never losing her smile.

A few minutes later, the phone on her desk rang. She nodded, writing on a small pad of paper. She tore it off with a flourish. "Mr. Walters says he'll meet you at this address in fifteen minutes."

CHAPTER EIGHTEEN

Jenna took a seat at the Landing, Hawks Mill's nicest restaurant. She arrived shortly before the height of the lunch rush and asked for a table for two. She felt self-conscious in her scrubs among the lawyers and executives and wealthy retirees who all were coming in wearing coats and ties and large rings. It was several years since Jenna had eaten at the Landing. Dr. Phillips, the founder of Hawks Mill Family Medicine, once brought the whole staff there for a holiday party. Other than an occasion like that, Jenna wouldn't spend the money on a place like the Landing. When the waiter asked her what she wanted to drink, she asked for a glass of water.

While she waited, sipping her water, she bounced her feet under the table and rested her hand on the cool glass to keep from tapping her fingers too much. She tried to think of the last time she and Ian had spent any time alone. She guessed it was before he and Celia started dating, long before the two of them were married. Celia missed school one day, so Jenna started walking home alone. She didn't mind the solitude. She let her mind drift, taking in the leaves that were just turning, the warm fall air that already carried a hint of decay. Her mind drifted so far she didn't notice Ian until he was walking beside her, a couple of books in one hand, the other tucked into the pocket of his jeans.

Even then he was taller than everyone else, almost to his adult height of six-four. His hair was longer then, a lock of it tumbling over his forehead, but he didn't give in to the grungy fashions that were sweeping through the high school. She never saw Ian in flannel or ripped jeans, never saw him in Chuck Taylor sneakers with the names of bands scrawled on the canvas in Magic Marker. She doubted his parents would allow it. They might not let him back in the house if he dressed that way.

When he showed up alongside her that day after school, she jumped a little as he said hello. He apologized, and she told him he'd materialized like a ghost.

"God, I hope not," he said. "Not yet."

He asked Jenna a lot of questions about her family and her life. What did her mom and dad do? What did she do for fun? Did she have siblings? She answered all his questions, trying to keep the nervous edge out of her voice so he didn't think she was a babbling, bumbling idiot. But when she turned the questions back to him, when she asked about his family and his friends and his life, he didn't reveal much. Even then, a screen existed, a barrier Ian didn't seem to want to let Jenna see behind.

They said good-bye in front of her house, and only

then did Jenna wonder about how far Ian would have to walk to get back home. She knew his family lived in a nice new subdivision, one a couple of miles on the other side of their school. She thought about calling him back, offering for her mother to give him a ride. But she didn't speak up. Ian seemed so at ease walking away, so sure of who he was and where he was going, that she figured he had it under control. People like Ian always had a way.

The next day, Jenna told Celia that she didn't have to worry about how she made it home, that Ian ended up walking her. Celia didn't say anything. She gave Jenna a knowing look, one that Jenna didn't fully understand at the time, but two days later she did when Celia and Ian were a couple, and the barrier that had always existed with Ian, the one Jenna hoped over time might fall away, became permanent. They spent time together over the years, but always with Celia there. And only in the context of Jenna being Celia's friend and not really Ian's.

The waiter came back one more time, as the restaurant started to fill. People stood near the front door, waiting for tables. And Jenna sat by herself with only a glass of water in front of her. She checked her watch. Twenty minutes had passed. Maybe Ian had been held up. Maybe he just didn't want to deal with her.

"Are you sure you don't want to order something?" he asked. Between the lines, Jenna heard what he really meant. *Are you* ever *going to order* something?

"My friend, the person I'm meeting, he should be here very soon."

And then the crowd at the door parted a little, and

Ian stepped through. He looked across the restaurant and made eye contact with Jenna. He nodded, his lips a compressed line.

He was there.

When Ian reached the table, Jenna didn't know what to do.

Since that awful November morning, the two of them had found themselves in the same room on more than one occasion. The police station, the volunteer head-quarters. But every time Jenna wanted to speak to Ian, to offer him some form of an apology for her part in the events that led to Celia's disappearance, she couldn't get close. Either circumstances beyond their control inter-vened, or Ian steered himself away, walking in the op-posite direction in a manner that didn't feel entirely purposeful but still left Jenna feeling shut out. And blamed.

Jenna stood up, and the waiter retreated. In full adult-hood, Ian stood six-four. He was long and lean like a basketball player, and his suit—the jacket and pants black, the white shirt open-necked without a tie—fit him as though it was custom-made, which it no doubt was. He wore a look of caution, his face impassive, his hands close to his body. Jenna took a half step forward, won-dering if they were going to hug. Wouldn't two old friends do that? Wouldn't two old friends who had shared a mutual loss do that very thing?

But Ian kept his distance. He reached for the chair and

not Jenna, so she had no choice but to follow suit and take her seat again, this time across from him. The waiter rematerialized and handed Ian a menu, which he set aside, ordering water and placing his hands on the table. Jenna was able to study his face and saw that the previous few months had taken a toll. His hair contained some strands of gray that Jenna swore had never been there before, and his eyes looked tired. Lines were starting to form in their corners, and she believed the lids looked heavier, weighted down by the seemingly endless days that had passed since Celia disappeared.

"If you're hungry you can order something," he said. "I'm not that hungry. I haven't had much of an appetite lately."

And Jenna noticed that change to his body as well. Ian wasn't just trim and fit. His face looked gaunter, the skin on his cheeks drawn tight.

"I guess I'm fine," she said.

"My treat."

"It's okay," Jenna said. "I can pay if I order something."

Ian reached out for his water and took a long drink, his Adam's apple bobbing as he swallowed. When he put the glass down, he said, "What did you want to talk to me about?"

What *did* she want to talk to him about?

How did she sum up the feelings of the past few months? "Detective Poole came and talked to me today. First time in almost a month."

Jenna let her statement hang in the air, expecting Ian

to ask what the detective wanted to talk to her about. But he didn't say anything. He waited for her to go on.

But Jenna couldn't do it. She couldn't talk about other things until the original problem between them was addressed. "Ian, I have to tell you something."

"Okay."

Jenna glanced out the window, where she saw people coming and going from the small clothing shop next door. She promised herself she wouldn't cry, that she wouldn't let the emotion of the moment get the best of her. She certainly didn't want to cry in front of Ian. He'd always been proper, always been a little reserved, but as an adult he'd become ever more serious. Stoic, withdrawn Ian.

She didn't look at him when she said, "You know I'm sorry about that night. I'm sorry I ever called Celia. I'm sorry I was late and that I even proposed meeting in that way. I've spent the last three months wishing I could undo that one phone call, those plans. You know I'd do anything to change that, and I'm sorry."

She thought she was out of words, so she turned back and faced him. She was surprised to see the emotion registering on his face. He looked down at the tabletop, and while she studied him, choking back her own tears, she thought she saw his chin quiver ever so slightly. Just as quickly, he composed himself, clearing his throat and reaching for the water again. When he put the glass down, he said, "I know. It's okay."

"I feel like the whole town blames me." She waited a moment. "Like you blame me."

He looked up at her, the most animation she'd seen in years spreading across his face. Some of the weight seemed to lift from his features. The lines smoothed; the skin became less taut. "Not at all. Never. Look at everything that could have happened. She thought someone was following her."

"Do you think that's true?" Jenna asked. "I mean, did you notice anything?"

Ian took a moment to answer. "No, certainly not. But I wasn't home a lot. Celia thought a car followed her a couple of times. And then she thought she saw the car parked on our street. If I'd known . . ." His top teeth bit down on his lower lip. "If I'd known there was really something to worry about, I'd have gone out to that car myself. But it could be nothing. She couldn't identify the car. It was always dark."

"And you told the police about it as soon as she disappeared, didn't you?" Jenna asked.

Ian gave her a look as if she were stupid. "Of course I did, Jenna. How could I not?" He leaned in. "I even gave them a name. A business associate of mine, someone I thought might have wanted to harass me or my family. They looked into it. Thoroughly."

"They did?"

"They followed a lot of leads, Jenna. If they could make something stick, they would."

"And now Benny Ludlow and the earring. You remember him from school, don't you?"

"Sure, he was a total weirdo. A scary guy."

"So, did he . . . Was he ever a threat to Celia?"

Ian bit down on his lower lip. "Who knows? Didn't he slime around every girl in the school? Maybe he was following her." Color rose in his cheeks. "If it's someone like that, some worthless little man who hurt Celia . . ." He looked angry and hurt. "I guess I should assume it's a worthless little man of some kind. Who else would go around hurting women?" His jaw clenched. "Jenna, I'm so damn tired of getting my hopes up. It just wears me the hell out, you know?"

"It's like being kicked in the stomach repeatedly."

"I was going to say 'kicked in the balls,'" Ian said, "but I get your point. Look, you were, *are*, Celia's best friend. You can't be held responsible for what happened. You were just living your life, doing the things you two always did. Don't worry about it. Lord knows every one of us could go back and find a million things we've done wrong."

Jenna wanted to feel immediately lighter, to sense the burden she'd been carrying floating away above and beyond the ceiling. When that didn't happen, she pressed ahead.

"Thank you," she said, her voice close to a whisper. "And Ursula?"

"She wouldn't think that way about you. She's always been crazy about you."

"Good. How is she doing?"

Ian's gesture, a slight lifting of his shoulders in a kind of shrug, said he wasn't entirely sure about his daughter. "She's doing her best. She's a little more like me than Celia in the sense that she doesn't open up. I know she's grieving and lost, but she puts on a brave face. I've offered to have her homeschooled or anything she wants really, but she tells me she's fine. She goes to school. She spends time with her friends. In some ways, her life is no different. But there's no mom in the house for her. My mother tries to fill in, but it's not the same."

"If I can help, let me know."

Ian nodded. "Thanks." He looked around the dining room until he made eye contact with the waiter. "I am hungry after all. Just a little. You?"

"Sure," Jenna said.

Ian ordered a sandwich and Jenna a salad. When the waiter was gone again and the menus cleared, Jenna contemplated the normality of the scene. There she was, sitting in a nice restaurant having lunch with Ian Walters. The scene could have happened at any time during the past twenty-seven years, but it took Celia's disappearance for the two of them to share the most commonplace experience.

"I saw the news last night," Ian said.

"Oh, God."

"Becky McGee called me too, trying to get me to show up out there at that crime scene that wasn't a crime scene. I told her no, of course."

"I guess you're smarter than me."

"It's not easy to say no. It feels like being there, if something happened, would somehow complete things."

"Yes, that's what I thought. I thought—"

She stopped the stream of words just in time.

Ian nodded, his face full of sympathy. "You didn't want Celia to be alone."

"Yes."

"I understand. I had to weigh that against . . . well,

against being a pawn in some journalist's game. Against being put on display like a monkey."

"I played right into their hands. They can loop video of me for the next few days. They can make the bleep louder and longer."

One end of Ian's mouth turned up as he laughed. A low, subtle sound, but a laugh nonetheless. "I don't normally watch that coverage. I can't stand to see that Reena Huffman and her hysterics. But Ursula saw the clip somewhere and showed it to me."

"Great. Everyone is seeing it. I've been trying to avoid my mother. She's thrilled, I'm sure."

"It's okay," he said. "It reminded me of what you were like in high school. Definitely a loose cannon."

"Some things never change, I guess."

"And your mom's still uptight? Thinks you're not ladylike enough?"

"Naturally." Jenna swallowed. "Ian, are the police still treating you like a suspect?"

"Lord, Jenna, you're not holding anything back, are you?"

"I'd like to think this isn't the right time, but who knows when I'll get to talk to you again?"

"It would be nice to have a break from all that."

"You can't expect that with me."

"I'm not a suspect. Officially. I'm sure plenty of people think I am."

He paused, as though he expected Jenna to contradict him, but she didn't.

He said, "They sure as hell treated me like one for the entire month of November. About the only thing they didn't do was give me a rectal exam."

"They always suspect the husband."

"Of course. And I cooperated fully." He looked around the room and nodded to an older man who seemed to know him. "My alibi's thin. I know that. I was home, with my daughter. I made a phone call to my mother. That's all I've got. I can't change what I was doing. It was late at night. Talk about hell . . . Your wife disappears and then you become a suspect. A nice double whammy."

The food came, and for a few minutes their conversation died while they ate. The voices around them murmured on. A middle-aged woman in a business suit came over and shook Ian's hand, making some comment about golfing together again in the spring.

Jenna was halfway through her salad and wishing she'd ordered an iced tea or a Coke when Ian asked, "What did the police want with you? As if I don't already know."

"You think you know?" Jenna asked.

Ian ignored her question, his voice taking on a new urgency. "You tell me. What exactly did they want?"

CHAPTER NINETEEN

Jenna set her silverware aside.

"Poole wanted to ask me about Holly Crenshaw. You know—the woman who disappeared from Clay County? She wanted to know if I knew her. Or I guess she wanted to know if I knew if Celia knew her."

"She didn't. Neither one of us did."

"Not even casually?"

"Okay, I can't account for everyone either of us ever said hello to at the club, but we didn't know her. She worked in the office. They're looking for a connection, and it isn't there. Not that way."

"But it could be the same person," Jenna said. "There could be someone hurting women. Celia and Holly Crenshaw do resemble each other. And maybe I only know this from watching TV shows, but don't these creeps have a type? You know, brown hair or blond hair or whatever. Maybe even Benny Ludlow."

Ian held his sandwich in his hands, but he set it down.

He looked as if he had a bad taste in his mouth, and Jenna wished she hadn't started offering half-baked theories about kidnappers.

"I'm sorry, Ian. I don't know what to make of any of it. But it seems like there hasn't been any progress in a long time, so if they follow this Holly Crenshaw trail and it takes them somewhere, I'm all for it." He wasn't looking at her, so she waited until he did. "I want her back. I want to know she's okay. If this maybe helps us, I don't mind answering the questions."

Ian moved his head the slightest bit, his attempt at an understanding nod. But he didn't look convinced by any of it. The things she spoke about weren't reaching him, and she still wondered what he meant when he said, "As if I don't know."

The waiter brought a piece of cake to the party next to them, and then came up to their table and asked how they were doing. Ian dismissed him with the slightest wave of his hand, almost like a magic trick, or as if the two of them had worked out a signal that said *Leave us alone.* But Jenna knew it wasn't a signal. It was power and class, the ability to barely lift your hand or arch your eyebrow and make someone go away.

She remembered another look, the one Detective Poole gave her when she asked about Ian and Celia's marriage.

"That wasn't all she wanted to ask me about," Jenna said, her tone tentative. "She was hinting around about your marriage."

"She shouldn't do that."

"Should or shouldn't, people do ask these things when someone disappears. It's the same as you being a suspect. It's natural."

"Natural?"

Jenna sipped her water. "Maybe I've been a fool. I've been going around ever since Celia disappeared telling everyone who asks what a great marriage the two of you have." She watched Ian's face. It didn't change as she spoke. "I just told that to Detective Poole again today. But do I really know that? Did I even really know Celia anymore? I certainly don't know you well."

"Jenna—"

"I don't want to be made a fool of anymore. I've been doing that well enough on my own. Tell me, Ian. Why was Poole asking about your marriage that way?"

He held her gaze a long time. Then he said, "You do know Celia very well. That's true. You're her best friend. I know her well too. But that doesn't mean I knew everything." He didn't look away as he spoke, so Jenna saw in his eyes the effort the words were costing him. Each one that emerged from his mouth added a layer of pain. "It wasn't the first time," he said. "This most recent one. The one going on right when she disappeared."

Jenna felt as if she'd fallen behind in the conversation. Had she missed something? Ian seemed to be talking in code, one that implied something about Celia.

"What do you mean?" she asked.

"I'm assuming you didn't know this, or you would have had the good sense to tell the police. Tell me you didn't know about this, Jenna. Celia said you didn't."

"Know what?"

And then the picture started to clear. Ian's hints, his inability to say it directly.

"About three years ago there was a guy. He wasn't from the country club. She met him—" He cleared his throat, lifting his fist to his mouth. "They met through a group she belonged to at church, of all things. It never got serious, I don't think. It's funny that in some ways that makes it worse. I mean, maybe it would be easier to swallow if they really loved each other or something, but this was apparently only about sex."

Jenna looked down at the nearly empty salad bowl. The remains of her lunch, greens and a few vegetables sitting in oil, looked so unappealing she couldn't stand to think she'd just eaten most of it.

"It ended," he said. "I found out when we bought new phones. She still had the texts right there. Times to meet and all that. I can tell you don't believe me."

"She never said a word. . . ."

"Did her behavior change three years ago, in the summer? Did you notice anything different about her?"

Three years. Around the time Celia and Ian joined the country club, around the time Jenna and Celia started seeing less of each other. Did their drifting apart begin in the summer? She couldn't say. She didn't answer Ian's question.

"We got it together after that. Mostly." The look in his eyes seemed far away. "I thought we were moving in the right direction at least. For a while, we spent more time together. We went away on that trip. You remember?"

"Europe. Ursula stayed with your mother."

"We were fine. Good, even. We were getting some-where, I thought."

"And then?" Jenna asked.

"Then she disappeared." He said the word casually, without any special emphasis or hesitation. *Disappeared*. It was a fact of life for both of them. "I never knew for sure about the most recent affair. I suspected it in the weeks leading up to her disappearance, but I didn't know with certainty. The police brought it up again over the last few days. They keep turning the same earth, hoping something new appears. I'm sure that's why Poole tracked you down and asked you the marriage question again. I can even see the smug look on her face when she asked you, like she was the all-knowing schoolteacher leading a precocious student toward a lesson."

"That is what she looked like."

"I don't know what they're thinking. They won't say, which seems ridiculous to me. I should be able to know as much about my wife's case as I can possibly know. Maybe they're so desperate for a lead they're just shaking the trees to see what falls out. The guy . . ." His voice dripped with distaste. "Some dentist who lives about twenty miles away from here, in Youngblood or someplace like that. I didn't listen much to the details. They hurt too much. Talk about getting kicked in the balls. But she'd been involved with him for a little while. A month or so, at least from what they can tell."

"So this guy, this dentist, he might be—"

"They cleared him. I asked the same thing. He has an alibi for that time. It's rock solid. He was with a group of his friends in a bar. Twenty people saw him. I wish it was different. . . ."

"I'm sure the cops wished it went that way too. But maybe one of these guys was following her. . . ."

"They've been through it all, Jenna. It's humiliating. Try having to go over your wife's two affairs with the cops."

"Ugh," Jenna said. "But if this is true about Celia and this dentist . . . how did you not know about it when it was happening?"

Ian smiled again, the same weak, wistful smile. "Celia could have been in the CIA apparently. They used some kind of throwaway cell phones, the ones drug dealers use. No paper or electronic trail. I worked a lot. We'd drifted some."

His gaze trailed out the window. Jenna followed it and didn't see anything worth noting. Ian appeared lost in his own thoughts, and she struggled with hers. She'd missed so much of Celia's life, and that life might be over. And again she wondered about the role she could have played if she had known everything that was going on with her friend.

But then she came back to the important questions at hand. "Did anybody else know about it? The thing with the dentist?"

"You think I haven't been thinking about that for the last week? You think I haven't been through every name of every person we knew?" Ian looked at his watch. "I can't look at anybody the same way again."

Jenna studied Ian's profile as he continued to stare out the window. "Is that the only reason you agreed to come out to meet me? To ask me what I knew? After you haven't said a word to me for months?"

He turned back to face her, a look on his face she couldn't read.

"You could have spoken to me a long time ago. Let me apologize or something. Instead I waited . . ."

Ian stopped her by reaching out and placing his hand over the top of hers. She felt the warmth of his skin, its surprising softness. He let it rest there for several moments, and then he squeezed it gently.

Without saying anything else, he stood up and left.

Jenna remained in her seat, processing the conversation, until well after Ian was gone. When the waiter came back, she asked for the bill. He informed her that it had already been taken care of by Mr. Walters.

CHAPTER TWENTY

The day felt like spring, the temperature climbing into the high forties. Jared walked home alone, his backpack bumping lightly against his body as he moved along, ignoring the passing streams of cars and buses filled with his fellow students. A few voices shouted at him as they went past, calling his name or just yelling. What else is there to do while riding a ridiculous school bus when you're in high school?

It took Jared ten minutes to reach the edge of downtown. He was south of Tabitha's neighborhood, and he stood still for a moment, his head turned toward the north where she lived. He could easily walk that way, swing by her house, and see what was going on. But did he really need to push? Mike had offered the unsolicited advice to move on, to find someone less complicated. Someone allowed out of the house after seven o'clock in the evening.

Jared understood why Mike said that, but he wasn't going to listen.

He didn't want anyone else. He only wanted Tabitha. He wanted everything to go back to the way it had been.

But he walked toward home, crossing through downtown. She'd be back in school the next day, he told himself. They'd pick up where they left off. But even as those thoughts trailed through his mind, he doubted them. There seemed to be too much to overcome. Her father's kiss, the rock through the window. His lack of any real knowledge about her.

His thoughts ping-ponged. Maybe Mike was right. If he could get one girlfriend, he could get another, right? But he didn't want another.

He was a few blocks from his house when the car pulled up alongside him. He didn't recognize it. An older Ford Taurus, green with fading spots around the fenders and on the roof. He thought they were going to ask for directions, or maybe it was someone from school wanting to talk to him.

Then he saw the face through the passenger window. Tabitha.

Jared looked past her to the driver's seat. It was her dad, his broad face staring straight ahead, looming over the steering wheel like a resting lion.

Tabitha stepped out and closed the door behind her. Jared's heart raced, the kind of excitement he felt when he was a kid on the verge of receiving a new toy. She was here. It was going to be okay.

But Tabitha wore a somber look. There was no light in her eyes.

She placed her hand gently on Jared's elbow and guided him a few feet away from the car. He wanted to hug her, to pull her close so he could take in the scent of her hair, the softness of her body, but she had a wall up. There was a stiffness to her posture, a formality as though the two of them were distant relatives and not two people who had spent the previous few weeks falling in love.

"Listen," Tabitha said. "I need to talk to you."

"Are you sick? Is that why you weren't in school?"

"Not exactly." She looked over her shoulder and back toward the car. Her father hadn't moved. He still stared straight ahead. But Jared got the sense he knew exactly what the two of them were doing, even if he wasn't looking. He seemed like the kind of guy who wouldn't miss a thing.

Jared assumed he knew about the night before. Jared lurking in the yard, the rock through the window right after the weird kiss on the lips.

"I'm sorry about last night," Jared said, trying to get his words in preemptively. If she could only hear him and know what he felt.

But Tabitha was shaking her head, the movement quick and urgent as if she was late for something. "It's okay," she said. "I know the whole thing is weird."

"It doesn't have to be. I don't care if it's weird or not weird."

Jared didn't know why, since he'd never dated anyone

before, but he felt her words coming before she said them. She was going to break up with him.

"We can't see each other anymore," she said. She hesitated, as though there was something else to add. She looked back at the car again. "We just can't," she said, her voice lower.

"That's not true."

"It is."

Jared saw the look in her eyes, something between fear and sadness. She had broken off physical contact with him, hadn't touched him since she first put her hand on his elbow. But she reached out again, quickly, and placed her hand over his. She gave it a quick squeeze.

"I'm sorry," she said. "This is all too messed up for both of us."

"I'll pay for the window. I have money saved. I'll apologize to your dad. I was just worried about you."

For a moment, she looked confused, and then the look on her face softened. "It's not that. Really. I have to go."

Jared took a step past her. "I'll talk to your dad. Man-to-man. I'll explain that everything was my fault. If we just talk—"

She took his arm in a tighter grip. "No, you can't talk to him." Her voice was sharp and biting, like the cold wind. It cut through everything. "He insisted on coming with me to keep an eye on me, to make sure I don't . . ."

"To make sure of what?"

"Just . . . talking to him won't work. He wants me with him."

"Sure. He's your dad, but we can still be together."

"I know how he is."

But Jared didn't listen. He slipped free and stepped to the car. He raised his fist and knocked on the passenger-side window. Up close he saw the pockmarks on the side of the man's face, saw the power behind his heavy-lidded eyes. He knocked again, and still the man didn't flinch. In fact, he turned away, showing Jared the back of his head. The gesture seemed defiant, as if the man wanted to prove how little he needed to heed anything Jared had to say. As if he wanted Jared to feel small.

"Sir? Mr. Burke?"

Jared straightened up and started around the car, heading for the driver's side. But Tabitha intercepted him. Her face looked desperate, more scared than he'd ever seen it. Even more scared than the day before when he tried to walk with her to her house and speak to her dad as he paced on the porch, cigarette glowing.

"That's it, Jared. I'm going. I have to go with my father. And you have to go home. Really, just go home. It's better that way, I promise."

Again she gave him a shove, lighter than the one she'd given him the day before. The message was the same. She didn't want him around. She wanted him away from her.

Jared lost his balance, the backpack pulling him toward the ground. He didn't fall, but by the time he righted himself, Tabitha was slipping into the passenger side of the car. He reached out, a fruitless attempt to stop her, but her father hit the gas and the car sped off before she even buckled her seat belt.

CHAPTER TWENTY-ONE

When Jenna came home, she found the door to Jared's room closed, the lights off. His backpack sat on a kitchen chair, dropped there as if he'd been in a hurry. It wasn't like him to do that, since he usually started on homework pretty soon after coming in the door.

Jenna stood in the hallway, her ear pressed to his door. Nothing. No fumbling, no moaning. No music or sounds of video games. She knocked lightly, using the knuckle of her index finger.

A muffled reply came back. "Yeah?"

"Just seeing if you're here."

"I'm here," he said. "And I'm alone."

Jenna felt chastened. But she had been worried about that. She didn't want her house to turn into a hookup location for her son or anyone else. As a single mother, she felt as though she was under greater scrutiny from other parents. If something went wrong, if some disaster occurred in her house, she knew what they'd say. *Well, she's trying to raise that boy alone. . . .*

And Tabitha's dad sounded so strict. She ran out of their house the day before in order to meet a curfew, an *early* curfew. Jenna didn't need the community's toughest dad on her case.

"Are you hungry?" Jenna asked, still standing before the closed door.

Jared offered her a soft grunting noise. She couldn't tell if it was a yes or a no. She placed her hand on the knob and turned. The door swung inward, and she stuck her head in. The room was dark, her son an indistinct lump beneath a pile of covers. His shoes and socks lay scattered on the carpet, his jeans tossed over a chair.

"Honey? What did you say? Are you hungry?"

"No."

She waited for more of an explanation but didn't get one.

"Is everything okay?" Jenna asked. She came closer to the bed, but Jared didn't move. "What is it?"

"I'm just . . . I'm not feeling well. I'm not going to eat."

Jenna placed her hand against his forehead. He didn't flinch or try to turn away. But he didn't feel warm. A little clammy from being wrapped in the covers, but no fever. "Are you sick to your stomach?"

"Sure."

"Sure? What is this about, really?"

"Mom, I just . . . I want to be alone."

Jenna remembered the night before, how she pushed too hard and drove him away. If he wanted to be in a mood and hole up in his room, so be it. He rarely acted like a depressed, angsty teenager, so she figured she could indulge him this once. If he wasn't sick, it must be girl trouble. And she didn't think he wanted her advice about that, not yet anyway.

"That's fine," she said. "I've had kind of a long day too. But I only had a salad for lunch, so I'm going to make grilled cheese or something." She threw out one of his favorites, hoping to see if he might go for it. But he didn't respond. He pulled the covers tighter around his body, returning to his cocoon. "If you want something later, just let me know."

He grunted again. She backed away and slipped out of the room, leaving him to his misery.

But Jenna didn't make anything.

She changed her clothes in the bedroom, kicking off her shoes and peeling off the scrubs and then changing into a pair of yoga pants and a favorite University of Kentucky basketball sweatshirt. On her way through the kitchen, she grabbed some carrots and a tub of feta cheese dip and carried them to the spare bedroom she used as an office. She kept a desk in there, a laptop, and a filing cabinet. She also kept the closet stuffed with summer clothes and papers she couldn't justify getting rid of. She placed the dip and the carrots on the desk and signed on to the computer.

Jenna always felt dirty when she did it. Almost as if she were logging on to look at pornography. In a way, she was. Before Celia disappeared, Jenna never realized an entire world existed online devoted to news and theories about missing persons cases and unsolved crimes. It made sense once she thought about it—there was something on the Internet for everybody. Every fetish, every hobby, every obscure interest or wish.

In the first weeks after Celia's disappearance, Jenna found herself visiting the sites, simply hoping for more information. The police only talked about so much, and the media, national and local, devoted only a certain amount of time and energy to any one case. And the reporters and journalists selected only the juiciest details to share, the ones that played best on a national stage.

But the Web sites and message boards struck the right balance. Yes, crazies and rumormongers jumped into every conversation, spinning the most outrageous theories possible, including alien abduction, satanic cults, and government conspiracy. But that was the lunatic fringe. A lot of people on the sites seemed to want to help. They approached the scant evidence with a logical mind-set and offered constructive ideas that managed to make Jenna feel comforted. She never knew what the police were doing or thinking, but she imagined they were tracing some of the same connections, no doubt with more thoroughness and more practical experience than the amateur sleuths on the Web.

Jenna went to the Dealey Society page first. They kept their breaking news section current, and the message boards were always active. A thread, dedicated to Celia's case, received constant traffic and updates from members. Jenna posted from time to time. If a thread or a conversation was going in an interesting direction, and she wanted the discussion to keep going, she would jump in and ask something pointed to keep things in motion. In an effort to avoid a flood of private messages and possible attacks, she used a pseudonym, Polly Baker, a name she chose at random, and she tried to never reveal anything that would let others know how close to the case she really was. When she clicked on the thread about Celia, a cascade of new information unrolled before her. Understandably so. A number of things had happened in the last couple of days, and everybody wanted to offer their opinions about them.

People went after Reena Huffman, calling her a sensationalistic hack who exploited the tragedies and vulnerabilities of crime victims. A few people dissented, defending her and giving her credit for keeping victims' stories in the news. But it wasn't a majority opinion.

A number of people talked about Jenna and her *f*-bomb on Reena's show. For the most part, the commenters sided with Jenna. Either they found her outburst funny or they took Reena to task for sticking a microphone in her face in the midst of tragedy, never mind the fact that it wasn't Reena who held the microphone. It was Becky, her local minion. A few people openly wondered about Jenna, picking up on Reena's comments from the previous night. Some even speculated that Jenna should be a suspect, that she might have killed her friend for some reason no one knew yet.

Jenna had seen those comments before, but they always hit her like a slap. To be thought capable of murder, even by the craziest of the crazy. To wonder how many people in Hawks Mill suspected her of a deeper, more sinister involvement. A convulsive shiver passed through her body, the equivalent of stepping on a slug while barefoot.

Was that part of the deal with the patient at work?

He attributed it to her "foul mouth," but what if it was something more? Some darker crime others suspected her of committing? And if that was the case, what if they never really found out what had happened to Celia? Would she live under that cloud forever? And when would it leak over and affect Jared's life as well?

She navigated away from that section. She couldn't give in to it, couldn't let the poisonous thoughts of others seep inside her head. She clicked the mouse a few times with her right hand and grabbed a couple of carrots with her left. Advanced multitasking, she and Jared called it. Eating while using the computer.

And then there was an entire thread devoted to the earring being found. New messages popped up in that thread every few seconds. The dominant theory seemed to be that Benjamin Ludlow was the guy who followed Celia. He killed her and held on to the earring until he needed the money and tried to pawn it. People called him scum, homeless, vagrant, worthless, and a hundred other names.

Jenna sat back. For a moment, just a moment, she felt a kinship with Benjamin Ludlow. He was being tried in the court of the Internet. A message board and a group of mostly anonymous posters as judge, jury, and executioner.

Hell, she'd judged him the same way based on how he'd acted in high school.

The private message icon lit up and dinged.

The site allowed any two registered members who were active at the same time to carry on their own conversation in private. Jenna suspected she knew who it would be. She experienced a mixture of dread and anticipation as she clicked the chat icon.

Just as she expected, it was Domino55.

Haven't "seen" you in a while, Domino55 wrote.

I've been busy. Work and other things.

I hear you.

Domino55 reached out to Jenna, or Polly, from time to time. He—she assumed Domino was a he—liked to ask probing questions about Celia's case, both on the public board and in their private conversations. He appeared to be one of the most informed posters, someone who absorbed every new tidbit of information that was made public and then used that knowledge to spin out ever more elaborate but still plausible theories. They often lacked consistency. If they contradicted one another, so be it. Domino didn't appear to care. He seemed more interested in playing the role of provocateur, a guy trying on a lot of different poses just to see if any of them stuck.

About once a week, he sent Jenna a private message. He liked to try some of his theories out on her in private before he took them public. Jenna didn't know if she was the only person he spoke to in this way. She suspected she wasn't. Domino needed an audience, and one person didn't add up to an audience.

Ten days ago they'd chatted. Domino's words felt more pointed that time, more probing. He started asking Jenna what part of the country she lived in and where her interest in Celia's case came from. When Jenna kept her answers vague or avoided engagement altogether, Domino told her he thought she was really close to the case, might even be a good friend or relative of Celia's. Jenna left the conversation, vowing to avoid the message boards. But she couldn't stay away. She liked, almost needed, the conversations and contact with other people who wanted to talk about the case.

That Reena is a hack, isn't she?

Sure, Jenna wrote. I never liked her show.

That stuff with the deer bones was insane.

Yes.

A ridiculous stunt.

Yes.

Jenna waited, but Domino wasn't writing anything else. The icon showed he was still there, still active, but no words came.

She chewed some more carrots, biting down and feeling the cold crunch against her teeth. She paused once, listening behind her, trying to see if Jared was up. The house remained silent except for the soft hum of the computer and her own crunching. One good thing about being single, she thought, no need to worry about chewing in a ladylike fashion. She crunched and crunched without worrying about the noise.

What do you think happened to Celia?

The directness of the question caught Jenna off guard. In her mind, she knew what happened. She couldn't contemplate anything else.

She was taken, she wrote. A crazy person. A killer.

No immediate response came, so Jenna added, Another woman just disappeared in the same area. Could be a connection.

Holly Crenshaw.

Yes.

Could be connected. A brief pause. Likely a coincidence.

Jenna took the bait. She knew he wanted a response, knew he sought the reaction on the other end. But she couldn't stop herself. She wanted to know what Domino was thinking.

Why do you seem so certain?

Another long pause, one that stretched so far Jenna started to think Domino had given up, withdrawn as he so often did when the conversation grew complicated.

You should know. You knew her well.

Jenna gasped.

What do you mean? Jenna typed.

You were there. I mean, you were almost there when it happened. A pause. Jenna.

Jenna stood up, the motion of her rising body knocking the chair backward and away, where it banged against the closet behind her. Her body heaved as if she'd just run a mile.

He knows who I am. Really.

She thought of the crank phone calls. Not the ones that took her to task for cursing on TV or for simply being late the night Celia disappeared. Other ones came during the previous months. Pointed questions asking Jenna *why* she'd been late that night. They didn't always sound like the same man. She felt certain they weren't. But could one of them be this guy, Domino55?

Don't talk to me anymore. Don't try to message me.

We should talk more. Maybe in person. Celia might be alive. People have reported seeing her—

Jenna slammed the lid of the computer down, severing the connection.

"No," she said.

She looked around the room. The blinds were closed. No one could see in, but she couldn't see out.

Was he out there? Watching?

Someone knocked at the door. Jenna jumped, gasping again.

"Mom?"

The door opened, revealing Jared. His hair messy, his eyes sleepy.

"Are you okay?" he asked. "I heard something."

"Where?"

"In here. You said something."

She brushed past him, heading for the front of the house. She checked the lock and chain, then breezed back down the hallway and through the kitchen.

"Mom? What is it?"

She reached the back door and checked the lock and chain there.

Jared came up behind her. "Mom, what's going on?"

"I have to call the police," she said. "Someone knows something about Celia, and they might be watching the house."

CHAPTER TWENTY-TWO

The police lingered for close to two hours. She felt safe with them inside the house and milling around outside. But what about once they left? Would a baseball bat and pepper spray be enough to let her sleep?

The first officers to respond checked the outside of the house. They walked around with flashlights, their jackets zipped to their chins in the cold night. Jenna imagined the neighbors taking in the show and just shaking their heads. The police had been to her house so many times over the past three months, the neighbors would have to work hard to summon any real outrage. The police visits also freed them from their mundane lives. They could judge Jenna, and then go to work or the beauty parlor the next day with yet another story to tell.

The cops were over there again last night. I don't know what it was this time, but did you see her on Reena Huffman? What a mouth.

While the cops poked around outside, Jared opened

cabinets in the kitchen. "What happened to that promise of grilled cheese?"

Jenna tried to take it as a good sign that her son could be so unconcerned by the arrival of the police. She went to work on the sandwich, hoping it would distract her. But her hands shook as she buttered the bread, and Jared stepped in.

"I'll finish," he said. "Thanks."

"Are you feeling all right now?" Jenna asked. "You said you were sick."

"I'm fine," he said.

"Was there a problem at school?" Jenna asked. "Or is this girl trouble?"

Recognition flickered across Jared's eyes. So it was girl trouble. But he didn't offer anything else, and before Jenna could follow up, the doorbell was ringing again.

"I . . . We can talk about this," she said.

"Just get the door, Mom," he said. "I'm fine."

"But you're not fine."

"I'm finer than you are right now." He placed his sandwich on the griddle. "That's probably the cops. Maybe they found an opossum sneaking around outside."

But then a small smile crossed his face. It looked forced, and Jenna imagined it said more about his own unhappiness than any judgment of her.

"Okay," she said. "But we will talk."

Detective Poole wore jeans and a sweater, and her white tennis shoes squeaked against the hardwood floors in the living room.

"I didn't think you'd be here," Jenna said as she took the detective's coat and hung it on a hook.

"These guys know to call me when the important stuff happens."

"I guess your evenings at home get interrupted a lot."

"The cat doesn't mind." Her clothes made her look older and more dowdy. She could have been anyone's mother just arriving home after an evening at Bible study or book club. "Tell me about these messages."

Naomi listened carefully and then asked if she could look at the conversation online. Jenna led her back to the office. They passed Jared in the kitchen. He sat at the table chewing his sandwich, staring straight ahead and looking lost.

Naomi patted him on the shoulder. "Hey, handsome."

"Hi, Detective."

"Naomi. Call me Naomi."

Jared smiled a little again, but he still didn't look like his usual self. Jenna felt a twinge of jealousy. She envied all the parents who had to worry only about typical teenage stuff. Broken hearts, parties, acne, proms.

Jenna opened the computer and logged on. The conversation came back up, although Domino had logged out. Naomi studied it for a few moments, reading it over a few times. She didn't take any notes, but her brow wrinkled as she read along.

She pointed at the computer. "I'm going to take a screen capture of this." And she did, the fake camera sound filling the room. "And this guy hasn't ever gotten too weird before?"

"No." She tried to keep her voice level. "Okay, the last time we chatted he asked more pointed questions. He wanted to know where I lived. He said I 'sounded' like a Southerner, whatever that means. And he asked me if I'd ever had the desire to visit famous crime scenes. He said he'd been to cities all over the country where these kinds of kidnappings had taken place."

"And that wasn't weird to you?" Naomi asked, her eyebrows lifting above the owlish glasses.

"Do you know what the people are like on these sites?" Jenna asked. "They all think they're some kind of junior Sherlock Holmes. It's a hobby. Some people collect stamps. These people study crimes."

Naomi leaned back in the chair. It creaked under her weight. "True. It's a great thing the members have been able to help solve a few crimes. Really, it's amazing. And rare. And now it's encouraged them. More and more probably joined the fun, thinking they could figure out things the police couldn't." She swiveled the chair a little, pointing her body toward Jenna. "I'll be honest with you—we just don't have the technology here to trace something like this. If the guy is using his own computer to talk to you, then the state crime lab could trace it. They have a unit devoted to online stalking and harassing. I can turn this over to them, and they can look into it."

"It seems like there's a but coming."

"It's all a long shot. The guy didn't threaten you or anything."

"He said my name."

"Did you reveal something personal about yourself?"

Naomi asked. "Something that would make him think you are who you are?"

Jenna felt like a fool, remembering. "We talked about Celia, of course. That's all we talked about. I think I gushed a little too much. I know I told him once that it was emotional for me to talk about. That was early on. I think I might have mentioned having a son too."

"He took a shot in the dark, and now you've let him know he was right." Naomi held up her hand. "I'm not blaming you. I'm just saying the guy got under your skin a little, and he knows it now. Mission accomplished as far as he's concerned."

"Ugh." Jenna raised her hand to her head and rubbed her eyes. "I shouldn't talk to anyone. It just makes things more complicated."

"You had a rough couple of days. Don't beat yourself up over it." Naomi's face looked placid, calm. She'd seen it all and didn't let any of it bother her. "I have a psychologist friend. She says when we make a mistake and then beat ourselves up over it, we hurt ourselves twice. Kind of makes sense, doesn't it?"

"Yeah. Too much sense. But this guy mentioned that Celia might be alive. He said he doesn't think there's a connection between Holly Crenshaw and Celia. He seemed so certain."

"Everyone seems certain online," Naomi said.

"Do you believe any of those sightings? The ones where people claim they've seen Celia?"

Naomi looked thoughtful. She lifted her hand to her chin. "There's a drawback to all this information circulating about a missing person case. It means everybody knows everything. So everyone suddenly decides they're seeing the victim somewhere. If I thought any of them were truly credible, I'd hop on the next plane myself. But we've looked into the ones that did seem credible. Nothing yet." She cocked her head. "You told me the other day she wouldn't run away from her life. Why are you asking me this now? Did something change?"

"No, it didn't. But I'd rather she ran away than accept the alternative. I'm trying hard not to accept the alternative."

One of the uniformed officers appeared in the doorway. He informed Detective Poole that they hadn't found anything unusual outside. No signs of break-in, no tracks in the mud. "Do you want us to do anything else?"

"Are you assigned to this sector tonight? Do you mind keeping a closer eye on things here for me?"

"No problem, Detective."

When the cop was gone, Jenna said, "I should tell you I saw Ian Walters today. We had lunch together."

Naomi's voice remained steady. "How did that come about?"

"I went to see him. After I talked to you this morning, and you asked about him, I couldn't stop thinking about it. Why hadn't I seen or talked to him since Celia disappeared?"

"Why hadn't you?"

"I don't know. It's always been a little weird between him and me. Like we were competing to see who could be closest to Celia. He was always going to win that one.

He and Ursula. It's pretty tough for an outsider to break into a tight family unit like that."

"That's what you think they are? A tight family unit?"

"They seemed that way to me," Jenna said. "Is that why you were probing me about the affairs this morning?"

"And you really didn't know about them?" Naomi asked.

"I didn't." Her voice was sharp. Jenna leaned back, resting her butt against the top of the desk. Her carrots and dip still sat by the laptop, but she didn't feel hungry anymore. Even the odor of Jared's grilled cheese hadn't tempted her stomach. "I had no idea." She picked at a loose piece of skin on her thumb. "I told you Celia and I weren't quite as tight as we once were these last few years. She had new friends. Different friends. But you know how it is with a best friend. You don't need to talk every day or know every detail about their life." She stopped picking. "Clearly I didn't know every detail."

"No one did."

"Why were you asking about it now?" Jenna asked. "Ian seemed to think you got a new tip or something."

"Not exactly," Naomi said. "More than anything, we just like to go over old leads and see if anything new turns up. Sometimes a second pass reveals something different."

"I guess that makes sense."

"Now that you have that little piece of news, do you have any new light to shed on their marriage?"

"I've been thinking about it all afternoon," Jenna

said. "I'm still processing it. I've been thinking about Ursula a lot, the effect the affair must have had on her."

"Naturally."

"Ian told me the guy, the dentist, isn't a suspect."

"He's not."

"But if she was having an affair, doesn't that make it more likely she'd run away?" Jenna asked.

"Without the guy she was having the affair with? Why would she do that?"

"Because . . . I don't know. Shit. Maybe one of those guys, her lovers, was following her."

"Unlikely as far as we can tell," Naomi said.

"Ian told me he even gave you a name, some business associate of his."

Naomi took a moment to answer. "We've looked into everyone Celia or her family ever came into contact with. We've looked into every possible motive."

"You didn't really answer my question."

"That's true. I didn't." She reached up and scratched her forehead. "Some of these leads haven't been completely closed. We're keeping our options open."

"Is there any news about Benny Ludlow?" she asked.

"I can't say much about him either."

"Of course."

"But he's denying he hurt Celia. Or Holly Crenshaw. We have to figure out where he was at the times these women disappeared. That's tough to do with a guy who mostly lives and travels alone."

"But it's possible," Jenna said, sounding like a kid wishing for a miracle snow day.

"He hasn't been cleared," Naomi said. "Like I said, we're keeping our options open."

The conversation seemed to have reached its natural end. Detective Poole rose from the chair and said, "I think I need to be heading home. Rosie and I were just about to watch *Sherlock*."

"Rosie?"

"My cat."

Jenna eyed the detective's hand. She still wore the wedding band. "And your husband?"

Naomi held her hand up, looking at the ring as though she'd forgotten it was there. "Oh. He died two years ago. I still wear the ring."

"I'm sorry."

"It's okay," Naomi said. "I'd have all these young guys chasing me if they thought I was single."

Jenna walked the detective to the front door and retrieved her coat. Jared was out of sight, the door to his room closed once again. The backpack was out of the kitchen, so at least he was doing homework. Once the detective was zipped up, she turned to Jenna. "I'd tell you to try not to think about this too much, but I know you will."

"I think you're getting to know me too well."

"It's kind of the job. You know, you mentioned Ian and Celia's daughter back there, Ursula. How is she doing?"

"I haven't seen her either."

"Good kid?" Naomi asked.

Jenna knew Naomi knew the answer to that question. She was a cop investigating the disappearance of Ursula's mother. If Naomi wanted to know something about the girl, she knew it. But Naomi clearly wanted to get Jenna's opinion. Someone who'd known Ursula since the day she was born.

"She's a smart girl," Jenna said. "Popular. She's become a little brattier over the last few years."

"Teenagers do that."

"Sure. But she has a tougher edge than most teenagers. She runs in a prominent crowd at school. Rich kids. Why do you ask?"

"You said you were worried about her. What did Ian say about her?"

"I asked him today. He said she's doing her best." Jenna remembered what a willful child Ursula was. Sweet most of the time, but also endlessly stubborn. When she and Jared played together as children, there was never any doubt as to who the leader would be in any game. It was always Ursula, not easygoing Jared. In her own mind, Jenna used to think how perfectly the girl was named. Ursula. The Bear. "I'm just remembering something."

"What?"

Jenna paused for a moment as the memory crystallized in her mind. "She shoved Jared once. They must have been three or four and were playing some game together. Jared didn't do things the way Ursula wanted. I guess he actually stood up to her and said no for a change, and she shoved him. Hard. He hit his head against the coffee table."

Naomi cringed. "Ouch."

"It was scary. I thought he was going to need stitches. You know how head wounds bleed. But it stopped eventually, and Ian and Celia fell all over themselves apologizing."

"That makes me glad I only have cats," Naomi said, her voice deadpan.

"She got into that fight at school right after Celia disappeared."

"I remember that," Naomi said. "Kids fight sometimes."

"Ursula always had Ian wrapped around her little finger. God, I hate when girls do that."

"Do what?" Naomi asked.

"That whole 'I'm Daddy's little girl' thing. You know? Climbing into her dad's lap? Acting like butter wouldn't melt in her mouth? Ursula always did that with Ian. I guess he went along with it because he wasn't around as much. With everyone else, Ursula could be a challenge. I guess she's more like her dad. Tough to read.

"It looks like her mom was tough to read too," Jenna said.

CHAPTER TWENTY-THREE

O n Friday, Jenna came into the break room where the employees drank coffee or ate their lunches or retreated when patient demands and craziness grew too intense. When she entered the room, two of her coworkers were already in there, and the moment she stepped through the door, the conversation halted. Jenna knew they were talking about her.

She looked at the two women, their faces sheepish. Emma was another nurse and Charlaine helped with the books. Jenna didn't know them well, didn't care much what they thought of her. She thought about just doing what she came to do—grab a cup of coffee and slip away without speaking—but why should she let things go unchallenged? If they had something to say to her, they should say it.

"You don't have to treat me like a china doll," she said to them. She went over to the pot, pulling a mug down from the cabinet above her head. "What is there to talk about now? I haven't cursed on TV for a few days, and none of my other friends have disappeared."

Jenna kept her back to them while she added sugar, stirring with a beat-up spoon, the metal clanking against the side of the mug the only sound until Charlaine cleared her throat. Jenna turned around. The two women looked sad and not offended. Their eyes were full of sympathy, the corners of their mouths turned down.

Something was going on.

"What?" Jenna asked, looking down. "Am I wearing two different shoes?"

"It's not that, honey," Charlaine said.

Honey? Charlaine never called her "honey." No one called her "honey" except her mother and maybe Sally.

"What, then?" Jenna asked.

Emma said, "Didn't you watch the news today?"

"No. I'm kind of done with the news these days." But her mind raced. News? Celia? She set the mug down and moved closer to the women. "What is it? What happened?"

The two women exchanged looks, each hoping the other would speak up.

"What?" Jenna asked as images of Celia rushed through her head.

A body found. A break in the case.

"You don't want to hear this kind of news from me," Emma said.

"What news?"

Finally Charlaine took one for the team.

"Why, Jenna, it's that Holly Crenshaw girl, the one who disappeared from Clay County? They found her body this morning. She's dead. We just thought you'd have heard."

Jenna paced in the break room, the phone to her ear. Everyone else had cleared out, giving her space, and word rippled through the office to stay out of Jenna's way.

She dialed Detective Poole over and over again, getting voice mail every time.

Sally came in once while Jenna dialed. She placed a reassuring hand on Jenna's shoulder and then folded her up in a hug. Jenna gave in to the human contact for a long moment, letting some of her weight fall into Sally's surprisingly strong grip. But then she just as quickly pulled out of it, straightening up and trying Naomi's number again, leaving her third voice mail of the morning.

"What are they saying on the news?" she asked Sally.

"Not much, of course. Are you sure you want to hear any of it?"

"Absolutely."

"I heard on the radio they found her in some remote area. I guess a farmer was out working his land in advance of spring, and he came across the body and called the police."

"Not the same barn?"

"Oh, no. This was near the county line, but on our side. Not close to where you were Monday."

"So it's murder," Jenna said. "She was murdered."

"They're not saying."

"What are we supposed to think? She wandered out into some field and had a heart attack? She's in her twenties."

Jenna's voice was harsh, sarcastic, and unforgiving.

Sally didn't even flinch. "I guess we'll know more as the day goes on," she said, stepping over to pour herself a cup of coffee. "Do you want water or something? I'd offer you wine, but they frown on that here."

"I want this cop to answer."

"I've been reading about this girl, this Holly Crenshaw," Sally said. "I understand if you've avoided it."

"I know a little," Jenna said. "Married. Young." She took it all in for a moment, the phone in her hand and away from her ear. "Her parents, Sally. God. They're going to have to bury their daughter."

"Maybe you should head home," Sally said.

Jenna didn't want to leave. She'd missed enough time already, but how was she expected to stay and work with all this craziness swirling through her mind?

"I'm staying," Jenna said. "I think. I don't know. Shit, Sally, I've missed a lot of work. I have a kid who wants to go to college. He wants to get a car. I need to work."

"That's fine," Sally said. "Would you like me to sit here with you?"

"I'll be out as soon as I can," Jenna said. "Thanks."

Then Naomi called back. Jenna answered, and she didn't even try to keep the eagerness out of her voice. "What can you tell me?" Jenna asked.

"My information is limited," Naomi said. "Why don't I call you back when I know more?"

"No," Jenna said. "You tell me now. I don't care if it's only part of the picture."

Naomi sighed. "Okay. I'll tell you what I know, which

isn't much. And really, I shouldn't be telling you anything at this point, but it's getting out on the news, so I'll share some things. We did find a body, a woman's body, out near the county line this morning."

"How do you know she isn't Celia?" Jenna asked.

Naomi paused. "Given the condition of the remains and other identifying factors at the scene, we can tell this body hasn't been there that long. Certainly not as long as Celia's been gone."

"But what if Celia didn't die right away?" Jenna asked, holding out hope as long as she could.

"It's not Celia," Naomi said. "It's Holly Crenshaw. The coroner will make an official identification and do an autopsy, but we can tell. It's Holly."

Jenna's hands shook as she pulled a chair out from the table. She sank into it, her weight dropping down like a sandbag.

Naomi said, "We don't know a cause of death yet. We don't know many other details. Some idiot talked when he shouldn't have talked and now it's all over Twitter and the rest of the news. I had to scramble to get in touch with her husband and parents before they found out from some disc jockey's tweets."

Jenna stared at the random scattering of items on the table. Napkins, a coffee cup, the newspaper, and some old full-color ads. The objects seemed foreign to her, artifacts from another world, one where women didn't disappear and end up dead.

"But she was murdered, right?" Jenna asked.

"I'm not going to jump to any conclusions, but we're certainly treating it as a crime scene."

"And you're searching the area. . . . What if whoever did this, what if Celia is there?"

"We're one step ahead of you," Naomi said. "I've done this job before, unfortunately. We're searching the area, of course. But, Jenna, don't get your hopes up for anything."

Jenna's elbow rested on the table, and she cupped her head in her hand. It all seemed like a bad dream. Months of her life seemed like the most horrible dream imaginable.

And then she thought of Holly Crenshaw's family again. They were suffering something unspeakable. The death of their child. The death of a spouse. A sister, a cousin, a friend. Would they ever know the truth about Celia? Would that day ever come for them?

"I have to get back to it," Naomi said. "I'll keep you in the loop as best I can, but it's going to be a long day of sorting things out. And in the end, this case may have no connection whatsoever to Celia's."

"I know. You told me that."

"Take care, Jenna."

"Benny Ludlow," Jenna said. "He's a suspect."

"Everyone is this early. We'll talk soon. Okay?"

"Naomi?"

"Yes?"

"Will you tell Holly's parents how sorry I am for them?"

"Sure I will."

CHAPTER TWENTY-FOUR

In the parking lot, someone called her name.

Along the horizon a red band stretched as the sun disappeared, and birds, black dots against the sky, flew past in a giant mass. A chill approached, encroaching on the town as the night came on. Jenna pulled her coat tighter, thinking she'd only imagined hearing her name.

But the voice said it again. It was faint, a soft, childlike voice. She looked around. Most of the cars were gone, the other employees and patients clearing out. Late Friday afternoon, just before five. People had plans, or else they just wanted to get home to their families, order pizza, and watch mindless TV. All of those things sounded appealing to Jenna. She'd survived the day, working as hard as she could, trying to keep Holly Crenshaw's death out of her mind. Nothing in her life, even raising a child, had ever required such deep wells of patience.

Jenna carried a canister of pepper spray in her right hand, and her grip on it tightened as she saw the figure approaching. But as the young woman emerged from the dark, Jenna decided she didn't intend to cause anyone harm. The girl looked scared, her eyes wide and pleading in the darkness.

"Tabitha?"

The girl wore the same old coat, the same scuffed shoes. She carried something in her hand, something awkward and blocky. Jenna saw it was a book, a thick paperback, its cover worn and its pages dog-eared. Had she seen it before?

"Mrs. Barton?" she said. "I wanted to ask you a favor."

"Is Jared with you?" Jenna asked, although it seemed obvious he wasn't. She'd texted her son before she left the office, letting him know she was on her way. He wrote back quickly, telling her he was home.

"No." She hesitated, looking around the lot as though someone might be spying on them. She acted as if they were two agents making a dead drop under watchful eyes. "He must have told you we broke up."

"No, he didn't." Jenna felt a little heartsick for her son, and she understood why he'd been in such an unpleasant mood. "But I could tell something was wrong."

"I know he's probably upset."

"Yeah. He seems like he is. Now I know why." She studied the girl, remembering Jared's question about the fatherly kiss. Had that been part of the breakup? "What are you doing here? Is there a problem?"

Tabitha held the book out in front of her. "Would you give this to Jared? I borrowed it from him, and I know it's one of his favorites." She hesitated, emotion flashing across her eyes. "It's hard for me to see him now, but I knew you worked here. I was out doing some other things, but I have to get home." She looked around at the darkening sky. "Would you mind?"

"No." Jenna took the paperback from her. *The Great Book of Amber* by Roger Zelazny. She'd seen it in Jared's room, seen him toting it around the house on more than one occasion. The thing must have had a thousand pages, and she shifted to tuck it under her arm. "Can I ask you something?"

The girl looked poised to go, but Jenna's voice stopped her.

"It's none of my business," Jenna said, "but was the decision to break up mutual or not?"

Tabitha's eyes darted around.

"It's okay," Jenna said. "I'm not trying to take sides here."

Tabitha relaxed a little, the rigidness in her shoulders easing. "It was my idea," she said. "I can't get involved with anyone now." She searched for the right words. "My dad, he wants me to go to college, and he says now isn't the time to get serious with a boy or spend my time doing other things."

The words came out in a torrent. Something about them sounded practiced, forced, as if Tabitha was just repeating what someone had told her to say.

"Your father's pretty strict, isn't he?"

"He wants what's best for me." The answer sounded less robotic. "He really does. That's part of the reason we moved here. The schools are better. He . . . he's trying to give me a better life."

The light slipped away, making it more difficult to see the girl's face. Jenna cocked her head to one side, studying Tabitha. Again she was struck by the familiarity of the girl's features: the set of her eyes, the shape of her chin. She'd seen this girl somewhere before, or more likely, a relative of hers. She got the same feeling when she saw Ursula, and embedded in the teenager's face was the ghost of her mother.

"And did you say your father isn't from Hawks Mill? I knew some other Burkes, not just Tommy. What's your dad's name?"

"His name is Ed."

"Ed Burke," Jenna said.

The girl nodded. "But he's not from Hawks Mill. He lived here once, a long time ago, I guess. But we don't have any other relatives from here."

"But he has friends here or something?" Jenna asked. "If he's lived here before."

"Work friends. He could get a job here."

"Where does he work?"

"I have to go, Mrs. Barton. I'm late. I shouldn't even be here. I really shouldn't. My dad's not home, and I need to get back."

"Are you a patient here?" Jenna asked, pressing. "Or is your dad? I've seen you somewhere, haven't I?"

Tabitha started backing away. "If you'll just give the book to Jared. Tell him I really liked it. I didn't finish it, but I liked it."

Jenna moved forward, following the girl. She wanted to reach out, to offer the girl a comforting pat on the arm or a hug. Tabitha didn't have a mother. She lived with a very strict father, one who might even be—

"Tabitha? Wait."

"Bye, Mrs. Barton."

"I can give you a ride. If you're in some kind of trouble."

Tabitha turned and broke into a run, hustling across the parking lot toward the far side where there was an opening in the fence.

Jenna broke in the same direction, running as best she could in her heavy coat. But she quickly saw she'd never catch up to the lightning-quick young girl.

"Tabitha?"

But she was gone.

CHAPTER TWENTY-FIVE

Jared was watching TV in the living room when Jenna walked in the door. She carried the book in her purse, its bulk pressing against her body like a cinder block. He looked up when she came in.

"Did you get stuck shooting the shit with someone?" he asked as he muted the TV. Jenna took a quick glance at the screen and saw it was a show about World War II. Grainy footage of airplanes diving and dropping bombs. She never knew what he'd find interesting. "Was it Sally? She always wants to bug you when you're trying to get out of there."

She sat on the couch, the bulky purse beside her. She still wore her coat, and Jared's eyebrows lifted when he saw the way she was acting. He knew something was up, since she usually made a beeline for the bedroom and changed into yoga pants as if her work clothes were on fire.

"I didn't talk to Sally. No."

He turned the TV off and sat up in his chair. He

tossed the remote aside as if it offended him. "Is it because of this body they found? I'm sorry—it kind of slipped my mind, but I read all about it on Twitter today. Did the cops want to talk to you?"

Holly Crenshaw. That name had slipped out of her mind ever since Tabitha walked up to her in the parking lot. "They did. This morning. I hate that stuff being all over Twitter."

"People like to talk," he said.

"Right. Look, honey, Tabitha came and talked to me as I was leaving work."

Jared's body jolted as if he'd been stuck with a knife. Every muscle went rigid, and his eyes widened. "Just now?"

"Just now. That's why I was a little late. I'd stayed late anyway to catch up on some things, but then she found me in the parking lot."

"What did she want? What did she say? Mom, she hasn't been in school for days."

Jenna brought out the book, its bulk making her hand sink toward the couch. She held it out to him, and Jared took it, handling it like something precious and fragile. "She said it belonged to you, and she wanted you to have it back. I tried to find out how she was doing, but she just took off. I even offered her a ride."

He stared at the cover of the book, one hand rubbing its surface while the other held it. "Why did she come and give this to you?" He asked the question absently, not really expecting a response. His words were the words of someone who'd been wounded, stung by another's rejection. "She could have brought it to me, here or at school."

"She told me the two of you broke up."

"She broke up with me," he said.

"I got that feeling."

"Was she okay?" he asked. "I haven't talked to her or seen her. She hasn't been in school. Did I mention that?"

"You did." Jenna removed her coat and tossed it over the back of the couch. "Did it ever occur to you that Tabitha might be having bigger problems than your relationship? Maybe she's in some kind of real trouble."

Jared told Jenna that he'd tried to search for information about Tabitha online but found nothing. No social media, no trace of the life she'd lived before she arrived in Hawks Mill. And then he told her about a discussion he'd had with his guidance counselor, the woman who dressed like a hippie and seemed to want to be everybody's friend. Jenna always felt put off by her clothes and demeanor, but Jared loved talking to her, and if she helped him navigate school and get into college, then so be it. Who cared what she wore?

"She said something about having to accept the fact that I may never see Tabitha again," he said. "She knew something, something she didn't or couldn't tell me. I'd swear it."

"Why don't you let me call Detective Poole?" Jenna said. "She could just do a little looking around if she has a free moment, which she may not."

"No, Mom."

Jared's voice was insistent, as hard as steel. He rarely

flashed an angry side, but when he did, he resembled his father more than Jenna wanted to admit. Marty had a short fuse and liked to play the role of the stern patriarch when he felt strongly about something.

"But if she's in danger, the police can help."

"No. You don't understand. What if you call the police and tell them about Tabitha, and then they go to her house and talk to her dad? She could end up in more trouble or she could . . ."

His voice trailed off. But Jenna understood.

"You think she'll blame you," she said. "She'll blame you and then what? You'll never be able to get back together with her?"

Jared looked down at the book cover. Jenna remembered those days when a fledgling little relationship meant more than anything else in life. There had been other boys in high school besides Ian. So many little crushes and flirtations, so many little disappointments and broken hearts. Hell, she felt that way when Marty left. He was no prince, but for close to six months after he walked out the door, she would have taken him back no questions asked. She had felt that desperate, that lonely and scared.

"Jared, there are more important things than a relationship sometimes," she said. "There's a person's safety."

"I'll go. I'll check on her."

"No." Jenna rarely told Jared not to do something. She trusted him to make his own decisions. Mostly. But she needed to play the parent this time. "You shouldn't go over there."

"Why not? It's better than calling the police."

"I thought you were worried about what she thought of you. What's she going to think if you come knocking on her door after she's dumped you?"

The word "dumped" sounded harsh and stinging, but Jared didn't react.

"Maybe you're right," he said, his voice lower.

"I won't call the police, if you don't want. Not right now. I'm holding on to that option, just so you know. If there's more trouble with her or other bad signs."

"Fine. That's fine."

Jared started paging through the book, not really stopping to read or look at anything. Just paging. It looked like a nervous gesture more than anything else.

"Are you hungry?" she asked. "I could call Stanley's and order a pizza. I'm not cooking, I can tell you that."

"Sure. That would be good."

"Are you seeing Syd and Mike tonight? Or are you staying home with Mom?"

He shrugged. "I'm just hungry. Can you call soon?"

"Sure."

She hung her coat up by the door, and on the way past the chair where Jared sat, she stopped. She wanted to hug him, pull him close the way she used to when he was little. He didn't look up or invite any contact, so she ruffled his hair with her hand. He tolerated the affection without resisting, and then Jenna went down the hall to the bedroom. It felt good to change her clothes, to shed the day and all of its problems. She hoped Jared would stay in, that they would watch a movie together while eating the pizza, a little mother-son bonding they both needed.

She heard a noise from the other room. Something opening and closing.

"Jared?"

She hurried back out to the living room. His coat was gone.

She knew right away what had happened.

He'd left to go check on Tabitha.

CHAPTER TWENTY-SIX

Jared knew what running out that way meant. It meant his mom would probably call the police.

But she didn't know where Tabitha lived. She didn't know how to find him.

He pulled his coat tighter around his body. It was close to six, the sky fully dark.

He decided to cut through Caldwell Park. It offered a more direct route, one that might shave a few minutes off his travel time. Kids from school hung out there in the afternoon and evening. On summer nights, it was impossible to go there without running into someone he knew. When he walked Tabitha home the other night, he'd bypassed the park for that very reason. He didn't want to share his limited time with Tabitha with anyone else. Alone, he didn't care.

He entered on the east side, a couple of blocks from where Celia disappeared. For a while, after her disappearance, the sidewalk was littered with candles and notes and stuffed animals. Most of that stuff was gone, the spot empty and back to normal. Jared wondered what the police did with all those trinkets. Did they keep them somewhere, as some kind of evidence or memento of the case? Or did they just trash them? He could imagine some cop with a garbage bag, showing up at night and sweeping it all away, tossing it in a Dumpster behind the police station.

There were swings and jungle gyms at the south end of the park. His mom had taken him there when he was little, letting him run around while she studied her anatomy textbooks. In the middle sat a statue of Abraham Lincoln, Kentucky's favorite son. Never mind that he lived in the state only until he was six years old and spent much more time in Illinois, people in the Bluegrass State liked to claim him.

On the far side of the park, the west side, the city had constructed a little band shell. They painted it light blue, and in the summers offered live music. Mostly old guys trying to play bluegrass, their banjos and fiddles twanging across the lawn while even older people in lawn chairs nodded along. In the winter, the place looked desolate. It filled with dead leaves, and only the skateboarders congregated there, using the place for dramatic takeoffs and landings.

As Jared passed by the band shell, he saw a group of four people, their figures dark outlines in the fading light. Kids from school, he figured, and he hoped he didn't know them. He didn't want to talk. He wanted to get to Tabitha's house and put his mind at ease.

"Look who it is," a voice said.

Jared turned to the right, toward the sound of the voice, but he kept walking quickly.

"Hey, hold it."

A girl's voice.

Jared slowed down, squinting as he peered into the quickening darkness. The girl was moving toward him, her long, wavy hair and tall boots growing visible. He thought he knew her, but it took a moment.

She reached the lit path he walked on, stepping into the glow of one of the lamps.

"Oh," he said.

"Hi, Jared."

He couldn't remember the last time he'd spoken to Ursula Walters. He knew it was before her mom disappeared, way before. Their moms made them play together when they were kids, sometimes on the very swings Jared was just remembering. She had fascinated him when they were little. She was bossy and brash, braver than any of the boys he knew. He never forgot the time she shoved him, causing him to crack his head against the corner of a coffee table. *With friends like that, who needs enemies, right?*

But he also used to go to sleep at night and think about her, imagining that they'd grow up and become more than friends. His mom and Celia liked to try to embarrass both of them by mentioning the way they used to bathe together as babies. Jared always felt his face turn red when one of the moms brought it up, but Ursula never blushed. She acted as though nothing in the world bothered her or knocked her off stride.

"Hey, Ursula," he said, hoping she didn't want to talk.

But she studied him up and down, taking in his clothes and his face, inspecting him as if she needed to know everything he was up to. A surprising amount of interest considering how little they spoke to each other. Around the time they became teenagers, Ursula had transformed into a mean girl, someone who ran with a crowd of rich kids. Their parents belonged to the country club, and they all wore the best clothes, as if they had Abercrombie & Fitch on speed dial. Jared felt squeezed out of her life, and he really didn't mind. Once she'd started acting that way, his nearly lifelong crush dissolved.

"Where are you going in such a hurry?" she asked.

He looked behind her. Three bigger, older-looking guys accompanied her. Ursula was that kind of kid. She couldn't spend time with people her own age.

"Just walking," Jared said, and started to move on.

But the voice of one of the guys stopped him again.

"Ursula, isn't that the kid whose mom got your mom killed?"

Two of the guys came forward, looming behind Ursula in the dark. The third guy, bigger than the other two, hung back, a red glow near his head telling Jared he was smoking. For the first time, Jared felt scared. The adrenaline and emotion that had fueled his rush toward Tabitha's house shifted to something more desperate and pointed. His own safety might be in jeopardy.

He wasn't a fighter. He'd skirmished with a couple of kids on the playground years ago, winning one battle by pinning his opponent to the ground and emerging with a bloody nose and a detention from the other. But these guys were bigger and older, and they sounded tougher.

"Don't blame my mother," he said. "She didn't do anything."

"She stood Mrs. Walters up," the kid on the left said, the one who had already spoken. He wore a puffy ski vest over a button-down shirt. Not exactly brawling clothes, but Jared had seen rich kids fight and he knew some of them were as tough as the poorest and most desperate students in town. Being rich didn't mean someone wasn't deeply pissed at the core of his being. "Handed her over to some killer on a silver platter."

The kid so casually threw the words "killed" and "killer" around. Everyone—the media, friends, family—took great pains to talk about Celia as though she were missing and might come back someday. Deep down, Jared suspected everyone knew the truth, but they never admitted it. This kid didn't try to sugarcoat it, and he assumed Ursula felt the same way or else they wouldn't be saying it around her.

"It wasn't her," Jared said. He needed to get to Tabitha, to check on her well-being, and then he needed to get home so his mom wouldn't worry too much. But he couldn't just walk away from the confrontation, letting these kids—and by extension everyone else in town— think that his mother was the one solely responsible for leaving Celia alone on the edge of Caldwell Park that night. "It was me," he said. "I made her late that night. Shit, she found some alcohol in my room, and we had to fucking talk about it. That's why she was late."

Ursula just stared at him in the dark, but one of the other guys spoke up.

"Oooo," he said. "Rebel without a cause. Alcohol in the room, and Mom caught him. You're lucky to be alive."

Jared ignored him. "Of course, if it were me, I'd blame the person who actually kidnapped your mother. But what do I know?"

Ursula studied him. The lamps that lined the walkway caught her brown eyes, making them shimmer like small reflecting pools. She was impossible to read, and he thought at any moment she might reach out and slap him.

Instead one corner of her mouth turned up, the beginning of a smirk. "Well, holy shit," she said. "Everyone has a little secret, don't they?"

"You can tell your dad or the police. I don't care, okay? But I have to get going now. You can get back to whatever worthless bullshit you were talking about before I came by. Like how your cleaning lady doesn't fold your underwear the right way, or which handicapped freshman you want to bully on the bus."

The guy on the left's hand shot out so fast Jared couldn't have avoided it. He half punched, half shoved Jared in the chest, knocking him off-balance. Jared caught himself and then moved forward, fists raised in a way he hoped didn't look ridiculous. The guy scrambled toward him, but before they could come close to each other, Ursula was in between them, her arms raised like a boxing referee's at the end of a round.

"Stop it," she said. "Knock it off."

They both stopped, Jared and the guy. Jared was

thankful for the darkness. It covered up the shaking of his hands, the unsteady quaking of his legs. His opponent betrayed no nerves, no uncertainty. He stood glaring at Jared, his eyes cold. But he clearly did whatever Ursula wanted him to do. He took a step back.

"Just leave him alone," she said, taking Jared in again. She seemed to be seeing something new, but he couldn't be sure if it was the information about the night her mother disappeared or his willingness to mouth off and fight a bigger and older kid. Jared tried to remember what impression she might have of him from growing up. It wouldn't be one that included toughness and grit. How could it when the lasting memory of their childhood was sitting in a bathtub together, splashing each other and playing with floating boats and animals? "Go on, get out of here, Jared. You've been very enlightening."

Jared saw that the kid who had been lying back, the one with the cigarette, had moved toward the group. He stood behind them, his hands jammed into his pockets. He wore his hair long and his face was covered with a scraggly beard. Bobby Allen. He was a junior, and he and Jared had played on the same soccer team back in grade school. Neither one of them was very good, and Jared had barely spoken to him since then.

Jared started backing away, his heart still racing.

Ursula said, "Go on and see your freaky girlfriend."

Again Jared stopped. "What do you know about her?"

"I know she's a freak," Ursula said. "And I know she's been out of school for a few days. It's kind of cute and sadly pathetic the way you two found each other. Is it time for your hookup? Is that why you're rushing over there through the park? So you can get your evening jollies?"

"He's not doing that, I can guarantee you."

It was Bobby Allen, and his voice didn't sound as threatening as the ones used by the others. He sounded almost friendly.

"What do you mean?" Ursula asked, turning her head slightly.

"Her dad, man. He's a fucking lunatic. He works for my dad. Or with him or something. He's not letting any boys near that house."

"What do you know about him?" Jared asked.

"Just what I heard from my dad. Guy's a weirdo. Listen, you're probably better off just finding a new girl. Hell, the school's full of them. Have you ever noticed, even some of the nerdiest guys are getting laid in our school? There's somebody for everybody."

"He doesn't want to do that, Bobby," Ursula said. "Look at him. He's in love. And now you made him even more worried about his girl."

As soon as she was done speaking, Jared started away, leaving their voices behind in the dark and not needing to tell Ursula she was right.

CHAPTER TWENTY-SEVEN

Jared passed the closed-up and quiet homes on Tabitha's street. He walked under a burned-out streetlight, its darkened shape showing against the sky. He felt determined, his steps heavier, his pace quicker. He couldn't just wander around the perimeter of the house, spying like a weirdo and hoping to catch a glimpse of Tabitha. He needed to talk to her, to know she was okay, even if that meant going straight to the door and knocking.

So he did.

Tabitha's house was dark. He saw that much. No lights glowed anywhere, not even from the back of the house where he'd seen them before. But Jared vowed not to accept that as enough. Maybe they were holed up inside, hiding out. Or maybe Tabitha was home, acting under orders from her father to lie low and show nothing.

Jared took the porch steps two at a time, and as he reached out for the bell, his heart raced twice as fast as it did in the park when Ursula's little gang confronted him.

He cursed himself for not figuring out what to say in advance if her dad answered the door. He decided he'd play it cool and simply ask to see her. If he said no, Jared wanted to rush in, right past the hulking body, and find Tabitha.

He rang the bell again. And waited. He pushed it again, but nothing happened.

"Shit."

He wasn't scared for himself anymore. He was scared for her. Was that love? When you worried more about someone else than yourself? It sounded like a good definition. He understood why his mom kept secret his role in her tardiness on the night Celia disappeared. She wanted to protect him. She cared more about him than about her own reputation.

Jared turned and went back down the steps. He walked around the side of the house, the side he'd spied from the other night when he threw the rock. The kitchen window was dark, and someone had taped a piece of cardboard over the hole he'd made.

Jared stood there, accepting the pointlessness of his trip. The sky above was clear, the stars beginning to speckle the sky. He faced the walk home and then explaining everything to his mother. And when all that was finished, he still might never see Tabitha again. He wouldn't know if she was safe or in danger, in town or gone somewhere else.

He headed back out to the street, his head sinking down into his shoulders. He kicked at a loose stone, which did nothing to make him feel better. An embarrassment settled over him, the sense of being a child who wanted something he could never have, something far out of his reach.

"Hey there."

Jared looked to his left. An old guy stood on the porch next door. He wore a T-shirt despite the cold. His hair was slicked back and long sideburns framed his face, making him look like some kind of throwback to the 1950s, the kind of dude who'd hang out shooting pool or leaning against a jukebox. He held a can of beer in one hand and a cigarette in the other.

The guy pointed with his cigarette. "You know them?"

"Kind of," Jared said.

"You're looking for them, though. Probably that girl, right?"

"We go to school together."

The man took a drag from the cigarette, shaking his head as he did so. When he blew out a plume of smoke, he said, "I wish girls looked like that when I was in school."

"Have you seen them?" Jared asked.

"No, sir. But there was some commotion over there a little over an hour ago. A fellow come over in a nice car, business type. You know, suit and tie and all that. I was out here smoking because I don't in the house anymore. I heard some yelling, I think, but that was it. I didn't see the girl, but I don't see her much."

"And that was all?"

"I ain't a spy," the man said. He flicked his cigarette out into the yard, the red glow falling like a star. "I didn't see or hear anything else."

"Did they move out?"

"Move out? I doubt it. I'd have seen a truck. I'm here most of the day. Somebody busted a window over there, but there are a lot of punks in the neighborhood. If they tried that over here, they'd answer to me."

"Thanks," Jared said.

"What's the girl's name?" the man asked.

"Tabitha."

"Tabitha. Her folks fans of *Bewitched*?"

"Of what?"

"Never mind." He tipped the beer can up to his mouth. "You know, I didn't see a van or anything when they moved in. Maybe they're the quiet types. Or maybe they don't have much. Lot of that going around."

"Thanks."

"You be careful going home. You heard there's some maniac on the loose. Took that woman right over in the park. Killed another one today."

"I heard."

"Like I said, if they were to come messing with me . . ."

His voice trailed off as Jared walked away.

CHAPTER TWENTY-EIGHT

Jenna calmed down a little as time went by. She didn't have a choice.

Right after Jared went out the door, she grabbed her car keys, intending to pick him up. But she knew better than that. Jared would have ducked down side streets and through backyards, probably even cut across the park, and she would have driven in circles, hoping to come across him by chance.

She also considered calling. But she knew he wouldn't answer. And if he did answer, she also knew what he'd say.

Don't worry. I've got this.

She stared at her phone, scrolling through her contacts. Detective Poole's name popped up. But then what? Bother a detective in the middle of two major crimes because her teenage son ran off?

She owed her mom a call, so she dialed. Her mom sounded distracted when she answered, and Jenna asked if it was a bad time.

"I'm playing cards," her mother said.

"Okay. We can talk another time."

"Honey? I don't want you to think I don't support you. I know you're having a difficult time."

"I know you know that."

"It's just that when you're on TV cursing, and then everyone compares you to Celia and how she conducted herself, well, it doesn't always look right."

"I get it, Mom. Celia's the pretty, polished one."

"I didn't say that."

"She's the one lucky enough to disappear before she cursed on TV."

"Honey, that's rude."

So Jenna hung up.

She made one more call, to Stanley's, to order a pizza. She felt hungry, and when Jared came back, even if he was angry with her, he'd be hungry as well. After ordering, Jenna admitted to herself she kind of liked the passion Jared displayed. It was young love, first love, but he cared enough about this girl to run after her, to do whatever he could to ensure her safety. She sometimes thought the passing years robbed everyone of the ability to make glorious, spectacular fools of themselves.

Just then the landline rang, making Jenna jump. Was it her mom again? The woman never apologized, so it couldn't be that.

When she answered she heard the comforting voice of Detective Poole on the other end, asking Jenna how she was doing. For an agonizing moment, Jenna worried that Detective Poole was calling with bad news about

Jared. He'd gotten in trouble or gone too far in his quest for finding Tabitha, but the thought left her mind just as quickly as it entered. Who on earth could get in trouble that quickly? And it wouldn't be like Jared.

"I'm okay. Is something wrong?"

"It might be," Naomi said. "I just got off the phone with Reena Huffman. Not an assistant, not a flunky. But the lady herself. She almost never does that."

"What did she want?"

"I think you need to prepare," Naomi said. "She's going to talk about you a little more on tonight's show."

"Because I cursed?"

"Not that. Although she may throw that in for good measure. No, she's learned about Celia's affairs."

"Who told her?" Jenna asked.

"Do you think Reena reveals her sources to me?" Naomi asked. "I have to ask you this, Jenna—"

"No, I didn't tell Reena. Why would I want my friend's name dragged through the mud by that awful witch?"

"I had to ask."

"I didn't, Naomi."

"Reena hasn't called you?"

"No." Jenna checked the clock. Fifteen minutes to showtime. "What does this mean for her case? Does it really affect anything? It's not relevant, is it?"

"When you don't know anything, everything is relevant."

"Naomi, do you ever do welfare checks on people? Kids especially?"

"Do you know someone who might be in danger?"

Jenna offered a quick rundown of what she knew about Tabitha, but as she related the facts she realized they still didn't amount to much. A kid who kind of looked familiar and had a strict father. Good luck with that.

"And you don't even know where this girl lives?" Naomi asked.

"No, I don't. Jared does."

Naomi sounded tired. "I suggest you monitor the situation. If something drastic happens, you can give us a call. For now . . ."

"I hear you. Thanks."

"I guess we'll all see what Reena has in store for us tonight."

CHAPTER TWENTY-NINE

Five minutes after she had hung up with Naomi, the phone rang again. As soon as Jenna answered, she heard the husky, overly dramatic voice of Reena Huffman on the other end. Even in a phone conversation off the air, the woman sounded as if she were pontificating and performing for a crowd.

"Jenna, how are you?" Her voice dripped with false concern, so much so that Jenna wondered if syrup was going to come oozing out of the receiver. "I've been thinking of you a lot lately. With everything going on this week, I can tell it's getting to you."

Jenna gritted her teeth. She held back so she didn't give Reena any other ammunition to use against her. "Did you want to ask me something, Reena?"

"I just did. I asked you how you were doing. You know, when Becky sent me that footage from the other day, I nearly fell out of my chair. I thought to myself,

'That can't be the sweet, friendly girl we've been getting to know so well ever since this tragedy happened.' That's why I thought the strain was getting to you."

"I'm fine, Reena. Actually my son will be home soon, and I have to feed him—"

"Perfect, I knew it. And such a good-looking boy. He resembles you some, but he must really favor his father. Is that true?"

"He got his dad's looks. That's about all my ex had to offer."

"Does he get to see him a lot? I know it's tough when a boy grows up without a father."

"You know, Reena, that's several questions you've asked me now, but I suspect none of them are the one you really called about."

"You're right," she said. Jenna could imagine the TV hostess patting her perfectly sculpted hair. "I'm about to go on the air with a story, and I wanted your comment on it. I would have called sooner, of course, maybe even arranged an interview, but we got this so late, and it's Friday and we want to get it on."

"You want to know if I knew if Celia was having an affair when she disappeared," Jenna said.

"News does travel fast out there in Kentucky. I need to know your sources."

"I didn't know. I just found out myself."

"Not about the affair in the past or the one at the time of her disappearance?"

"Neither."

"How did you learn about them, then?" Reena asked.

"I'm sure the police will be wondering why you didn't know and how you found out."

"I've already talked to the police," Jenna said.

"Well, this is all fascinating." Someone said something on Reena's end of the line. The voice sounded harsh and rushed. "I'm on my way," Reena said, her voice muffled a little. And then she was back. "I do have to go now, Jenna. But you should watch tonight, since I'll be covering this."

"Yeah. Maybe."

"You're not still mad at me about last time?" Reena asked, her voice as sweet as buttermilk. "I just had to follow the story and show the human drama. And this is a very human drama."

"You don't want them to find Celia, do you?" Jenna asked.

She hadn't planned it, hadn't thought it, but the words rushed out. Was there a benefit to Reena if a crime was solved? Not if it happened quickly. There must have been a sweet spot where she hoped an answer would come. Long enough to stretch the ratings out but not so long that people grew sick of hearing about the story.

Reena didn't lose her cool. That was the problem with challenging someone like Reena, a true believer. She never lost her cool. She'd argued in courtrooms and on national TV. Did Jenna think she could shake this woman's composure or knock her off stride? More important, did Jenna think Reena cared about anything she had to say to her?

"See?" Reena said. "You're getting angry again. I

worry about you. I really do. Think about your son and the example you're setting. And think about your health. You want to be around for him, and that stress is toxic. It eats us up inside."

"Listen, Reena, I only care about Celia's—"

But the connection was terminated. Reena had had the last word.

CHAPTER THIRTY

J enna stared at the dead phone in her hand.

She slammed it down against the base. The act gave her little satisfaction. It served only to jar her wrist and leave her with an aching shoulder.

"Fuck."

Then the doorbell rang.

"Who the hell?"

She remembered she'd ordered pizza. She grabbed her wallet and walked over to the door, pausing to peek through the window, since a murdering lunatic was on the loose in the area.

It wasn't Stanley's Pizza.

Even with his back turned, Jenna recognized Ian from his clothes, his hair, his posture. She opened the door and let him in.

Jenna tried to estimate how many times Ian had been inside her house. She remembered him coming over for a few of Jared's birthday parties, maybe stopping by to pick up Ursula when Jenna had watched her. But it wasn't often. No more than ten or fifteen times and probably not once during the previous five years.

He stepped into the living room, his long, lean frame seeming to reach the ceiling. Jenna took a quick look around, seeing the space through his eyes. It was clean and picked up, just like always. And Jared, thank God, hadn't left any dirty dishes or socks or books on the floor. But it was nothing like what Ian had grown up with or how he lived as an adult. If you looked at the house that way, it suddenly seemed small and insignificant.

"This is kind of a surprise," she said.

"I know. I realized, well, I didn't have your number saved in my phone. I could have found it at home, of course, but I wanted to talk to you sooner rather than later."

Jenna offered him a seat on the couch and asked if he wanted anything to eat or drink. He declined politely, and she told him she had a pizza on the way.

"You know Jared and I do that a lot on Friday nights," she said. "It's a tradition. I guess I have to enjoy it before he's off to college."

"Maybe Ursula and I need to think of some things we can do like that." He looked lost in thought for a moment, as though he wanted to formulate a plan for bonding with his daughter right then and there. "It's tough with a girl. I have to be honest—I don't even know what she's into. It was easy when she was little. It was pretty much all princesses and horses."

"I think . . . maybe you don't want my advice."

"No, I do." He smiled, the light in his eyes flirtatious. "You're a girl, after all. You'd know."

Jenna felt herself blush. *Dammit. Blushing when the big man on campus acts a little flirtatious?* "I was just going to say that it doesn't matter so much *what* the thing is, just that there's something you do together. Even if it's as mundane as eating pizza."

"You're right, of course," he said. "With work and everything . . . I never imagined I'd be a single parent."

"You're not," she said, her voice urgent, trying to believe what she said. "You know what I mean."

"Sure. But I am a single dad for now, no matter what happens next." An awkwardness settled over their conversation, like an engine that just wouldn't turn over. Ian brought them out of the nosedive. "I guess you're wondering why I came by out of the blue like this."

"I think I know."

She told him about the calls from Naomi Poole and Reena Huffman. As she spoke, she knew Reena was on the air, broadcasting the story about Celia's affair and, likely, Jenna's lack of knowledge of it.

"Turn it on," Ian said.

"Really? You want to watch it? I thought you stayed away from all that."

"I watch sometimes," he said. "It's good to know what people are saying and thinking. Do you mind?"

"Not if you don't."

She flipped on the TV. The show was in its early stages, with Reena giving a rundown of all the stories she intended to cover during the hour. Apparently other things did happen in the world. She planned on discussing a priest who molested children in Idaho and a dog who rescued a family from a burning building in Michigan.

And, of course, she intended to devote a lot of time to the latest crime in Hawks Mill: the murder of Holly Crenshaw.

But then she was ready to launch into her first topic for the night: *Breaking news in the case of the Diamond Mom, Celia Walters.*

Reena delivered the news of Celia's affairs to the viewing public. She took her time, milking the story for all it was worth and placing forceful emphasis on certain salacious words. *Extramarital. Sexual. Lying.*

Jenna snuck a couple of glances over at Ian as Reena went on and on. His face showed nothing, just a simple curiosity about what was being said. He could have been watching a weather report.

"I hate this 'Diamond Mom' shit," Jenna said.

"Celia would think it's ridiculous."

Reena mentioned Ian only in passing. She told the audience that Celia's husband, Ian, had no knowledge of the most recent affair and was as blindsided by the whole thing as anybody else.

Jenna thought of her mom and the earlier phone call. Celia wasn't as perfect as everyone thought, and everyone knew. Jenna hated herself for it, but she felt a little glee, the smallest hint of a fuck-you to her mother.

"Earlier tonight," Reena said, "I spoke with Ian Walters on the phone. He was too upset to speak on the air, and I completely understand that. I do. But he told me how devastating these affairs are, especially considering that he has a young daughter at home. Think about that, folks: The Diamond Mom's daughter is now learning that her mother, who is already a crime victim, was being unfaithful at the time of her disappearance."

Reena gave the camera one of her patented headshakes, a gesture meant to indicate how confounding and crazy the things she was forced to talk about were. *If only I didn't have to do this,* she wanted everyone to understand.

"Did you really talk to her?" Jenna asked.

"Briefly," Ian said. "I didn't want her smearing Celia without saying something."

"I can't reveal my source on this breaking news," Reena said, "but I can promise you it's been checked and double-checked, with confirmation coming from individuals very close to the situation."

"Do you want to turn it off now?" Jenna asked.

Ian held up his index finger without looking at Jenna, so she left it on.

"But do you want to know what really confounds me?" Reena said. "Do you want to know what really has me scratching my head? The best friend. Jenna Barton. I spoke to her earlier tonight as well. Obviously we didn't want to speak to her live on the air given her proclivity for using profanity." A little bit of an eye roll. "But I did want to get her take on this story, since she claims to be the Diamond Mom's best friend." She made air quotes when she said "best friend." "And guess what—Jenna told me on the phone that she had no idea there was an affair going on. None. No idea that her best friend was involved with another man. Also no idea about the previous affair that we learned about. Does that seem a little odd to any of you?"

Jenna picked up the remote control. She placed her finger over the on/off switch, but didn't press. Ian still appeared to be watching.

"What all this means to me is that there's a lot of lying and deceiving going on. And it's my job, as a journalist, to get to the bottom of it. But first, we're going to go out to Becky McGee in Hawks Mill for more. And frankly, I don't know what to even think of this. Another beautiful young woman murdered in this small town. Do we have a serial killer on the loose out there, preying on the women of Kentucky—"

Jenna turned the TV off.

CHAPTER THIRTY-ONE

The driver from Stanley's Pizza came as soon as the TV was off. Ian stood up and tried to pay, but Jenna waved him off. She might be publicly called out as a foulmouthed liar by a bloviating cable news host, but she could pay to feed her own son.

Her son. Who hadn't come home yet. Her pulse sped up as she closed the front door. *He's okay,* she told herself. *Give him another twenty minutes or so.*

She and Ian went out to the kitchen, where she brought down plates and asked him if he wanted anything to drink. He accepted her offer of a beer—something bitter and expensive someone from her book club left behind one night—and they sat down to eat.

"I haven't had Stanley's in years," Ian said. "Since high school."

"We went there all the time after basketball games," Jenna said. "After watching you play. It was always a big deal when the guys from the team came in."

"I need to eat this more." He bit into the pizza with gusto and took a couple of long swallows of the beer. Jenna excused herself and checked her phone. Nothing from Jared. She sent him a message, asking him to let her know where he was before she had to call the police. He wrote back right away.

On my way home.

Jenna sighed with relief. She walked to the refrigerator and took out a bottle of wine. She told herself she'd earned it. Just one glass to take the edge off. "So you just came by to warn me about the TV show? Is that it?" She filled her glass and sipped off the top. Then she added more and came back to the table.

Ian patted the corners of his mouth with a napkin. "Not the only thing. Our conversation the other day got me thinking. About Celia. About everything that's happened."

Jenna leaned back in her chair, the wineglass held in front of her chest. She felt wary and wanted to consider Ian from as much distance as she could. All that time without any contact, and suddenly he showed up on her doorstep, wanting to talk.

But another impulse competed with the caution. She felt light-headed, a little giddy, the sensation pushed along by the alcohol. She hadn't felt that way since . . . since before Marty left? Since the occasional dates and short-term relationships she'd experienced over the previous ten years of being single? Since that time in high school when Ian walked her home, those fleeting moments she held his undivided attention before Celia moved in?

"And what were you thinking?" Jenna asked, acutely aware that none of it would be happening, she wouldn't be enjoying the time alone with Ian if Celia hadn't disappeared.

"Celia kept secrets," Ian said. He rested his hand on the beer bottle but didn't drink any more. He wore concentration on his face, his brow slightly furrowed, his eyes staring at a fixed point somewhere just above the table. "We know that now. I've known it for a while, I guess. Maybe the two of you shared more over the years. Maybe you were closer than she and I."

"I was clearly in the dark about some things as well," Jenna said. "I think Celia liked to remind those closest to her that she didn't need us as much as we needed her."

"Maybe that's it," he said, although he didn't sound convinced. He used his index finger to pick at the label on the beer. It made a small ticking noise beneath their conversation. *Tick. Tick. Tick.* "I'm sure you've seen or heard the rumors about Celia. The stuff people say on the Internet or sometimes even right in the papers."

"I've made the mistake of getting on those sites," Jenna said.

"People think they've seen her other places. Other cities and states, like she ran away and started a new life."

Jenna's heart beat even faster. And she felt a cold chill on the back of her neck as if a draft were blowing through the house. "You don't believe any of that, do you?"

"The police know about something. For some reason, it hasn't leaked out to the media, but maybe it will. I guess nothing's really private anymore, is it?"

"What are you talking about?"

Tick. Tick. Tick. Then he stopped and wiped his fingertip on a napkin.

"We kept cash in the house," he said. "Not a lot. A few hundred dollars, maybe a thousand at the most. Just emergency money, if there was a sudden crisis."

"Yeah, I have the same thing. It's a jar of loose change."

Ian ignored her comment. "It was gone around the time she disappeared." He held up his hands right away to silence any comment. "Now, it could have been used for something else. I hadn't checked it for a long time, and it's possible Celia used it on a shopping trip or something. She did that sometimes. She'd go to Lexington or Cincinnati with her friends, her *new* friends, and they'd shop. If I complained about the credit card bills, she might get into the cash, so that could be it."

"Or?"

"Or I don't know," he said. "A thousand dollars can't take a person very far, but it's enough to start a new life somewhere, isn't it?"

CHAPTER THIRTY-TWO

Are you saying you think she ran away? That she's not the victim of a crime?"

Jenna needed the wine. She needed water too, but she liked the wine more.

"We got a really good lead once. Somebody who followed the case online saw a woman in Chicago. Outside Chicago, actually, in some suburb. This person swore it was Celia, the so-called Diamond Mom. That's what he called her, like she doesn't have a real name. He even snapped a photo of her once at the mall."

"Are you kidding?" Jenna felt an ache in the pit of her stomach. She hadn't touched the pizza and then she drank. And then the news. It was all making her feel a little sick.

Ian looked doubtful. "The police went and checked it out. They couldn't find the woman who was supposed to be Celia. Maybe she'd moved on, or maybe the person who saw her was a kook."

"Did you see the photo?"

"I did. It could have been Celia. But it could have been any one of a million middle-aged women with brown hair. The cops couldn't prove anything. Nobody could. When the cops struck out, I hired a private investigator to look as well. He talked to people who knew this woman. She moved to town and then left pretty quickly. She said her name was Amelia something or other. She didn't leave a trail, so the investigator couldn't find anything. There've been a few other incidents like that. Not as promising as that one, but we followed up on them."

"So crazy people think they see her," Jenna said. "There are people who think they see Elvis in gas stations. People see Jesus on a potato chip. Do you think Celia would leave you? Okay, even if you guys were having trouble, would she leave Ursula? Her daughter, who is just entering the most vulnerable and important period of her life?"

Ian seemed to snap out of something, some memory trance and reflection he'd fallen into when he started talking. He picked up the beer and drank. "You're right."

"And why would she leave . . . I'm sorry, Ian, but why would she leave without the guy she was having a relationship with?"

"It's okay. I've learned to discuss these painful things." His smile looked more like a wince. "Maybe there was another guy, somewhere else. Maybe in another state. I guess I don't know."

"I'm sorry, Ian. I'm sorry for you and Ursula."

"I think about this all the time and wonder if I want to believe these things the way someone would believe in a fairy tale. It's just been so long now and nothing. And they found Holly Crenshaw so quickly. This isn't a big community. People see things; they know people. How does something like this remain hidden for so long?"

"I don't know. Maybe Benjamin Ludlow will lead to something."

"Can you think of anything?" Ian asked. "Anything she said or did that might suggest . . . that might suggest anything? Anything besides this being a random crime?"

"Have you talked to her other friends? The ladies from the country club? The golf-and-bridge set?"

Jenna failed to keep the contempt out of her voice. What the heck? They were sharing secrets over pizza. Why hide how she felt?

"They didn't know her well," Ian said. "Not like you. I know you guys seemed to be drifting a little too, but you were always her closest friend. That could never change. If Celia didn't open up to you about these relationships, it was because she feared your judgment. She knew you'd tell her the truth, and I don't think she wanted to hear it."

"What if there's a killer on the loose? A serial killer like Reena said. Celia isn't the only one." The full weight of the idea settled on Jenna's shoulders. "It's terrifying, Ian. Who could ever have thought this would happen in Hawks Mill?"

He picked up the empty beer bottle and rose from his chair. He rinsed it out at the sink and then turned. "I need to get going. Jared will be home soon, and you have food waiting for him. I have to check in with Ursula."

"You must worry about her a lot more now."

"I've always worried. And I try not to smother her because of Celia. But it's tough. My mother stays at our house most days. Between the two of us we're managing with Ursula."

He put the bottle upside down in the drying rack and came over to the table, where Jenna still sat. He held his hand out, as if he wanted to shake. Jenna reached up and they clasped. It seemed like an odd gesture, awkward and formal for two people who'd known each other so long. She remembered the way he'd placed his hand on hers in the restaurant, squeezing before he left.

His hand lingered longer this time, and the racing of her heart began again. He used his thumb to rub the soft skin on the back of her hand, and they were just slipping out of each other's grip when someone called from the front of the house.

"Mom?"

It took Jenna a slow moment to respond. Then she said, "Out here."

She kept her eyes on Ian as Jared came to the doorway. "Oh," he said. "Hi, Ian."

"Jared." He moved across the room and they shook hands as well, formal and still natural. "I was just leaving. I came by to bother your mom, but I have to go."

"Okay," Jared said, unable to hide his confusion. He'd heard his mother complain about Ian's aloofness many times over the years. Jared had no doubt witnessed it first-hand at the few gatherings Ian bothered to attend. To see this man in his kitchen, standing over a Stanley's pizza, must have thrown him off-balance. "I just got home."

"Will you walk Ian out, honey?" Jenna asked.

"Sure."

She watched them disappear toward the front of the house. And when they were out of sight she had no choice but to throw back the rest of the wine.

CHAPTER THIRTY-THREE

Jared closed the door. On Ursula's dad.

Ursula's dad just walked out the door of their house. Right after Jared had seen Ursula in the park.

And had he really seen what he thought he saw in the kitchen? When he came through the entryway after calling out for his mom, it looked as though the two of them had been holding hands or something. Holding hands? His mom and Ursula's dad?

Jared walked slowly to the kitchen, trying to process all of it.

And he tried to process what he'd learned at Tabitha's house. If Tabitha wasn't in the house, and it didn't look as though anybody else was, where had they gone? Were they gone for good?

He smelled the pizza as he approached the kitchen. When he walked out there again, his mom was staring into space, the glass of wine in her hand empty. She must have drained it while he walked Ian to the door.

"Mom?"

"Are you hungry?" she asked. "There's plenty."

"I'm sorry about running out before. I just had to know what was going on."

"Running out? Oh, yeah. You really shouldn't do that, but I understand."

She still looked as if her mind was somewhere else, which only added to his belief that something more was going on with Ian than met the eye. But he wasn't sure he could ask her about it.

Jared went to the refrigerator and grabbed a can of Coke. Then he sat at the table, pulling on the metal tab, hearing the liquid *pfft* as it opened. He grabbed for the pizza and took a bite, his hunger surprising him. He'd spent the whole week worrying about Tabitha, and when he worried that way, which was rare, he didn't like to eat. Maybe it was the Stanley's, but Jared's appetite roared back as he sat at the table across from his mom.

While he chewed, she rose and poured herself more wine.

"Do you want to hear what I found out? About Tabitha?"

"Sure," she said. "Did you talk to her?"

"The house was dark, and no one answered. The neighbor told me he hadn't seen them, but that maybe her dad got in an argument with some guy in a suit earlier. Bizarre, isn't it?"

His mom stood with the bottle of wine still in her hand. "What's her dad like? You've met him, haven't you?"

"Briefly. I guess."

She put the cork back in the wine. "You guess?"

"I mean I've seen him. I don't really know him."

"And nothing about her mom?"

"She doesn't talk about her. Never. And I don't push. I figure someday I'll get the story."

His mom closed the refrigerator again and came back to the table with her wine. She seemed more focused on him, whatever fog she'd been swimming in when he first came home having lifted.

"This is all strange. I think maybe you need to stay away from that house for now," she said. "You don't know what's going on. And if she asked for space, you need to give it to her. You don't want to come across like a weird, desperate guy."

Her words stung. *A weird, desperate guy.*

"Jesus, Mom. Thanks."

"I'm not trying to put you down," she said. "You're young. It's your first love. It's easy to let your emotions get the best of you."

Her words sank in while he chewed another piece. She seemed to be speaking from hard-won experience. And he knew on some level she was right. He'd been dating Tabitha for what? Three weeks or so? And what did he think was going to happen? They would stay together and get married? Have kids and grow old? But it wasn't just about the relationship. He sensed something wrong, not with Tabitha but with her life. And she might be in danger or distress. Could he just stand by while who knew what happened to her?

"I think there's something I need to tell you." He swallowed. "I ran into Ursula in the park tonight. That's why it was kind of weird that her dad was here when I got back."

"What about running into Ursula?" she asked.

"Her friends started mouthing off about you. How you were the cause of what happened to Celia."

"Have they done that before?" she asked.

"It happens from time to time. Just stuff they say in the halls at school when I pass by."

"Are you serious? Do you want me to call the school and ask them to stop it?"

"Mom, easy. I can handle it."

"It sounds like bullying to me."

"Not everything is bullying, Mom. Well, I guess when Ursula tried to pummel that girl back in November, that was kind of bullying."

"Her mother had just disappeared."

"Sure, Mom, I get it. Well, here's the thing, and you're not going to like it," Jared said. "They started mouthing off, and I got mad. So I told them the truth. I told them that I was the one who made you late that night. And why."

For a moment, his mom remained calm, and Jared thought—hoped—it would be one of the many times she took bad news in stride, let it roll off her back like nothing. He hoped the wine would make a difference as well. Maybe the wine combined with the end of a long week would keep her mellow.

But her eyes opened wide.

"Tell me you didn't," she said.

"I lost my cool. It just came out. I don't want people to think the worst of you. I deserve a share of the blame."

A flush rose in her cheeks, and it wasn't from the wine. She was pissed. She slammed the wineglass down on the table, making the liquid slosh up the side like waves on a storm-tossed ocean. Jared was surprised it hadn't broken. "Dammit, Jared. I asked you never to say anything about that. To anybody. I lied to the police. Do you understand that? I told the police a different story to keep you out of it. I said I was just a dumbass who was running late because I couldn't find my keys and my phone. I could get in a lot of trouble for that. And then, once that starts to spread and everybody knows . . ."

"It was just Ursula and a few of her asshole friends."

She gave him a withering look. "'Just Ursula'? The biggest pain in the ass in town."

"I thought you liked her. You felt sympathy for her."

"I do. And I liked her more when she was a sweet kid. Not a nasty teenager. And those other kids . . . They could tell their parents or anybody else—"

"Okay. I get it. I'm sorry." He held his hands out like a televangelist beseeching the crowd. "You know, most parents would like it if their kid stood up for them. And most parents would like it if their kid decided not to tell a lie."

His mom studied him for a moment, her cheeks even redder. "I'm done with you for the night."

She grabbed her wineglass and left the kitchen.

CHAPTER THIRTY-FOUR

Jenna and Jared circled each other warily that weekend. Neither one mentioned the tension between them, and neither one apologized. They both did their own thing and passed by each other like roommates, answering each other's questions with grunts, politely informing the other person where they would be.

Jenna spent most of her Saturday with Sally. In the afternoon they went shopping at the small mall in Hawks Mill. Sally needed to buy a dress for a wedding she was attending, and she wanted to bring Jenna along as an extra set of eyes.

"You're younger than me," Sally said. "You can keep me from looking like the bride's grandmother."

That evening, they met up with some friends from their book club at a Mexican restaurant. They all ordered giant margaritas and fried ice cream, and Jenna made a point of not saying anything about Ian or Celia or Reena

Huffman. To their great credit, her friends didn't bring them up either.

While they drank and talked and laughed, Jenna was also aware of where Jared was. He told her that morning that he and Syd and Mike were going to a movie—some horror movie they'd all been hearing about for weeks—and then they were heading back to Mike's house to play video games and hang out. Jenna knew Mike's parents and had been to their house on numerous occasions to pick Jared up or drop him off. They were attentive parents, and even though Mike was already developing into a bit of a smarmy smart-ass, she trusted them to keep an eye on the boys while she went out.

She told Jared, as she always did, to text her if he went anywhere else.

Jenna returned home around eight thirty and started reading a book. Her reading habits had changed as soon as Celia disappeared. She used to read mysteries and thrillers, books about serial killers and disappearances, but she quickly found she couldn't stand to experience those kinds of stories anymore. She'd taken to reading historical romance novels, dramas that ended with the man and the woman riding off into the sunset together, all their troubles behind them. Just a few months earlier she would have laughed if someone suggested she read something like *The Stranger Carried Me Away* or *The Knave Who Stole My Heart.* That night, waiting for Jared to come home, she read the last thirty pages of one of them and ended up getting a little teary-eyed when the hero and heroine finally got together.

"God," she said out loud, "what's become of me?"

Jared returned home just after nine. He told her that Mike's dad had given him a ride, and then he started for his room as if he couldn't wait to get away from her.

"Do you want to watch a movie or something?" Jenna asked.

"I already watched one today," he said, and kept on going.

His words had some bite to them, but Jenna shrugged them off. She knew she couldn't take a teenager's mouthing off personally, and she remembered the awful things she'd said to her parents while she was growing up. *"What goes around comes around,"* her mother always told her. *"Someday you'll have kids of your own."*

Indeed.

She went to bed early.

She spent Sunday cleaning while Jared studied in his room. He emerged from his sanctuary from time to time, helping with the laundry and carrying the garbage out to the curb, but otherwise they remained in their mutually imposed détente.

Jenna knew she shouldn't have lied to the police. And she shouldn't have asked Jared to keep a secret. She never wanted either one of them, especially Jared, to get into the habit of lying, even about the most inconsequential thing. But she made her decision early on and felt she had to live with it. She wanted to protect Jared from the kind of scrutiny she had endured in the wake of Celia's disappearance. Maybe he'd thank her for it later.

On Sunday night, after the laundry and the cleaning were done, Jenna didn't feel like reading. She'd finished her latest romantic adventure and wasn't quite ready to start a new one. She faced another week of work and liked the idea of giving her brain even more of a rest than a romance novel could provide. So she turned on the TV, making a conscious choice to avoid any channel that carried anything resembling news. She didn't want to come across some weekend host offering their half-baked opinions on Celia's affairs or Jenna's lies.

She settled on a nature show, something about hippos wallowing in the middle of Africa. But just like with the romance novels, she found herself tearing up when they showed a mother hippo with one of her calves. *What's wrong with me?*

And then Jared came into the room, throwing himself into a chair. He propped his feet up on an overstuffed ottoman and stared at the screen.

She saw his presence as a peace offering, a gesture of reconciliation.

"What's this?" he asked.

"Hippos."

"Cool."

"Do you want to change it? I'm not really paying attention."

He held out his hand and she tossed him the remote.

"But no news," she said. "I don't want to see my face or hear my name."

"Neither do I," Jared said. And then he laughed. "I mean on the TV."

"Nice."

He flipped around carefully, skipping the channels

that might show news or crime stories. Jenna watched him and tried to sound casual.

"I Googled Tabitha yesterday," she said. "Just curious."

"There's nothing there, right?"

"No. But that's not so unusual. She's young."

"Did you Google me?" he asked.

"Yes. For comparison. And Syd and Mike."

"And?" he asked.

"You all came up for something. But not Tabitha."

"Weird, huh?"

"Yeah. A little. I tried her dad as well. Also nothing, but there are a lot of Edward Burkes. Do you know her mom's name?"

"I don't. I never asked."

"But they're separated. Is that it?"

"It seems that way."

"And her mom still lives in Florida? Is that where you said she was from?"

"Mom, do you know that my answers to these questions aren't going to change? I said I don't know anything about her mom."

"I hear you."

Jared didn't seem to want to say more, and she felt relieved. He surfed some more and then settled on a show about the life of JFK.

"Is this okay?" he asked.

"Sure. Just don't expect a happy ending."

"I know what happens," he said.

Together they watched, and Jenna felt somewhat normal again.

CHAPTER THIRTY-FIVE

During lunch, Sally came into the break room and informed Jenna she had a phone call.

"Here?" Jenna asked. "Did they say who it was?"

"No, but it's a guy. He sounds kind of formal. Maybe it's Manuel, the waiter from Saturday night. I could tell he liked you."

"He was what, seventeen? And gay?"

"He had to be twenty-one. He served us margaritas. Line three for your mystery call."

Jenna stepped into the records room. Jared would have called on the cell or texted if he had a problem. So would the school. She picked up and pushed the flashing light. "Hello?"

"Hi, Jenna. It's Ian."

She would have recognized the voice even without his identification. It took her a moment to answer. "Oh, hi. Is something wrong?"

She assumed there had been a break in Celia's case, something Ian needed to let her know about.

"No, nothing's wrong. And I would have called your cell or something, but I don't have it. I just knew where you worked and figured you'd be there on a Monday afternoon."

"I'm here. I'm pretty much always here."

"And I don't want to take up a lot of your time. I just wanted to tell you I'm glad we talked on Friday. You were right at lunch that day when you said I should have spoken to you sooner and given you a chance to say whatever you needed to say."

"Okay. Thanks." Jenna kept her voice low. Even though she'd pulled the door to the records room closed behind her, coworkers and patients passed by talking and laughing. "I wasn't up nights worrying about that. In the big picture, how I feel or what we talk about isn't the most important thing."

"But maybe it is in a way. It helped me, talking to you. Sure, Ursula and I have a bond and a relationship to Celia. But it's nice to talk to another adult who knows her as well as you do."

Jenna remembered the feel of his hand against hers, both in the restaurant and then in her kitchen. Had he really been caressing her skin with his thumb that night? Or had she imagined it, like a foolish schoolgirl? Either way, the memory of the touch made every nerve end in her body tingle. And as soon as she realized that, she told herself to make it stop.

"I wish we could talk about the good things," Ian

said. "All we've talked about is this awful stuff. This stuff that has blindsided us. When Celia disappeared, it felt like I'd been hit by a truck. And now this news of the affair . . . it feels like I got hit by another truck."

"Or kicked in the balls?"

Jenna cringed. Had she said too much?

Ian laughed a little. "Right."

Ian never seemed like the kind of person who needed sympathy, but what else could she say to him? "I'm sorry."

"No, it's good. Let's just make sure the next time we talk, we focus on something else. Maybe we can involve Ursula like we talked about. She's at an age when she's going to want to know what her mom was like as a teenager. Who better to tell her, right?"

"You know, Ian, I haven't stopped thinking Celia can tell Ursula herself. I—"

But she stopped herself. She wasn't sure if she believed the words coming out of her own mouth. And she didn't want to sound completely fake.

"It's okay, Jenna," Ian said. "We all know where we stand."

A silence settled over the call, so Jenna broke it by giving him her cell number. "Call me or text me if you want to share those good memories with Ursula. Or anybody else. I think you're right. It would be a good thing."

"Sure." He paused. Jenna heard someone talking in the hallway. Then Ian said, "It's been good reconnecting with you, Jenna. It's, well, it's a part of the past that had been shut off for a while."

"You're right," she said. When she hung up the phone, her hand was shaking.

She walked out with Sally at the end of the day, both of them moving slowly, tired from a busy Monday.

"So, who was your mysterious caller today?" Sally asked.

"Oh." Mention of the call made her feel guilty, even though she wasn't sure why. She'd spent the day thinking about Ian a lot. The two times their hands touched, the desire to reconnect and share old memories. Wasn't that a perfectly normal thing to do when someone . . . "Just a friend."

"'Just a friend'? Just a man friend? Why so defensive? Do you say that about me? 'Oh, that's Sally. She's just a friend.'"

They stopped by Sally's car, a black Jetta. Sally leaned back against the trunk as if she had all the time in the world.

"It's Ian." Sally didn't react. "Celia's husband."

"Oh, I get it." A knowing look spread across Sally's face. "You're worried what it looks like if you two start buddying up."

"We're not buddying up. We're old friends too."

"I thought he was such a stick-in-the-mud. Didn't you always refer to him as Mr. Uptight or something like that?"

"He is like that now, but he wasn't always. In high school he could be funny. He partied like anyone else at times. He has a warmer side."

"So did Celia, apparently. I saw that stuff on the news over the weekend." Sally studied Jenna, waiting to see if she wanted to talk. When she didn't say anything, Sally said, "I'm sorry you got dragged through the mud again."

"It's fine. I just didn't know my best friend as well as I thought I did."

"Hey, who knows anyone as well as they think they do? Derrick, my oldest, he called me over the weekend. His whole family is converting to Catholicism. The whole family."

Jenna was only half paying attention. She saw her conversation and contact with Ian through Sally's eyes, through the eyes of anyone else in town. No, it might not look right, even if they were old friends. Even when things with Marty were at their worst, their most unfulfilling, she never cheated. Not that she had a lot of choices as the stay-at-home mother of a four-year-old boy. But how far she'd come, how much more confidence she possessed about her own place in the world.

"Do you have time for a drink?" Sally asked.

Jenna came back to the conversation. "A drink? No, I should get home. Jared and I had a rough patch over the weekend. I feel like I should be there. And his girlfriend dumped him."

"No way. That little bitch. And after she mounted him that way? Got him all stirred up?" Sally offered a sympathetic smile. "Those poor boys. They never talk about their feelings, but when they get hurt, look out. There's a well of emotion just waiting to come out."

"I know. He was really into this girl, I think. It's a long story."

"Maybe that's what's going on with your gentleman caller," Sally said.

"What do you mean?"

"Celia's husband. He's hurting. His heart's broken. The disappearance. The affair. Hell, the guy's been crushed. He probably sees you as someone he can open up to. An old friend, right?"

Sally's logical explanation disappointed her a little. Disappointed because it made sense.

"Maybe," Jenna said. "You're probably right."

CHAPTER THIRTY-SIX

When she came in the door, Jared was at the kitchen table, doing his homework. He had books and papers spread all over and headphones covering his ears. He slipped them off when he saw her and offered a small smile.

He still looked as if someone had run over his puppy.

"How's it going?" she asked, trying not to sound falsely chipper.

"I'm fine."

"I thought I'd make spaghetti. Are you hungry?"

He nodded. "Sure."

"Clear your stuff and I'll get it going."

He ate quickly and didn't say much. Jenna wanted to give him his space, let him lick his wounds over being dumped by Tabitha. Jared was more outgoing than Marty, better able to express himself and open up. It was likely a consequence of growing up with a single mom. She edged toward bringing up the elephant in the room rather than ignoring it, but before she said anything, Jared spoke up.

"So Celia was really having an affair before she disappeared?" he asked.

"It looks that way."

"And she kept it hidden from everybody?"

"People usually hide affairs." Jenna pushed the food around on her plate. At least he was talking. Not what she wanted to talk about, but at least the boy was talking. "For all I know, she has friends who knew. Just because we were close for a lot of years doesn't mean I knew everything about her."

"Yeah." He nodded as though he were listening to music. He wasn't. The headphones were off. Jenna could tell he was absorbing the knowledge about Celia, processing it, learning some things about the adult world. "And this weird, random guy shows up trying to pawn her earring?"

"He's a suspect," Jenna said. "Or he might be. We went to high school with him."

"Really?"

"Yeah. He was a total oddball back then. Just thinking about the way he used to creep around the school in his army jacket makes my skin crawl. Even after all these years. I need to call Detective Poole and see if they've learned anything."

"I guess it takes a lot of trust to be in a relationship."

"It does." She twirled spaghetti on her plate. "Do you think you trusted Tabitha that much?"

He grew defensive. "She didn't betray my trust."

"I didn't say she did." They ate in silence for a few

minutes. "Who am I to talk? I don't think I've ever trusted a man that much in a relationship. Not your dad. Not anybody else."

Jared looked up, his face showing surprise. And not just at the content of the revelation, but also the raw nature of it. They were moving into that territory where parent and child found themselves standing on the same level for a short time, sharing the same view. It could be invigorating and unnerving for both parties.

"I just thought Tabitha and I would go on and be together. For a while. And you know what the really frustrating part is?"

"What?"

"I don't know *why* she did it. I don't know if I did something wrong or what it was."

"I doubt it was you. And I'm not just saying that because I'm your mom. When I talked to her the other day in the parking lot, I could tell she cared about you a great deal. That's why she brought that book back to me. She wanted me to tell you that. She cared."

"Really?"

"Really. I suspect it's her dad. Or something else we don't know about. Has she been back in school?"

"No. No one's seen her. They think she's gone. Moved away."

"Are they looking into it?"

"I asked Mrs. Timmons. You know, the counselor. The one who looks like a hippie? She said they have to file some reports when a kid stops coming to school. They're doing that with the proper authorities." He shrugged, trying to put away all his awful feelings with one gesture. Jenna knew it wouldn't work. Nothing was ever that easy.

Jared took a second serving, and Jenna poured some wine for herself while he ate. She offered him ice cream for dessert, but he shook his head, saying he might eat some later.

"Can I ask you something else?" he said.

"Sure."

"I always thought Ian was kind of cold and, you know, had a stick up his ass. Like, way up. Not mean or anything. Just . . . distant."

Jenna tensed at the mention of Ian's name. Her hand tingled where his thumb had rubbed. In that very room, at that very table.

"He can seem that way," she said. "But he's not. He's just serious about work. He has a lot of responsibility at the foundry."

"I know he's your friend. And you know him well, right?"

He gave her a sidelong look, one that seemed to anticipate her response, as though the words she used to answer him might be surprising or revelatory in some way. She kept her eyes on Jared, her hand on the wineglass, resisting the urge to look down at the back of her hand. Had he seen something the other night when he came home?

"Pretty well. We were better friends in high school. Why are you asking about this?"

"The other night when he was here, and I walked to

the door with him, he was pretty chill. You know, friendly and everything. Friendlier than I've ever seen him."

"You're older now. Maybe he feels more comfortable around someone your age than a little kid."

"Maybe. And Celia was cool. *Is* cool. Sorry. I always . . . I like her. She's friendly and warm."

"What is this all about?" Jenna asked.

"How did Ursula end up being such a royal bitch?"

Jenna held in a laugh and a mouthful of wine, which burned against the back of her throat. She finally swallowed. "She's going through a brutal time. Cut her some slack."

"She wasn't that bad when she was a little kid. She was tough and bossy, but not mean. You don't see her at school. She picks on other kids, weaker kids. She's always trying to undermine everybody's confidence in class. I think I really hate her."

"I always thought you had a crush on her," Jenna said. "Celia did too. We could tell the way you looked at her."

"That's gross."

"Look, some people in our lives are just difficult," Jenna said. "Hell, look at Grandma."

"That's true. But she's old. Ursula's young. She's always had a lot going for her."

"She's a pretty girl." Jenna paused. "Just like her mom."

Jenna heard the moroseness creeping into her voice and wished she'd cut it off.

Jared must have heard it too. He tried to keep it light, and he did. "I may be single now, after my three-week relationship, but that's one girl I'm not interested in."

CHAPTER THIRTY-SEVEN

Detective Poole called as Jenna finished cleaning the kitchen. She dried her hands on a towel and answered, trying not to guess about what the detective was calling for.

"I was thinking of calling you," Jenna said.

"Great minds think alike," Naomi said. "I promised I'd do my best to keep you in the loop, so I'm letting you know the latest on Benjamin Ludlow."

Jenna felt cold. She shivered, even though she'd been working in the small kitchen. "I'm guessing this isn't the news we're looking for."

"He has a rock-solid alibi for the time Celia disappeared. It took us a while to follow up on it, but it's solid. There's no way he could have harmed Celia."

Jenna pulled a chair out from the table and sank down into it, her butt hitting the wood with a solid thump. She didn't even feel relief. She felt fear, a tugging, dragging ache in her heart. *It's not over*, she thought. *It's still not over.*

238 DAVID BELL

"Jenna?"

"I'm here. I'm just . . . worn down, I guess."

"There's more," Naomi said.

Jenna almost hung up. She took the phone away from her ear and looked at the screen, her thumb hovering over the red button. *More?*

She returned the phone to the side of her head. "What else could there be?" she asked.

"Ludlow's story about finding the earring keeps changing. He's told a couple of versions." She paused. "I'm not sure what it means, but we're still looking into all of it."

"Is he in jail?" Jenna asked.

"We can't just hold him forever. He has a couple of outstanding misdemeanor charges we can use to make his life unpleasant. But he'll be out soon. Don't worry—we'll keep an eye on him."

"You said he's a vagrant. He could leave town."

"He won't."

"What about Holly Crenshaw? Maybe Benny is behind it all. Maybe we're safe with him behind bars, and you'll make the case."

"We'll consider everything," Naomi said. "Believe me."

"People are scared, Naomi. I'm scared."

"I know. The police are well aware of that."

Naomi sounded understanding, but her tone didn't comfort Jenna at all. She wanted something to end, something to conclude. And nothing seemed to be. Doors kept opening, leading to more long hallways and doors. She didn't know where she was in all of it.

"Thanks, then," Jenna said.

"We'll talk soon."

Jenna had things to do online. She paid a few bills. She responded to a few e-mails. Later in the month, she was scheduled to volunteer at a community health day in Hawks Mill, an event where local doctors and nurses provided free blood pressure and cholesterol screenings to people without health insurance. Jenna checked the Web site, making sure to mark the correct time and date in her calendar.

She didn't walk away. She tried another search for Tabitha's name. She used a variety of search engines and people finders. No results came back. Nothing on social media—no Facebook, Twitter, or Instagram accounts. None that she could find. But Jenna knew people sometimes used different names and odd handles on social media. And it was possible Tabitha was one of the few teenagers in the country without those accounts.

The girl looked a little economically disadvantaged. And intense. With a strict father and an absent mother. Maybe she was the smart one. Maybe the girl just put her head down and worked, hoping to finish high school and go to college and have a better life than her parents.

But Tabitha clearly believed in having some fun. She'd come back to the house with Jared and climbed on top of him. Jenna wondered if they were having sex already. She'd had the "talk" when he was twelve, offering him plenty of words of wisdom from a woman's perspective, including lots of information about birth control. He squirmed through the conversation, admitting to his mother that he'd heard most of it already from his friends. Did Jared need to hear it from a man? Jenna's dad was dead. She didn't have brothers. Who the hell served as a masculine role model in his life?

She almost felt a measure of relief that Tabitha was out of the picture. Maybe she was too fast for Jared. Jenna always swore she'd never be one of those overprotective mothers, the ones who guarded their sons, believing that no girl who came along would ever be good enough for their little boy. But she felt a twinge, something between jealousy and fear, when she thought about Jared and Tabitha spending time together. He'd started dating. He had just over two years of high school left, and very soon he'd be driving.

It was all going by so fast, like a film stuck in fast-forward.

So why would she spend time online looking at that nonsense?

Because she couldn't look away once she came near it.

She took a quick glance at the Dealey Society page. She avoided all mention of Celia. She could guess what they would be talking about on the new threads, the ones that rose to the top of the page with a flaming icon next to them indicating they were the most popular discussions of the day. They'd be talking about the affairs. They'd be talking about her.

She skipped past them and went to the index, the listing of the names and details of thousands of missing persons cases going back to the turn of the twentieth century. Jenna scanned through them. So many were familiar to her after so much time looking, but she scrolled past the faces anyway.

They progressed from black and white to color, from slicked-back pompadours to hippie curls to mullets. Some of the faces looked happy and optimistic in their photos, just people smiling for the camera before some unimaginable tragedy befell them. Others looked haunted and scared, as though they could already see some doom rushing toward them, and they merely hoped to stay out of its way as long as possible.

The faces haunted Jenna. They scared her. As they paraded by, her skin crawled, a deep and profound unease settling over her body. *We are all so vulnerable,* she realized. *We all dance on the knife's edge. One push, and we are over.* Even someone like Celia. The wrong place at the wrong time and you became a statistic, one of the many missing, their faces fading into the past with every day that went by.

Jenna shivered. She looked behind her like a scared child.

Nothing there. A closed closet door, a shoebox full of photos. All the things people would find if she disappeared or died. A collection of dead objects that might not even mean anything to her son. He'd just have to dispose of it someday.

"Why are you thinking this way?" she whispered to herself.

Because you're scared.

She clicked the back button a few times, reversing to the home page.

She saw the story about a suspect in an abduction and murder being spotted in Louisville, just an hour away.

And then she saw the photo that froze her.

She knew where she'd seen Tabitha before.

She stared at the screen for what felt like an eternity. While she stared, her mouth went dry. She felt a tingling along her scalp, something uncomfortable and itchy.

A man named William Rose was a suspect in the murder of his ex-wife and the abduction of his daughter. His daughter, the girl who had stood right there in her house, the girl she'd stood face-to-face with in the parking lot of Hawks Mill Family Medicine, was named Natalie Jane Rose.

In the photo, she looked younger, her features less defined and more childlike. It appeared to be a school photo, and the girl—Tabitha!—wore a plain red sweater, the ruffled collar of a white shirt peeking out of the top. She looked nervous in the photo as lots of kids did on school picture day. Her eyes were wide, her smile forced.

But she was the same girl. Tabitha.

Jenna had read about it a few times during her search for information about Celia. Unlike the amateur sleuths online, Jenna never believed she'd actually solve a crime herself, never thought she'd stumble across a missing person in the grocery store or cross paths with a suspect at a gas station.

And yet she had. The details came back to her, vague and sketchy. A man in Nebraska who was believed to have murdered his wife and maybe even his daughter. Their bodies were never found. The man was on the run, possibly headed to Mexico.

Jenna remembered seeing the girl's face on the Dealey Society site, that awkward school portrait. Even the nervous look, the deer-in-the-headlights stare as some photographer told her to smile before the flash went off, couldn't hide the girl's beauty. *What a pretty girl,* Jenna thought then. What a tragedy that she was likely dead, her short life snuffed out while she was still a teenager.

Jenna couldn't say how many times she'd scrolled past Tabitha's face over the past few months. Ten? Twenty? Enough that it stuck somewhere in the folds of her subconscious.

She was even more beautiful two years later when she stood in Jenna's hallway. When Jenna had made the bumbling comment about her mother, and the girl answered her like someone who had seen so much more of the world than most adults.

But not the girl. The girl *wasn't* dead, as the authorities feared, at least not as of a few days ago. Her father, the murder suspect, had shoplifted from a store and been filmed on a closed-circuit camera. A cop working security in the store recognized him from a wanted poster. A new alert was issued . . . but no one had seen the girl with him. And the story was front and center again.

Jenna stood up. Her legs felt wobbly. She needed to remain calm. She needed to tell the police.

And she needed to tell Jared.

How on earth was she going to tell Jared?

CHAPTER THIRTY-EIGHT

Jared felt sleepy. He'd spent the past two hours reading *A Connecticut Yankee in King Arthur's Court* for English class. At times the book was funny, and at other times it became quite disturbing. He liked it okay but probably not as much as other things they'd read, such as *Lord of the Flies* or even *The Last of the Mohicans*. But the book passed the time, and he knew a quiz and a paper were coming up, and he needed to do well on both.

He'd spent the weekend thinking about his life and what he wanted to do next. He liked his friends a lot. He liked Hawks Mill, even if it did seem small compared with most places in the world. But there was enough to do—a bookstore, a movie theater, a comic shop.

But he decided he wanted to get out. He needed to dedicate himself to school and not his friends or a girl-friend. If he pushed himself hard enough and got the best grades possible, he could try to go to school anywhere he wanted. Maybe California or New England.

Maybe he could use his dad's address and apply to the University of Texas, which he'd heard was a great place to go and live.

He laid Mark Twain aside and stared at the book Tabitha had returned to his mom. He hoped the book would carry some piece of Tabitha with it. Maybe a strand of her hair that fell into the pages, or maybe a lingering whiff of the flowery shampoo he loved to take deep breaths of when they were close. But the book smelled kind of gross, as if it had sat in a dirty kitchen where someone fried a greasy hamburger. He didn't have any other mementoes of her. No articles of clothing, no real gifts.

He received a text from Mike, asking him to provide a refresher on the book during lunch the next day. Mike never read anything, never even tried. Jared wrote back, promising the information in exchange for a dessert or a chocolate milk. Mike agreed, and Jared decided he needed to start raising his prices.

And then his mom pushed the door to his room open.

She always knocked. The only time she didn't was the day she found Tabitha on top of him, her hand doing things he could only fantasize about with her gone.

Jared sat up because his mom looked scared, the book sliding off his chest and onto the bed. His mom's cheeks were pale, her eyes nervous and darting.

"What is it, Mom?"

"I need you to come and look at something." It sounded more like an order than a request. His mother didn't usually bark orders, even when she was at her most pissed. She made it seem as if it were his choice to do something, even when it clearly wasn't. She added, "Now."

"Okay, okay."

He followed her across the house to the little office she kept in a spare bedroom. She pointed to the chair in front of her laptop, indicating he should sit down, and she stayed back, just behind him, while he looked at the news story she had open on the screen.

None of it made sense at first. A picture of Tabitha's dad appeared on the screen. Next to it a photo of Tabitha. Why? Was it some social media site he'd never heard of but his mom had?

Then he saw it was a news site.

"What is this?" he asked, although he wasn't directing the question at anyone in particular. He was talking to himself.

He studied the screen more, and as he did, he felt his legs becoming weaker, felt a cold stain of fear spread from the center of his body to the tips of his fingers and toes.

Tabitha's picture. But with a different name underneath it.

It said she was from Grand Junction, Nebraska. Not Florida.

Tabitha and her father. In the newspaper.

And a headline with the word "murder" in it.

The wheels in his head moved slowly, like a car stuck in the mud. He couldn't seem to keep up, to process everything he was meant to process. It was like a dream he didn't understand even as he was having it.

His body started to shake.

"Is that Tabitha's father?" his mom asked. "Is it?"

"It is. But his name's not William Rose. What is this?"

He saw the headline. SUSPECT IN MURDER SPOTTED IN LOUISVILLE.

Louisville. Not far away. Not far away at all.

His mom had her phone out, pressing the buttons. "Somebody saw him in a store up there. We have to call the police. You said the school reported something, so they're already looking to some extent. I'm calling Detective Poole."

While she dialed, Jared scanned the story. The words didn't make sense. They might as well have been a jumble, like those puzzles in the newspaper. But he caught certain things. "The man was alone when spotted . . . no sign of his wife or daughter . . . believed to be dead, a victim of Mr. Rose . . ."

But Tabitha wasn't dead. Not a few days ago.

"No one saw her?" Jared asked, his voice faint.

"That doesn't mean anything."

He saw the darkened house in his mind, the closed doors and pulled shades. He'd been right there, knocking and looking around.

Had Tabitha been inside while he spoke to the neighbor?

Could she have been in the house dead?

He was up, brushing past his mother.

"No," she said, her voice harsh and authoritative. "You need to stay here. The police need to talk to you."

"But Tabitha—"

"No. They need the address. It's dangerous. What if that man is back?"

But Jared was gone, out the front door without a coat, without a plan.

For the second time, he ran to Tabitha's house, hoping to save her.

CHAPTER THIRTY-NINE

The house still looked shut up and dark. Abandoned. Devoid of hope and life.

Jared glanced at the neighbor's house and saw no sign of Mr. Fifties, his cigarette or his beer.

He remembered the news story they saw on the Web, the one with Tabitha's—Natalie's?—picture. A witness saw her dad. A cop. But they didn't see her. And the authorities thought he'd killed her mother. . . .

Where was she if she wasn't with her dad?

Maybe she was in the bathroom of the store, and that was why the witness missed her. Maybe she was hunched down in the back of the car. Maybe she'd blended into the crowd.

Or maybe . . .

He stared at the house, its locked doors and drawn blinds. It looked like a place that held its secrets close and tight, as impenetrable as a bank vault.

But maybe it all made sense—the curfew, the isolation,

the restricted texting and calling. Tabitha and her dad
were on the run, living under different names. Her father
was a murderer, someone who had killed her mother and
then taken Tabitha away from her home to live there in
Hawks Mill. And they were on the run again.

Maybe. If Tabitha or Natalie or whoever she was really
had gone with him.

He checked the back door, hoping for something with
a large window he could break. He wanted to smash the
glass and just reach in and undo the lock. Or he could
crawl through the window.

And look for what? Tabitha's dead body?

Jared shook the thought out of his mind. No time for
that. He just wanted to concentrate on getting inside.

The back door was locked and made out of wood. No
window, no opening. He pushed against it and it didn't
budge.

He went back down the steps to the side of the house
and stood under the window he had previously broken.
The cardboard still covered the opening, but the window
was too high to reach or boost his body through. Above
the roof, low clouds started to build, blotting out the
stars and the rising moon. It was getting tougher to see.

Jared scrambled around on the ground again, searching with his hands. He found a large stone, one that
someone had once used to create a border around the
landscaping. The stones were scattered now, the flower
bed overgrown with dead weeds and grasses. He clutched
the rock in his hand. It was bigger than a softball, filling
his palm and then some.

He spotted a basement window, small but still big enough for him to squeeze through if he knocked all the glass out. He didn't try to disguise the noise. He pulled his hand back, making sure to keep his fingers out of the way as best he could, and brought the rock forward. The window crunched, the shards of glass falling inside and making a sound like discordant music.

He checked his hand. He didn't see any blood in the dark, didn't feel the stinging of any cuts. He used the rock to clear the rest of the glass out of the pane, swiping it away so there were no jagged edges sticking up, and then he tossed it away. He took off his sweatshirt, since he hadn't bothered to grab a coat on his way out, and used it to line the pane, hoping for a little more protection against any pieces he'd missed.

He looked around one more time, checking to see if anyone was watching him or had heard the glass breaking. But there was no one in sight. The night was quiet except for the soft creaking of tree limbs rubbing against one another when the faint breeze moved.

Jared bent down and slithered through the opening, not sure where he would land.

CHAPTER FORTY

Nothing broke his fall but the cement.

Jared managed to twist his body a bit before impact, allowing his shoulder to take most of the force instead of his head. It still hurt, and he lay on the floor for a moment, letting out a low groan that he quickly repressed. He doubted anyone was in the house, at least no one who was alive, but did he really want to telegraph his arrival by moaning and groaning?

He yanked his sweatshirt in and shook it out, making sure no more glass was embedded in its material. A cool draft followed him through the broken window, and he pulled the sweatshirt back on as his eyes adjusted to the even darker space. When they began to acclimate, he looked around. He saw an old washer and dryer, some boxes, and a set of golf clubs that looked as though they hadn't been touched since Jack Nicklaus was an infant. But the large open space was mostly empty.

Across the room, a staircase, wooden and rickety, led to

the next level of the house, so Jared headed that way, stepping lightly, hoping that when he reached the top the door wouldn't be locked. He eased up the stairs, every creak amplified in the dark, quiet space. As he climbed, he wished he'd kept the rock he'd used to break the window. He possessed no weapon, no way to defend himself on the off chance someone was in there. But he also figured if someone was in there, someone who meant to do him harm, a rock wasn't going to be much help.

The door at the top of the stairs gave way when he turned the knob. He pushed it open slowly, and in the meager light saw he was in the kitchen.

The smell hit him, a sickly stench that burned his nostrils. Like poop. Maybe a pipe had burst or a toilet had backed up. Or could it be something worse, some kind of decay from someone who had died?

Jared's will and determination took a hit. If someone was dead in the house. If *Tabitha* was dead in the house, did he really want to be the person to find her? Did he want to see her body and remember her that way for the rest of his life?

But if she was there, if she'd been killed and abandoned by her father, Jared didn't want to leave her there unattended. Her life had already been violent and shitty. No one, least of all the girl he really and truly loved, deserved to be left to die and rot alone.

Or what if she was just hurt? Bleeding or injured?

He moved through the kitchen, past the table where he had spied her dad planting that creepy kiss on Tabitha's lips. He shivered at the memory, which had been enhanced and made even worse by the information he'd learned on-line. Again, he reminded himself not to dwell. There'd be time later to deal with those things. Hopefully there would be, he thought. Hopefully there would be.

He reached a hallway that ran to the front of the house. The smell seemed to be coming from somewhere in that direction. He hadn't adjusted to it, not at all. He took off his sweatshirt again, feeling the cold chill of the house against his bare arms, and pressed it against his nose, hoping to block out the odor.

There were doors on either side of the hallway. One of them was open, and Jared peered inside. A bathroom. The sink was streaked with rust stains, the shower curtain torn and hanging loose. A pang of regret stabbed his heart, an aching sorrow he felt to his core. He hated to think Tabitha lived in these conditions in a dirty run-down house. She showered there in the crude little room. Went to the bathroom and combed her hair.

Then he saw the door on the left, one that must have led to a bedroom. It hung open, but there was a hasp attached to the wood on the outside. No padlock was in sight, but it meant that someone had been kept locked inside there. The hasp was new, the metal clean and shiny in the dingy gloom.

Tabitha.

Had she been a prisoner in her own house? Held by her father?

Jared rushed into the room. He saw a mattress on the floor and some cardboard boxes against the wall. The closet hung open but was empty.

Jared saw scattered papers and a textbook he recognized from school. He also saw a notebook, one with scribbles on the front. He recognized Tabitha's handwriting and bent down to pick it up. It was full of drawings. Flowers and horses and a unicorn. The kind of things lots of kids, especially girls, drew. Page after page of them.

He flipped back and looked at the inside front cover. Someone had signed their name there in large flowing script.

Natalie Lynn Rose.

And under the name, a photograph. Taped to the notebook. A beautiful woman who looked a lot like the girl he knew as Tabitha. But older, probably in her thirties.

Her mother. Had to be.

Jared gently peeled the photo off the notebook and slid it into his back pocket.

He tucked the notebook under his arm and left the bedroom.

He brought the sweatshirt back up to his face. As he moved down the hallway toward the front of the house, the smell grew stronger. Even through the thick material of the sweatshirt, the odor reached him. His eyes watered from the stinging stench.

Faint light leaked into the front room through a small opening in the blinds. Jared saw two overstuffed and dirty chairs, a small out-of-date TV with an antenna sitting on a plastic milk crate. An inert lump, fat and bloated, lay sprawled on the floor.

It was a man. Jared could see that. But not Tabitha's dad. This man wore a business suit, the tie knotted against the thick folds of skin at his neck. A giant pool of blood spread around his head like a halo. The blood was thick and black, and Jared could tell no one could survive losing that much from his body. A few feet away from the body sat a small ceramic statue of Santa Claus, the weapon that was probably used to smack the fat man over the head.

Jared stared a moment longer, making sure, really sure, the man was dead and beyond help. He clearly was. His mouth hung open, the jaw slack. His eyes behind half-closed lids were sunken. At the moment of his death, the man's bowels had emptied, the main source of the nasty odor in the house.

Jared backed away. He went down the hallway and through the kitchen. He saw the back door, the one he'd tried earlier. He turned the lock and pulled it open, stepping out onto the small back porch and letting the cool air wash over his face. He took the sweatshirt away, gulping in the mercifully clean and cold air of the late-winter night.

He huffed in the air for a few moments. Then he called the police.

CHAPTER FORTY-ONE

The first two police officers to arrive on the scene asked Jared a lot of questions. He couldn't answer many of them. He told them who had lived in the house as of a few days ago, and he related the story online identifying Tabitha's dad as a fugitive and a murderer. The officers—one of them young and stocky, the other middle-aged and wiry—made him go over that a few times before it was all clear, and once it was, they decided to go into the house.

One of the officers, the stocky one who wore a name tag that said "Jones," asked Jared if he knew the dead man inside. Jared shook his head. The image of the bloated, bloody body came back to him, and even though he stood outside, the rotten smell lingered in his nostrils. He wished for something pleasant to sniff—a bunch of flowers or a peppermint patty or a wet dog. Anything.

"You broke into the house because you thought your girlfriend was in danger?" the older cop asked him. His name tag said "Bradford," and he sounded a little suspicious. Jared understood what the whole thing looked like. He'd already confessed to the crime of breaking into the house. But considering what he'd found and how shitty the house was to begin with, he hoped they'd cut him some slack.

"I thought she was dead," Jared said, trying not to sound pathetic. "She still might be."

Another car approached, and the three of them watched it pull over to the curb. Jared knew who it was. He'd called his mom as soon as he contacted the police and she said she would be right over. She popped out of the car, her face worried. Jared knew she'd be freaked, but then again, what parent wouldn't be? Her son had called her up and said he'd just found a dead body in a house in a bad neighborhood a few months after her best friend disappeared. Yeah, she could be freaked out if she wanted.

"Are you okay?" she asked when she came up to them. She placed her hand on his shoulder, and then she pulled him close into a hug.

Even though the two cops watched, Jared didn't mind. The hug felt good, warm, and safe. It made him feel like a little kid again.

"You're his mom," Jones said.

"I am. He called me."

"Do you know the people who live here?"

"No, I don't. Well, wait—I knew the girl who lived here. I met her a couple of times."

"This is your son's girlfriend? The girl who might be the victim of a custodial kidnapping?"

"I guess that's what you call it," his mom said, sounding a little impatient.

"And your name is Jenna Barton, right?" Bradford asked.

Jared saw the look cross his mom's face, the tired one that always showed up when she was recognized simply because of her connection to Celia. It was as if some power drained from his mother every time that came up.

"Yes," she said, her voice short. "I know Detective Poole very well."

"But you don't have any reason to believe the two things are related, do you?" Jones asked. "The dead body in there and . . ." For a moment, it seemed he wouldn't even finish the thought, but then he said, "Mrs. Walters's case."

His mom answered right away, her voice assured and confident. "No, I don't think so. Do you?"

The cops didn't offer any opinion. Over the past few months of watching them up close, he'd learned they usually didn't. They said as little as possible that might obligate them to something later. They liked to ask questions and then sit back and let the other person, the non-cop, talk. Then they'd ask another question and another.

The notion that the two things were related—Celia's disappearance and Tabitha's—had never crossed Jared's mind until Jones brought it up. And once he did, the idea wedged in Jared's brain like a large splinter.

Could they be? And Holly Crenshaw as well?

"Do you mind if I take him home?" his mom asked, her hands still resting on Jared's shoulders, even though he was taller than his mom by a few inches. It was one of those protective gestures parents like to make. It said to the world, *This one is mine, and you better believe you're going to have to go through me first.* "It's cold. He doesn't have a coat, and he's been through something awful."

"Mom," Jared said. She seemed to be laying it on pretty thick, making him sound like a baby. But he did want to go home, to get out of the cold and away from the stench of the dead man inside. If he ever could fully get away from it. His mom ignored him and waited for the cops to say something.

"Are you going right home?" Bradford asked. "Because a detective will want to speak to you. Tonight."

"Believe me," his mom said, her voice sounding tired, "they all know where I live."

Bradford nodded and Jared's mom didn't break contact with him until he sat down inside the car.

CHAPTER FORTY-TWO

Early the next morning Detective Poole came by, looking tired and worn. She wore a navy pantsuit, the jacket wrinkled, and her hair seemed frazzled and unkempt, as if she'd ridden to their house with the windows down in her car, despite the cold temperatures. When Jenna offered her coffee, she accepted it as if it were manna from heaven.

The three of them sat at the kitchen table. Detective Poole started with a rundown of everything Jared knew about Tabitha and her dad. But before she started asking questions, Jared said, "Her real name is Natalie, isn't it?"

Naomi nodded. "It looks that way."

"Maybe we should call her that. I need to get used to that, I guess, and I think someone would like to be called by their real name."

"Fair enough," Naomi said.

Jared told the detective the little he knew about them. Natalie said her parents were separated, her father strict.

She said she came from Florida. Jared admitted that he had never really met her dad, never set foot inside the house until he broke in.

"I'm sorry about that," Jared said to the detective. "But I was scared. I thought Tabitha—Natalie—might be in there. Hurt. Or worse."

Naomi gave him a reassuring pat on his hand. "I don't think anyone's going to be pressing charges over a broken window."

"It's not the only window I broke on that house. Did you see the kitchen window was all taped up?"

"We did," Naomi said. "Did you try to get in that way first?"

Jared looked at Jenna and then over at the detective. He told her he'd broken the window one night when he saw Natalie's dad kissing her on the lips in the kitchen.

"I lost my shit," he said. "I got so angry. And jealous. I couldn't stop myself."

"Is that why you asked me about fathers kissing daughters?" Jenna asked.

"Sure. It seemed weird, but I didn't know. You and I never kiss, not that way. But I don't know about fathers and daughters."

Jenna pulled her sweater tighter around her body. "Your instincts were probably right. Is it possible this girl was being abused by her father?" Jenna asked Naomi.

Naomi kept her face a blank mask, revealing nothing. "We're looking into everything." She turned to Jared again. "Is that all of it? Any other relevant details? Anything at all?"

"That lock on the bedroom door," Jared said. "Do you think he kept her in there?"

"He let her go to school," Naomi said. "She wasn't a prisoner all the time. And she didn't tell you or anyone else at the school that she was being mistreated or abused. She could have run away, and she didn't. Right?"

Jared's shoulders rose and fell, a hopeless shrug. Or an admission of defeat. "I wish to God I knew more. I really do. I'd give anything to be able to see her again and learn more about her. But most of the things she told me were lies."

Jenna reached over and rubbed his back. She ached for him. It was bad enough to get dumped, to lose his first love, but to lose it all in such a shocking way. She felt powerless to ease the boy's pain. She might have to get him help. Real help.

"Is that all, Detective?" Jenna asked.

"No," Naomi said. "I have to keep bugging you two." She reached into the pocket on the inside of her jacket. Jenna thought only men's clothes had a pocket there. "We've identified the body we found in that house. Or I should say, you found in that house. I need to know if you know him."

She brought out a photo of a balding, middle-aged man wearing very unstylish glasses. "Recognize him?"

"No," Jenna said.

But Jared said, "Sure. That's Mr. Allen. I go to school with his son."

CHAPTER FORTY-THREE

Jared picked up the photo, staring at the awkward posed portrait. It looked like something taken at work, maybe for a company Web site, and the smile on the man's face looked as if he'd rather be anywhere than sitting in front of a camera.

"How do you know him?" Detective Poole asked.

"I don't really know him," he said. "I know his son, Bobby. Bobby and I were on a soccer team once." He looked up at his mom. "Remember that year I played soccer for the Optimists' Club? Bobby was on the team."

His mom nodded, although he couldn't tell if she really knew who the kid was or not.

He said to the detective, "His dad used to come to some of the games. Once he got into an argument with a referee over something stupid. He thought Bobby had been fouled, but the ref didn't make the call. The whole thing was insane. We were losing, like, ten to one. We were kids. But he ended up getting the team a red card.

I felt awful for Bobby. He stood there with his head down while his dad made an ass of himself. That's who it is, isn't it?"

Detective Poole nodded. "Indeed. Henry Allen is the man you found deceased in that house."

Jared stared at the picture again. It was hard to imagine that lump in the living room, that still, cold, bloated body, had once been a living man, someone capable of fathering a son and arguing with a referee. He had felt the same way at his grandfather's funeral years earlier. He couldn't reconcile the stiff, overly made-up body in the casket with the vigorous man who had once lifted him in the air and swung him around. Jared knew everyone ended up that way, dead and cold, empty and lifeless. It didn't matter if the body was in a funeral home or on the floor of a shitty house. Dead was dead.

Had Tabitha—Natalie—met the same fate?

"He was murdered, right?" Jared asked. "That's why all the blood was behind his head."

"We're treating it as a homicide," Naomi said. "Did you ever see Mr. Allen in the vicinity of Natalie's house?"

"Never."

"And Natalie never mentioned him to you?"

"Never."

"But you went to school with his son, Bobby?"

"He's a grade ahead of me."

"Did Natalie know him?" she asked.

Jared paused to think about it. "She didn't have many friends. She'd only been in the school a few weeks. I can't say for sure she didn't know him, but I never saw them together. She never mentioned him to me. Bobby ran with a different crowd than us."

"What kind of crowd is that?" Naomi asked.

"The rich kids. In fact, you know who he's friends with? Bobby? I just saw them together the other night. He hangs out with Ursula Walters. They were in the park a few days ago when I went walking through."

Something crossed Detective Poole's face, a look of mild surprise or curiosity. She didn't have to say anything about it. Everyone in the room saw the strangeness of the circumstances: Bobby Allen, the son of a murder victim, was friends with Ursula Walters, the daughter of a kidnapping victim. And Bobby's father was found dead at the home of another girl who was apparently kidnapped and in danger.

"And Ursula and Natalie weren't friends?" Naomi asked.

"No. They were in a couple of classes together, I know that. The other night, when I saw Ursula in the park, she called . . . Natalie weird. You could tell she said it just to be hurtful. She didn't really know her. Natalie. She just wanted to be nasty in some way. She's a raving bitch."

"Jared," his mom said, "don't say that. Ursula's probably just jealous."

"Jealous of what?" Jared asked. "Of me?"

"Not exactly," his mom said. "Mean girls don't like it when anyone makes them look bad. Let's face it—Natalie is a gorgeous girl. Have you seen a picture, Detective?"

"I have. We got one from the school."

"Maybe it's just mean-girl jealousy," his mom said.

"Or maybe she really thinks Tab—Natalie is weird. Who knows?"

"Let me ask you something else, Jared," Naomi said. "When Natalie broke up with you, did she mention another guy? Do you think she was seeing someone else?"

Her words twisted in Jared's guts a little. He knew she was just doing her job, and he didn't want to react like a sniveling little baby. But he didn't like the question. He didn't like it at all because he knew so little about Natalie that the answer to the question might just be yes.

"How could she?" he said. "She could barely get out of the house to see me."

Naomi looked sympathetic, maybe even a little sorry she'd asked the question. "So she didn't mention anyone?"

"No. She never mentioned any other guys. None."

A silence settled over the kitchen. He couldn't hide his real feelings, his fears that Natalie simply didn't want him anymore because she found someone else.

But he knew the detective had bigger things on her mind. She wasn't concerned with a silly little high school love triangle. She was hunting bigger game.

Naomi reached out and picked up the photo of Henry Allen, tucking it back into her coat pocket. She checked her watch.

"We've sent out an AMBER Alert about Natalie. Her description and her father's description are going to be all over. They won't be able to go many places without being recognized." She stared at both of them, a serious look on her face. The light from above reflected off her oversize glasses. "If you hear anything from Natalie, anything at all. A text. A phone call. An e-mail or a social media message. If you get any of those things, let us know right away. Don't continue the conversation. Don't say anything. Just call us. And needless to say, if you see her or her father, call the police immediately. That man is dangerous. Don't approach him. Don't play the hero, okay?" She shifted her gaze to Jared when she said the last part.

"I hear you."

She patted his hand again. "I know you want to rush in and help this girl. It's noble. It really is. What girl wouldn't want a boyfriend like you? But let the police handle it, okay? Don't play Junior James Bond anymore."

"Can I ask you something, Detective?" Jared said.

Naomi kept her hand resting on his. "I don't know if she's alive or not, Jared. But until we know otherwise, we're going to assume she is."

CHAPTER FORTY-FOUR

———————

Jenna walked to the door with Detective Poole while Jared went to his room, and the two women went outside together, stopping on the small front porch to talk some more.

The late-winter sky was gray and low. The sun seemed to have given up. It was cold, too cold for Kentucky in February, and Jenna again found herself wishing she could live someplace warm. Once the glory of spring came, she'd talk about how there was no place better to live than Kentucky, and she couldn't imagine being anywhere else.

"Thank you for being so encouraging with Jared," Jenna said. "I don't really know what to say to him about this girl. Here I've spent a couple of months complaining about people who don't know what to say to me, and now I'm in the same boat. I don't know what sounds right or makes sense."

"I try to be positive," Naomi said, "until I can't be anymore."

"Do you really think this Natalie might still be alive?" Jenna asked.

"Her dad brought her here for some reason instead of killing her back at home. That means he had something in mind for her. It can't be easy bringing a teenage girl along with you."

"No. I guess I'm holding out hope he really cared about her in some way. Like you said, he let her go to school."

"She didn't run. If she was scared enough, that might motivate her to stay. He could have threatened her. Intimidated her. We don't even know if the girl is aware that her father is a suspect in the mother's death. That might change her tune if she knew that. But it doesn't look like she has much family. She could be completely dependent on him."

Jenna thought of the kiss Jared described. If you combined that with her father's controlling, domineering nature, it seemed hard to come up with a benevolent scenario.

Detective Poole considered Jenna. The wind rose and tossed the detective's short hair around on top of her head. "So, you don't know Henry Allen, do you?"

"No. I don't remember him from the soccer games."

"Did Celia know him?" Naomi asked.

Jenna knew she should have expected the question, but it still knocked her off-balance. "I have no idea, Detective. It's a small town. Anything's possible, and Jared said their kids are friends."

"But you don't know the parents of all of Jared's friends."

"Not his girlfriend's dad. Thank God."

The detective didn't walk off. She seemed to be lingering, to be taking her time as if she were retired without a care or a deadline in the world. "Have you spoken with Ian anymore?" she asked.

"He came over the night the news broke about the affair."

"He came over?"

"He didn't have my number. I guess he was worried about the impact the news would have on me. He knew Reena was going to be targeting me and he wanted to offer support."

"Did you talk about the case?"

"Not really. No."

"It's good you two are supporting each other that way."

"Can I ask you something, Detective?"

"Sure."

"Ian has a solid alibi for the night Celia disappeared, right?"

Naomi shifted her weight from one foot to the other. She winced a little as if something pained her, and she rubbed her back with her right hand. "Why do you ask?"

"No particular reason. People online have always said things about Ian needing to be investigated more closely. And I know the statistics. Usually it's someone very close to the victim who commits the crime. Parents kill children. Husbands kill wives. . . ." Her voice trailed off. Just giving voice to the thought felt like a betrayal of Ian, even though she wasn't sure what loyalty she owed him. Wasn't her greater loyalty to Celia?

"This has all been made public, you know," Naomi said.

"Two people can place Ian at home at the time Celia disappeared. His mother, to whom he was speaking on the phone, and his daughter. Now, usually we want more than a family member's account of things, but the phone records back it up. He was thoroughly questioned. More than once. Do you have reason to think he was involved?"

"No, of course not. And you asked me all this when Celia disappeared. I never saw any abuse or violence between them. Celia never mentioned being afraid of him. There was nothing."

"But you didn't know about the affair, so . . ."

"It's not that. With Ian talking to me again I started thinking about it."

Naomi studied Jenna for a long time. "The media have been a little rough on you lately," she said. "A Reena Huffman type doesn't like it when someone doesn't keep jumping through her hoop. The media giveth and the media taketh away."

"What does that mean?" Jenna asked.

"It means they'll have a field day if you keep getting closer to Ian. They're distracted by Holly Crenshaw now, but they may get back to you if they get bored."

Jenna wanted to be offended, to protest her innocence, but she knew the detective had seen through her. It was her job, and Jenna had opened herself up enough to be read like an X-ray.

"Talk soon," Naomi said as she walked away into the cold morning.

CHAPTER FORTY-FIVE

Jared felt like a prisoner in his own house.

News of the discovery of the body broke quickly and spread through town like a rushing tide of water. The phone started ringing off the hook again, and local reporters in their makeup and perfectly tailored clothes showed up at their house. They parked their news vans at the edge of the property and crept up to the door, smiling ever so brightly and trying hard to convince Jenna to let Jared just say a few words on the air.

It was a frenzy like nothing Hawks Mill had ever seen: a missing woman, a dead woman, and a dead man . . . all within the space of a few months.

Jared felt as if he'd been transported to the set of a TV show or movie. So much craziness. So many rumors and ideas and theories.

So much fear.

His mom turned all the reporters away, begging them to give her son his space.

"He's only fifteen," she said over and over as he listened from his bedroom.

Then the reporters tried her, asking for her comments on the, as they put it, bizarre turn of events. His mom refused to comment, except to remind the reporters that a family in town had suffered a terrible loss and everyone should be thinking about them.

She also called the police, asking Detective Poole to send someone around to shoo the reporters away. A patrol car arrived, and two beefy cops in dark jackets, their badges and shiny zippers visible from the house, stepped out. They smiled as they talked to the reporters, but Jared could tell they were trying to get them to leave. The reporters kept pointing at the house, and he could imagine the case they were making. The public's right to know. The first amendment.

The reporters moved back to the property line, but they didn't leave. Jared considered it a small victory.

He tried to concentrate on school. He worked ahead in his classes, tackling the readings and assignments for the next day and the day after that. But he had a hard time getting anything accomplished. His mom buzzed around the house, cleaning the kitchen floor and then the bathrooms, her usual routine when something was bothering her that she couldn't do anything about.

Around noon, Detective Poole called and suggested Jared and his mom put out a statement, something asking for privacy and referring all future questions to the police. So they did, hoping everything would calm down.

Jared's phone pinged all day. His closest friends called

and texted, and then kids he barely knew wrote to him through e-mail and social media. The friends wanted to know how he was doing. The acquaintances said all kinds of things. They wanted to know how bad the body smelled or why weird shit kept happening to his family.

He heard his mom talking to his grandma. He knew what Grandma was saying. The old lady was like clockwork with her complaints.

How do you expect to raise a child with the police there all the time?

Jared didn't know how his mom put up with it. And he didn't know how she turned out so well adjusted with his grandma for a mother.

He also tried to ease off on feeling too sorry for himself or thinking of himself as a prisoner. Natalie had been a prisoner of some kind. He'd seen the lock on the outside of her door. He knew the strict curfew she lived under. And her father had simply taken her away, swept her up and out of town. Back on the run. If she was lucky. If something worse hadn't happened to her.

Could his first love really end that way?

Shortly after dinner, while the reporters were still out on the lawn but seemed to be wrapping up after doing some kind of live shot of their house for the evening broadcasts, his mom retreated to her office. Jared sat in the kitchen picking at the remains of the leftover spaghetti he'd heated in the microwave. His mom said she didn't have an appetite.

Jared thought he'd imagined the light knocking

against the door. It could have been the house settling or a squirrel running through the gutters.

But then the knock came again.

He didn't bother his mom. He figured it was a rogue reporter, one who hopped the fence into the backyard because he felt bold, hoping to get a scoop by bugging the family while they sat in the kitchen. Jared intended to tell him to get lost, refer him to the statement the police had issued on their behalf.

He eased the door open.

Ursula blinked as the light from the kitchen spilled out onto the small back stoop. Jared jumped a little. Hers was the last face he'd expected to see out there.

"What do you want?" he asked.

Ursula raised her finger to her lips. "I need you," she said, her voice just above a whisper. "Someone needs to talk to you."

"Who?"

"Look, can you just come out? There aren't any reporters back here. We can cut through the yard behind us and talk to my friend. It won't take long."

"Who is your friend?" Jared asked, his heart rate rising a little with anticipation.

Ursula looked past him into the brightly lit kitchen. She took the whole scene in—the cramped space, the out-of-date table, the plate of spaghetti. Then she looked at Jared again. "Get your coat if you want. It's kind of cold."

CHAPTER FORTY-SIX

———————

Jared stepped into the backyard, the stiff frozen grass crunching under his feet. He looked around and didn't see Ursula.

He walked toward the back of their property to the chain-link fence bordering the neighbor's yard. Someone emerged from the darkness. It was Ursula. She stood in the neighbor's yard, her hands dangling at her sides. Jared found the way she stood—hips cocked, chin up— attractive, and he wished he didn't. Seeing Ursula that way made him feel like a little kid again.

And he thought of Natalie. He really missed Natalie.

"Climb over," she said. "It's easy."

"I know. I've done it a million times in my life."

When they'd first moved in, a family with two sons around his age lived behind them. Jared used to climb the fence whenever they were out in their yard, and the three of them ran around playing football and war and hide-and-seek until the family moved away, the dad having taken a job in Pennsylvania. Jared couldn't remember if he'd even said good-bye to them. There seemed to be a lot of that going around.

He easily scaled the fence and landed next to Ursula. She didn't look at him or say anything. She just started walking, heading for the front of the neighbor's house and the street that ran parallel to Jared's.

Jared watched the way Ursula's hips moved as she walked, her jeans fitting her shapely body perfectly. No surprise. She'd have the best of the best. The best-fitting clothes, the most expensive brands.

They reached the next street, and Ursula turned to the left. A black SUV sat at the curb, its parking lights burning in the dark. Ursula walked over and tugged open the passenger-side door.

"Go ahead," she said, sweeping her arm like a game show hostess.

In the glow of the dome light, Jared saw Bobby Allen.

Jared climbed in. Ursula pulled open the rear door and came inside, a gust of cool air following her. In the faint glow from the dashboard, Bobby looked tired. His eyes were red, his mouth turned down.

"I'm sorry, Bobby."

Bobby nodded. He took a deep breath, his broad shoulders rising and falling beneath his coat. They were practically the first words Jared had spoken to Bobby since they'd played soccer together.

The car's engine hummed. It was warm in the cabin, the soft rush of heat coming out of the vents. Jared loosened the top buttons on his coat, letting the heat dig in against his body. Bobby didn't look at him. He stared straight ahead, as if something were coming down the street at him. Jared even turned and looked through the windshield, but the horizon was empty and quiet.

"Are you going to ask him?" Ursula said from behind.

Bobby didn't move when she spoke, but his eyes narrowed just a bit as though her question annoyed him. Jared wanted to know if the two of them were dating, or did Ursula even confine herself to just one boyfriend at a time? He knew a lot of kids at school were like that, even though he'd been content with just the one person in his life. Natalie.

"I want to know what it was like," Bobby said. "Seeing my old man that way." He took another deep breath, this one shuddering a little as if he might be about to cry. But no tears came, and Bobby collected himself. "Somebody bashed his fucking head in. It's a shitty way to die, and I just want to know what you saw."

Jared hadn't expected that. His mind raced as he searched for the proper response. "Are you sure—"

"He's sure," Ursula said. "We talked about it all day. Just tell him what you saw. You don't have to pull any punches."

Jared hesitated. Then he said, "I didn't see too much. It was dark. He, your dad, was on the floor in the living room. On his back by the TV. I could tell he wasn't breathing, and . . . there was a pool of blood around his head. I didn't get close and look. If I'd seen his face clearly, I would have recognized him as your dad. I remember him from when we were kids. But I left. The cops showed me a picture and told me who he was."

"So you didn't see his face?"

"Not really. Like I said, it was dark."

"Could you tell if he suffered?" Bobby asked.

Jared knew what the right thing to say was. "I bet not. With the way he was lying there, and the blood on the floor, he probably got hit pretty hard. He was probably out right away."

"Did he smell?" Ursula asked.

Jared turned a little, but knew he couldn't see Ursula since she was sitting right behind him. So he looked at Bobby. "Yeah, it smelled. It smelled pretty bad. I had to put my sweatshirt over my face. You know, when people die . . ."

"They shit themselves," Ursula said.

Bobby winced a little, as if he'd felt a sharp pain in his stomach.

"I'm sorry," Jared said.

"I asked," he said.

"I went over there once, a few days ago, and the neighbor next door told me that he'd seen a guy in a suit going into the house. And then he thought he heard people arguing. Maybe that was your dad going in."

"Probably was," Bobby said.

"He doesn't know anything, Bobby," Ursula said, sounding bored. "Can he go?"

Bobby held out his hand, and Jared shook it. "Thanks, man," Bobby said. "I appreciate it."

"I want to ask you something," Jared said.

His hand slipped out of Bobby's. Bobby nodded, indicating he could go on.

"Do you know what your dad had to do with Tabitha's dad?" Jared asked. "Why was he there at all? They don't seem like they travel in the same circles."

Bobby said, "I don't know exactly. That lunatic, Mr. Burke or Mr. Rose or whoever he is, did some kind of work for my dad a few years ago. I kind of remember hearing my dad say his name. Then Dad said something about him coming back to town and they were working together again, although Dad acted kind of weird about it, like he didn't want to say too much."

"Mr. Rose was here a few years ago?" Jared asked.

"Yeah. He's one of those guys who comes and goes. My dad once said he was rootless."

"But you don't know what kind of work he did?" Jared asked.

"No, I don't. Something at the plant, but I don't know what."

"I think it was something illegal," Ursula said. "Why else would he kill your dad? Somebody had dirt on somebody."

"The point is I don't know," Bobby said, speaking to Ursula's reflection in the rearview mirror. "Neither do the cops. Not yet anyway." He turned to Jared. "Do you know what he did for a living? Did he ever say?"

"I never really talked to him. I never formally met him. The first time I ever set foot in the house was when I found your dad."

Bobby nodded as though some profound truth had just been confirmed. "Well, I'm sorry about Tabitha. Or . . . What's her real name?"

"Natalie," Jared said.

"I'm sorry about Natalie." They shook hands again. "The whole town's kind of gone crazy. I hope they find her."

He turned and stared out the window, his gaze distant and unfocused. Jared wondered if he was remembering something about his dad, some happy childhood memory like a Christmas morning or learning to ride a bike. Or was he focusing on the bad stuff? Stuff like the soccer game or whatever he was involved in with Natalie's dad? When his own dad left the family, Jared spent a lot of time thinking about the good stuff. Times they'd gone for car rides together or played a game. And then the more time went by, he stopped thinking about him much at all. It was hard to remember any of the good stuff.

"I have to get back to my mom," Bobby said.

"Sure," Jared said. "Take care."

"If you hear anything," Bobby said, "will you let us know?"

"I will."

He stepped out into the cold, expecting Ursula to move to the front seat, but she didn't budge. He shut the door and watched them drive off.

CHAPTER FORTY-SEVEN

Sally insisted on getting a drink after work. A couple of days had passed since the revelations about Natalie and William Rose broke. The news media and the cops seemed to be stuck in a loop, running on a wheel like hamsters. No additional credible sightings of them came in. No one saw Natalie anywhere.

They drove in Sally's car to Haley's Taproom, a bit of a dive in a strip mall near the office. The place was rarely crowded, and the owner kept the lights down low. No one had to make eye contact in Haley's. No doubt most of the patrons didn't want to.

Sally went to the bar and brought back two bottles of beer. Budweiser. Cheap. Jenna took a long swallow, and it tasted like liquid heaven. She enjoyed the sting of the alcohol against the back of her throat, the tingling in her bloodstream as the buzz started.

"I shouldn't be here," she said.

"Why not? You've earned a drink. And so have I."

"I should be home with Jared."

"I thought you called him," Sally said.

"I did."

"And?"

"And he's home," Jenna said. "His friend Syd came over. They're playing video games."

"And probably looking at porn. Normal boy stuff."

"Sally, that's gross."

"Honey, every boy does it. They can't get enough of the stuff."

"Not Jared."

Sally raised her eyes. "All of them, Jenna. Even the pope. All of them."

Jenna took another drink. She'd spent the week lying low at work, trying to stay out of the way of patients who had once again seen her all over the news. She wished more than anything her life could return to being normal. *No chance of that,* she thought. *No chance of that anytime soon.*

"See," Sally said, "you wanted that beer. And to think you said you didn't want to come out."

"You're right."

And Sally was. She always was. It felt good to get out of the house and away from work, to go somewhere and not talk about any crimes. Jenna wasn't naive. She knew everyone in that bar had heard of Celia and Holly and Natalie. She felt certain some of them recognized her, if not from before, then certainly from the previous few days of coverage. Local and national news talked about the cases, covering every angle. And speculation ran wild that everything was related.

"Jared's doing okay otherwise?" Sally asked. "I know he got his little heart broken, and now this with the girl . . ."

"He's doing fine," Jenna said. "I'm sure he's talking to his friends about it."

"Boys talking about feelings?" Sally said. "Playing video games together is as much as you'll get. They aren't going to talk."

"Maybe. He hasn't said much to me. I think I need to get him in to see a therapist. He's a teenager, and he's dealing with all this."

"Has he been having nightmares?" Sally asked.

"Not that I can tell. He isn't eating as much. He's a little down, a little distracted. I'm walking a tightrope here. I don't want to keep asking and push him away, but I don't want to ignore him."

"He'll talk when he's ready," Sally said, her voice certain. "I'm sure he's just glad to have you around and to know you care as much as you do. Really. If he feels loved, he's doing okay."

"I hope he does."

"He does." Sally emptied her beer and without asking went to the bar for more. She also brought back two shots. Kamikazes by the looks of them. "Drink up."

"Sally, what are you trying to do?"

"We're not driving for a while."

"All I'd need right now is to get pulled over or arrested for public drunkenness on top of everything else. That would enhance the story."

"You see that guy over there?" Sally pointed at an overweight man with a walrus mustache and a leather wallet on a chain. His belly had slipped out from beneath his shirt, exposing a pale roll of fat.

"What about him?" Jenna's nose curled.

"He's going to take you home."

They laughed, and then they threw back the shots. Jenna felt good. Really good. Better than she deserved to. She also felt her tongue loosening, even more than usual. She wanted to talk to Sally, to say some things out loud she hadn't said to anybody.

Sally seemed to read her mind. Her face grew a little more serious, and she said, "I'm really wondering how you're doing. That's what we're here for. *Your* therapy."

"All I need is alcohol," Jenna said, pushing aside her pledge to drink less. The alcohol made her feel philosophical, expansive. She asked, "Do you ever wonder about all the paths you didn't follow in your life?"

Sally's look told Jenna there were too many unwalked paths to ever think about all of them. "Where did that come from?"

"All of this. Everything. Thinking about Celia so much, seeing Jared growing up, it's all making me feel old."

"What does that make me? I'm ten years older than you."

Jenna stared at her bottle of beer, the faint light from above reflecting dully off the brown bottle. "Did I ever tell you Ian and I were almost an item in high school? This was before he started dating Celia."

"You told me once. You made it sound like Celia swooped in and took him away from you."

"She did. It was no big deal. It was inevitable in a way."

"No big deal?" Sally said. "It seemed like a big deal when you told me about it the first time."

"It did?"

"I think it was a couple of months ago. We were talking after happy hour one night, maybe at the Downtowner. You still sounded pissed."

Jenna couldn't argue with Sally's memory. It made sense. She was a little pissed, had been for almost twenty-five years. "I didn't know I was so transparent."

"Hey, I get it. High school's a bitch. And it's full of bitches too. No offense to Celia, of course. But those wounds stay with us. And so do first loves."

"He wasn't—" She stopped. "Not exactly." But he was the heaviest of her teenage crushes. Even after he and Celia were married, even after she married Marty, she held Ian up as a kind of ideal, the model against which she measured all other men. She knew she was more likely to do that precisely because they never dated. "But nothing happened. We were friends. We flirted. We skated up to the edge, and then that was it."

"That's the worst. What might have been. Heck, if you'd dated back then, you might have found out he was boring or a bad kisser or he farted in bed. And that would have been the end of the romantic dream. Now he's always out there, a big question mark floating over his head."

"It's still here," Jenna said. "A little bit."

"What?"

"The question mark."

Sally raised her eyebrows. "Oh, boy. I think this is beyond my expertise."

Someone dropped coins into the jukebox, and a Glen Campbell song started playing. "Wichita Lineman." Sally swayed a little in her seat as the intro came out of the speakers.

"You're right," Jenna said. "I need to let it go."

"You're not sixteen anymore."

"I know."

"And he's married to your best friend. If you think you've seen a media shit storm so far, you ain't seen nothing yet. Tell me that you hear me on this one."

"I do. I get it." Jenna swallowed more beer. "But he's been opening up to me. We've been connecting. He and I, we're the ones who knew her best. I think he just feels good being able to talk to someone about her in the way we can. Her new friends probably can't do that."

"Of course that comforts him. You feel old because Jared is growing up. How old do you think he feels with a missing wife?"

"When I look at him, even though he's aged some, I see that same guy from high school. I think he sees the same thing with me."

Sally pushed her bottle and the two empty shot glasses aside. She leaned forward, her elbows resting on the tabletop. "Are you listening to yourself?" she asked.

Sally's tone had shifted. She'd shed the joking edge and sounded like someone on a mission. The sharpness of her words made Jenna sit up a little straighter. "Of course I'm listening to myself. I thought we came here to talk."

"Then listen closely." Sally looked around the room, her eyes wandering as though she was looking for someone else.

"Sally, he and I were friends in high school. We've both suffered a loss. Maybe a permanent loss. Are you saying we shouldn't talk to each other?"

Sally turned back. "I get that. I do." She picked up her empty beer bottle and shook it. There was nothing left. She frowned and pushed it aside again. "And if that's all it was, if that's all you wanted . . ."

Another song started playing. Something darker and heavier Jenna didn't recognize. The fat guy at the bar drummed his hands against his thighs. Something felt tight and raw in her chest. It was the realization of how transparent she'd been to her friend. "I've been single a long time. My mom thinks I'll never get another man to look at me as long as I live."

"Forget her. My cousin would still like to meet you."

Jenna had seen the pictures of Sally's cousin. A harmless enough looking guy, but she hated to think Sally thought he was her match. He was balding, slightly overweight, and wore a goatee that hadn't been in style in fifteen years. The pictures always depressed Jenna.

Jenna said, "I know what I'm doing, Sally."

"I hope so."

Jenna started to protest. She started to say, *He's not interested in me that way*, but she couldn't. He was, a little bit. He probably just needed someone: a friend, an emotional crutch. It wouldn't be right for anything more to happen, but she kind of enjoyed his attention.

"I need to get home," Jenna said. "Jared is there."

"Don't go away huffy," Sally said. "I'm looking out for you."

"Yeah, I know. Everybody seems to be doing that these days."

The two women walked out in the cold night. The sky was purple, the stars scattered. They hugged good-bye at their cars, and Sally held Jenna a moment longer than normal.

"Remember what I said about that shit storm. Watch out for it."

Jenna wanted to but didn't say she'd already been living in one for the past three months.

CHAPTER FORTY-EIGHT

When Jenna came home she found Detective Poole sitting in her living room, talking to Jared. Jared seemed to be in the middle of a long, complicated explanation of something.

"Hi there," Naomi said. "Don't worry. I wasn't interrogating him. He's explaining *Minecraft* to me. I have a nephew who plays it all the time, and I wanted to know what it was about."

"That's fine," Jenna said. "Are you here to talk to me?"

"I am. If you don't mind."

"No." Jenna slipped out of her coat and set her purse down. "I'm going to run to the bathroom first, okay?"

"Sure. Jared can finish what he's telling me."

Jared gestured toward Jenna. "She never wants to play these games."

Jenna went into the bathroom and scrubbed her face and hands. She felt as if the smell of the bar—the collection of spilled drinks and fried food—clung to her body like a second skin. She gargled with mouthwash twice, making sure to mask the odor of alcohol from the detective. Why? She wasn't sure. She just didn't want Detective Poole to see her coming in the door to greet her son with beer on her breath.

But she'd smell the mouthwash and know.

Jenna caught a glimpse of herself in the mirror. A little tired, a little angry from the conversation with Sally. Couldn't she do anything in this town without someone knowing about it? And once again a cop waited in her living room.

She came back out and took a seat on the opposite end of the couch from Jared. He smiled at her when she sat, apparently pleased that he knew something the detective wanted to know.

"Syd left?" Jenna asked.

"He did. Right before the detective got here."

"I haven't been here long," Naomi said. "I've been running all day."

"Do you want a drink or something?" Jenna asked.

"Jared already offered. You've trained him well."

"I did, Mom. I remembered to offer. But she turned me down."

"My work here is done," Jenna said, but she felt uneasy. The conversation with Sally lingered, the complicated feelings for Ian plaguing her like a committed sin. "What's on your mind, Detective? I hope it's not bad news."

"That depends on how you look at it."

"How am I going to look at it?" Jenna asked.

Detective Poole cut her eyes over to Jared. Jenna read

the look, and so did Jared. The detective wanted to know whether it was okay to talk in front of him. Jenna had long ago stopped covering his eyes or sending him out of the room when scary things came on the TV. She'd seen the movies he watched and the games he played. Blood sprayed and splattered everywhere. People screamed. Monsters roared.

But they were living in real life. With real monsters.

Jared had handled the stuff with Natalie well so far, as she'd told Sally. He'd fallen for the girl hard. He'd been burned like an adult. *Welcome to the world*, she wanted to say.

"It's up to him," Jenna said. "Do you want to hear this?"

"Is it about Natalie?" he asked, hope rising in his voice. Like Jenna, he couldn't hide his feelings either. He put it all out there. He sounded desperate for any information about the girl, and Jenna felt a mixture of pride and fear for him. Pride that he didn't hide what he felt. Fear that the transparency and vulnerability would be used against him. And hurt him.

But she couldn't protect him from all that.

"Indirectly," Naomi said. "We haven't found her. In fact, we really don't have many leads about her whereabouts, although we're continuing to look."

"Is this about her dad?" Jenna asked.

"Yes."

"Go ahead," Jenna said. "We can handle it."

Naomi accepted her verdict and started talking. "We got some results back concerning the death of Holly

Crenshaw. Ordinarily it can take a while to get these types of DNA results back. The state lab is backed up, and they don't just wave a magic wand like they do on TV. But the case has been getting a lot of attention, and apparently Ian's family has some pull in Frankfort."

"His grandfather was a state senator for years and years," Jenna said.

"That might do it. They've tested DNA on Holly Crenshaw's body and entered it in the national database. They got a hit. William Rose."

"What does that mean?" Jenna asked, the words coming out slowly.

"It means he's a sex offender, right?" Jared said. "You had his DNA in the system from another crime he committed. And it means he killed Holly Crenshaw."

"That's it," Naomi said. "He's now wanted for the murders of both Holly Crenshaw and Henry Allen. And he's wanted for the kidnapping of his daughter. And he's suspected of killing his former wife."

The news hollowed Jenna out. It felt like too much to bear, too much to absorb in one moment.

"And Celia?" Jenna asked. "Does this have anything to do with her?"

"We can't say anything conclusively. There's no evidence tying William Rose to Celia, but we'd be fools to think it isn't a real possibility. We certainly want to talk to him about it."

The detective seemed to have left something unspoken. Her words hovered in the space between them like dark clouds.

"So you do suspect something?" Jenna said.

"I can't go beyond what I've already said. And needless to say, this is top secret and off the record. I just wanted the two of you to be in the loop before the public hears about all of it. I know how invested you both are in this."

The dark clouds conjured by the detective's words stayed. Jenna didn't know what to say, whether to feel relief over knowing something or fear that her life as well as the life of her son had veered so close to such a monster.

She looked to Jared. She wasn't sure if she needed to go to him, to place a comforting hand on his shoulder.

His eyes were wide and unfocused. He didn't glance at either one of them.

Detective Poole seemed uncertain about what to do next. Jenna looked at her and asked, "Was there anything else we could do for you, Detective?"

Naomi took a deep breath. She looked at her watch and pushed herself out of the chair. "No, I don't think there is. Like I said, I just wanted to give you the heads-up." She took a couple of steps toward Jared and placed her hand on his shoulder. The gesture managed to appear heartfelt and forced at the same time.

"You hang in there, okay?" she said. "Sorry to keep bringing you heavy news."

Jared didn't look up. He nodded. "I get it," he said. "I'm glad to know. It looks like her dad's a murderer. And she's either with him or dead."

"Remember what I said. Don't jump to conclusions about anything yet."

Jenna followed the detective to the door and asked her in a low voice, "I assume you've told Ian about this?"

"Just a little while ago."

"And he's doing okay?" Jenna asked.

"He understands that William Rose could be connected to Celia's disappearance. He also understands there could be no connection."

Jenna thanked her and closed the door.

CHAPTER FORTY-NINE

The ringing phone, the landline, brought Jenna out of a deep sleep. Ian walked through her dreams, talking to her, smiling at her. Reaching out to her, touching her hair. Her eyes opened with a tinge of regret and a stab of guilt. Ian. She dreamed about him instead of Celia.

"Hello?"

"Jenna? Becky McGee." The reporter's voice was so chipper it could break glass. Jenna moved the phone an inch away from her ear, hoping to create a buffer. "I hope I didn't wake you."

Jenna looked at the clock. Six ten. Becky McGee and her chirping voice had just robbed her of twenty minutes of sleep. And maybe the conclusion of her dream.

"Is something going on?" Jenna asked.

"It is. You know, I didn't really want to call you after the way you talked to me the last time. That time out at the barn? You remember that, right?"

"You mean the clip that played endlessly on CNN? I'd almost forgotten."

"Do you know no one's ever talked to me that way? In my life."

"I doubt that," Jenna said.

Becky's end of the line went silent for a moment. Then she said, "Well, be that as it may . . . I'm calling with an opportunity for you. I figured you wouldn't want to miss it." The more she talked, the more the pep returned to her voice. "Guess what."

Rather than telling Jenna, she waited, forcing Jenna to provide the prompt.

"What?" Jenna asked.

"Reena's coming."

Jenna sat up straighter, the covers pooling around her body. It was cold in the house. They turned the heat down at night to save money, and Jenna felt the chill in the air, the draft from the imperfect windows. The skin on her arms prickled with gooseflesh. "Coming where?" she asked.

"To Hawks Mill. She hasn't been here since early December, but with everything going on in the town—Celia, Holly Crenshaw, the earring being found, this William Rose and that poor girl, Natalie—she just feels the time is right for her to come back and try to help people sort through it."

"Help people?"

"I told her I could handle it on this end," Becky said. Jenna imagined the reporter reaching around and patting herself on the back while she talked. "I've been handling things for her for the last couple of months. But you know Reena. She wants to be where the action is. We're like that in the news game."

"Becky, what does this have to do with me?" Jenna asked.

"A lot." Becky seemed surprised Jenna didn't get it. "Reena wants to talk to you. She wants to interview you. She's going to put you on her show live tomorrow night."

Jenna felt deflated. She fell back against her pillows. "I'm not doing that, Becky. I was on TV so much when Celia disappeared. I never liked it. It made me so uncomfortable."

"But you're doing it for Celia. And Natalie."

"Not after the way I was treated the last time," Jenna said. "I'm not going to be Reena's puppet. Forget it. Find another stooge."

"Reena wanted to call and apologize."

"She did?"

"She did."

"So why didn't she?" Jenna asked.

"She's busy. Look, between you and me, I think she's feeling the heat at the network. She's an older woman. Her ratings are a little down."

"Good-bye, Becky. Don't snow me."

"Jenna, wait. They're both still out there, and we want to bring them home. Both of them. Don't you want to make this happen? If you want the cops to keep searching, if you want the story to stay alive, you have to go on the air and talk about it from time to time."

"I can talk to *any* reporter."

"Not one with this much reach. And that girl, Natalie, she could be anywhere in the country now. So could Celia, for that matter."

Jenna had to admit—Becky was no dummy. She knew the right buttons to push at the right time. She had managed to get Jenna out to that barn for the discovery of a set of deer bones. And she'd made it nearly impossible for Jenna to say no to Reena's request. What had Jenna been told ever since Celia disappeared? *You never know which piece of information would solve the case. You never know what might help.*

"How long is it? I mean, this is going to be a short segment, right? Just a few minutes?"

"Well, probably a little longer than that." Becky sounded cagey. She was going to turn over another card. "We wanted to have another guest on with you."

"Who?" Jenna asked. "Ian?"

"Ian? Lord no. He won't go on TV. He barely talks to us. No, we were really hoping to make this as personal as possible, to get someone on who really knew the victims. The missing victims. You know Celia, of course. Very well. And then we were hoping to have someone on who knows Natalie Rose well. We wanted Jared to come on with you."

"No," Jenna said. "No. No way. He's not going on TV."

"But—"

"No. You need to drop this about him. If you want me on, you need to leave him out of it."

"Can you at least think about it?" Becky asked, her

voice rising higher as she pled her case. "It would be fantastic."

"No," Jenna said. "Nonnegotiable. In fact, you know what?"

"What?"

"Forget the whole thing. You don't get me, and you certainly don't get my son."

She hung up before Becky could say anything else.

CHAPTER FIFTY

The din of the cafeteria went on and on around them. Every once in a while, Jared stopped and listened to it. *Really* listened to it. The voices and shouts, the clattering of trays and silverware and scooting chairs, made a racket that assaulted the ears. Jared wondered how they all could handle being surrounded by it day after day.

But they did. Everybody sat there day after day. And their lives went on as they always had. So much human activity, so much life. So much of it mundane and pointless.

Jared chewed his food, his history textbook open before him. He'd told Syd and Mike about the detective coming by the night before, about the DNA match between Holly Crenshaw's body and Natalie's father. They both listened with their mouths hanging open, even though they'd heard a lot of it from their parents. Even Mike, who never acted as if he cared about anything, appeared captivated by the news. He hung on every word as if Jared were a celebrity. Or the president.

When Jared finished talking, Syd looked crushed. "And I left right before the cop showed up? If I'd stayed longer I would have heard all this myself."

"It's not that exciting," Jared said. "The detective looks like she's someone's grandma. She looks like one of our teachers, kind of old and frumpy. I don't even think she has a gun." Jared made a mental note to check the next time he saw Detective Poole.

"Still," Mike said, "it's pretty wild. And it's happening right here in Hawks Mill. It's shitty for you and everything, but it's kind of fascinating. If you could separate the part about human beings, real human beings, suffering from the crazy details, it would be pretty cool. I mean, like, if it were a movie or a TV show."

Jared turned back to his book. "You can't really separate that part. Ever."

Jared lost himself in the reading, blocking out the noise as best he could. He read about Rome, the fall of the empire, and just as the barbarians invaded, he noticed Mike squirming around in his seat, looking above Jared's head at something or someone moving behind him. Mike usually stopped and paid attention to the world around him only if a beautiful girl was walking by.

Somebody tapped Jared on the shoulder. He looked back.

It was Ursula. She stood over him, her face determined.

"I need to talk to you," she said.

"Again?"

"Yes. Again."

She wore a long-sleeve T-shirt and black leggings. Her boots came up to her knees, and Jared couldn't help thinking of Nazis from World War II movies, the actors strutting around in crisp uniforms, their heels clicking as they saluted and talked.

He wanted to beg off, citing the history book in front of him, but a fact remained just as true in high school as it was in their childhood—he couldn't say no to Ursula. Back then it was because Ursula was three months older than he was. And maybe when he was a kid, the memory of his sore head from the coffee table edge had kept him in line. As a teenager, he thought it was because she knew how to talk in a way that didn't allow for arguments.

Jared packed his things and stood up. As they walked away, Mike said, "You know I'm always available to talk, Ursula, if you ever get tired of the snotty country club boys."

She turned on her heel and looked at Mike as if he were a bug. "I'd have to get awfully tired to come talk to you."

Jared followed her outside. He couldn't help it—he again watched the movement of her hips, the shape of her butt, only this time, in the daylight, he was better able to see it all and feel the bubbling surge of lust in the middle of his body. He hated to think Mike was right, that there were many, many more fish in the sea besides Natalie, but he knew it was true. And even if Natalie came back, would they be together? One of the last things she did was break up with him and return his book.

Ursula led him to an area outside the cafeteria where students were allowed to mill around and talk before the next period started. In the old days, even before Jared's mom went to school there, it was the smoking area where students could light up cigarettes and who knew what else.

It wasn't miserably cold, and Jared was thankful for that, but it was cold enough that most of his fellow students stayed away. They opted to remain in the cafeteria, shooting the shit with their friends or preparing for all the tests and quizzes they hadn't already studied for. About fifteen kids sat outside, mostly burnouts and freaks, the ones who wore black clothes and listened to the darkest, dreariest music imaginable. They never went to dances or football games, never joined any clubs. Jared knew he didn't fit in everywhere, but he wasn't as low on the social ladder as they were.

Ursula sat on a short wall, away from the other kids. A couple looked up, and one sneered when he saw them. Jared sat next to her, making sure not to get too close. They made an interesting pair—the girl whose mom disappeared and the guy whose mom everyone thought left her hanging on the night she was taken.

Ursula crossed her legs and stared off into the distance. She acted as if Jared weren't there, and he wondered if she'd brought him along for any real reason, or if she just wanted to sit and intensely ignore him for a few minutes. He was on the brink of reaching for his history book when she said, "I hear you got invited to go on TV tomorrow night."

"I did? What are you talking about?"

"No one told you?"

"No. How do you know anything about it?"

She still didn't look at him. "That Reena Huffman bitch is coming to town to do interviews. She wants to talk to your mom. And you. She also wants to talk to my dad, but he won't do it. She told him she invited you both on. I guess she thinks that will move him to reconsider, which it won't." She finally turned to face him. "He's hopeless. Doesn't he know how bad that makes him look?"

"You mean it makes him look guilty?" Jared asked.

Ursula studied him. In the dull winter sun, he saw the spray of freckles across her nose, fainter than when they were kids but still there. "Or unfeeling. Take your pick. Everybody already thinks of him as the ice man. He's just feeding into it."

"My mom didn't mention it," Jared said. But he had to admit she had seemed a little off her game as they got ready that morning. She didn't talk as much, and she seemed to lack energy. He thought he'd heard the phone ring while he was still deep asleep. Had that been the cause of her mood? An invitation to Reena's show? "She tries to shield me from the media and stuff."

"I get it," Ursula said, looking back off into the distance. "Here's the thing—my dad thinks your mom said no. That's the vibe he got from Reena's people. They called him again and again, trying to get more out of him. The media, they're vultures. Reena just comes around and tries to get ratings off our suffering. It's all bullshit." A light breeze picked up, making Jared shiver a little. The breeze also brought a sweet scent from Ursula, something that smelled like flowers, either her shampoo or her body spray. "People think I'm unfeeling too," she said. "It's my mom this happened to. I'm closer to this than anybody."

Even though she was in profile, Jared saw the emotion in Ursula's eyes. He felt for her because she looked so lonely and small, no longer the invincible tough girl everybody imagined her to be.

"I'm sorry," he said.

"It's fine. You know, whatever."

"I really don't want to go on TV," Jared said. "You're right—it's kind of bullshit. I'm glad my mom took care of it."

Ursula turned back to him quickly, her eyes boring in on his. She held his gaze for a long, uncomfortable amount of time, her gaze appearing to absorb information about him as if her brain were a supercomputer.

"What?" Jared asked.

"I think you *should* go on. With Reena. Your mom too."

"Why? I thought it was bullshit."

"It is. But we're both in the same boat here. That guy, that William Rose or whoever he is, he took something important away from both of us. My mom and your girlfriend. And I'm thinking of Bobby too. You saw him the other night. He's so torn up. His dad was murdered. Somebody has to tell the story for us, don't you think?"

"You suddenly care about Natalie and me?" Jared asked.

Ursula shrugged. "Not exactly. I care about my mom. You care about Natalie."

"Why don't you go on, then?" Jared asked.

"My dad won't let me. He hasn't really let me near the media in a long time. It's like your mom. He wants to protect me. He certainly won't let me go on if he's not willing to go on. How would that look? But your mom could go on. And so could you."

"And how do you know all this?" Jared asked.

"My dad. He talked to Reena, and he told me. He's been talking to me more than ever. You know, he's trying to be both parents and all that. It's kind of sweet in a way, how much he's trying. He's a little lost." She looked sad but determined. "Anyway, if you just talk to your mom, explain to her how important it all is, she'll probably go along." She licked her lips. "Your mom hasn't made the best impression on the media lately. So maybe you could both work on that."

Jared ignored the criticism of his mother, but he couldn't ignore Ursula's ability to persuade him. Something about the way she spoke, the certainty of her tone, the force of her voice, made him feel as though saying no simply wasn't an alternative.

But he didn't trust her. He knew someone like Ursula used people only for her own ends, but what if her goals and his overlapped? He wanted Natalie brought home safe. If he had to deal with Ursula to make that happen, then so be it.

And it didn't hurt that she looked so good. Over the years, his mom had complained more than once about how easy and simpleminded men were when it came to attractive women. She was right. It was tough to say no to one.

"I'll talk to her," Jared said. He found himself already reconsidering his gut-level position against going on TV. He was the only one who could speak for Natalie. Her mother was dead. Her father a brutal criminal. And his mom didn't know her the way he did. She wasn't as invested in her safe return. She cared, of course, but not as much as he did. "I'll try."

"Do that." Her hand came over and landed on his knee. Through the denim he felt her gently squeeze, and he couldn't stop the reaction that rose again in the center of his body. His stomach tingled, and he felt the first stirrings of an erection. She just as quickly removed her hand. "I know I've been kind of a bitch to you and your friends." She looked into the distance again. "It's not you. I'm like that with everybody. I just, you know, get impatient. I get shitty with people. My mom . . . all this stuff makes it worse."

"I know."

She didn't react to what he said. She squeezed his knee again and walked away, leaving Jared to wonder what exactly she was up to.

But in the end, if he got on TV and helped Natalie, did Ursula's motivations really matter?

CHAPTER FIFTY-ONE

During her lunch hour, Jenna slipped out to the parking lot to make a phone call. The sun had appeared and reflected painfully off windshields and hubcaps, although it brought little warmth. Jenna had packed a sandwich and a bottle of water, and she carried them to the car with her, seeking privacy.

She dialed the number at Walters Foundry, the one from the business card Ian had given her. While the phone rang, she flicked the card with her thumbnail, making a satisfying clicking noise inside the car.

A secretary answered, and Jenna asked to speak with Ian. When the woman asked who was calling, Jenna hesitated for the briefest of moments. And why? She couldn't say. On some level, she thought Sally was right. Maybe she shouldn't be calling Ian at all. But she wanted to talk to him before she went on TV.

"Jenna Barton."

Did she imagine the pause by the secretary? She heard

another phone chirping in the background, the low murmur of music. Had the secretary been instructed to put
her through or turn her away?

"One moment, please."

Then the music was in her ear, some canned, whispery
Muzak, the kind of stuff her grandmother used to play in
the afternoons when Jenna visited. She remembered the
old woman humming along to "Theme from *A Summer
Place*," her mind someplace other than Hawks Mill.

Jenna expected the secretary to come back and take a
message, but then Ian answered, saying hello in a formal
voice.

"Are you busy?" Jenna asked. "Is this a bad time?"

"It's good," he said, his voice warming. "Is something
going on?"

"Not really. Well, I've been thinking about something
you said the other day, something about Celia."

"About Celia?" His voice grew lower, as though he
didn't want someone to hear him speak her name. "What
about her?"

"It's nothing bad. It's good. You said we needed to talk
about happy memories instead of just always talking about
the awful things that have happened. Are happening."

"I saw the news," Ian said, his voice rushed. "That
girl . . . and she was right there in your house, spending
time with Jared. To think of that. Well, Detective Poole
gave me the lowdown on the whole situation. They want
to see if this man, this William Rose, had anything to do
with Celia."

Jenna heard the struggle for composure and control in

Ian's voice. She wondered if it was a mistake to call. They had a suspect now, a man with a name and a face they could try to tie to Celia's disappearance. They'd gone so long with nothing, not a hint or a lead, that she wanted to view the identification of a potential suspect as something to be celebrated, even mildly. But how could anyone think to celebrate or feel good about news like that?

"It scares the hell out of me to be so close to these things," Jenna said. "How did this end up being my life?"

"I don't know." His voice sounded distant and hollow, like a corn husk rustled by an autumn wind.

Jenna rushed to fill the silence before it settled between them forever. "I got invited to do an interview on TV tomorrow night. Reena Huffman's show. I know she tried to get you on as well, but I told her no. She's awful, and she's been saying such horrible things about me."

"I don't blame you for that. You've been trying to be accommodating, to be loyal to Celia, but you don't need to go on TV with that monster."

"Are you sure, Ian? It might help."

"No. Forget it."

"It's an opportunity to spread the word about Celia and Natalie. You know there's a chance—"

She stopped herself. The words fell out of her mouth in a rush, so she slammed on her verbal brakes before she finished the sentence.

But Ian knew what she was going to say. He finished the thought for her. "There's a better chance for this Natalie girl than for Celia. I get it. He's her father. He's kept her alive this long."

"I'm sorry, Ian."

"It's okay," he said. "You don't have to go on there. When I first heard your voice today, I thought you were calling to talk me into going on."

"I wasn't going to try to talk you into anything. I just wanted to make sure you were okay with me saying no. I could go on and on about Celia, as you know. I could never run out of things to say about her, especially from when we were growing up."

Ian grew silent. Jenna heard two deep breaths through the phone.

When Ian spoke again, his voice was phlegmy. "What I want everyone to know . . . I know what's important." He cleared his throat, once and then twice. "I know Celia was a very good mother. I hope everyone knows that about her. You know that, right?"

"I do."

"I have to go, Jenna. I have someone coming by."

He was off the phone before Jenna could apologize.

CHAPTER FIFTY-TWO

———————

Jenna was walking in the front door of her house when her cell phone rang. She answered and heard the familiar voice of Sally. "Can I bend your ear for a moment?"

"Sure. I'm just getting home."

When she came into the living room, the phone pressed to her ear, Jared appeared from his bedroom, an anxious look on his face. He started to speak but stopped when he saw she was talking to someone else.

"I just feel like we kind of gave each other the cold shoulder today," Sally said. "I think that conversation last night at Haley's didn't go the way either one of us wanted."

Jared lingered in the room, pacing back and forth with his hands swinging at his side. He looked like a hungry dog wanting to be fed.

"You're looking out for me," Jenna said. "I get it."

"I am looking out for you. I know you've been through a lot these last few months. It's really intense."

Jenna went to her bedroom and kicked off her shoes. She sat on the bed, working her toes into the thick carpet. "I can take care of myself, you know? I've been doing it a long time." As she spoke, she remembered all the other times Sally offered unsolicited advice and opinions. Jenna knew she was no one to throw stones considering her own tendency to verbally fire from the hip and ask questions later. It was part of the reason she liked Sally so much—they both spoke their minds to each other, consequences be damned. But she'd spent the day thinking of Ian, thinking of the way they'd reached each other as they talked. No, she hadn't been close to Ian over the years, but weren't the normal rules out the window with someone from high school? Growing up together was almost like sharing the same DNA. How much talking did it take to feel that rekindled connection?

"I suspect you snuck out to see him or call him today," Sally said. "You weren't in the office for your break."

"Wow, you're really keeping tabs on me."

"We're friends. I'm curious."

"I already have a mom, Sally." The words came out like a slap. Jenna even cringed after they were out of her mouth, but Sally didn't say anything. Only silence came from the other end of the line. How many people was she going to put off that day? "Look, Sally, I'm sorry, but—" She looked up. Jared was pacing in the hallway, right outside her bedroom door. He was listening to everything. But more important, what was his problem? He was acting like a child. "I have to go, okay? Can we talk more about this another time?"

"We don't have to talk about it at all," Sally said. "You know what you're doing."

"I don't, Sally, not really, but—"

"It's your life, Jenna. Whatever." Her friend hung up.

Jenna stepped into the hallway and tried to stop thinking of Sally. "Okay, what is it? You're pacing like a caged tiger."

"You have to hear this."

She followed Jared out to the living room, where the combination cordless phone and answering machine, a relic from when Jenna and Marty were first married, sat on a small table. The message light was blinking, and Jenna's heart jumped.

"What gives, Jared?" she asked, running through every scenario in her mind. Had Celia called? Natalie?

Jared reached out and pressed PLAY.

The voice sounded pleasant, a little high-pitched but still a man's.

"Jenna, I'm so glad I reached out this way. I'm coming to town and I want to talk to you about Celia some more. I think you'll be interested to hear what I have to say." Pause. "Oh, I didn't say who I was. This is Domino fifty-five."

Jenna stared at the phone and its blinking red light as though it were a poisonous snake. The light mesmerized her, held her in place unable to move or speak.

"Is that the guy from the Web site?"

She found her voice again. "Yeah. He's the one who

wrote the other night when I called the police. He never said he was showing up before."

"You are going to call the police again, right? He says he's coming here. He must know our address. I told you not to leave the number listed. Celia wouldn't need it."

"He must be joking, right? He's just a nut."

"Do you want to take that chance?" Jared asked.

"No, of course not. Go make sure the doors are locked."

CHAPTER FIFTY-THREE

Jared went to every door, making sure they were locked. And they were. Then he checked a few windows, but the windows in the house hadn't been opened since November when the last Indian summer days blew away. Right when Celia disappeared.

If the guy on the answering machine really possessed the information he claimed, why hadn't he gone to the cops and collected a reward? And besides, his voice sounded like air leaking out of a balloon, high and squeaky and annoying.

But they couldn't take chances, could they?

As he returned to the living room where his mom was still on the phone with Detective Poole, a bizarre possibility popped into his mind: What if Domino55 and William Rose were the same person? Jared had never heard William Rose's voice, so it was possible. Or what if they were friends, working together as partners in crime?

Then why show up in Hawks Mill, where everyone was after them?

His mom got off the phone. He saw two lines along the side of her mouth, lines he would have sworn weren't there just a few months earlier. She'd always looked and acted so young compared to a lot of other parents, even ones the same age. Celia's disappearance was etching itself on her face.

"They're sending a car around to keep an eye on things," she said.

"Good."

"They're busy, though. They've stepped up the patrols with William Rose on the loose. And they're having some kind of press conference tonight. Just an update on everything, something about a connection between William Rose and Henry Allen. I'm curious, but I don't want to watch it."

"Right. I heard—"

"You heard what?"

Jared stopped. He took a mental step back. He wanted something from his mom, so he couldn't just go wandering into the conversation as if it were an unseen minefield. He needed to be careful. He knew she would be reluctant to let him go on TV. But he could try to bargain. . . .

He desperately wanted to speak on Natalie's behalf. To plead for her on TV.

To do something to save her from William Rose.

"I know what that stuff's all about. The Henry Allen and William Rose stuff."

"What is it?" she asked. She wore the same serious look she had when she worked on her taxes or paid bills.

"I need something from you first."

"What?"

"It's a big favor."

"Are you trying to negotiate with me? You know, I can talk to Detective Poole anytime I want. I can read about this in the paper. What do you want?"

"I want to go on TV tomorrow night. With you."

His mom stared at him for a long moment. Her eyes blinked a few times. "Are you nuts?"

"Listen to me, Mom."

"Who told you about that? Did Becky call you?" Her voice rose with every word.

Jared felt as if he were trying to outwit a Jedi master. "No, Ursula did."

"Ursula? What does she have to do with it?"

"She heard they wanted me to go on. They called her too, but her dad won't let her. But she wants me to go on. She thinks it will be more emotional, more real if I'm on there. And it will keep the story alive."

His voice sounded weak and unconvincing. Even though he was a teenager, his mom could make him feel like a little kid if she wanted to just by looking at him the right way.

"And what do you know about Henry Allen and William Rose?" she asked.

"Ursula . . . she came to the house the other night. She and Bobby Allen. And I went out and talked to them."

"What did they want to talk about?" she asked.

"Bobby wanted to talk about his dad. About what I saw in that house. His body and how he died."

"Shit." Her eyes widened. "I guess I understand the curiosity. It's a little morbid. . . ." She looked as though she wasn't sure what to say next. "I really don't like you having to keep thinking about it."

"It's fine, Mom."

"But what is this about Bobby Allen and William Rose?" she asked. "They know each other? And what does that have to do with Ursula?"

"William Rose worked for Bobby Allen's dad. That's what I found out when they came to the house."

Confusion crossed his mom's face first, and then she looked determined.

"And they just came to the door? Out of the blue?" she asked.

"They hang out in the park a lot," he said. "They're always just kind of around."

His mom looked distracted. She talked almost to herself. "I could call Ian and ask to talk to her."

"Talk to Ursula?" he asked.

"Or . . . Get your coat."

"Why?"

"I want to talk to these kids. If they're in the park, it's a sign I was meant to find them. Otherwise, I'll call Ian."

"Mom, don't embarrass me."

"You want both of us to go on TV with Reena? Then you'll be embarrassed."

She had him there. Check.

"What about Domino fifty-five?" he asked.

"If the guy's dangerous, then it's better if we're gone. Right?"

He couldn't argue with her logic. He put his coat on.

CHAPTER FIFTY-FOUR

Jenna opted to drive instead of walk. It was cold, too cold for her to be wandering around in the evening. And what if the kids weren't there? It seemed easier to jump in and out of the car.

Jared rode slumped down in the passenger seat, embarrassed. If there had been a hole in the floor of the car, something he could slip through and disappear into, he would have used it. But Jenna was tired of hearing pieces of the story from a lot of different people. She could wait for the information to filter to her through the police, or she could go straight to the source. Bobby Allen. She barely remembered him from when he and Jared had played sports together.

And Ursula. Shouldn't she be reaching out to the girl more? They hadn't spoken in weeks, and she was spending her time hanging out in the same park her mother was kidnapped from. Jenna imagined it made sense—someone might go to the last place their loved one was seen alive. Someone might feel a connection that way, a bond to a place in the absence of the actual person.

As she thought those things, she rolled past the corner where she was supposed to pick Celia up on that November night. They found the earring there, but no one heard a scream. No one saw anything. People drove or walked by places where unspeakable and awful events happened all the time. A spot where someone dropped dead of a heart attack. A place where one lover told another he or she was leaving. Those spots weren't marked. Nobody knew. Life went on.

Her body tensed as they went past, but Jared didn't say anything. He stared out the window, the back of his head toward her. She let the scene go by without comment.

"Where are they?" she asked.

"By the band shell. Usually."

Jenna went around to the far side of the park and pulled into the small public lot over there. The place had always held happy memories. She had brought Jared there when he was little, and her father had brought her before that, pushing her on the swings and watching her chase butterflies. And she and Celia—the park had been their spot. Where they met, where they planned.

"It looks empty," Jared said. "We should go."

"Hold it."

"If you want to talk to Ursula, just call her. Or Bobby."

"I don't want to wait." Jenna paused. "If you're going to sit here, I'll leave the car on."

He heaved a heavy sigh, then pushed his door open.

They walked toward the band shell, the lights along the path casting their shadows ahead of them. The place did look deserted, locked up and shut down for winter. In just a couple of months, the flowers would be starting to bloom, the world returning to life again. Would everyone have forgotten about Celia by then? Would they possibly know some kind of answers by that point?

Jenna was glad Jared had stepped out of the car with her and walked along the path by her side. It seemed crazy to be in the same park where her friend was kidnapped, but the kidnapper was likely hundreds of miles away. It was a big world, one so big she wondered how anyone—living or dead—ever got found when they disappeared. So many places to run to or hide in. So many places to be discarded or buried. Hidden away forever . . .

Jenna stopped. A pang of nostalgia jabbed her in the heart. As a teenager, she'd come here, sometimes with a group of friends that included Celia and sometimes not. On more than one occasion, she'd spent a hot summer night making out with a guy from school in a deep recess of the band shell, their bodies wedged against a stack of chairs or sprawled over a collection of discarded cushions. In the darkness, she could have gone back in time, back to a place she once knew. Only Jared's presence and the heavy weight of Celia's loss reminded her she was well and truly an adult.

You can't go back again. You can't undo what's been done.

"We can leave now, right?" Jared asked.

Jenna looked around some more. "Is this the only place?"

"I guess so. I don't get invited—"

"This is the place," a voice said.

Jenna spun to her right, toward the sound of the voice. A figure emerged from the side of the band shell, one that looked so familiar to Jenna that her heart stopped for a moment. She really felt as if she'd gone back in time because Ursula looked more like Celia than ever. Same posture, same height. Younger than Celia was on the day she disappeared, but compared to Celia at age fifteen, almost identical.

"What are you two doing here?" Ursula asked.

She didn't approach them, but stood with her arms folded across her chest. She looked cold or uncertain. Or both.

Jenna walked toward her. "We were looking for you."

"Why?"

As Jenna came closer she saw a hard cast to Ursula's features, something that had developed during her teenage years. She'd always been strong-willed, always tough, but becoming a teenager seemed to have added an extra shell to her that repelled any and all attempts to break through.

Maybe Jared had been right. Maybe Ursula was just a bitch.

Or . . . Jenna thought of what she'd learned from Ian. Celia's first affair had happened three years earlier, just as Ursula was entering adolescence. It was hard enough being a kid without having the added stress of your parents' marital problems. Ian hadn't said if Ursula knew, but even if she didn't, she might have picked up on the negative vibes in the house. That would be enough to make anybody mad at the world.

"Do you just hang out here alone?" Jenna asked.

"Sometimes."

"Is it safe?"

"I'm not spooked by what happened to Mom, if that's what you mean."

"Not just that," Jenna said. "I wouldn't think a young girl would hang out in any park alone when it's dark out."

"I usually have Bobby or other friends with me." She looked around, flipping her hair off her shoulders. Her voice lost some of its edge when she said, "It is good to see you, Jenna. I always think of calling you, but I never do."

"I should call you more. I've been derelict."

"It's okay," Ursula said. "We're all kind of living in a swirl. It's like one of those snow globes you have at Christmas. Except this is real, and it's been shaken up and a bunch of bad stuff keeps blowing past our faces."

"Yeah," Jenna said, struck by the appropriateness of the metaphor. "I still should have reached out to you. Just to talk if nothing else."

"I know you've been talking to Dad more. That's nice."

Jenna couldn't read the girl's tone. She thought she detected a slight judgmental edge, but she decided to give Ursula the benefit of the doubt.

"How's Bobby doing?" Jenna asked. "He lost his father."

Ursula moved her upper body. It might have been a shrug, but Jenna again wasn't sure how to read it. "The viewing is tonight. They're laying him out over at Marcum and Sons."

"Oh. Tonight? Are you going later?"

"Bobby and I had a huge fight over something, something that belongs to me. I don't think I'm going."

"Maybe we should go home, Mom," Jared said.

"Wait a minute," Jenna said. "Jared told me that Bobby's dad worked with this William Rose guy. That's the connection between the two of them. But what kind of work did he do for Bobby's dad? How did that lead to his dad being dead in that house?"

"I'm not sure I understand it," Ursula said.

"Try me. I bet you understand it better than you think."

Ursula fixed Jenna with an impertinent stare, one intended to burn holes in Jenna's flesh. The girl didn't like to be challenged. Jenna knew she came by that honestly. Celia didn't like to be pushed or challenged either. Queen bees don't like to have the drones rise up against them. But Jenna had been in stare-downs with Celia. She didn't always defer to her more polished friend. Jenna's spine had plenty of steel, especially after the past few months. She could handle Ursula.

"It was some security stuff," she said. "I guess Mr. Allen had employees he didn't trust, and he wanted to keep an eye on them. Maybe it was even like blackmail. You know, get some dirt on the employees and then they wouldn't act out or maybe they'd even get fired. I think William Rose was doing that."

"Spying," Jenna said, cutting to the chase.

"Right."

"But Bobby doesn't know why William Rose killed his dad?"

"Something went wrong. It usually does, especially if you're dealing with lowlifes." The girl sounded wise beyond her years. And she probably was.

"And that's it?" Jenna asked.

"Could there be more?"

"Why do you want Jared to go on TV so much?" Jenna asked.

"Mom?"

Jenna looked over at Jared, and even in the dark she could read the look on his face. It said, *Let it go. Let it rest.*

"Can't we discuss this at home? Just you and me?"

Jenna ignored him and waited for Ursula to reply.

The girl said, "Isn't it obvious? He's a new voice. He can plead for the safe return of his girlfriend. Don't you want her to come back safely?"

"Of course," Jenna said.

"I'd be happy to go on TV and talk about Mom. Do you remember I did it a few times when she first disappeared? I talked to Reena. I talked to a couple of other shows. I did whatever I thought would help."

"I remember."

It was one of the saddest spectacles of those first days, watching Ursula on the TV. She squinted against the lights, her eyes fixed on the camera. Her voice quavered as she spoke from a combination of nerves and grief. Jenna understood why Ian wouldn't let her back on. It was the same reason she didn't want to let Jared do it—why expose your kids to that? It was bad enough the adults had to publicly grieve.

"And I'm worried about Bobby," Ursula said. "His dad was murdered. Even if I'm mad at him, he's a good friend." She looked down at the ground and kicked a small rock out of the way. When she spoke again, her voice was lower. "I have a lot of reasons."

"Sure," Jenna said.

"Don't you want to go on?" Ursula asked, turning to Jared.

"I do," he said, his voice low in the cold night.

"Look, Jenna, you just have to do the right thing here," Ursula said. "You just do. It's one of the best chances we have to find this guy. And we need to find this guy. We all benefit. We can learn what happened to Mom. And Natalie." Ursula lifted her arms and then let them fall to her sides. "We have to."

Her voice grew faint, disappearing into the traffic sounds and the soft whooshing of the wind through the naked trees. Ursula looked small, more like a child than a teenager. The wind lifted her hair, brushing it across her face.

Jenna closed the distance between them, reaching out as she came alongside Ursula. She'd known her since the day she was born. Had held her and changed her, babysat for her and bathed her. She placed her arm around Ursula's back, felt the girl stiffen at her touch.

"This isn't easy for any of us," Jenna said. "Maybe you're right. But I'm not crazy about any of us going on

TV right now. Maybe we can reach out to a different reporter. I'm not getting burned by Reena."

Ursula's body remained stiff, as if infused with iron. But Jenna didn't let her go.

"I just want it all to be over," Ursula said. "You know? I just want it all to be over. I'm sick of this limbo life we're all living."

"I know," Jenna said.

She felt the girl soften a little under her touch. Ursula didn't give in and fully accept the hug, but she moved closer to Jenna, her body easing in.

"Your mom . . . she loves you very much," Jenna said. "I'm sure you know that."

Ursula closed her eyes. Jenna thought tears would come then, bursting out through the girl's closed lids. But they didn't. She kept that look on her face for a moment, and then slipped out of Jenna's grasp.

"Do you want a ride?" Jenna asked. "I drove and it's cold."

"I'm meeting a friend."

"Will you call me if you need anything?" Jenna asked. "You can. I hope you know that."

Ursula stopped on her way to the side of the band shell, the place she'd emerged from minutes earlier.

"I need this to be over," she said. "That's all."

CHAPTER FIFTY-FIVE

When they returned home, Jenna approached the house cautiously.

Domino55 might be around. Whoever he was.

Jenna carried her pepper spray in one hand and insisted on walking ahead of Jared.

"Shouldn't I go first?" he asked. "I'm supposed to be the man of the house."

"Not until you pay rent," she said. "Until then, *I'm* the man of the house."

But there were no problems. No sign of anyone lurking in the bushes. No sign of any break-in. As Jenna slipped her key into the lock, the bright glare of the porch light illuminating her work, a police cruiser rolled by, the extra protection promised by Naomi Poole.

Jenna breathed easier as they went inside. But she still made sure to turn the dead bolt behind her, to do whatever she could to keep out everything that needed to be kept out.

Jared went out to the kitchen and opened the refrigerator. He slid containers and jars around while Jenna stopped behind him, leaning against the counter.

"Do you want me to make you something?" she asked.

"I'm good. I'm not really hungry. I'm just looking."

"I feel terrible for Ursula," Jenna said. "She seemed so alone. So small and lost."

Jared took out a jar of pickles and closed the refrigerator. "Sure. You're right." He opened the jar and started munching, pickle juice dripping onto the floor.

Jenna pointed at the mess.

"Sorry," he said and leaned over the sink. "She's . . . Yeah, I feel bad for her. She lost her mom. She's trying to get by as best she can. I should be sympathetic when she's cold."

"I need to do a better job for her," Jenna said. "I hope getting back in touch with Ian allows me to do that. Celia would have liked it, don't you think?"

"You talking to Ursula? Or Ian?"

"Ursula," Jenna said quickly. "Well, both."

Jared shrugged and took another pickle from the jar. "Sure. I guess."

Jenna's phone rang. She looked at the screen. "Shit. It's Naomi."

"So?"

"I jump out of my skin every time she calls."

The phone kept ringing.

"Not answering it doesn't change whatever she has to tell you," Jared said.

Jenna watched him wipe pickle juice off his chin. "When did you get so wise?"

She took the call.

"Can I bend your ear for a minute?" Naomi asked.

"Is something wrong?"

"No, no. There's no news."

Jenna's heart was beating fast. She took deep breaths, trying to slow it down. Would she be jumping this way at the sound of a phone for the rest of her life?

"I guess that's good," Jenna said.

"I hear Reena is on your case to do the show again," Naomi said.

"She is." Jenna felt angry just thinking of Reena's smug face. "I told her I'd think about it. She wants Jared to go on as well."

"So, what are you thinking?" Naomi asked.

"I think I'd hate myself if I could have gone on that show and made a difference. If one person knew something about Celia or Natalie and my going on there could have tipped the scales. I know it's crazy."

"Not entirely. But you don't sound certain."

"I'm not, Naomi." Jenna tried to keep her voice level. "I hate that bitch. I hate her overly made-up, sanctimonious guts. And I'll be damned if I'll let her anywhere near my son."

"That's good."

"You know who I'd feel like if I went on there?"

"Who?" Naomi asked.

"Charlie Brown."

"Trying to kick the football every year?"

"Exactly. Tell me, Naomi, tell me I don't have to go on. Tell me it won't really make a difference."

"Jenna, the word about Celia and Natalie is out on loads of news outlets and social media sites. You don't have to carry the whole burden alone. You know that, don't you? You're not in this alone."

The detective's words brought a catch of emotion to Jenna's throat. Simple. Direct. Calming.

She wasn't alone.

"Then can I tell Reena to screw off?" she asked.

"I wish you would," Naomi said.

CHAPTER FIFTY-SIX

Jenna didn't want to watch the next night.

She tried to channel Ian, his detached calm, his refusal to get drawn into any of the messy emotional scenes surrounding Celia's disappearance.

She tried reading another romance novel. She tried cooking. She stood over the stove with her hair pulled back into a tight ponytail and made an omelet and bacon, the little splatters of grease hitting her wrist and hands and decorating the backsplash.

But she knew Reena was in town. In town and on TV.

And she wouldn't be in town and on TV unless she had something important to say.

Jenna shook her head. She didn't regret skipping the interview. Not at all. She wasn't sure how she would have reacted if she'd been in the same room with Reena. She wasn't a violent person, never had been. And it was rare for one woman to ask another to step outside and solve a problem with their fists.

But Jenna wanted to. She wanted to channel months of frustration and fear and sadness into one punch that connected with Reena's overly powdered nose.

So Jenna was glad to be at home.

But she found herself in front of the TV when the ominous and overly dramatic theme music for Reena's show started playing.

Jared came into the room and sat on the end of the couch. "You're going to watch the freak show?"

"I'm ashamed of myself."

"It's kind of like porn, I guess," he said.

Jenna looked up. She remembered Sally's assertion that all men, including Jared, looked at porn. She started to ask but stopped herself.

"I'm glad we didn't go on there," Jared said.

"Are you?"

"Yeah. I don't think it's a good scene. I don't think it helps. Like I said, it's a freak show."

"I think you're right," Jenna said. "No, I know you're right. I just want Celia and Natalie to be found. I'd give anything for that."

"I know you would," Jared said. He slid down off the arm and onto the couch seat. "God, her makeup is horrible."

Reena came on the screen. A live shot in front of the police station. The scenery around her looked so wholesome, so safe and homey, it was hard to believe such horrible crimes had happened in Hawks Mill. That people looked at each other with suspicion, that no one felt safe in their houses anymore.

Reena loved the contrast. It played right into her hands. She loved to sit on TV and scare middle America.

Reena jumped right in. She didn't bother to bring her audience up to speed on either Celia's or Natalie's cases. She acted as if the unseen audience were an old friend, someone who was able to just pick up on the neverending story of murder and betrayal and mayhem that Reena brought to their homes every night.

"I'm here in Hawks Mill, live in front of the police station in this beautiful town, because there is breaking news in the case of Celia Waters, the missing Diamond Mom. And, of course, we have the latest news on the case of Holly Crenshaw and yet another murder here in this picturesque little town. And this time the victim was a middle-aged man."

Jenna's hand moved toward the remote, an involuntary gesture. She knew she should turn it off. She knew she should look away.

But Jared was there, watching. And Jenna knew she couldn't avert her eyes. Reena's show was too much of a train wreck.

". . . and you know I've had my doubts about Jenna Barton, the friend of Celia Walters who showed up late that night, that tragic night Celia disappeared. Snatched away by some animal."

Reena's bright red lips pursed. She shook her head, so disgusted by all of it. Jenna knew Reena loved every minute, every controversial, overblown minute of the spectacle.

"We've now learned why Jenna Barton was late that

night. This is an exclusive, people, one you need to pay attention to. One that involves a lie Jenna Barton told, and a crime committed by a minor."

Jenna looked over and locked eyes with Jared. He paled, his lips parting but no words coming out.

"What is she talking about?" Jenna asked, not expecting an answer.

"She couldn't," Jared said.

They turned back to the TV.

"As it happens, Jenna was late to meet Celia that night—and this information comes from a reliable source. A rock-solid source. Believe me, I never bring anything on the air unless it's rock solid." She pointed a manicured nail at the screen. "You can count on that."

"What a fake-ass bitch," Jenna said.

"It turns out Jenna's son was involved in an underage drinking incident. He's fifteen. That's why Jenna was late that fateful night. That's why she didn't meet her best friend. That's why Celia Walters was taken off the streets by a maniac. And yet Jenna Barton lied about it—"

Jenna threw the remote as hard as she could. It missed the TV—fortunately—but shattered against the wall.

"Mom?"

"Turn it off," she said, her voice barely under control. "Just turn it off so I don't have to see that witch's face ever again."

CHAPTER FIFTY-SEVEN

Jared's fingers scrambled around the edges of the TV until he found the power switch. He pressed it, and Reena's face disappeared. He looked down at the floor. The remote was in a few pieces, the batteries scattered.

He couldn't remember ever seeing his mom throw anything in anger.

He turned to face her.

"Did you tell anybody else?" she asked, her voice level and strong. Every word fell like a brick.

"I told you. I mentioned it in the park to those guys and—"

"Ursula," she said, finishing the thought. "What about Mike?"

"He wouldn't say anything. Never."

His mom pulled her phone out.

"Mom? What are you doing? I mean, this is all over the TV. She just called me a criminal. You too, I guess. Are we going to get in trouble for this?"

She looked up from the phone. "No. Not at all. You have nothing to worry about. I promise."

Her firmness made him feel better. A little.

He guessed there were worse things than being outed for holding alcohol. Maybe it would make other kids at school think he was a wild partier, even if it wasn't true.

"Who are you calling?" he asked.

But she didn't answer. He saw the veins standing out in her neck, the whiteness of the knuckles that held the phone.

Ursula.

His mom's voice went up a little bit on the phone. He heard her say, "Ian."

He'd expected that. First Ursula pushed Jared to go on TV. Jared could remember, like probing a healing bruise with his index finger, the touch of Ursula's hand against his knee.

And then she went to the media—to Reena—with the story about his mom's lie. The lie that covered up for Jared.

Why?

Jared wandered back to his room, giving his mom privacy. It was Friday night, and he had no plans. That wasn't unusual, since he didn't always have plans. And even when he did, they consisted of going to Syd's or Mike's, or having one or both of them come over to his house.

He wished Natalie could be there. He wished they could go out and do something.

His mom came by his room. Her cheeks were red, and she carried her phone in her hand. "Are you okay if I step out for a minute?"

"Sure."

"Really, Jared. You'll be here alone. Maybe I shouldn't go."

"What's going to happen to me?" he asked. "Will I get a ticket for underage drinking?"

She smirked and raised her eyebrows, as if to say, *We all know what can happen to people. We know it all too well.*

"Are you worried about this Domino guy too?" Jared asked.

"That's part of it."

"I'll lock the door," he said. "I promise."

"Do you want me to call Grandma? She can come over and sit with you. Or Sally?"

"Grandma? She's going to call and chew you out now that she knows I had booze in the house. And I'm not a child. Remember?"

"I'm going to call Detective Poole. She'll send a patrol car by just to be safe. Okay?"

Jared sighed. "Okay. Hey, Mom? Are you okay?"

His mom let out a sound of throaty frustration. "I'm fine. Thanks for asking. I'm just pissed. Very, very pissed."

"We're going to need a new remote."

She laughed a little. "I guess I'm not always a good example, am I?"

"I kind of thought it was cool. Just like when you cursed on TV that day."

"I'm teaching you a lot of good lessons." She started to go, then stopped. "Hey, aren't you wondering where I'm going?"

"I know where you're going."

"Where?"

"You're going to ask Ian what the hell's wrong with his daughter."

She nodded. "Doors locked. You hear?"

"I hear."

"Yeah?"

"Yeah."

Once she was gone, Jared pulled out his phone. He sent a text to Mike, asking what he was doing.

Nada, he replied.

Are the country clubbers partying tonight?

Probably.

Can u find out where?

Will check my sources.

Jared changed his clothes and pulled on sneakers. He checked his hair in the mirror once, tousled it around with his hands, and decided he looked relatively cool. Certainly not rich, but also not someone who would hang out on the bottom rung of the social ladder. He was somewhere in the middle, which wasn't a bad place to be most of the time. It might not be enough to get into a rich kids' party, but he intended to try.

His phone chimed.

You know that asshole Kirk Embry? His house.

We have 2 go.

Can't. Grounded. Mom caught me w cigs. Take big Syd.

Need you. Get out.

There was a long pause. Jared thought Mike had ended the conversation. Or had his phone snatched away by his mother.

But then one more text came through.

K. Meet u behind school in 15.

He knew the cops might be out there, checking on the house. But they couldn't watch every door all the time. Not because of a phone call that might be a prank.

Jared grabbed his coat and slipped out the back.

CHAPTER FIFTY-EIGHT

It felt surreal for Jenna to be back in that house again.

Ian opened the door for her, and as she stepped into the foyer, the light above providing a soft glow, every surface below dusted and polished to perfection, she tried to remember that last time she'd been there. Two days after Celia disappeared. A flurry of activity that day. Cops and volunteers and media. People in the kitchen making signs and brewing coffee, hangers-on milling and gawking at the edge of the property line.

Ian closed the door, but before he did, he stuck his head out, looking first one way and then the other. She didn't know if he was checking for nosy neighbors or media, and she didn't ask.

He led her out to the kitchen. Jenna expected Celia to appear at any time. Up until a few years ago, it was always that way. Jenna would arrive at the house—late as usual—and she'd walk out to the kitchen, where she'd find Celia languidly enjoying a glass of wine or a gin and tonic.

Maybe she'd be sitting with a much younger Ursula working on homework, or maybe she'd have a magazine or her cell phone in front of her, and when Jenna would walk in she'd look up, her face breaking into a smile.

"At long last," she always said.

Jenna shivered at the memory, felt the icy hand of regret and grief grabbing her around the back of the neck.

Ian walked over to the refrigerator. "Wine?" he asked. "Or a beer?"

"Nothing. Is Ursula home?"

"She's out. I told you. It's Friday night. What teenager wants to be home? We never were."

He was right. They played and partied hard, and they didn't have computers and video games and streaming movies to keep them occupied. If they wanted something they had to go out and get it. Good or ill.

"Are you sure you don't want anything?" Ian asked. He pulled out two beer bottles. "I get the feeling this is going to be an unfriendly conversation. Maybe beer would help?"

Jenna nodded. She still felt cold and so kept her coat on. She slipped into a seat at the kitchen table, remembering the hundreds of nights she and Celia had sat there, talking and eating and drinking and talking some more. She never thought about any one of them being the last, even as their lives slowly changed the more Celia became involved with her country club life. She knew someday one of them would die, knew there'd be an end of some kind, but pushed it away, further and further out into the future. She wished they'd been closer in those final few years, wished she'd taken an emotional snapshot of every moment.

Ian placed the beers on the table, the caps off. He slid one over to Jenna, the bottom of the bottle leaving a condensation trail on the tabletop.

"So? You said something about the TV tonight and Ursula. You know, I told you not to trust Reena. She's a snake."

"Yeah. But that's not really my problem right now. Why did Ursula go to her and tell her—" She stopped. "Shit, you don't even know. Nobody knows."

"Know what?"

She told him why she'd been late the night Celia disappeared. The discussion with Jared that kept her from getting out the door on time. Ian listened, his lips slightly parted.

"So you lied to the cops back then?" he asked.

"I didn't tell them the whole truth. I think there's a difference."

He leaned back, sighing a little. "I understand if you didn't want to involve Jared in all this," he said. "I told you that before. I'd defend anyone who wanted to do that."

"Listen to me. Nobody knew Jared made me late. Just Jared and me. And he told Ursula and a couple of her friends the other night. Now Reena Huffman knows about it, and she broadcast that news on TV tonight. The whole friggin' world knows now. So either Ursula or one of her friends told Reena."

He was slowly shaking his head, the corners of his mouth turned down. "I don't think Ursula would do that."

"She went to Jared and encouraged him to go on TV tonight. She practically begged him to do it when I wouldn't let him. What's her interest in all this?"

Ian pushed away from the table and stood up. He carried the beer with him as he walked to the sink, his back to Jenna. He stopped, staring at something on the wall Jenna couldn't see, and then he turned around.

"I know how Ursula is," he said. "I know what she can be like."

"She's been through a lot, Ian. I can tell."

He held up his hand. "Maybe if I'd been around more, I could have taken some of her edge off. Maybe a father's influence . . . I don't know." He swallowed some beer. "But you're accusing her of something. And I don't like the way it sounds."

"Why did she want Jared to go on TV so much?" Jenna asked. "Why did she try to lead us into an ambush?"

"She didn't do that, Jenna. She wants her mother to be found. She wants this murderer to be arrested."

"And how does humiliating us on national TV accomplish that?"

"You said yourself it could have been those other kids who said something."

"Do any of them do anything without Ursula saying it's okay? We know who the queen bee is, don't we? And let's be honest: We knew who the queen bee was when we were in school. We know who always got what she wanted."

"I guess I should have expected that comparison."

Jenna knew she'd pushed. Too hard, maybe. Her emotions had turned on a dime, from the wistful loss she'd experienced when she walked into the house to the vein of anger she carried with her best friend's name on it. Talking to Ian dug it out of her, brought it up into the light.

Ian didn't say anything right away. He drained his beer and contemplated the empty for a moment. Then he turned on the tap and rinsed the bottle out, his movements methodical and precise.

While he worked at the sink, Jenna watched, her stomach churning. She'd jumped the track, taken them down a path she hadn't intended to travel. But Jenna always believed, always had and always would, that it was better for things to be out in the open than bottled up inside.

He dried his hands on a towel and turned to face her. His expression was calm except for his eyes, which seemed alive with a new energy.

"You think you understand everything, don't you?" he asked.

And Jenna knew the question didn't require an answer. Ian was going to keep on talking.

CHAPTER FIFTY-NINE

Jared and Mike tried to blend in. They passed through the crowds of kids, music thumping in the background. Kirk Embry lived in one of the big old homes around downtown. His father ran a consulting business, and his mother was a lawyer who appeared every day in TV commercials advertising her firm. They were out of town, attending a family wedding, and Kirk stayed behind. He was a junior who came to school every day in a sleek black BMW.

A few people gave them funny looks as they navigated the rooms. Jared tried not to imagine questioning stares and sneers where there weren't any, but he knew they didn't belong with this group. He and his friends were a little too young, a little too unpolished, even Mike. Jared simply wanted to find Ursula and then get out.

"I have to tell you something," Jared said.

"What?"

"The booze came up on national TV tonight."

"Are you kidding me?"

Jared explained about Reena's revelation. "Don't worry," he said. "Your name wasn't mentioned."

"Shit," Mike said. "What if my parents see that? They'll get pissed all over again. They always blame me, even when I didn't do anything."

"I'm the one in hot water now," Jared said.

"Why can't everybody keep their fucking mouths shut?" Mike said, and he stormed off.

Jared thought about following him, but he let his friend go. He slipped through the kitchen, where a keg of beer in a large plastic tub drew a crowd of his classmates like flies to sugar. They held plastic cups before them, supplicants to the senior who held the nozzle. The guy filled the cups of the pretty girls first, and when the pretty girls were gone, he turned to everyone else.

Jared went out the back door onto the patio. The crowd was smaller there. The night air was cool, and the people on the patio smoked and drank, filling the air with the fumes of alcohol and cigarettes. A little farther in the darkness, near the covered swimming pool, two kids were making out, their heads rolling from side to side in search of the best kissing angle possible. Jared thought of Natalie when he saw them. He couldn't help it. And it wasn't just the kissing and the fooling around he missed, although he very much missed that. Even in a few weeks' time, he knew he could count on Natalie, knew she'd take his side no matter what was wrong. Seeing the couple together, two people so wrapped up in each other, made him feel lonely, as if he were the last man on earth even in the midst of the crowded party.

Someone sat on the diving board, his feet dangling over the thick green tarp that was pulled tight over the pool with a series of dark ropes. The tarp looked like part of the ground, something a person could walk across and never know there was water underneath. The guy on the diving board took a drink from a bottle of whiskey, tossing his head back as he threw down the liquor. He smacked his lips, the noise reaching Jared in the dark. It was Bobby Allen.

Jared walked over, his shoes scuffing against the concrete pool deck. Bobby looked up when Jared approached, his eyes heavy lidded and wary. Jared remembered what Ursula had said in the park the night before, her mention of a falling-out between them.

"Hey, Bobby."

"Hey."

Jared looked around. The couple that had been making out suddenly stood up and walked inside, hand in hand, no doubt searching for a vacant bedroom. The music still thumped but was muffled by the walls and doors of the house. Jared knew how these parties ended. Some neighbor would call the police. They'd break it up, send all the kids scattering into the night.

"Have you seen Ursula?" Jared asked, cutting to the chase.

Bobby made a noise somewhere between a snort and a laugh. "She was here earlier."

"She left?"

Bobby took another drink and then he tilted his head back, taking Jared in. "You love her, don't you? Ursula."

"No, I don't."

"You want to fuck her."

Jared didn't feel like arguing or verbally sparring with a drunk rich kid. "I'm sorry about your dad, Bobby. I'll see you around."

"You don't have a dad either, do you?"

Jared didn't say anything. He looked at the house. If Ursula was gone, there was nothing and no one for him to find in there. He wanted to just slip away, maybe even leave Mike to whatever adventures he had found.

"Ursula told me all about you," Bobby said.

"Why was Ursula talking about me?" Jared asked.

"Who knows? The girl talks. She talks and talks." He held up the bottle. "Want some?"

"No, thanks. I guess there's nothing new about your dad's case."

Bobby shrugged. "Cops say they keep getting reports about this William Rose guy. Once they put the word out, everybody thinks they know where he is. Like with Ursula's mom. People think they see her everyplace, just because her face is all over TV. I guess they all think they're going to be the hero and save the day. What do you want Ursula for if you don't want to fuck her? I mean, you guys aren't friends or anything."

"I just wanted to talk to her about something."

"She probably went home." He pointed to an empty space next to him on the diving board. "She was right here. Right in this spot."

"She told me you two had a falling-out."

"We always do." Bobby shrugged, the liquor bottle

waving in the air. "She's always mad at someone. Me, you. Her mom, her dad, her cat. Always mad."

"She was like that as a kid too," Jared said. "She told me off all the time when we were little. I guess some things never change."

"They don't."

Jared started to walk away.

"Hey," Bobby said.

Jared turned back. Bobby had shifted his body a little. He sat farther out on the diving board, his legs dangling more quickly.

"It feels a little like spring, doesn't it?" he said.

Jared hadn't noticed. It still felt cold, as far as he was concerned. But Bobby was right that the temperature was a little higher, the air and the wind less biting. He'd seen the forecast and knew some warmer temperatures would be arriving during the next week. Highs in the mid-fifties, maybe even near sixty, a little hope amid the gloom.

"I wish I was graduating," Bobby said. "I'd be getting out of here, moving someplace else. When the warm weather comes, it's time to go. Am I right?"

"Sure," Jared said, although he didn't know exactly what Bobby was talking about. Maybe rich kids thought that way. They could imagine doing anything and getting away with it, even dropping out of school. But he and Bobby weren't that different after all. Jared dreamed of leaving Hawks Mill, of going someplace very different. Everybody must at one time or another.

"Everything will be different then," Bobby said. "So maybe I'll go."

CHAPTER SIXTY

Ian walked across the room and sat again. He placed his hands on the tabletop, and he looked calm, almost professorial. "I've already told you I wasn't perfect, as a husband or as a father."

Jenna felt uncomfortable as she sensed a revelation coming.

"I felt I had to protect my family. After Celia . . . wandered, I didn't know what to do. I wanted to protect Ursula. And Celia, frankly."

"And you wanted to protect yourself."

He nodded. "Self-preservation was part of it. Sure. I just knew if Celia strayed again, she could be putting not only our family in jeopardy but also herself. See, I always worried something like this would happen."

"Something like a kidnapping?" Jenna asked.

"Something dangerous. When someone, a woman, puts herself out there that way, she risks the consequences of being around a man who doesn't feel any loyalty to her.

No commitment. No honesty. An affair is built upon lies, isn't it? So what's to stop that man from doing nothing but lying to the woman?"

A clock above the kitchen doorway ticked. Jenna remembered going along with Celia when she registered for wedding gifts. The two friends laughed a lot that day, joking about the kinds of things they could add to the registry to shock the guests. Silk sheets. Or a box of rubbers. One of the things they selected—in all seriousness—was the clock that still ticked in the Walterses' kitchen seventeen years later. Something itched below the surface of Jenna's mind.

"What form did this 'self-preservation' take?" Jenna asked.

"It's more complicated than that. I want to explain myself."

"You were worried about an affair, or Celia being in danger. You were also worried about your reputation. The family's reputation. The foundry. A straying wife in a small town isn't good for business."

Ian made an exasperated noise in his throat. "Don't try to reduce me. Or my family."

"You weren't worried about that?" Jenna asked.

"I worried about my family more."

"So, what did you do with all this worry?" Jenna asked.

"Jenna . . . because of my job, I have access to certain people and things that an ordinary person might not have access to. You're right—a company needs to protect its reputation. And there are people who can do that for us."

"You mean PR people?"

"No, I don't mean that."

"Then what?"

"I've been clear about this with the police," he said. "I talked to them again when that man died. Henry Allen. His son and Ursula—"

"Holy crap," Jenna said. She remembered her conversation with Ursula in the park. "Did you know Henry Allen?" she asked. "The guy who was just murdered in William Rose's house?"

Ian sounded reluctant. "I knew him. Some."

"Did Celia?"

"No," Ian said. "He and I were once in a foursome at the country club. Some tournament thing to raise money for charity. Golf and then drinks. The usual bullshit."

"But you knew him well enough," Jenna said. "Well enough to enlist his services?"

Ian didn't respond. A flush rose on his cheeks. He looked down at his folded hands, staring at them as though he could open them up and find some wisdom hidden there.

"So, what happened? You had drinks together at the club and that loosened your tongue?" Jenna said. "And then how did it come up? You started bemoaning the fact that you couldn't keep your woman at home?"

Ian looked up. "Hold on. You're making it sound so nefarious. I told you I was trying to keep the family together."

"So you talked, and he told you what? That he knew a guy? A guy who could do the job for you? And you asked Henry Allen to have someone follow Celia?"

"I did. And yes, Henry did have employees who could follow Celia. It was supposed to be simple. Keep an eye on her when she left the house in the evenings and let Henry know if they saw anything suspicious. I called a number when she was going out and told them. Or I'd call them if I wasn't going to be home. If they didn't see anything, they didn't tell Henry anything. No news was supposed to be good news. I was trying to protect Celia. And the truth is, they never saw anything. Nothing was ever reported back to me."

"She was right," Jenna said. "Celia was right. Someone was following her."

"Maybe. We don't know—"

"And you trusted these guys?" Jenna asked.

"I trusted Henry. He's a prominent businessman in town. He wouldn't hurt anybody."

"Businessmen never hurt people, do they?"

"Jenna, you know I'd never put my family in danger."

"What did you tell the police about it?" Jenna asked.

"I gave them Henry Allen's name, Jenna. I told them the whole thing." He tapped his fingers against the table a few times. "They questioned him, but I don't know what he said. And when Henry Allen turned up dead, I told them again. Even though I didn't need to. They remembered, of course. What are they supposed to think when a guy who might have been involved with having my missing wife followed turns up dead? It looks bad, doesn't it?"

"Bad for who?"

"Everybody."

"So they're all connected. Ian . . . you . . ."

"I was trying to protect all three of us. To ensure that our family would make it. Celia had been wandering. Hell, I thought about having Ursula followed, but I couldn't bring myself to do it. I think kids should be free to make mistakes and learn from them."

"But not wives?"

Ian started to say something, but then he just nodded, almost like admitting defeat.

"Jesus, Ian. Celia said she thought someone was following her. You know what? I thought she was just being paranoid, seeing shadows that weren't there. But she wasn't crazy, was she? She was being followed."

Jenna was up, grabbing her coat and heading for the door.

CHAPTER SIXTY-ONE

Jared felt as if he was on a wild-goose chase, walking through the streets of Hawks Mill hoping he'd come across Ursula. All he knew from Bobby was that she'd left the party early, possibly heading home. But she could be anywhere in town—another party, a friend's house, a restaurant, a store. Jared didn't have a car, didn't have any easy way to find her.

And once he did find her, then what?

He wanted to ask her about her insistence that he do the interview as well as the information Reena revealed on TV.

Ursula and her family lived six blocks east of downtown in a neighborhood called Teakwood, on the opposite side of the heart of Hawks Mill from where Natalie's father lived. As Jared walked away from downtown, the houses were newer, built mostly after World War II, and the streets felt more suburban, like something you'd see in a movie about kids who were rich but not too rich. Jared didn't know, but he suspected Ursula's family could afford to live someplace more expensive, out in one of the fancier suburbs where the doctors and lawyers—new money, his mom called it—lived with their three-car garages and giant swing sets. But Jared knew Celia's family lived in Teakwood when she was growing up. She must have felt comfortable there.

Jared thought about turning around. The more he walked, the farther he knew he had to walk back to his house as the night grew colder. He thought about calling his mom for a ride, but then he remembered: She was already at Ursula's house. Maybe she'd even started back home.

At least that seemed to be her plan.

He started checking the cars that passed. If he saw his mom driving by, heading for home, he'd wave his arms, flag her down, and get out of the cold. But it was dark, and the headlight beams glowed bright, almost blinding him.

And then he saw a figure up ahead.

He thought he recognized the size of the body, the gentle rolling bounce of her hips.

Was it Ursula? The girl was two blocks ahead of him, walking slowly in and out of the glow of the streetlights. He quickened his pace and saw he'd catch up to her easily. He tried to land gently, to make sure his footfalls didn't startle her in the dark. As he came closer, though, she slowed down, and he saw it was Ursula. She came to a stop next to a bench and slumped down. For a moment she stared straight ahead, her eyes fixed on the pavement, and then her body shook as she started to cry, her hands rising to her face to brush the tears away.

Jared felt like an intruder.

She was sobbing, her body shaking. Jared thought about walking away, turning around and leaving her to her private moment. But he stood still under a street-light, and Ursula looked over and saw him, her face coated with tears.

He couldn't leave then. Not unless he wanted to act like a completely heartless bastard.

So he moved forward. He expected Ursula to stand up and leave or tell him to get lost, but she didn't. He came alongside her and said the idiotic thing everybody says to someone who is horribly upset.

"Are you okay?"

She didn't answer with sarcasm. She shook her head as her breathing started to return to normal. Jared's hands were jammed in the pockets of his coat. He brought one out and gently, cautiously, placed it on Ursula's shoulder. He felt like a man testing a stove to see how hot it was.

"Is there something I can do?" he asked.

Ursula wiped at her face with both hands.

"I'm leaving," she said. "I'm sick of all these fucking people. And this fucking town."

"Do you want me to at least walk you the rest of the way home?"

"I don't care."

"Did something happen at the party?" he asked.

She looked up. "You were at Kirk's house?" Even through her tears, she managed to convey the appropriate amount of shock and dismay at the fact that Jared attended a party given by one of her friends.

"I was. Just for a minute. I saw Bobby."

Something flashed in her eyes at the mention of Bobby's name. But she said, "I had to get out of there."

"It seemed kind of lame."

"Not because of the party," she said. "Other stuff."

"Sure. I understand."

"No, you don't." She paused, sniffling. "Or maybe you do."

"I'm not sure what I know," he said.

Ursula stood up. She straightened her coat and wiped at her face one more time. Her breathing seemed to have calmed, and she wasn't crying anymore. She didn't say anything to Jared but just started walking, so he followed along. If she wanted him gone, she could tell him so.

But she didn't.

They walked side by side on the sidewalk, their arms occasionally brushing. Jared didn't know what to say, but it didn't seem right to not say anything. "I didn't go on TV tonight."

"So?"

"Reena revealed something really personal about me. And my mom."

"I don't care anymore, Jared. I really don't."

She seemed like the Ursula of the last few years, the one who acted as if someone had just slammed one of her fingers in a car door. Her behavior emboldened Jared to push.

"For some reason, Reena knew the stuff I'd told you.

The stuff about me making my mom late the night your mom disappeared. You must have told her, Ursula. Why did you do that to us after you wanted me to go on the show?"

Ursula stopped. Fifty feet away was the street she lived on. A right turn and she'd be home. She looked back at Jared.

"You don't understand any of this," she said.

"I know. That's why I'm asking."

"Get lost," she said.

"I'm going with you. I'm pretty sure my mom is over there asking your dad these very same questions. And it's too cold to walk home."

"Your mom is at our house? Talking to Dad?"

"Yes."

"Fuck this," she said. And kept on walking.

CHAPTER SIXTY-TWO

Jenna reached her car and pulled the door open. She climbed in, tossing her purse into the backseat. When she started the engine, the lights came on, adding illumination to the Walterses' front yard. Ian dashed from the house, coatless, and came across the lawn before she could pull away.

He gestured for her to roll down the window.

Jenna thought about backing away, dropping the car into gear and leaving Ian standing there in his own driveway watching her go. She tried to process what he'd just told her—what she'd guessed at and been correct: that Ian used Henry Allen's employees to follow Celia.

Jenna pressed the switch and powered the window down.

"Did *he* follow her?" she asked.

"Who?"

"Goddammit, Ian. William Rose. The guy they suspect of killing Celia. Is he the one who followed her? Tell

me you have something to say about this that makes
sense."

"I don't know who followed her," he said. "I don't
know if it was William Rose."

"What did the police think when you first told them
about this?"

"What do you think they thought? It was unpleasant."

"Unpleasant? Ian. What did they think?"

"They didn't like the way it made me look."

Jenna pressed the button, starting the window up.

"Wait," Ian said, his hand against the glass.

Jenna stopped the upward progress of the window.
But she didn't move it any lower.

"Can I get in the car and talk to you?" he asked. "It's
cold, and I feel like you need to hear this."

Jenna didn't answer right away. She checked the clock
on the console. It was getting later.

"Or you can come back into the house," Ian said.
"I'm okay with either one."

Jenna undid the locks. "Get in," she said. "But I don't
want any evasions."

"Have I been evading?" he said. "I've been telling you
everything. I'm trying to tell you more."

He moved around the front of the car, his body passing through the cone of the still-glowing headlights. He
opened the door and settled into the passenger seat. He
rubbed his hands together once he was sitting, and Jenna
reached forward and turned up the heat.

"Okay," she said. "Tell me why I shouldn't be completely outraged about this."

She waited for Ian to start. She saw him in profile. She would have sworn there was more gray at his temples than the day in the Landing, as if even more layers of strain had been piled on top of him in the matter of a week.

"When Jenna cheated on me the first time," he said, "we tried to keep it between the two of us. We didn't want anyone to know. And we really, really didn't want Ursula to know."

"I can understand that."

"She was only twelve at the time. Not that her age really mattered, but we both felt strongly that she shouldn't find out." When he looked at Jenna, his eyes were wide and pleading. She saw the remnants of the long-ago hurt inflicted by Celia, and it tempered her anger. She'd been wounded too. Deceived by Celia. Not like him, but she understood the feeling. "I felt strongly Ursula shouldn't know. I couldn't imagine our daughter, my daughter, looking at her mother with that kind of contempt or disappointment. Could you?"

"No. I get that." Jenna was listening, taking in his story.

"Best-laid plans. Ursula found out. She heard us arguing one night when we thought she was asleep. Looking back, it seems foolish to think we could have kept it from her when there were just the three of us living together. She could feel and see the strain. She could hear the fights. We thought about sending her to live with Celia's mom for a while, so she wouldn't find out, but how would we explain that to anyone?"

The engine hummed beneath their words, a soft rumbling bass line.

"So Ursula found out?" Jenna said. "And?"

"It was bad. It was really bad. You know what Ursula's like. She's so . . ." He snapped his fingers in the air, searching for the right word.

"Hard," Jenna said.

"Yes, that's it. But she hadn't always been quite like that. You know it."

"She's always had a temper."

"Oh, Jenna. The coffee table thing was over ten years ago. They were practically babies."

"Okay. I hear you. I can't imagine what it would be like to learn that about your mother. It could change a person."

"Right. She became *hard*. Difficult. It was like she'd grown an exoskeleton around her body. An armor. Not just normal teenage stuff. Quite frankly, and I say this with all the love in my heart for her, but if she wasn't my daughter . . ."

He left the thought unfinished, but Jenna knew what he meant to say. *If she wasn't my daughter, I wouldn't like her at all.*

"You two always seemed pretty tight," Jenna said. "You and Ursula."

"You mean she knew how to get whatever she wanted from me?" Ian smiled as he said it.

"Lots of daughters can do that with their fathers."

"I guess I'm a softie. Maybe that happened because she's an only child. Who knows?"

"I've noticed the change in her over the last few years," Jenna said.

"All teenagers get a little mouthy and a little standoffish. It's a difficult time. But it became more than that with Ursula. She was openly contemptuous with both of us, and she really turned on Celia. She was furious at her. Barely spoke to her. She really shut her out. I caught some of it too, but not as much." He rubbed his chin, his face lit up by the dashboard display. "I never understood why she held it against *me*. I was as much a victim of the affair as she was."

"God, Ian. Don't be a martyr. You're her parent. You were in the cross fire."

"I guess so." He continued to rub his chin. His face grew more somber. "When I suspected it was happening again, this last time, I didn't know what to do. I saw our lives just unraveling. It was like tugging on a loose thread and then everything coming apart. I had to stop it. Or try to contain it at least."

"So you spied on your wife."

"I'm not proud of it." His face turned more serious. He wore a look of wincing, searing pain. "I have to live with this, Jenna. No matter what happened to Celia, I have to live with the fact that I may very well have put her in grave danger. It keeps me up at night just thinking about it. I feel sick. Physically sick. And sick of myself." He let out a long, slow breath. "I have to live with that the rest of my life. I just want you to understand it. I wasn't making some rash, heartless decision."

Jenna wanted to be mad but couldn't. Even in high school, she'd never heard Ian so open, so vulnerable. And she could relate to the desire to protect her family at almost any cost.

"Like I said, I don't know if it was actually William Rose or someone else who Henry Allen found to keep an eye on Celia. I certainly wouldn't have gone along with it if I knew a madman was going to be involved. Never in a million years."

Jenna couldn't decide if she felt better or worse knowing what she knew. The knowledge that Ian had invited a possible connection between Celia and her killer sat like a heavy stone in her gut.

She leaned back, letting her head rest against the seat. "And whoever followed her didn't bring you evidence of an affair?"

"No. How do I even know how good a spy he was? Maybe he just wanted to take someone's money."

Jenna couldn't sort through it. The blowing heat made the car feel close and confined. It was getting late, and her eyes felt tired.

"I have to go," she said. "I have to get home to Jared."

Ian shifted in his seat. Jenna thought he was getting ready to leave, reaching for the door handle. But he kept talking.

"None of us are perfect here, Jenna. We've all made mistakes."

Jenna wasn't sure what else she could say to him, wasn't sure how to offer support. She reached out and patted him on the shoulder, a gesture that felt both weak and ineffectual. But she wasn't sure there was anything else she could do.

He leaned over, and they hugged. It too felt awkward, and Jenna made sure not to hold on too tight or too long. Sally was right. There couldn't be anything else between them. Not even the remnants of a teenage fantasy.

She moved back, still disgusted by his revelations. "Let's talk another time. Just let me know if you need anything."

And then someone knocked against the window on Ian's side of the car.

Jenna jumped. Ian turned and looked through the glass. It was Ursula, her mouth open, her face emanating disgust.

"Jesus, Dad," she said, her voice muffled by the glass but still audible. "Fuck you."

"Honey, wait."

He was opening the door, letting the cold air of night into the car.

CHAPTER SIXTY-THREE

When they came in sight of the house and saw his mom's car parked in the driveway, Ursula quickened her pace. She moved so quickly Jared couldn't keep up, even though he started jogging to make up the gap.

He could tell the car was running. The lights were on and a faint trail of exhaust puffed out of the back. He saw people inside, sitting in the front seat, their bodies silhouetted in the glow from the console display. His mom. And? Ursula's dad?

Ursula stopped when she came alongside the car. She stared in the passenger window for a moment, and then she stepped forward and beat against the glass with the side of her fist. Then the door was opening, and Ursula's dad was stepping out into the cold just as Jared arrived.

"Jesus, Dad," Ursula said, her voice becoming thin and brittle in the cold. She sounded like a little girl. "First Mom. And now you?"

"Ursula . . ."

Her dad held his hands out in front of him, trying to get her to calm down and listen. Jared couldn't tell what she'd seen in the car that set her off.

"And you're doing it with her," Ursula said, the words coming out of her mouth like spittle.

"We were just talking."

"You were fucking kissing her."

"No, I wasn't. Ursula, calm down."

Ursula stormed off toward the front of the house with her dad following along, calling her name. Jared watched as they went through the front door and inside.

When they were gone, he looked into the car, through the still-open passenger door.

"Mom?" he said.

"Get in."

"Is everything okay?" he asked.

"It's fine. Come on, it's cold."

Jared got in and closed the door. The car felt warm, mercifully warm, and he held his hands up to the vents as his mom backed out of the driveway. When they were in the street and moving away, she asked, "What the hell are you doing running around at night? After I called the police and told you to stay inside?"

"I went to find Ursula. I wanted to see why she was saying those things."

"And? Do you think that gets you off the hook?"

"She just acted like it was more complicated than I could understand." He pictured her sitting there on that bench, wiping the tears off her face. He felt awful for her. Even Ursula, tough-minded, sharp-tongued Ursula, broke down sometimes and lost her shit. "She was crying. I think there was something else going on. I went to a party at Kirk Embry's house. That's where Ursula was. Bobby Allen was there too. They both said kind of the same thing, even though they weren't together when I saw them. They both said they were leaving. Like they both were thinking of getting out of town for good."

His mom didn't respond. She stared straight ahead, her eyes on the road. Jared could see she'd learned something, that ideas and thoughts percolated through her brain.

And he wondered what they could have been doing in the car that made Ursula freak out so much. Had Ursula said they were kissing? He couldn't just ask, could he?

"Did you learn anything, Mom?"

They turned onto their street. His mom didn't answer. She just shook her head as if she'd been made privy to some piece of particularly disturbing information. He wanted to press her for more, but the distant look on her face told him to hold his tongue. They were pulling into the driveway, and he knew if he gave her time to cool down, she'd probably tell him everything he wanted to know.

Not that he wanted to know if she was making out with Ian.

That he might be happy to remain in ignorance about.

His mom seemed to read his mind. Like always. "For the record, we were not kissing. I gave Ian a hug. He's upset."

"That's cool," he said. "I'm not worried about it."

She stopped the car and killed the engine. Before the

lights went off, something moved near the front of the house. A person. Only the legs were visible at first as they moved toward the car. Khaki pants and white sneakers moving across the lawn. Then he passed through the cone of the headlights. A man, tall and thin and almost sixty, whom Jared had never seen before.

His mom gasped.

"Do you know that guy?" she asked.

"No."

"That's not—"

"No, it's not her dad. It's not William Rose."

"Then who the hell is it?" she asked.

His mother reached for her purse. She pulled out her phone and a canister of pepper spray. The man walked to the driver's side of the car and waved. He wore a lopsided grin, and the zipper of his winter coat was open, revealing an untucked checked shirt.

"I'm calling the police," she said.

"Hold it, Mom."

"Who knows who this creep is?"

She lifted the phone. The man gestured. He wanted the window rolled down.

"Mom, just crack the window. See what he wants. Maybe he's selling something."

"This late?" His mom handed Jared the phone. She kept the pepper spray. "If he tries anything, he's getting a face full of this. And then you call the police."

"I'm on the case, Mom."

She pressed the button, opening the window less than an inch.

"Hi," the man said. His grin grew wider. He looked like somebody's grandpa.

"Who are you?" his mom asked.

"Are you Jenna?" he asked. "Of course you are. I recognize you. I recognize Jared too. I've seen you on TV and the papers."

"Are you a cop?" Jared asked. "Or a reporter?"

The man laughed. "Heavens no. I'm Rick Stearns."

He said the name as though it would mean something to them. Jared looked at his mom. Was he some kind of relative he'd never met and his mom had forgotten about? Jared hated when he met those people, the ones who knew who he was and he couldn't remember them to save his life.

"Who?" his mom asked. "I'm going to call the police if you don't explain yourself. Now."

"Okay, okay." The man laughed again. "Of course. Silly me. You don't know me as Rick Stearns. You know me by my other name."

"What other name?" she asked.

Then the guy said something weird.

"Domino fifty-five."

CHAPTER SIXTY-FOUR

Jenna told Jared to get out of the car and go to the house.

"Mom—"

"Just go," she said. "Walk to the door."

She kept her eyes on the goofy, smiling face of Domino55. Rick Stearns. He looked as though he should be coming to the door to sell insurance. Or else teaching math at the local community college.

Jared's door opened and closed, and only then did she turn away and watch her son climb the front steps and use his key to enter the house. Like a good boy, he flipped the porch light on, and then she saw the curtains move as he stuck his head out to check on her.

"Move back," Jenna said. "I'm getting out. And I have my pepper spray ready."

"Oh," he said, backing away from the car as she pushed the door open.

She stepped out onto the driveway, her shoes scraping

against the pavement. She kept the pepper spray clutched in her right hand and her keys, their tips sticking out through her fingers like jagged claws, in her left.

Rick Stearns took all this in and moved back farther. "I can go if this is a bad time."

"What are you doing here?" Jenna asked. "Why do you keep writing me and saying those things about Celia?"

He blinked a couple of times. "Because I'm like anyone else on those boards. I want to help."

"If you want to help, go to the police. If you know something, call the tip line."

Rick looked wounded, as if she'd reached out with the keys and poked him in his soft belly. "Do you think they listen to a guy like me? Hundreds of people, maybe thousands, call those tip lines. Some of them are nuts. They don't get taken seriously. And I live in northern Indiana, a few hundred miles away from here. I can't just talk in person to the detective investigating the case. Naomi Poole, right?"

"She's here in town. And now so are you. Go talk to her. Go right to the station. They're open twenty-four hours, I hear."

He lifted his hands, as though he were surrendering. "I wanted to talk to you first. You know Celia better than anyone. I want your opinion before I go to the police." He lowered his hands and sounded resigned. "I wanted to show you something. It's something you're going to want to see."

Jenna wavered. She looked to the house where Jared was still peeking out through the front window. It would be so easy just to dash inside and call the police, have Rick taken away, off her lawn and out of her life.

But what if he really did know something? What if he was one of those amateur online sleuths who managed to piece something together? Could she stand to turn him away?

"Where's your car?" she asked.

He nodded toward the street. A dark-colored Prius sat at the curb. In the glow of the streetlight, she saw the Indiana plate.

"Did you come here through downtown?" she asked.

"Yes. On Highway Fifty-nine."

"Go back the way you came."

"Wait a minute—"

"Downtown there's a place called Webb's Diner. It's also open twenty-four hours. Go there. Get a table. It's usually fairly crowded . . . and it's a block from the police station. I'll be there in fifteen minutes."

He smiled, his teeth straight and white. "Okay. Do you want me to order you something?"

"No. Just go."

He nodded and started off across the lawn. Before he crossed the street to his car, he turned back. "You really are going to want to see this. It's a picture. I think I found her."

Jenna watched him go and then she entered the house.

Jared waited for her in the living room, his phone in his hand. "Should I call the police?" he asked.

"Not yet."

"Where's he going? Are you just letting him get away?"

"Relax," Jenna said. She kept her coat on. "I'm going to meet him at Webb's."

"What for?" Jared asked.

"He claims he has information about Celia. And before you tell me the cops should be involved, I know. I've already covered this with him, okay?" She came forward and placed her hands on his upper arms. "You need to trust me on this one. I'm not going to endanger myself. We're going to be right by the police station, in a public place."

"Let me go with you."

"No. Stay here."

"Mom—"

"No. Stay here. I'm going to text you every fifteen minutes. If I miss one, call the cops. Okay? I need to know what he knows. He says he knows where Celia is."

Jared's mouth opened a little. "Do you believe him?"

Jenna hugged him, pulling him close. When she let him go, she looked him right in the eye. "I desperately want to. Don't you?"

CHAPTER SIXTY-FIVE

Jenna walked into Webb's, a greasy spoon that had been serving the residents of Hawks Mill since shortly after World War II. Several different families had owned the place, and Jenna remembered going there as a kid, her dad buying her a milk shake and a plate of french fries. She and Celia went there after school for hamburgers at least once a month, and Jenna had never imagined that the smell of fried food and coffee could summon so much nostalgia. The smells and the nostalgia washed over her in waves.

Rick smiled at her from a booth near the back. He faced the door, his lopsided grin almost sliding off one side of his face. The diner was about a quarter full, a mix of high school kids and families and elderly couples just marking time. Jenna walked through them to the back and sat down across from Rick.

"I ordered coffee and a sandwich," he said. "Do you want something?"

"No."

"My treat."

"What do you have to show me?" Jenna asked.

Rick looked hurt, but he recovered quickly. "Can I just shake your hand?"

"Come again?"

"I'd like to shake your hand." He held his out over the table, his sleeve just above the ceramic mug of coffee.

"Why do you want to do that?" Jenna asked.

"I've never met anyone like you," he said. He took his hand down when he saw Jenna wasn't going to shake. Again hurt passed across his face, and again it left quickly. "You see, I live in a little town up in Indiana. It's called Leesburg. Nothing really ever happens there. My dad farmed, but I worked in a factory. I'm retired now."

"Rick, is this relevant?"

"Now, hold up. You see, I live a little life up there. It's nice but slow." He held up his left hand. Jenna saw the gold wedding band. "I lost my wife four years ago, and since then I've been spending more time online, looking at missing persons cases."

Jenna swallowed hard. "Wait a minute. Lost her? Did she disappear?"

"No. Cancer. I'm lonely, so I'm online a lot."

"Oh." Jenna felt relief. She didn't need to hear another sad tale. Not that a lonely old widower wasn't sad enough. "I'm sorry."

"What I'm saying, Jenna, is I've never met a celebrity before. That's why I wanted to shake your hand. You're famous. You're on TV and everything."

He looked so sincere and pathetic it was sickening. Jenna held her hand out and they shook. Rick even placed his left hand over top of hers, a two-hand shake. The waitress came by and Jenna ordered coffee and a blueberry muffin. When the coffee came, Jenna poured more sugar in than she needed. But she loved coffee only when it was supersweet. She didn't understand the people who drank it black.

"Okay, Rick, you've got to tell me what's going on."

"Right. Sure. So I've been following this case ever since I first heard about it. And I've read all about the recent events, the things having to do with your son and that missing girl. You know, I'm sorry I didn't get to talk to him more. He seemed like a nice kid."

"He has to stay out of this stuff. It doesn't concern him. Not directly."

"I didn't like what Reena said about you tonight. I watched it in my hotel room here. I like her show, but sometimes it seems as though . . ." He seemed to be grasping for the right way to say what he wanted to say. "She has this tendency to turn against people." He spoke about the TV host as though she were a close personal friend. "She builds people up, has them on the show, and then at some point, she turns against them and tears them down. I guess it's for the ratings."

The waitress brought the muffin, and Jenna checked her watch. "About Celia?"

"Okay, I've been following the case. She had that affair. And they haven't found her body. They found that other girl's body."

"Holly Crenshaw."

"Right. And they found this man's body in the house where he was killed. But people have seen Celia other places, so maybe she ran away."

"She wouldn't leave her daughter."

"I'm sure you know this, Jenna. But Celia's grandparents used to own a house on a lake up near where I live. Sawmill Lake, it's called. Her grandparents grew up in Indiana."

Jenna sat back in the booth. Celia's grandparents did come from northern Indiana. They had died before Jenna and Celia met, but Jenna remembered Celia talking about family trips up there when she was little.

"How did you know she had family in Indiana?" Jenna asked. "Was it in the news?"

"Now, that's the funny part. It was someone on the message boards. At first, I thought this person was you because they seemed to know so much about Celia. But then I figured out who you were. To be honest, I just kind of guessed about you. Took a shot in the dark."

"How exactly did you figure that out?" Jenna asked. "It's kind of creepy, if you don't mind my being honest."

Rick looked hurt again. "No one's ever called me that."

"You'll get over it," she said. "How did you guess it was me?"

"Like I said, it was a guess. But you were so passionate about the case. You talked on the boards like you really knew Celia." He reached up and rubbed at his forehead. "I don't know how else to say it, except I felt your pain through the computer. It was palpable. You cared about Celia. Not because she was missing, but because you really knew her. Does that make sense?"

It didn't surprise Jenna that she'd revealed too much. She always did. "I guess it does," she said. "Who told you about the grandparents and Indiana?"

"This other person is just someone else who is curious about the case. But she's really encouraged me. I think she's a she. She says the picture I have really shows Celia living in northern Indiana."

Despite her misgivings and her desire to see Rick as a harmless kook, she felt her hopes rising, building in her chest and making her hands shake. She felt anticipation she hadn't felt in a long time, a swirl of rising emotion. "You have a picture? Of someone you believe is Celia?"

"I sure do. Right here on my iPad."

Jenna pushed her muffin and coffee mug aside. "You have to show it to me, Rick. Now."

CHAPTER SIXTY-SIX

Rick reached down below the table and brought out his iPad. He started swiping the screen while Jenna's heart rate increased, a steady thumping she imagined the other diners had to be able to hear above the clatter of dishes and murmur of conversation.

"It's not the best set of photos," he said. "It's tough to take pictures of someone when they don't know you're taking them and they don't want anyone to see them." He continued to tap and swipe. "My theory is Celia wanted to get away for a while, and it made sense for her to go someplace familiar, someplace she went as a child. It would be like returning to a simpler time. We can all relate to that. See, maybe she left the earrings behind to make people think she'd been taken. One in one place and one in another. Like she was dragged away or something. I read in an article that they were her favorite earrings."

"They're a family heirloom." Jenna reached across the table. "Can I just see it?"

"There's a few of them. Swipe left to see them all."

The first one showed a woman from behind. She appeared to be in line in a store. Maybe a hardware store, given the screwdrivers and socket sets in the background. She had brown hair, just like Celia's, but unless Celia had gained some weight since she disappeared, it couldn't be her. The woman in the photo was wider through the hips and butt than Celia had ever been. Or would ever let herself be.

Jenna swiped again. This time the woman was photographed at a gas pump, filling up her car. Her hair hung across her face, obscuring most of it. Same color, yes. But it could have been just about any middle-aged woman with brown hair. The clothes, functional and plain, didn't look like anything Celia would ever wear.

She swiped to another one. The woman wore sunglasses and carried grocery bags. There was no way to tell who it was, and disappointment crept through the center of Jenna's body. She felt like a deflated balloon.

"These don't prove anything," she said. "This could be anybody with brown hair. And Celia wouldn't wear these clothes."

"She would if she was hiding out," Rick said, his voice full of triumphant pride.

"Did you talk to this woman? Did you approach her?"

"I called her name once. I shouted, 'Celia!' And she stopped and looked at me. And then she kept going."

Jenna put the iPad down. She felt sorry for the old guy. Sorry for his enthusiasm and his loneliness and the disappointment he was about to feel when he understood he hadn't solved anything or moved them any closer to finding Celia. She could tell he desperately wanted to do something important and relevant, to be one of the stars of the Dealey Society, but some blurry photos of a middle-aged woman going through her daily life and a half-baked theory about Celia escaping to a place she went to as a child weren't going to cut it.

"It's not her, Rick."

"How do you know?"

"She wouldn't wear those clothes and you can't see her face. And Celia's body didn't look like that."

"Maybe she gained weight or something. To blend in."

"She wouldn't gain weight if her life depended on it," Jenna said. She reached across the table, past the iPad and the mugs of coffee, and placed her hand on top of Rick's. "I really appreciate you trying so hard. It does make me feel good that so many people care about finding Celia. It does. I've been on those message boards. I know how much people want to help. But I think you have a blind spot here. It's not Celia."

Rick managed to smile even though she could see the disappointment—and some sadness—in his eyes. "Are you sure I'm not onto something here?" he asked. "It felt so right."

"Did you show these to the police?" Jenna asked. "You said you didn't think they'd listen to you, but they might look at these photos."

"I talked to a detective back home," he said. "He basically blew me off."

"The photos aren't very conclusive." Jenna reached back

to earlier in their conversation, before the ridiculous photos appeared. "You said someone on one of the message boards told you about Celia's grandparents being from Indiana?"

"Yes. I showed her the pictures too. Online, in a private chat. See, I didn't want to share them publicly and make a big stink before I knew more. But I showed them to this lady, and she had a different reaction from you. She said she thought they *were* Celia."

"And this is the same person who told you about Indiana?"

"That's right."

"And who is this?" Jenna asked. Her phone rang. *Jared*. She had forgotten to check in. She held up her finger. "I'm sorry, Rick. I have to take this. It's my son."

"Jared."

Jenna gave him a look, one she hoped said *Back off*. She didn't like him acting so familiar with her son. Rick looked down.

"Hey, bud, I'm sorry," Jenna said. "I'm fine. I just forgot to call."

"Mom, you've got to get home."

He sounded frantic.

"What happened?"

"Just get home. You need to get back here."

"Did you call the police?" Jenna asked.

"We don't need the police. Just get here. I need your help. We need your help."

We?

"I'm on my way." She grabbed her purse and coat and stood up. "I have to get home."

"Do you want a ride? You said something about the police. I can help—"

"No."

She started to go, but Rick's voice brought her back. "Do you want to know the person's name so you can check her out?"

"Whose name?"

"On the message board. The one who saw the pictures."

"I don't care, Rick."

"Teddy Bear," he said. "That's it. Teddy Bear."

"Thanks for the muffin." Jenna rushed out of the diner.

CHAPTER SIXTY-SEVEN

Jenna raced across the lawn. Then she was up the stairs and trying the front door, which was locked. She fumbled for her keys and knocked at the same time. She was worried something had happened inside, that whatever was upsetting Jared had rendered him unable to open the door.

But before she pulled her keys out, she heard the lock unlatching from the other side. Jared yanked the door open, stepping back as Jenna came in. He looked unhurt, but his eyes were wide.

"What's the matter?" she asked.

He closed the door behind her and locked it again. She spun to see him better and asked the question once more.

He placed his hand on her arm and started guiding her toward the kitchen. "You've got to be cool, Mom."

"About what?"

"I thought about not calling you. I really did. I

thought about leaving and maybe telling you later where we were."

"Why would you do that? And who's we?"

"But I think we need your help," he said. "I think we're all in over our heads at this point."

They reached the entrance to the kitchen, his hand still on her arm.

Jenna saw Natalie Rose sitting at their table.

The girl looked scared. And dirty.

Her left cheek was smeared with something that might have been blood and might have been mud. Her jeans were streaked with dirt, and the material on her right knee was torn, exposing her skin. Her hair was greasy and matted as though she hadn't bathed for days.

"Shit," Jenna said. "Are you okay?"

The girl nodded, averting her eyes.

Jenna dropped her purse and coat on the floor. She moved away from Jared and toward the girl she knew was named Natalie. She watched Jenna with big, scared eyes. Jenna came alongside her and did the only thing she could think to do. She wrapped her arms around Natalie and pulled her close. Natalie didn't resist. She smelled musty and rank, but Jenna wouldn't let go. She didn't care about anything else but making sure the girl felt safe.

"Thank you," Natalie said, her voice just above a whisper.

Her mother was probably dead. How long had it been

since someone had held her this way? The way only a mother could?

Jenna straightened up. "How did you end up here?"

"Mom, can we go easy on her? She's been through hell to get here. She came to the door right after you left, so it hasn't even been that long."

He was right. She knew he was. Jenna turned back to Natalie and once again took in her condition. Dirty, ragged, smelly, and scared. No one wanted to sit around like that.

"Are you hurt?" Jenna asked. "I'm a nurse, you know. Is anything on your body hurt?"

"No. Not really."

"Do you want to take a shower?" Jenna asked. "Have you eaten anything?"

"I ate a little. But I would like a shower, if you don't mind."

"We don't mind. I have some clothes you can borrow. We can . . . Let's put these in the laundry room."

"You can throw them away," Natalie said. "I don't even want to see them again."

"Sure. Do you know where the bathroom is? You were here once before. At least."

"Only once," Jared said, his voice defensive.

"You can show her to the bathroom, then. Show her the towels and all that. I'll find some clothes for her to wear."

Jenna went to her bedroom and fumbled through her drawers in a haze. She tried to imagine the trail of craziness that had brought that girl to their door. She had nowhere else in the world to go, no one else she trusted or cared about. She looked so young, scared, and alone. Such a young age to be so adrift.

Jenna carried a small stack of things back to the bathroom door. She had sweatpants, yoga pants, a couple of T-shirts, and a sweatshirt. Jenna knocked lightly on the door and handed them through the narrow opening. "Take your time, honey."

Natalie thanked her. Once the door was closed and locked, the water started running.

Jenna nodded to Jared and they walked out to the living room together.

"Do you know what happened?" Jenna asked.

"Not really. She got away from her dad and came back here. She was looking for me. I don't think she trusted anyone else, not even the police."

"I don't doubt that. But we are going to have to call them."

"Mom, no way. You can see what kind of shape she's in. It's like she's shell-shocked or whatever. You know, PTSD. You can't have the cops come and question her."

"She's part of an investigation," Jenna said. "If we don't call, we get in trouble."

"Is that all you care about?"

"I'll ignore that remark. You know better than that." She went out to the kitchen and started pulling food out of the refrigerator. She could make grilled cheese or soup. Maybe heat up a leftover chicken breast and potatoes. She put the kettle on for tea or hot chocolate. Or both. Whatever the girl wanted. She felt Jared behind her, watching her movements in the kitchen. She waited for him to speak.

"Mom?"

"Yeah."

"Can we just take it slow? Let her get cleaned up. Let her eat."

And let her tell the story. Jenna wanted to hear it as much as Jared. Maybe more.

"Okay," Jenna said. "I'll be patient. For a short time."

CHAPTER SIXTY-EIGHT

W hen Jared saw Natalie enter the kitchen—her hair and face clean, a shy smile on her face—he felt the electric desire rising inside his body again. She looked so beautiful, so fresh and perfect, like a vision, even though she wore just an old sweatshirt of his mom's, one that advertised a clothing store in the mall nobody went to anymore.

Natalie placed her hand on his shoulder as she passed by, and then she trailed down his arm and squeezed his hand. Her skin felt warm, and he didn't even mind sharing the moment of affection in front of his mother.

His mom pulled out a chair at the kitchen table and handed Natalie a plate of food. Chicken, potatoes, a cup of hot tea. Natalie thanked her, and then they all ate together. There wasn't much conversation. Natalie ate quickly, and between almost every mouthful she stopped to thank his mom for her hospitality. His mom brushed it off, saying it was no big deal and she was just happy to see Natalie okay.

Jared had to admit, as he watched the two of them interact, that his mom really could handle herself in a crisis. She knew just the right things to say and the right things to do when someone needed help. She might push too hard sometimes and overstep her bounds, but he was thrilled to have her here taking care of Natalie.

Natalie ate two plates of food. When they were finished, Jared cleared the table and his mom sat at her place, her eyes fixed on Natalie. Jared knew what was coming. They all did. He knew they were all so quiet during the meal because they still needed to have the larger conversation, and everyone—especially Natalie—was saving up their energy for it.

His mom didn't hesitate. "Natalie, honey, we need to get in touch with the police. Everybody's been looking for you."

Jared finished what he was doing at the sink and came back to the table. Natalie sat between them, her eyes staring at the tabletop, her hands tucked into her lap. Jared wanted to reach out and take one of them, and so he did, lifting her hand in his. She looked over at him and smiled, their fingers intertwining.

"I'm afraid," Natalie said. "I don't have anywhere to go."

"What do you mean?" Jared asked. "You can stay here as long as you want. Right, Mom?"

"It probably doesn't work that way," his mom said.

"No, it doesn't," Natalie said, looking at his mom, her voice gathering force. "I know. My mom . . . I think she's dead. My dad . . . My grandparents are all dead too. I have an aunt, my mom's sister, but they were never close. I don't think she wants anything to do with me." She looked over at Jared, looking sad and resigned. "I'm a minor. I'm only fifteen. That means foster care. I'll get placed somewhere, maybe even back in Nebraska. I know kids that's happened to, and it's really shitty."

"But we can—we must be able to do something." He looked at Natalie and then back at his mom. She was giving him that look she always gave him when he acted naive or idealistic, a look he hated because it made him feel like a child. And by certain measures he still was. Certainly compared to Natalie, who had been through several lifetimes of experience in her fifteen years, maybe in the last couple of weeks alone. "There's nothing?"

Natalie was shaking her head. "That's why I came here instead of going to the police or anyplace else. I wanted to see you again. One more time before all this hit the fan." She squeezed his hand again, and her eyes filled with tears. "You've been so good to me. I know that."

Her words gave Jared a surge of pride. He reached out and wiped the tears from her cheeks.

"I love you," he said. "I do."

"I love you too," Natalie said.

He knew it was crazy to say it and think it so quickly, but he didn't know what the future held. Not even close. He wanted to say it. He wanted Natalie to hear it.

And so they sat like that for a long moment, holding hands and locking eyes, as though no one and nothing else in the world existed. Jared wished that moment could stretch out for eternity.

CHAPTER SIXTY-NINE

But his mom pierced the bubble.

"How did you manage to get here?" she asked. "Somebody spotted your dad in Louisville, and everybody's been looking for him. And you. But to be honest, a lot of people thought you might be dead. It's kind of amazing you're not."

"Do you think I can have more tea?" she asked.

"Sure." His mom took her mug and filled it at the stove. She dropped a new tea bag in and brought it back. "There you go."

"I haven't been very warm lately." She sipped the hot drink, her cheeks flushed. When she spoke her voice was as flat as the tabletop. "My dad killed that man in our house. Mr. Allen. I don't know what they were fighting about. It was something to do with the work my dad was doing for him."

His mom perked up. "Yeah, what was he doing for Mr. Allen?"

"I don't know."

"Was your dad following people?"

Natalie looked confused. "Following people? Like who?"

"Anyone," his mom said. She tried to sound casual, but Jared could tell she knew more than what they'd heard in the park from Ursula. "Anyone like maybe my friend Celia."

"Where did that come from, Mom?"

"Let her answer."

"It's okay, Jared." Natalie shook her head. "I swear I never heard anything about your friend, Mrs. Barton. I got the feeling they were doing something that might have been illegal. I'm pretty sure my dad knew Mr. Allen from some time before. My dad lived here once and came back because he knew Mr. Allen. My dad wasn't always with us when I was growing up. There were long stretches when I didn't see him, so he could have lived anywhere."

His mom leaned forward. She started to ask another question but stopped. Natalie knew what she wanted to ask. "I was there when it happened," she said. "I was locked in my room. He did that sometimes, just to control me. He didn't trust me because technically he had kidnapped me. He didn't have custody of me. He wasn't supposed to have me, but I went along with him. He's my dad. I didn't feel like I could say no or run away. That's why we lived under the other names. That's why he never let me out. I was locked in my room that night, and I heard them arguing. And then I heard them struggle like there was a fight going on. Then it all went quiet." She swallowed. "They didn't mention Celia. Not that I could hear. But I think I heard a couple of names mentioned. I'm almost positive."

"Who?" his mom asked.

"Ursula and Bobby."

Jared watched his mom's face. She looked as if she'd taken a blow, something sharp and unexpectedly painful. "But you're not sure?" she asked.

"I'm pretty sure. About an hour later, my dad came into my room. He told me to pack, and he told me I couldn't go in the living room. I didn't think there was a body there, but it didn't surprise me when I heard it on the news."

"Where did you hear about it?" Jared asked.

"He kept the radio on in the car sometimes," she said. "We knew people were looking for me. For us. Dad had some cash. He used that for shitty little motel rooms and fast-food restaurants. We hung out in rest areas and mall parking lots a lot. It was scary. Terrifying at times, running around like criminals, looking over our shoulders no matter what we did. But it was boring too. Just amazingly boring. I didn't have my books or anything. It was just driving around and driving around, like we were in a maze with no exit."

She sipped more of the tea, holding the mug with two hands. "Dad drove west for a while, like he was going back to Nebraska. And then he turned around and came back toward Kentucky. I didn't know what his plan was. I don't think he had one. I don't know that he was thinking clearly. He was floundering, I think."

"Why didn't you run away earlier?" Jared asked. He'd watched enough crime shows to know what Stockholm syndrome was and that kidnappers could exert such fear and control over someone that they wouldn't even attempt to get away. But Natalie seemed so clearheaded and logical, he didn't think she'd been completely controlled or subjugated by her dad.

"He promised me something, something I couldn't say no to," she said. Her eyes filled with tears again, and she let go of the mug and wiped them off her face. His mom stood up and found a box of tissues. She brought them to the table, and Natalie thanked her while she cleaned her face. "He told me my mom was still alive."

"And you believed him?" his mom asked.

"Mom."

"I'm sorry," his mom said. "Go on, honey."

"It's okay," Natalie said. "He told me he'd take me to her, that I could see her again. He kind of hinted she lived here. And then he hinted she lived somewhere else, somewhere back East. Maybe that's why he came back this way, to make me think I was going to see Mom."

"You must have asked a lot of questions," Jenna said. "You must have been curious about what was going on."

"I was," Natalie said. "You have to understand something about my dad. He can be very charming. Persuasive, you know? He knows how to talk. And he knows how to intimidate people. I didn't want to ask too much. He told me my mom was having problems. He hinted she was involved with drugs."

"Was she?" Jenna asked.

"I don't know. I doubt it. But she was depressed a lot. She tried to kill herself once after Dad left. I was really young, but I remember when she was in the hospital. I stayed with my grandma, who was alive back then." She swallowed. "What I'm saying is my mom wasn't really stable either. I know she loved me, but when Dad told me she'd left, it wasn't far-fetched. My mom hadn't been home for a couple of days. That happened sometimes. I just took care of myself."

"Really?" his mom asked. "You stayed alone?"

"I could cook. And wake up on time. I did my homework. And she always came back. She did. I didn't ask where she went. I figured she partied or was with guys." Natalie shivered. "I didn't ask."

"That's smart," his mom said.

"But this time Dad showed up at the house, and he said we needed to leave. He said Mom was gone, and we needed to go find her. I hadn't seen him in about six months. But he said he had a job, and he thought he knew where Mom was. That's why I went. She always had problems, and I thought we'd be helping her if we found her."

"But the police thought your mom might have been dead. They thought your dad—"

"I know." Natalie looked down at the table for a moment. She looked back up and said, "When I heard about your friend disappearing, about Celia, it just hit me in a strange way. I knew what that was like. My mom was gone, and I didn't know where she was. You were all going through the same thing. I understood. I really did."

"I wish we had talked about it," Jenna said.

"But I held out hope I'd see Mom again. He kept me in check that way, making me think there was a chance I'd see her. He said he hoped that someday we could all live as a family again. God, I wanted to believe it. I really did. Even though I was never able to call her or talk to her, I wanted to believe it." She looked at both of them and regained her composure. "Once we were out there on the road, and he kept promising without delivering, I knew he was lying. It hit me like a ton of lead one day. He was just lying. I started to believe Mom was dead. Gone." She stared ahead, her eyes flat, the emotion gone. "When I realized the truth a few days ago, I felt lower than ever. I didn't care if I died or not. I kind of accepted that I was going to die out there somewhere, that he'd kill me and just leave me on the side of the road. I thought it was all over."

"So what made you go on?" Jared asked.

"I had a dream about my mom," she said. "I saw her face. She told me to keep fighting. So I did. I decided I needed to get back here to see you. My dad was so tired from the driving and the sneaking around, he started falling asleep all the time. And when he slept he slept really deep. A couple of nights ago we were in a shitty motel, and he zonked out. It was about a four-hour drive from here. I just walked out. I didn't look back. And he didn't come after me. Some part of me kind of thinks he wanted me to get away. He could have killed me at any time. He could have tied me up. But he didn't. So I just got away."

"And how did you get from there to here?" Jared asked.

"I walked. I got a ride once from a trucker. He was nice, but he wanted me to pray with him. He brought me most of the way. I snuck into town here once it was dark. I didn't want anyone from school seeing me. Not the police or anybody else. I came here, and I saw that guy creeping around out front."

"He's harmless. I think," his mom said.

"Once you left with the guy, I saw my chance. I hoped Jared was home, so I went to the back door and knocked."

"And there you were," Jared said.

CHAPTER SEVENTY

_____

Jenna sat back.

She felt a terrible and profound sadness. This girl—and at age fifteen she was still very much a girl—had been through so much and lost so much. And somehow she'd survived it all.

And the girl loved her son. Jenna could see that. As much as two fifteen-year-olds could be in love, they were. And maybe someone like Natalie, someone who had seen so much of life so fast, understood the value and the meaning of love better than anybody.

Jenna wanted to protect them both, to wrap them both up and hide them away.

But Jenna couldn't hide from what Natalie had just revealed: William Rose and Henry Allen argued before Henry Allen's death. And the men mentioned Ursula and Bobby.

"You know, they think your dad might have killed my friend Celia."

"Mom—"

Jenna held up her hand, asking for silence from Jared. Jenna wondered if the girl knew anything about it. "I'm not sure they have any hard evidence, but they want to talk to him because he's been involved with some other things."

"I know," Natalie said. "Like that woman they found. The body in the woods."

"Holly Crenshaw."

"Dad always had girlfriends. Younger girls usually. I don't know if he was involved with this Holly Crenshaw lady. He didn't tell me much of what he did. But my mom always told me he had a perverted streak, that he liked to hurt women. I guess both my parents sound like real winners, don't they? But I don't know anything about your friend, Mrs. Barton."

"Jenna."

"Jenna. I don't know your friend. I never saw her, and I never heard my dad mention her. But I didn't know everything he did or everyone he talked to. I knew very little about him. He wasn't always a big part of my life. My parents were off and on. And Dad just kind of came around when it suited him. When he wanted or needed something. Mom had a hard time saying no to him when he did show up. She couldn't turn him away. I guess I couldn't either."

Jenna tried to focus. She had so many things she wanted to ask the girl, so much she wanted to know but couldn't push. She remembered that kiss Jared had witnessed, the one that prompted him to throw a rock through their window. Jenna wanted to know exactly how much the girl had suffered at the hands of her father, but that was all too much and too soon. She might never know what went on between the two of them. And maybe that wasn't what Natalie needed from her.

She looked at the clock. It was nearing midnight. She felt newly tired from the long day, wrung out and empty.

But the day wasn't finished. Not close.

"It's time we called the police and let them know you're here," she said.

"Mom, no." Jared was up out of his seat so fast he sent it tumbling backward to clatter against the floor. He moved next to Natalie, placing his hand on her shoulder as though protecting her from attack. "You can't do that. Not now. It's so late."

"Jared, the police need to know."

"And they can't wait until morning?" he asked, his face indignant.

"No, they can't. They're the police. And Natalie is involved in a crime. She's a witness. She knows where her dad was last. The man's dangerous, Jared. What if what she tells the police prevents him from hurting someone else?"

Her words brought him up short. He stood frozen in place, his hand still resting on Natalie's shoulder.

Natalie looked up. "She's right, Jared. The whole time I was coming here, I knew I was going to have to face this. I've been preparing for it." She made a sound like a short, bitter laugh. "I guess I've known my whole life I might have to testify against my dad. It was always going to come to this."

"Are you ready now?" Jenna asked. "Do you want to eat something else?"

"I'm good. I'm tired, but I'm good."

"You'll like Detective Poole," Jenna said. "She's very understanding."

"As understanding as the two of you?" Natalie asked.

"She's pretty good. But she might not heat up leftovers for you." Jenna reached for her phone and dialed.

CHAPTER SEVENTY-ONE

It was nearly four in the morning by the time Detective Poole finished with Natalie. The detective conducted most of her questioning in the kitchen, after Jenna brewed a pot of coffee and she and Jared retreated to the living room to give them space. Jenna turned the TV on, and the two of them channel-surfed, breezing past shows about dolphins and biplanes and priceless junk people found in their attics. They settled on a soccer match, the endless bouncing of the ball from one side of the green grass pitch to the other soothing their minds.

Jenna saw the tension and sadness on Jared's face, even as her own eyelids grew heavier. She tried to say something to soothe him, something that would make the whole thing easier, but the right words didn't come.

She dozed off at some point. She came awake with Naomi Poole standing over her, the detective's large glasses pushed up on top of her head and resting in the cottony billows of her hair. Jenna looked over and saw that Jared was gone. The TV still played, only it showed an infomercial for a chicken roaster.

"He's in the kitchen with Natalie," Naomi said. "They're having a moment."

"Are you finished?" Jenna asked, stretching.

Naomi took a seat in the spot on the couch Jared had vacated. "For now. I've already called in her father's last known location. At least as close as we could get based on Natalie's description. She's young. She doesn't know the highways and towns the way an experienced driver would. She didn't even catch the name of the place."

"She's not from around here."

"Right. Anyway, she was very helpful. And she's quite strong, considering everything she's been through."

"I was thinking the same thing."

Naomi spoke in a lower voice. "It's too early to tell about any physical or sexual abuse. Psychological abuse, yes. The girl's been pretty close to a prisoner. But it actually seems like her father wanted to keep her from harm. In a twisted kind of way."

"That's a relief. I guess."

"It's a hard one to unravel. He let the girl go to school. She was able to go out other times. He didn't have to take her away from here and go on the road with her. He could have . . . he could have been done with her."

"I thought of that. He seemed to want to have her around."

Naomi nodded. "I hate to use this word, since it seems like a perversion of the word and the idea, but maybe he really did love her. Maybe he really felt some-thing for the girl."

Jenna found the remote and turned the TV off. The more it ran, showing nonsense, the more her brain cells died. "What about that other stuff she said? The stuff about Ursula and Bobby?"

Naomi raised her eyebrows. "We'll certainly be look-ing into that. Very soon."

"What else happens now?"

"I send all this information to the state police, the State Bureau of Investigation, and the FBI. They share it along their networks and with the media. We hope some-body sees him. He's getting tired and desperate, accord-ing to Natalie. That's mostly to our advantage."

"She said she thought he might have wanted her to get away. Do you think that's true?"

"My experience is guys like this don't give up their toys so easily. He was probably just exhausted and she took advantage of it."

Jenna rubbed her eyes. Sleeping in the chair gave her a crick in her neck. "What happens to Natalie? She's wel-come to stay here as long as she wants."

Naomi was shaking her head. "I'm going to have to call Child Protective Services. She's only fifteen, and they need to open a file on her and get her examined by a doc-tor and a shrink. They're going to want to give her a full workup. As they should."

"And then?"

"She's going to go into the foster system temporarily, Jenna. They'll try to locate a family member, but from what Natalie says, there aren't any. They'll find her a place to stay."

Jenna sat up straighter, her neck pain forgotten. "Let her stay here. We've got room. We care about her."

"It doesn't work that way. I wish it did, but there's a whole process in place."

"Goddammit."

Jenna placed her head in her hands. She wished she could remain in that position long enough—not looking, not seeing—that the problems around her would be resolved in some favorable and benevolent manner. But she knew they wouldn't be. She wasn't a little kid who could play hide-and-seek until somebody else—somebody older and more capable—shouted the all clear.

It was her life. The swirl around her belonged to her.

"I don't want to let this girl go, Naomi." She kept shaking her head and spoke through hands still cupped over her face. "I had a couple of chances with her. Once when she was here and again when Jared hinted at some problems. And then I saw her, Naomi. She came to me in the parking lot at work. Why didn't I just grab her by the arm and not let her go?"

"Because you can't just do that to somebody else's kid," Naomi said. "And I don't have a degree in psychology, but you can't save every girl in the world just because your best friend disappeared and you hold yourself responsible."

Jenna took her hands away from her face. She studied the odd little woman on her couch. "Do you charge for this therapy?"

"Your tax dollars at work." She checked her watch. "If she goes into the system locally, they'll keep her in the area. You can both stay in touch with her no matter where she goes."

"But if she goes back to Nebraska to live with relatives, I'm going to have a teenager with a shattered heart."

"I think you already do." Naomi stood up. She smoothed her knit pants around her thighs. "I'm going to call them. It's Saturday now, so they'll be moving slower. It will give the kids a little time to say good-bye."

"Good."

"I don't want to leave her here without protection, so I'm going to stay until they show up. Unless you want me to take her to the station with me."

"No, I wouldn't want that." Jenna shivered. "But please, some extra protection would be nice. If that maniac is out there . . ."

"I'll be here. And there will be extra patrols." Naomi was starting to look even more tired. "I forgot to tell you. Benjamin Ludlow is finally sticking to one story. He's saying he didn't just find the earring the day he tried to sell it at the pawnshop. He said he's been carrying it around for almost three months. Almost as long as Celia's been gone."

"What does that mean?"

"He says he was out looking for cans, like he said before, but he saw a man throw the earring into the field where Ludlow found it. A young man, but he couldn't give much of a description. He says it was dark."

Jenna waited for Naomi to add something, and when she didn't, Jenna asked, "Does that help us?"

"A young man. Who knows? But no description and an unreliable witness." Naomi shrugged. "I'll let you know what I hear."

"I guess it's not William Rose."

"Probably not. If Ludlow is telling the truth."

Then Jenna asked, "This whole thing with William Rose, though. If he really hurt Celia . . . and Ian hired him, Ian put him onto her."

"He may have."

"Was Ian really forthright with the police about it?" Jenna asked. Her mouth felt dry, her chest tight. "I know you'll just tell me I can't know, but I have to ask. Was he honest with you?"

"In my opinion," she said, "he was. He directed us to Henry Allen right after Celia disappeared. We didn't find anything. We don't know if William Rose was in town then. As far as we can tell, he came and went a lot. We're still piecing together his movements at that time. Remember, Natalie started school here in Hawks Mill just about a month ago. When Henry Allen turned up dead, we looked again. William Rose's name came up, of course, but he'd already committed that murder. He was long gone."

"Thanks." But Jenna didn't feel much better. She felt sick.

"Ian's got a lot to live with, I'm sure."

"Thanks, Naomi. By the way, I met someone tonight. Domino fifty-five."

"The Internet troll? He came here?"

"The man himself," Jenna said. "He showed up claiming to have a photograph of Celia. Said she's staying up in northern Indiana where her grandparents used to have a place." Jenna read the interest on the detective's face. "I saw the photos. They're not of Celia. Just a woman with brown hair. He's a lonely old crackpot who likes to hang out on message boards and try to solve crimes."

"He should get a cat."

Jenna made a lot of noise as she went out to the kitchen. She walked with a heavy tread and cleared her throat once or twice.

But she found the two kids sitting side by side and holding hands. They both looked as though they'd been crying, and they both wiped at their eyes when she came to the doorway. She felt as though she was intruding, so she looked down at her feet and waited while they collected themselves.

"I think we're all tired," Jenna said. "It might make sense if we slept. I don't know if I'll be able to, but I might try."

"I am tired," Natalie said. "I haven't been sleeping much."

"Did Detective Poole explain everything to you?" Jenna asked.

"She did," Natalie said. "It's about what I expected."

"You can stay here as long—until—"

"Until they take me away," Natalie said. "I appreciate that. Thanks."

"You're safe here," Jenna said. "Detective Poole is going to sit right in the living room, and there are extra patrols in the neighborhood."

"Good," Jared said.

Jenna looked at the two of them. They looked perfect together. Battered and torn but perfect. She'd do anything for either one of them.

"I'm going to my room," she said. "I'm sure you guys can— Well, there's a futon in the spare room, Natalie, but . . . whatever."

She turned and went to bed.

CHAPTER SEVENTY-TWO

The morning sun leaked through the blinds.

Jared came awake, blinking his eyes against the light.

He held Natalie's body tight against his own, her breathing soft and even. Their clothes lay in a pile on the floor, and Jared realized he still wore the limp, wet condom. He made a mental note to thank Mike for giving him a couple when he first started spending time with Natalie, along with the advice *"Better safe than sorry."* Jared never dreamed he'd actually get to use them.

He stared at the ceiling. Natalie had shown him the way, guiding him through everything with patience and understanding. Once they started, Jared understood that certain instincts just took over. People had been performing the act for . . . however long there'd been people. He felt a momentary ease, lying there in the bed, a sense of amazement unlike anything else he'd ever experienced.

Natalie snuggled closer. Her eyes came open as she rubbed her hand over his pale, bony chest. Very little hair, and even fewer muscles. He knew he didn't look like anyone on TV or in the movies, and it didn't matter.

"Are you okay?" Natalie asked. "Go back to sleep."

"I have to go to the bathroom."

"Mmmm."

He couldn't tell if she was still awake. "You know, I'll see you wherever you are. I promise."

"I know."

"I can travel at school breaks and stuff."

"Sure."

"Hey," Jared said. "I have something for you."

He went over to his desk, trying not to feel self-conscious of his bare butt, and opened the top drawer. He came back to bed and handed a photograph to Natalie.

"I found that in the house when I went in looking for you," he said. "I thought you'd want it."

Natalie held the photo, her eyes filling with tears. She lifted her hand to her mouth and just stared at the image of her mother. Then she leaned over and threw her arms around Jared's neck, pulling him tight.

"That's the sweetest thing," she said. "This is my favorite picture of her."

She held on to him. And he let himself be held. The sex had felt better than he could have imagined. And so did the tight embrace.

"She looks just like you," he said.

"Everybody says that."

They held each other for a while. When they let go,

Natalie kept glancing at the photo, the tears wiped from her face.

Jared finally asked the question that had been on his mind. "Do you think my mom heard us?" he asked.

"No. And I don't think she'd care. She practically let us sleep together."

"That's true."

Jared tried not to think too much about his mom while he lay in bed with his naked girlfriend just after losing his virginity, but thoughts of her came through again. He knew she wouldn't have turned a blind eye to their sleeping together under just any circumstances. But she understood the world, understood how difficult things had been for Natalie. Given what had happened to Celia, his mom probably understood better than just about anybody alive.

Life is short. Time is short. You never know.

"What about Detective Poole?" Jared asked. "She's a cop. She hears everything."

"She probably ignored it." Natalie looked at the clock. "My escorts from the foster system haven't shown up yet. Maybe they believe in young love too. It is almost Valentine's Day."

"How romantic," he said. "I'll be right back."

He took care of the condom and then pulled on shorts and a T-shirt. Natalie tugged the covers higher up on her body and said, "Don't be gone long."

"Do you want me to stay?" he asked.

"I want you to pee if you have to. But do it quickly. I'm not crazy about being alone."

Jared bent down and kissed her on the forehead. He eased the door open and stepped softly toward the end of the hall. He stuck his head around the doorframe. Detective Poole sat in a chair, reading a magazine. She looked up.

"Hey, tiger," she said.

"Hey."

"Can't sleep?" she asked.

"Bathroom trip."

The detective nodded, a small smile on her face. "I understand." She looked at her watch. "The child welfare folks are backed up. You probably have another hour together."

"Thanks. You look tired."

"I'm no spring chicken. But I can sit a watch with the best of them. Even now." She tossed the magazine aside. "Go on. Time's wasting."

"Thanks." Before he went in the bathroom, he moved over toward his mom's closed bedroom door, pressing his ear against it. He didn't hear anything. Satisfied, he went back to the bathroom and stepped in.

While he peed, he tried to maintain the sense of euphoria the sex brought on but found it slipping away. True—Natalie was safe. That was the only thing that mattered. She was safe and away from her father. Even in foster care or whatever system they'd place her in, she'd be safer there than out on the road with a maniac. But she'd be going anytime, maybe forever. He felt the hole in his heart growing and spreading like a crater.

He flushed and then washed his hands. He paused for a moment before the mirror and studied himself. His hair stood up and his eyes looked puffy and tired. Other than that, no real differences. Would people at school see he'd lost his virginity? Would Mike and Syd know when he sat down at the lunch table on Monday morning? If they didn't, he would tell them. Maybe not right away, but eventually he'd tell them.

He reached for the knob. He heard a noise in the hallway. He pulled the door open, the adrenaline shooting through his body like ice water. He stood in the hallway listening, and then moved back to his bedroom. The door was shut. He could have sworn he'd left it cracked when he went to the bathroom. He pushed in. The bed was empty, the clothes gone from the floor.

Jared spun, and he saw Detective Poole at the end of the hallway.

"She's in the kitchen, Romeo. Getting a glass of water. I'm using the little girls' room, if you don't mind."

"Sure."

Jared went to the end of the hallway, scratching himself absently as he went. He had decided to turn around and wait back in bed when he heard the thump from the back of the house.

He waited. Head cocked.

He heard it again. And something like a muffled cry.

"Natalie?"

He ran for the kitchen and the source of the noise. When he entered he saw Natalie's dad, William Rose, and he held Natalie by the arm, trying to drag her through the back door and out of the house.

CHAPTER SEVENTY-THREE

William Rose stood in the doorway, his hand clamped around Natalie's arm. Jared saw the brute force exerted through the man's hands as he squeezed her flesh. He saw the ugly, offending lips that sneered his way.

"She's my daughter, and we'll be leaving now," he said.

Jared spoke with the simplest clarity. "No."

His heart pounded and his hands shook. He felt a strange, jangling electricity in every part of his body, something that compelled him to move forward into the kitchen, his steps cautious and catlike.

Natalie looked more resigned than scared. Tears covered her pale face, but she seemed in control of her emotions. She wasn't pulling against her father or fighting him. She didn't scream.

"It's okay, Jared," she said. "I'll just go with him."

"No," Jared said again, moving closer.

"Stop right there," her father said, holding out his free

hand. It was meaty and thick, like a fat holiday ham stuck on the end of his arm. His voice sounded like ground glass. "You're going to get hurt, boy. If you don't step off, you're going to get hurt real bad."

Jared heard someone behind him. He didn't turn, didn't take his eyes off Natalie and her father, but he knew Detective Poole and his mom had arrived and stood in the doorway. He heard his mother gasp, heard her breathing grow heavier as she watched the spectacle unfold.

Detective Poole spoke into a radio, requesting— *demanding*—backup. "We have a hostage situation."

Jared kept moving forward. He stood ten feet away from them. If he lunged forward, moving as quickly as possible, he could be on the man. He was about to when Natalie's voice stopped him.

"I'll go," she said again. "Just let me go. No one else will get hurt."

"Jared," his mom said. "Get back. Let the police handle it."

William Rose stood in the doorway to the backyard. He gave one more tug, pulling Natalie with him. But then Natalie gripped the door. She locked eyes with Jared.

Detective Poole came up next to Jared. She had her gun drawn. The overhead lights reflected off the black metal barrel.

"She's right. Get back." Poole's face looked determined, steely. A far cry from her usual grandmotherly appearance. Jared didn't doubt that she could—and would—use the gun. "Sir," she said to William Rose, "let the girl go."

"She's my daughter."

"Let her go and get down on the floor. We don't want anyone to get hurt."

"Jared, back up," his mom said.

"Sir, get down."

"I love you," Natalie said.

Jared sprang forward. He led with his right hand and clamped it up and under William's chin, grabbing hold of his thick, fleshy neck. He felt his nails sink into the soft skin, and he squeezed as hard as he could, the muscles and tendons in his fingers and forearms straining to their breaking points.

Something hit him once and then twice in the side of the body. William Rose's fist swung wildly, smashing against Jared, blows he couldn't feel in the heat of the moment. The fist swung a third time, connecting with the side of Jared's head, knocking him off-balance and causing bells to ring deep inside his skull.

But he saw Natalie pull free.

She made a quick dash to her left, breaking loose from her dad's grip.

William was then free to use both of his hands on Jared, and he did. He came forward while Jared still held on to his neck, adding pressure as much as he could.

Detective Poole came closer. She held a small canister in her hand.

Pepper spray.

She ordered Jared back. But he couldn't move. William Rose held him by his shirt, his grip like iron.

The blows from the meaty fists rained down on Jared.

He swung his right leg up, kicking with as much force as he could generate. His first attempt missed, glancing off William's shin. But when he tried again, he connected with flesh. Jared wasn't sure where—either the enormous man's groin or his gut. He didn't care. It stopped the assault for a moment, allowed Jared to reassert his grip.

But then one more punch fell, landing against the side of his head. Brightly colored stars and whirligigs swirled before his eyes, and then his vision clouded. Before the picture faded, something flashed behind William Rose.

A quick, blurring movement. Something swinging once and then again. William's eyelids grew wide and then fluttered, and he fell forward while Jared jumped back, avoiding the falling body like a lumberjack ducking a large tree.

William Rose hit the floor, his eyes closed. He groaned, reaching for the back of his head, where blood was visible.

Jared looked to the open doorway, expecting to see the police. Instead he saw Rick Stearns, Domino55, the old guy who had come to see his mom. He stood there holding a thick branch like a baseball bat, and he posed like a triumphant hunter over his prey.

"I got him," he said.

When William Rose stirred, as though he was about to stand up, Rick lifted the branch higher, ready to swing again.

"Hold it," Natalie said. "Hold it." She held her hand out, protecting him, and Rick stopped.

Detective Poole moved in. She pulled out a set of handcuffs and worked them over the man's wrists. She snapped them closed and then straightened, the pepper spray and the gun out of sight as quickly as they had appeared.

"I hear a siren," his mom said.

Within moments, the police were inside the house, swarming over the kitchen like uniformed ants.

Jared had never seen so many cops.

Some of them dragged William Rose out of the house while he continued to groan about the injury to his head. Different cops spoke to Natalie, Jared, Rick, and his mom. Paramedics hovered around as well, checking them all out. Jared told them he was fine, even though his side and his head started to hurt, dull aches from the blows William Rose had showered him with. He didn't care. He sat close to Natalie, their bodies touching.

Detective Poole drank a glass of water. And then another. She said to Jared, "I thought he had you in the last round, but you hung in there."

The paramedics paid a lot of attention to Rick Stearns. He sat at the kitchen table, drinking a glass of water someone brought him. Jared's mom stood close by him while they checked his blood pressure and heart rate.

"I came by the house to say good-bye," he said. "I was on my way out of town, and I wanted to thank you for listening to me." He smiled up at Jared's mom, but it looked as though it cost him some effort. Sweat beaded on his forehead, and his face looked pale and ashen. "I saw that guy creeping around like he wanted to come in. I recognized him from the TV and the Web. I really did. I knew who he was, so I dialed the police. They weren't far."

"That's why they got here so fast," Jenna said.

"He worked his way in the back door," Rick said. "Jimmied it or something. So I watched. Then I saw him coming back out with the girl. I heard the talking and the fighting. I figured he meant to hurt you or your son. I found that log out in the yard. I played some ball in high school. I knew what I was doing when I swung."

"Do you have a history of high blood pressure?" one of the paramedics, a woman with brown hair pulled into a tight bun, asked.

"I do. I had a small stroke—a TIA, they called it—two years ago."

"His pressure's sky-high," she said. "We're taking you to the hospital, Mr. Stearns."

"No, no," he said. "I don't want to miss anything."

"If you don't go to the hospital, you're going to miss everything," she said.

"You should go, Rick," his mom said, placing her hand on Rick's arm. "You've done more than enough. You saved us."

He smiled but still looked ill. "Thanks, Jenna. I guess I'm kind of a hero."

"You are," she said. "Wait until they hear about this on the Dealey Society page."

They brought a gurney in for Rick, and he protested a little as he climbed on board. While they wheeled him out the front door, he said to Jared's mom, "I wanted to tell you something else."

The paramedic shushed him.

"No," he said. "Wait."

"We can talk later, Rick. I'll visit you."

"No."

They stopped the gurney, and he sat up a little straighter and called to Jenna.

"I told you 'Teddy Bear' was online," he said. "It's not Teddy Bear. It's 'Little Bear.' Little Bear's been talking to me. She's the one who pushed me to think that picture really was of Celia."

Then they wheeled him out.

CHAPTER SEVENTY-FOUR

Jenna made sure Jared was okay. The social worker had finally taken Natalie away, after a painful good-bye, and he was alone in his room.

"I have to go somewhere," she said, standing in the doorway of his room, "but I'm not going if you don't want me to."

He sat on his bed, his eyes staring at the floor. He looked tired and worn-out.

"You know what?" she said. "Forget it. I'm not leaving you here."

"What are you doing now?" he asked.

She didn't want to tell him, didn't want to dig into all of it in case she was wrong. She *hoped* she was wrong.

She feared she was right. And if she was . . . "It's just—it's private. Personal."

He looked up then, a strange curiosity on his face. "Like a date?"

"Not a date. I can tell you all about it another time. Why don't you come with me?"

"No, thanks. I'm tired."

"But I can't leave you here—"

"They just caught the bad guy, remember? And if you try to get Grandma to babysit me, I'll scream."

"Are you sure you're okay here?"

"Mom, how many times in my life are you going to ask me that question?"

She hated the jaded tone in his voice. She knew he'd been through a lot, but she didn't want to think his soul was growing disenchanted with the world. He flopped back on the bed, closing his eyes.

"I'm okay, Mom," he said. "Lock the door behind you and I'll be fine. They arrested him. About fifty cops dragged the guy away. It's over." He rolled over and spoke into his pillow, his voice muffled. "They took Natalie away too. Remember? It's all over."

His words pierced her heart.

But she really needed to go.

"I've got my phone," she said.

She drove to Ian's house.

On the way, Jenna's phone rang. Her mother.

She considered not answering, letting it go to voice mail. She didn't need another lecture or scolding. But something in Jenna didn't allow her to just ignore her mother.

What if it's an emergency? What if she needs me?

So she answered.

"Jenna? I want to talk to you about that TV show last night."

"I don't have time, Mom. I know it was awful."

"*Awful*'s not the word for the way you were treated." Her mother sounded breathless. "It was . . . abysmal."

"The way *I* was treated?" Jenna said.

"Of course. There was no excuse for it. They shouldn't share your private business on TV like that. It's a violation."

"So you're taking my side?" Jenna asked.

"Don't I always?"

Jenna almost laughed. A million responses raced through her mind, but she held them all in. She felt real gratitude, a warmth in the center of her chest. Her mother could be counted on when the chips were really down. Jenna always knew that.

"Thanks, Mom," she said.

"Do you want to talk about this more?"

"I can't now," Jenna said. "I'm on my way . . . I'm going somewhere. But really. Thanks."

"Always, honey. Always."

Ian opened the door, wearing a button-down shirt and jeans. He held a pair of reading glasses in one hand and looked surprised to see Jenna standing on the porch.

She'd driven away from his house the night before feeling sick about his admission that he'd had Celia spied on, and he looked like a different person—one without the stardust glow she'd seen encircling him ever since the day they first met.

Jenna stepped inside and looked around. She smelled coffee brewing and maybe something baking. "Is Ursula home?"

"She's asleep. It's only nine o'clock."

"Have the police been here?" Jenna asked.

"Detective Poole called. She said she needs to come by later. What is this about, Jenna?"

"I need to ask Ursula something."

Ian closed the door and stood in front of Jenna, blocking her access to the rest of the house. He was a good eight inches taller than she was. His body was still trim, his shoulders still broad and thick. "What do you need to ask Ursula?" Then a knowing look crossed his face. "Are you still on this kick about why she wanted Jared to go on TV? Look, Jenna, I'm going to have to ask you to lay off of her. I saw the news today. They arrested that man." He lifted his hand and rubbed his eyes. He kept his hand there, obscuring Jenna's view of most of his face. "I've wanted this to end for so long, to just know something. And now that we might learn something, the real truth about it all, I'm terrified. I just don't want to find out. I don't want to get some final answer. What would I do then? Do you know?"

"Ursula didn't just push Jared to do it," Jenna said. "She went online, to message boards where they talk about missing persons cases. She went on there and she led another man on, making him think these photos he was taking in another state were photos of Celia. She encouraged this guy to think Celia was alive and living in his town."

Ian looked like a man who understood only half the story. He tilted his head to one side, as though her words might register in his brain and make more sense if he pointed his ears a different direction. "I don't follow any of this. Can we go out to the kitchen? Ursula's bedroom is right up there, and I'd like to know what you're saying about my daughter before she hears it."

Jenna looked up the staircase. She wanted to break past him, shove Ian aside, and go right to the source. But she held herself in check. No need to make a scene. No need to run wild.

Yet.

She followed Ian out to the kitchen, where he offered her coffee, which she accepted as she sat at the table. Her body felt energized, but she knew it wouldn't last. The mixture of adrenaline, fear, and lack of sleep would bring her back to earth soon. She'd crash like a meteor.

As clearly and patiently as possible, she explained about Rick Stearns, their conversations online and his firm belief that he had found Celia living in Indiana.

"Someone using the handle 'Little Bear' went online and told him that the pictures he took of this other woman were of Celia, even though they clearly weren't. 'Little Bear,' Ian. Ursula."

"Do you know how many girls in this country are named Ursula? And do you know how many people might call themselves 'Little Bear'? It hardly seems like proof that my Ursula was involved."

"But she told him Celia used to go to Indiana when she was a kid, that her grandparents lived there when she was little. How many people know that? I barely remembered."

Ian tapped his fingers on the tabletop. His nails were neatly manicured and even. "Any of her good friends would remember that. Maybe it was on the news. Knowing that one fact about Celia doesn't make someone special."

"Why did she push us to go on TV? Why did she tell Reena about Jared and the alcohol?"

"You don't know that."

"Ursula seems to be in the middle of a lot of things. Hell, Ian, she's friends with the kid whose father was murdered by William Rose. She's connected in a number of ways. Why?"

"Because her mother disappeared." Ian's voice rose, and he thumped the table with his right hand.

Jenna sat back. The volume of his outburst and the display of emotion caught her short.

Ian looked angry. A flush rose in his cheeks.

But he regained control of his voice. "Goddammit, Jenna. Her mother disappeared. Of course she's involved."

Jenna didn't know what to say.

Had she pushed too hard again?

But Jenna was in the middle of it too. And Jared.

She needed to know.

"Let's ask her, then," she said. "Natalie, the missing girl, she came back. To my house."

"She did?"

"She was there when Henry Allen was killed. And

Henry Allen and William Rose mentioned Bobby's name and Ursula's name. Why, Ian?"

"What are you implying?"

"Let's go ask her. We'll just ask her why those men, the men you had following Celia, were saying her name right before one of them killed the other."

"You want me to wake her up on a Saturday for this nonsense?" His eyes looked cold, skeptical. His voice still maintained an edge of anger. "You say you don't want Jared dragged into this. Don't you think I feel the same way about my daughter?" His voice sounded choked. "Our baby. She had a shitty night last night, in case you don't remember."

"I had a shitty one too. And you know Ursula has always had a temper. She's even been violent a few times."

Ian's eyes looked like glass. "Really, Jenna? You'd say that?"

"Do you want me to go up there and wake her?"

Ian rubbed his freshly shaven cheeks. His eyes remained cold. "Goddammit, Jenna, it's always something with you. You're always shooting off your mouth about something, always pushing people to talk when they don't want to. Or do things. If you'd left Celia alone that night—"

He stopped. But Jenna's cheeks burned. She ground her teeth together, holding her tongue.

Ian stood up, the chair scraping against the floor. "*I'll* ask her. She's my daughter."

She heard him walk to the front of the house, heard his shoes on the stairs, rising above her.

Little Bear. She trusted her hunch.

It was nothing but a feeling. But it felt right.

It made sense. And she didn't want to wait anymore.

She went out to the foyer, where the stairs rose to the second floor.

When she arrived, she saw Ian coming down, his face perplexed.

"What is it?" she asked.

Ian paused halfway. He pointed behind him, somewhere up the stairs.

"She's not there," he said. "I thought she was home, but she must have . . ."

Jenna went up, moving past him, and entered Ursula's bedroom. The bed was made, possibly never slept in. She looked around, pulled open some drawers. It looked as though things had been removed. Underwear, socks. She stepped into the bathroom. No toiletries were visible, no jewelry, no retainer or toothbrush or makeup.

She ran back out. "Ian? She left. Did you know this?"

"No. I swear. She was here last night."

"So she didn't hear they arrested William Rose?"

"Not from me."

"She ran away." Jenna moved down past Ian. She didn't know where she was going, but she needed to move. "Her things are gone."

He stayed rooted in place on the stairs. "My God. What have I done? How did I let her get past me and out of the house?"

"She's not a baby, Ian. She's fifteen. You can't control her."

"But her mother's missing. And now she . . ." He fumbled in his pockets, his hands shaking. He brought out his phone. "Let me call her. She wouldn't just . . . leave. Leave me."

Jenna watched his face while Ursula's phone rang. It rang and rang, and Ian's complexion grew more pale. He hung up and tried again. He still didn't get an answer, so he left a message.

"Ursula, honey . . ." He managed to keep his voice level, but Jenna could sense his struggle. "I need you to call me. As soon as possible. I need to know where you are. Right away, honey. Okay?" He paused but didn't hang up. "You're kind of scaring me, honey. I need to know where you are."

He lowered the phone and stared straight ahead, his body slumping back against the wall of the staircase.

"Why don't you come downstairs?" Jenna asked. "You can sit."

"I have to call the police, don't I?"

"Yes, you should. Right away. She could be in danger or running away. You need to know why she's doing this. Why now."

Ian nodded as he started dialing. "Why would she run now? After everything."

"I have no idea," Jenna said. "But you're right when you say we need to know."

CHAPTER SEVENTY-FIVE

Jared walked across town. The day promised to be bright and clear and warmer, but it was early enough for his breath to puff like little clouds as he moved.

He thought of Natalie. He didn't know where she was or who she was with. Detective Poole said she'd go to the doctor and then into foster care. She told him to be patient, to wait as the process played out.

The time ahead of him stretched out like an endless highway, like walking through quicksand toward a destination that receded farther and farther away.

He needed to do something besides sit in his room and wait.

His mom. She was off looking into something about Celia. He knew it. Something that old guy Domino said. It set her off. The old guy who saved his bacon. He hoped he was okay, that his blood pressure hadn't soared off the charts or blown up his brain.

After fifteen minutes of walking, the sweat forming in

his armpits and on his back, he came to Bobby Allen's street. It was the same house he'd lived in when they were kids, just a half mile from Ursula.

Jared walked up to the front door and was about to ring the bell when he heard a car coming down the driveway. Bobby sat in the driver's seat, and he looked over at Jared standing on the porch with his hand raised.

Bobby didn't look completely surprised. He stopped the car and rolled down the window as Jared moved across the grass.

"You looking for me?" Bobby asked.

Jared said yes, although it seemed obvious.

"I guess this isn't strictly a social call," Bobby said. "We didn't even do that when we were kids."

"I wanted to ask you something. I'm sorry, Bobby, but it's something about your dad. And Natalie."

Bobby didn't look surprised or offended. He waved his hand. "Get in."

Bobby looked as tired as Jared felt. As he drove, he gave off a jittery energy, the kind kids had when they'd been up all night studying and throwing down coffee to stay awake for a test. Jared chalked his behavior up to the weird aftereffects of grief.

"Where are we going?" Jared asked.

Bobby stared straight ahead. "That depends on what you ask me."

The first budding of fear sprouted in Jared's chest. Bobby drove downtown and around the square. He did it once and then he did it again, circling while Jared sat in the passenger seat.

Jared started. "Okay, so Natalie—"

"Your girl."

"Right."

"And the daughter of the guy who killed my dad." They were starting a third circuit around the square. "My mom told me they caught him today, by the way. At your house."

"Yeah," Jared said. "I'm glad they did."

"I was supposed to have gone somewhere sooner, but when that news broke . . . well, my mom was kind of upset. My sister too. I had to stick around, and then the cops came by again."

"You have somewhere to be?" Jared asked.

"It's probably too late," Bobby said. "I was meeting a chick."

"Ursula?"

"The cops say this guy William Rose is claiming he's innocent, that he didn't hurt anyone, including Ursula's mom."

"No surprise, I guess," Jared said.

"There could be a trial," Bobby said. "That would be shitty for my mom."

"Yeah, right."

"Your mom too."

Bobby left the square, heading west. No music played, and he seemed to be driving faster than the speed limit.

"Do you need to call your friend?" Jared asked.

"She keeps calling me. I turned the phone off."

Jared went ahead and asked the question on his mind, the one that had driven him to leave his warm bed when he was dead-dog tired and trudge over to Bobby's house in the late-winter cold.

Jared said, "Your dad, the night he was killed . . . you know, Natalie was in the house. She heard it happen. She heard them arguing and then fighting."

Bobby's lips were pressed tight. He stared straight ahead.

"You see, Natalie swears she heard your name come up. And Ursula's. During the argument. She told this to me and then to the police. Maybe she misunderstood, but I was just wondering if you thought that was possible."

Bobby didn't answer right away. They were out near the old state road, the one people used to take to Lexington before the interstate went in, leaving this one kind of forgotten. They came to a four-way stop, and Bobby let the car sit there, the heater humming softly, the engine a low purr.

"They talked about that, huh?" he asked.

"Yes. She heard them."

"And Natalie told the police this?" Bobby asked.

"She did. She told them a lot of stuff, but that's the part I noticed. I kind of figured they'd be talking to you and Ursula soon."

"They did talk to me," Bobby said. "This morning. But they didn't push too hard. I told them it kind of made sense my dad might say my name to someone who wanted to kill him. Right?"

"And Ursula's name?" Jared asked.

"I don't know if they talked to her yet."

"What does it mean, Bobby?" Jared asked.

"I think I have to show you something."

"Do you know why your dad and William Rose mentioned you?" Jared asked. "Or did Natalie hear them wrong?"

"I could drive away," Bobby said. "Put this thing in drive and just go. I could take you with me, if you wanted. We could get away from it all."

Jared felt confused. "And go where?"

"Anywhere."

"What about your family?" Jared asked. "You said your mom, your sister—"

"Yeah. Them. Everyone." He tapped his fingers on the steering wheel. "Things never really end, do they? Even if you run away."

"Not really."

Bobby turned the car around. They headed back toward town, retracing the route they'd just taken.

CHAPTER SEVENTY-SIX

Ian walked into the living room after calling the police. He had reported Ursula missing, a possible runaway. He couldn't give them a motive or explain anything, but he asked that they inform Naomi Poole.

Then he sat down and looked to Jenna.

A few long moments passed, and then Ian slipped back into the guise of the rational, detached businessman.

"I want to find her first," he said. "I don't want my daughter just pursued and questioned by the police. You understand wanting to protect your child, don't you? She hasn't done anything wrong. Not that we know of."

Jenna's heart beat a bass drum rhythm while she studied Ian's face. "You should stay here. She might come home. You should be here."

"No. I can't do nothing."

"I'll go drive around and look for her. I'll look in the park."

"Let's go look for her together," Ian said. "You and me. We can drive around. The police can call me if they need me. Poole or whoever. We have our phones."

He sounded so reasonable, so believable, that Jenna found herself nodding before he was even finished.

"Okay," she said. "Okay. Let's go look for her."

Jared recognized the alley they drove down. Bobby moved the car slowly, his forehead creased with concentration. It had only been the previous night Jared was there, moving through the party in search of Ursula.

Kirk Embry's house.

Jared saw the gate he'd come through at the back of the property, the tall privacy fence that protected the pool. Bobby opened his door and climbed out without saying anything, so Jared followed him.

The back gate hung open. Bobby strolled through and when Jared entered the pool area, he saw a few scattered Solo cups and empty beer bottles. A discarded UK sweatshirt lay next to the thick tarp covering the pool, and Jared wondered how Mike had fared at the party.

Bobby walked over to the side of the pool and crouched down next to one of the thick cords that held the tarp in place. He started unwinding the knot, looking like a deckhand preparing a ship to sail. He sprang a few of the cords loose near the deep end, never once looking up at Jared.

"What are you doing?" Jared asked.

But Bobby kept working, as patient as a carpenter.

Jared thought back about twelve hours, to Bobby sitting on the diving board and waxing philosophic about the coming of spring and his desire to get away from Hawks Mill. Jared's throat felt dry.

When Bobby was half done with the cords, he strolled back to the deep end of the pool and pulled on the tarp, rolling it back.

It looked heavy. Jared saw the strain on his face as he tugged, the tendons in his neck flexing.

When Bobby had it rolled back, he sat down on the side of the pool, his feet dangling above the water, which only reached half as high as it did during summer. Bobby stared into the depths as something grotesque settled over his face. A deep pain and sadness that seemed to age him twenty years as he sat and looked.

"Isn't this what you wanted to see?" he asked without looking up.

Jared took a couple of steps closer.

No, he didn't want to see. But he couldn't stop himself. He edged toward the lip of the pool.

He saw a human shape, facedown, floating in the scummy water.

CHAPTER SEVENTY-SEVEN

J ared stared into the partially frozen, dirty water.

He saw the back of a head, hair fanning out.

"Ursula?" Jared asked.

Bobby shook his head.

Then it made sense.

"It's her," Jared said. "Celia."

Bobby remained in place, his feet hanging over the water, his eyes vacant.

A cold knot of revulsion and fear grew inside Jared.

"That's what I meant about things changing in the spring," Bobby said. His voice echoed off the concrete surface of the pool. "Pretty soon, Kirk's family would open this up, and they'd see what was in there."

"But Kirk didn't kill her," Jared said. Not asking. Stating a fact.

"He doesn't know anything about it. Unless he's looking out a window right now."

Jared looked up at the house. The morning sun was

hitting the windows, reflecting and obscuring anyone who might be looking outside.

"He's probably hungover."

Jared watched as Bobby started to cry, his face dissolving into tears, his body shuddering. "My dad. Her. All of it."

Jared couldn't move. The body in the water kept him transfixed.

The only sound in the quiet morning was Bobby's sobs, which grew quieter and less frequent.

"Who did it?" Jared asked.

Bobby looked up, wiping his face. He stared at Jared, not saying anything.

And then Jared saw that Bobby was looking past him. His eyes were fixed on a spot behind Jared.

Something. Or someone.

Before Jared could turn he was hit in the back and knocked forward.

Jared was propelled into the air, out over the lip of the pool, and he landed in the screaming-cold water, his body bumping up against the frozen block of a human being.

Ursula didn't answer calls or texts.

Jenna and Ian checked the park, the school—anywhere she might be spending time. Thirty minutes passed, then forty-five.

Detective Poole called. Ian answered and explained the situation. Naomi promised to spread the word about Ursula.

"But don't make a big deal out of it," Ian said. "Don't embarrass her. This may be nothing."

Ian hung up. Jenna was driving so that Ian could keep trying Ursula.

"We know she came home last night for some amount of time, right?" Jenna asked. "And you didn't see her this morning?"

"No. I didn't hear her either. And I was up early."

"Could she have gone back to the party last night? Maybe to meet people or drink more?"

"Worth a try."

"Do you know where she was?" Jenna asked.

"The Embrys' house. Kirk Embry is the kid's name."

Jenna turned at the next stop sign and accelerated.

"Ian," she said, "I have to ask you a question. Did anything else happen in your house the night Celia disappeared? Is there something we all don't know?"

"Oh, Jenna . . ." Ian had the phone out again. Dialing and dialing.

They came to another stop sign, one on the edge of downtown. When it was her turn to go, Jenna didn't. She put the car in park and turned toward Ian. "What else is there, Ian? Is this something about Ursula?"

"I don't know," he said.

"You don't know?"

Ian stared straight ahead for a moment. Then he reached out and banged his fist against the dashboard. The noise made Jenna jump.

Ian still didn't look at her.

His breathing grew heavy. "I wasn't home that night."

A car pulled up behind them and then went around when it saw they weren't moving. Jenna struggled to put her thoughts together. And then she struggled to find words. "Where were you?"

"It only happened one time. I swear, Jenna. One time. Celia probably went out that night because I wasn't home either. I was gone and you called . . ."

"A woman? You were with another woman? And all this time you've let everyone think—everyone know—that Celia had affairs? And you weren't even there when she left?"

"I said we've all done things we aren't proud of."

"So you don't know where Ursula was that night? Or what Celia was doing before she left the house?"

Ian didn't answer. He looked at his phone.

"Wait," Jenna said, reaching out and placing her hand on Ian's phone. "You lied to the police? You lied to everybody?"

"What did it matter where I was? What matters is where Celia was."

Jenna felt a pressure in her chest, a combination of anger and shock. "But if you lied, Ian, do you know what that makes you look like?" She stared at him, her lips parted. "Did you hurt Celia?"

Ian's forehead creased. "Are you kidding, Jenna? Never. Never."

"So Ursula lied for you?"

"Jenna, can we talk about this later?"

"No. Now. Ursula lied for you? Your own daughter."

"We agreed it was best."

"Where was she that night if you weren't home?" Jenna asked.

"Home."

"How do you know?" Jenna asked.

Ian didn't answer.

Jenna continued to the Embrys'.

Jared scrambled away from the stiff body, reaching for the metal ladder above him.

The water in the deep end of the pool came up to his chest, and it helped to break his fall. But he was freezing, his lips chattering, his insides burning with cold.

He reached for the ladder and looked up. He used one hand to clear his eyes and saw Ursula standing on the edge of the pool where he had just been. She looked down on him imperiously, her face hard, her jaw set.

She looked over at Bobby. "What the fuck is wrong with you?" she asked, her voice harsh and brittle in the cold air.

"He knows. Everybody's going to know. And I'm glad."

"You didn't meet me. I waited at school with my fucking bag, you moron. We could be gone. Long gone."

"Don't call me that," Bobby said. "You can't bully your way out of this one."

Jared reached into his pocket and pulled out his phone. It was soaked, the screen blank. His hands were cold, and it slipped out of his grip and plopped into the water next to Celia's body, sinking down beneath it to the bottom of the pool.

Ursula came closer to the ladder, staring down at Jared where he shivered. She stepped away, and Jared started climbing, his hands so cold he struggled to grip the railing.

Before he reached the top, Ursula was back. And she held a long metal pole in her hand, the kind people attached a skimmer to in order to remove leaves.

Jared thought she was going to hand it down to him, to use it to help pull him up.

But then he saw the look on her face. She swung it at his knuckles, intending to knock him off the ladder and back into the water.

He ducked her first swing and her second.

And then someone called her name.

Ian went through the gate first.

He called for Ursula, and when Jenna came through behind him, she saw Ursula standing at the edge, a long metal rod in her hand, and Bobby Allen sitting on the rim staring down into the water.

Jenna wondered: *Why are these two rich kids cleaning their friend's pool on a Saturday morning in February?*

Then Ursula dropped the pole. It clattered down into the pool.

And Bobby stood up and leaned over, extending his hand down the ladder to the deep end.

Ursula locked eyes with Ian. She clutched her arms across her midsection as though she was about to be sick.

"Oh, Daddy," she said. She folded in half, as if she'd

been struck in the stomach. She sank onto the concrete that surrounded the pool, her body curling into a ball.

Ian rushed to her. Jenna tried not to be cynical. She tried not to see Ursula's wheedling behavior as manipulation of her father.

But then she saw Jared, soaking wet and shivering, lifted out of the pool by Bobby Allen.

Jenna rushed across, taking her coat off as she went. She reached him and wrapped him in her coat. "What are you doing, Jared? You'll freeze."

"Mom, don't look down there," he said, his lips blue, his teeth chattering.

But Jenna looked.

And she understood.

CHAPTER SEVENTY-EIGHT

I didn't mean for it to happen," Ursula was saying. She said it over and over.

Ian continued to hold her.

Jenna listened. She felt far away, as though she were watching the scene unfold from a great remove. A million miles or more.

But it was real. She was there, hearing the nightmare words.

"We fought that night, the night she disappeared." Ursula leaned back and stared directly into Ian's eyes. "I knew you were out. I thought . . . I thought Mom was going to see someone, a man. I heard her making plans on the phone."

"It wasn't a man," Jenna said. "It was me."

"I didn't know that," Ursula said, her voice rising to a higher pitch like that of a wronged child.

"Honey, what happened?" Ian asked.

"I tried to stop her from going, and she wouldn't listen to me. I thought she was lying to me when she said she wasn't meeting a man. She'd lied to you about other men. Why else would she be sneaking out late at night if it wasn't for a man?" Ursula's voice grew more petulant as she went on. "She insisted on going. And I couldn't stop her." She wasn't crying. "I didn't mean to shove her as hard as I did, but she wouldn't listen. She fell by the laundry room and hit her head against the wall. She didn't bleed. But her neck was turned kind of funny. Her eyes were open. I could tell . . ."

Jenna's arm slipped from around Jared's back. She felt nauseated, felt her mouth filling with saliva. She raised her hand and bent down on one knee as though genuflecting. She heaved, her mouth filling with bile, and she spit it onto the concrete.

"I helped her cover it up." Bobby stood to the side of the scene, his face vacant. "She called and we brought the body over here. The Embrys are always gone. They'd just closed their pool. And we dropped that earring at the spot where Ursula said her mom and Mrs. Barton always met. Ursula knew right where to put it. Mrs. Walters said she was going to meet you, so we thought that would throw people off. I thought it was a shitty idea. I didn't think anyone would even see it. But Ursula said the cops would look over every inch of that area. She was right." He looked over at Ursula. "She tried to keep the other earring. Like a keepsake of her mother, after she'd killed her."

"It belonged to me," Ursula said.

"We would have gotten caught," Bobby said. "I had to take the earring from her and throw it out. I should have thrown it in the fucking river, but she wouldn't shut up about it. I barely got it away from her."

"Bobby—"

Bobby didn't stop. "You'd already taken money from the house. She said it would make her dad think her mom had run off on him. Then she went on message boards and tried to make people think her mom was alive, that she'd just run away."

"I met one of the lonely people she convinced," Jenna said. "You convinced him so well he showed up here."

"We were going to come back here and move it— *her*—when the weather got warm," Bobby said.

Jenna looked up at Bobby. His cheeks were red, but otherwise he looked so normal, so innocent. The all-American kid. And he was discussing hiding a body as though he were talking about hiding a case of beer.

"And William Rose found out," Jenna said from one knee. "He was supposed to be following Celia, but he must have seen you two. You went out that night, Ian. Did you call to have Celia followed?"

Ian moved his head. It was barely a nod.

"Somehow he saw us moving the body," Bobby said. "He knew what we were doing."

"And what then? He wanted to blackmail your dad?"

"I think that's why William Rose killed him," Bobby said. "I think something went wrong there. Dad might have been tired of it. Maybe he didn't have the money as fast as Rose wanted it." His eyes filled with tears. "I might as well have killed him myself. I caused it to happen."

"That's why Natalie heard your names the night your dad was killed," Jared said. "He was threatening your dad."

"Ian?" Jenna said. "What about you?"

Ian nodded. Slowly. "He kept his distance from me after Celia disappeared. Maybe it was just a matter of time and he would have blackmailed me as well."

Jenna stood up. Jared was shivering and scared. She placed her arm around his shoulder and led him away. When they passed Ursula and Ian, Jenna said, "I'm calling the police."

"Wait," Ian said. He looked pale. Terrified. "Jenna, you understand. These are . . . they might be my last moments with my daughter for a long time. Can you wait?"

"Please, Jenna," Ursula said, her eyes pleading. "Mom wouldn't want you to do this. You were such good friends. She'd want you to protect me."

Jenna didn't bend. "She'd want you to tell the truth. But you put her . . ." Jenna made a vague gesture toward the pool. Toward the secret floating below them. "You did everything to hide it. To cover it up. To try to get away with it. You told Reena about the affairs, didn't you?"

Ursula didn't answer.

Jenna and Jared walked out of the pool area and back toward her car. When they were inside, she started the engine and cranked the heat.

She took a deep breath and dialed the police.

After she made her report, insisting that the cop on the other line find and tell Detective Poole right away, she turned to her son.

"It wasn't your fault, Mom," he said. "Celia was dead and never even left the house that night. No one hurt her at the park."

"Yeah." Her own voice sounded distant. "I think they call that cold comfort. I still called her. She was leaving the house for me when Ursula . . ."

"You can't think that way," he said.

But Jenna wasn't sure.

Two police cars arrived in the alley. The officers jumped out and headed onto the Embrys' property.

"We should get going," Jenna said. "You're cold."

"Sure."

"You can change at home and get warmed up. The police know where to find us. They know that very well. And we'll be talking to them for a while, but maybe we can visit Natalie later," she said, trying to give them some hope. "We'll find out where she is, and we'll go by. What do you say?"

"Sounds great."

She took one look back at the property where Celia rested and drove them home.

ACKNOWLEDGMENTS

Once again I'd like to thank the many booksellers, librarians, bloggers, and reviewers who help spread the word about my books. With special thanks to Jennifer Plane Bailey and the staff of the Barnes & Noble store in Bowling Green, Kentucky, and Lisa Rice and the staff of the Warren County Public Library.

Thanks to my friends and family, especially Tomitha Blair, J. T. Ellison, John Hagaman, David Lenoir, Andrew McMichael, Mary Ellen Miller, Jane Olmsted, and Craig and Tracy Williams. Big thanks to Samantha McAllister for all her help and assistance. And thanks to Kara Thurmond for designing and maintaining my Web site.

Special thanks to Loren Jaggers and the publicity team at NAL/Berkley for getting the word out about my books.

Once again my amazing agent, Laney Katz Becker, guided me with her wisdom, high standards, and determination.

And, of course, my amazing editor, Danielle Perez, showed the way with her commitment, insights, and patience. And special thanks to everyone at NAL/Berkley.

And thanks to Molly McCaffrey for everything else.

SINCE SHE WENT AWAY

DAVID BELL

QUESTIONS FOR DISCUSSION

1. At the beginning of the novel, Celia has been missing for several months. In what ways are the various characters—Jenna, Jared, Ian, and Ursula—responding to and coping with the stress of her disappearance?

2. Jenna and Jared seem to have a solid mother/son relationship. Do you think this is because Jenna is a single parent? Do you understand why she sometimes worries about the job she is doing and the lack of a male role model in Jared's life?

3. Since Jared is only fifteen and inexperienced with girls, does it make sense that he would fall so hard and so fast for Tabitha (Natalie)? Are you surprised that he would go to such great lengths to find out what happened to her, including breaking into her house? Do you believe that Tabitha (Natalie) would fall for Jared so quickly as well?

4. Jenna and Celia have been close friends since childhood, but they have drifted apart in the years before Celia's disappearance. Is it unusual for close friends to drift apart like this

as their adult lives change? Do you think Jenna and Celia drifted apart because Celia had moved into a higher social class? Is it possible for friends to grow close again at some point? Draw from examples in your own life, if possible.

5. On the night Celia disappeared, Jenna was late to meet her because she discovered alcohol in Jared's room and wanted to talk to him about it. Do you think Jenna handled this the right way? Do you blame her for putting her son ahead of her friend? Why do you think Jenna feels as guilty as she does about Celia's disappearance? Should she feel so guilty?

6. Jenna and Ian have a complicated relationship, starting all the way back in high school when the two of them almost started dating. Do you think they have unresolved feelings for each other? Are you surprised that Celia "stole" Ian away from Jenna? Would Jenna have harbored anger toward Celia? Have there been times in your life when a friend betrayed you? Were you able to forgive?

7. What role does Sally play in Jenna's life? Is she the kind of friend who tells someone the truth even when they don't want to hear it? Do we all need a friend like that? Do you have a friend like that, or are you that friend?

8. What did you think of Reena Huffman? What part do the news media have to play when someone like Celia dis-

appears? Do they sometimes overstep their bounds in an effort to get a story? How can the media affect people's perceptions of a crime? Do you think Jenna made the right decision by not going on Reena's show?

9. William Rose is obviously not a role model as a father, so why do you think he kept Natalie with him as he traveled around? Do you think in some way he really cared for his daughter?

10. Were you surprised to find out that Ian had Celia followed in the wake of her infidelity? Do you understand why he felt he had to take extreme measures to try to keep his family together? Do you agree or disagree with what he did? What would you do if you found out your spouse was having you followed?

11. Were you surprised to find out that Ursula was responsible for Celia's death? Can you understand at all the pressures that might have contributed to her violent outburst against her mother? How difficult would it be as a teenager to watch your parents' marriage almost fall apart as the result of infidelity?

12. How difficult will it be for Jenna and Jared to put their lives together and move on after the end of the novel? Do you think they will maintain a relationship with Natalie?

Read on for an excerpt from
David Bell's latest novel of suspense,

THE FINALISTS

Available now

CHAPTER ONE

The house sits on the far eastern edge of campus, nestled in the woods among the sycamores, the maples, and the white oaks, all older than the college. Older than Kentucky itself. To reach it by car, one must turn left off the main road that circles campus and onto Ezekiel Hyde Lane, a narrow, winding strip of asphalt that cuts through the trees, enters the clearing, and ends in the small parking lot on the side of Hyde House. On foot, the house can be reached by way of the numerous paths that cut through the trees and give the campus its natural beauty.

I step out of my car and look back up the road I just traveled, and it's easy to believe the world doesn't exist even though the rest of campus is just a third of a mile away. Standing on the Hyde House grounds can feel like standing in another century, which is exactly the way Ezekiel Hyde, the founder of the college and its first president, had wanted it to stay.

The sun is bright, and its rays hit the windows of Hyde House, reflecting the light, capturing the morning glow.

Is it weird to say the sight of that house still lifts my spirits?

It's eight fifteen, and I'm early. Which is good. I want to be here before the students. More than anything, I want to be here before Ezekiel Hyde's great-great-great-great-grandson, Nicholas, arrives.

I climb the portico steps to the Neo-Federal structure. Up close the brick is more weathered than I realized. I reach for the brass knob, which is tarnished. The heavy black door needs to be repainted. For years, the college's board of trustees has wanted to renovate the house, but the money is never there. The college has a list of projects that never get done.

I pull on the knob and, not surprisingly, find the door locked.

I step off the right side of the portico, my shoes sinking into the soft soil, and press my face against the window. I've been in Hyde House many times for college events and know the layout well. I'm staring into the music room, the space where Major Hyde, his family, and subsequent generations of Hydes came to listen to recitals on the piano. The piano originally moved to the house by Major Hyde fell into disrepair and was sold in the 1990s, but a music stand remains along with a bust of Major Hyde's favorite composer, Wagner.

The sun warms the back of my neck. I wait on the lawn in front of the house. In the distance, the campus is quiet on a Saturday morning in April. The students sleep off the night before. Purple hyacinths bloom in the flower beds, and I catch their overwhelming scent. A robin chirps in a nearby tree.

I want to call Rachel, apologize for our fight earlier. Money. We only fight about money. We have to decide whether to get new windows or a new roof, and we disagree about which is the higher priority. Our household is like the college—there's never enough money to go around.

But before I can hit the call button, the phone rings.

"Shoot," I say, then answer. "Hello?"

"Hey, Troy. It's Grace."

"Hey, Grace." I try to keep my voice buoyant and not let any irritation show, even though my boss—the president of the college—is calling to check up on me. But she's not just my boss—she's my friend. She and Rachel belong to the same book club, and just last weekend Grace and her husband, Doug, came over to our house for drinks. "How are you on this fine morning?"

"Is he there?" she asks. She cuts to the chase. Today is about business. On another day, we would talk about our kids—Grace's oldest son, Michael, is in the same grade as my oldest daughter, Rebecca—but I know Grace has other things on her mind.

"If by 'he' you mean Nicholas Hyde, then no, he isn't here yet. No one is."

"Damn it. When did you talk to him last?"

"It's been about a month. And that was just a short e-mail."

"Yeah." Grace sounds defeated. She never sounds defeated. "I can't get ahold of him either. Did you know he left Kentucky and moved to California?"

"He did? I thought he was still living in Lexington. He didn't tell me."

"He's lost both his parents in the last year. That's a terrible blow for anyone. And I know he was close to his mother. Very close."

"Maybe that's why he moved to California. His mom was his last real family tie here."

"I'm worried about this, Troy. He's not connected to the college or to Kentucky the way the Hydes always have been. You know as well as I do his father would never have left us twisting in the wind."

"You're absolutely right. I'm worried too. Nicholas is pretty much the only living heir of Ezekiel Hyde. Certainly the only direct descendant. And he controls the estate."

"And they've been giving us less and less every year. For the last decade. And it's been coming to us later and later every year, which makes it harder to budget and plan. Is it too early for a drink?"

"A bit. But if you want to get one tonight, you know our patio bar is always open to you and Doug."

A car comes down the main road and turns onto Ezekiel Hyde Lane. It makes the slow, winding run in my direction and pulls up and parks next to mine. An older model with a dent in the fender. A middle-aged man steps out, trim and tall. He wears a dark suit with a white shirt and a thin black tie.

"The students are starting to arrive. I think this is—"

"Troy," Grace says, "remember what we talked about."

I know right away what she means. The 100 More Initiative I've been working on for the past two years.

"I think it's fantastic you want to increase the number of minority and first-time students at the college. That's why we promoted you to this position. It's not just because you're my friend and a nice guy. It's to raise money. But we've been falling short. *You've* been falling short. The Hydes are giving less, so we need to raise more from other sources. And the board is—"

"Nicholas promised us the money for One Hundred More. Two million dollars. We shook hands on it."

"Do you know how much a handshake is worth?" Grace asks. "Don't let him leave without getting a real commitment. Okay?"

"That's my plan."

"I'm sorry, Troy. You know I am, but I don't have to remind you of what's at stake. For the college or for you personally."

"I get it, Grace. We'll toast our success tonight, have a drink around the fire."

The man in the dark suit comes my way, almost marching. Back straight as a flagpole. A chin made of granite. His heels clack off the pavement, and his hair is cut close to his head.

"Grace, the students are—"

"Wait, Troy. There's one more—"

The man reaches me, extends his hand. He doesn't seem to notice or care that I'm on the phone.

"Vice President Gaines, sir. It's a pleasure to meet you.

I'm James Stephenson. Retired, United States Army. Thank you for the opportunity to compete for this scholarship, sir."

We shake. My hand feels like it's been slammed between two bricks.

"Sir, I know no Black student—indeed, no student of color—has ever won the Hyde Scholarship. I'm intent on being the first, and I want to thank you for the chance."

"Well, it's not me. It's the Hyde family and their board—"

"Sir, I was wondering if I could express some concerns to you before we begin—"

"Troy, are you there?" Grace asks.

"Just a minute, Grace. Can we speak in a moment, Mr. Stephenson?"

"Call me Captain Stephenson, sir."

"Okay, Captain Stephenson. Can we speak in a moment?"

"Yes, sir."

He remains in front of me, hands folded behind his back. Parade rest. His shoes are so polished and clean, they reflect the sky like the windows of Hyde House.

I hold up my index finger. "Just one moment."

I walk fifteen feet away and switch the phone to my other ear. "Okay, Grace, I'm back. But you don't have to tell me again that I've missed my fundraising quotas two years in a row. I'm well aware—"

"No, Troy, not that. Something else. Something about the scholarship process today. I'm afraid we have a situation brewing there. And you need to be ready for it."

CHAPTER TWO

Before I ask Grace what is going on—and before she is able to tell me—two campus police cruisers turn off the main road and come down Ezekiel Hyde Lane. They stop at the boundary of the grounds of Hyde House, a couple of hundred feet from where I stand.

Two officers step out of each cruiser, and a cool wave of relief passes through me.

"Grace, don't worry about it. The campus police are here, and I see Chief. He'll let us in now. Problem solved."

"Troy, that's not it."

The four police officers open the trunks of the two cars and pull wooden sawhorses out. They stand them up across the entrance to the Hyde House grounds, creating a barricade that shuts off vehicle traffic. Even Captain Stephenson has turned away from staring at me and fixed his eyes on the activities of the police.

"What's going on, Grace? The cops are making some

kind of perimeter at the edge of the lawn. They've never done that before."

"That's what I'm trying to tell you, Troy." Grace speaks to me in the way I speak to my daughters when they are slow to understand something. "We've received word there are going to be protests during the process today. A number of students are going to gather, so I notified the campus police. We want them to keep the protestors back as far as possible."

"They're protesting *against* their fellow students competing for a big scholarship?"

"No, it's not that."

A couple of students come walking toward the house from one of the paths that cuts through the woods from the south. A man and a woman. They appear to be having a passionate conversation. The young woman—who is tall and lanky like an athlete—seems to be trying to convince the guy—who is almost strutting like he's in a movie—of something. He's listening, nodding his head as she speaks. Captain Stephenson has noticed them as well and turns in their direction.

"Then what's the problem, Grace?"

"It's the Hyde family they're going to protest. They want us to divest from the Hyde family fortune. You know they think money made in coal is blood money."

"I thought the Hydes settled that. They have a plan to move away from coal to green energy during the next two decades."

"You know that's not nearly fast enough for the students," Grace says.

"What good does it do to block the road?" I ask. "Can't someone reach us by one of the paths?"

"They met outside the student union. Then they're marching over to Hyde House as a group. We know which way they're going."

The police appear to have the sawhorses all in place. And just in time. About thirty students carrying signs and chanting approach Hyde House from the direction of campus. They walk down the main road, the one I just drove over to get here, and then turn down Ezekiel Hyde Lane, heading in the direction of the police barricades. It's hard for me to make out the chant from this distance, but I can kind of read one of the signs, which a student holds high in the air. It's written in red paint—at least I hope it's paint—on white poster board.

NO BLOOD MONEY!

Captain Stephenson turns his whole body in that direction, facing the protestors. "I don't like the looks of that," he says, shaking his head.

For a moment, I worry. What will happen when they reach the cops? I don't want anyone to get hurt. And I don't want any arrests or fights. The police are outnumbered, but I know they're armed. The cops tense, their bodies primed for action. They all stand with hands on hips, but I know that puts their hands closer to weapons— pepper spray, Tasers, guns.

The protestors continue to chant as they approach the edge of the lawn, their faces angry and determined.

"Grace, I think we . . ."

"What is it, Troy?"

My body tenses like I'm about to brawl.

But the protestors stop behind the barricade. They don't appear interested in pushing their way through or making any more trouble. They chant and wave their signs, but there's no actual trouble.

I breathe a sigh of relief.

"It's okay, Grace. They stopped. They're facing the cops, but they're not too loud. Once we're inside, the students should be able to concentrate. The house is old and keeps sound out pretty well. But they are blocking the driveway to the house."

"The cops are going to take care of that," she says. "They can protest, but they can't block traffic."

The young man and woman continue their discussion off to the side. They stand close together. The woman wipes at the corner of her eye. A tear?

"Grace, I think I need to go. The students are arriving."

"There's one more thing."

"What else could there be?"

"Can you read any of the other signs?"

"I can try, but you're testing my middle-aged eyesight. They're kind of far away." I watch, squinting as the signs move up and down. Someone beats on a tambourine, making an oddly discordant jingling. "I think there are a couple about blood money. One about paying for education with coal. Another about killing Mother Earth. Oh, and one nasty one about slaughtering the innocents. I guess it has a nice biblical touch. You can tell the protestors I appreciate the large type they're using."

"*That's* the one I was worried about," Grace says.

"What about it?"

Grace sighs into the phone again. "Well, we were trying to keep this under wraps until we could fully investigate the claim, but word leaked out on social media this morning. It's about Ezekiel Hyde's service in the Civil War."

"You mean *Major* Ezekiel Hyde."

When I say the word "Major," Captain Stephenson looks my way. He raises his hand like we're in a classroom, reminding me he still wants to talk. I hold up my index finger again and then point to the phone.

"Yes," Grace says, "*Major* Ezekiel Ellis Hyde. This is courtesy of Charlie Porter in History." She sighs. "Oh, Charlie. He's uncovered something about Major Hyde's service in the Civil War."

"What could possibly be uncovered? Everyone knows that Ezekiel Hyde served with the Union Army."

"That's what we say on the tour when everyone goes past the statue of Ezekiel on his horse Lancer by the campus gates. But . . . Charlie uncovered something in his research."

"You mean something not related to the family destroying the earth with their coal?"

"It's about the Palmyra Massacre."

"The what?"

"Exactly. Not many people remember it, but the Union Army massacred ten Confederate troops rather than take them off as prisoners. A horrific atrocity." I can hear Grace shudder through the phone. "There was always speculation that Ezekiel was there, but no proof. Well . . ."

"Charlie found the proof."

"He did." Grace sighs. "Ugh. He posted about it on his blog and tweeted about it. And he's writing a book too. So not only has the Hyde family made their money off coal—and continue to do so. Now everyone knows that Ezekiel Hyde, founder of our beloved college, participated in a slaughter. How do you think the students feel about that?"

"Not good. Is there a statute of limitations on mass slaughter?"

"Troy. That's not funny."

"Sorry, sorry. I'm just not sure what we're supposed to do. Dig Ezekiel and Lancer up and scold them?"

"You need to know that the mood on the campus is tense because of these things."

A dusty black Ford pickup turns down Hyde Lane and approaches the protestors and the police barricade. It looks like trouble, like someone from town has shown up intending to counterprotest. Someone who remains a big fan of Major Hyde. The pickup truck looms large and intimidating, like a vehicle of destruction.

But the protestors move aside, and the driver—a guy in a cowboy hat—leans out and speaks to the police. The cops move the barricade, letting him through. The protestors increase the volume of their chants as he maneuvers his vehicle onto the Hyde House grounds, but no one tries to run through in his wake, and the cops quickly shut the opening.

The truck approaches my position, its muffler rumbling, the large tires squealing slightly. Once it's parked, a slender, muscular young man wearing pointy-toe boots and the aforementioned cowboy hat slides out, the ornamental clasp on his bolo tie glinting in the sun.

"I'm glad to know this, Grace. Once all the students arrive, we'll go inside and get started. The protestors will get bored or hungry or tired, and they'll go home."

"I don't think Nicholas knows about the stuff concerning Ezekiel."

"You've met Nicholas, Grace. He's a wealthy playboy. He struggles to remember my name, and I've had several meals with him. I don't think he's going to be upset about the . . . What did you call it? Palmyra Massacre?"

"I mean the protestors. He's going to see that when he arrives. There's no other way for him to drive in except right past them. What if that makes him pull all the money from the school?"

"You could tell Charlie to put a lid on his research."

"Yeah, right. He has tenure. You know the administration can't muzzle the faculty. You used to be a professor, remember?"

"Barely. I sold out for money. My fault for having three kids who want to go to college. Look, Grace, it's all going to be fine. Nicholas likes me, even if he isn't sure of my name. He's a baseball fan, and so am I. When we get together, we talk about the Reds and the designated-hitter rule and how defensive shifts are ruining the game. We have *rapport*. I'll smooth any ruffled feathers, I promise. I'll nail down the One Hundred More donation, and we'll all be in fat city. Okay?"

"Okay, Troy. I *do* believe in you. I know the board is putting a lot of heat on you. They're putting heat on the whole administration. Shit, you know my contract is up this year. We're all facing the reality of how hard it is for private colleges to survive. It's daunting, Troy."

"I know. But Hyde College is a special place. It's been here for a hundred fifty-two years. It's like these oak trees I'm standing by. Strong. Powerful. Unbending."

"You really believe that, Troy?"

"I'm suffused with the Hyde spirit."

"Okay. Let's concentrate on something good. One of those six students is going to win a really nice scholarship."

"That's right," I say. "And more of them are arriving, so I'd better go."

"Thanks, Troy."

"Try to enjoy your Saturday," I say.

Before Grace can answer, a fat red bird comes streaking through the sky, heading right for me.

Ready to find
your next great read?

Let us help.

Visit prh.com/nextread

Penguin
Random
House